Peter Watt has spent time as a soldier, articled clerk, prawn trawler deckhand, builder's labourer, pipe layer, real estate salesman, private investigator, police sergeant, surveyor's chairman and advisor to the Royal Papua New Guinea Constabulary. He speaks, reads and writes Vietnamese and Pidgin. He now lives at Maclean on the Clarence River in northern New South Wales. He has volunteered with the Volunteer Rescue Association, Queensland Ambulance Service and currently with the Rural Fire Service. Fishing and the vast open spaces of outback Queensland are his main interests in life.

Peter Watt can be contacted at www.peterwatt.com.

Author Photo: Shawn Peene

Excerpts from emails sent to Peter Watt

'. . . you are by far and away my favourite author. Your portrayal of an early Australia and its rich, and not so rich history told by a skilled storyteller should have gained more accolades than has been the case.'

'Wow . . . another sensational story, I have just finished reading *And Fire Falls*. I would like to take this opportunity to say how much I love your stories, the ability to capture you at page 1 and keep you reading page after page, not wanting to put the book down. The same, book after book, every book, for that matter. All I can say is . . . write faster, because I'm running out of books to read!'

'Thank you for such an inspiring yarn.'

'I have come lately to your works, and what a cracking good read they are . . . What I like about your books is that you capture the frailties of human nature pretty much as I see it, and see people for what they are, with station in life and the colour of your skin counting for nought other than to show how prejudice and bigotry can still be so prevalent because of them . . . I am not filling your pockets when I say this, but I reckon from your books I have read so far (including the Papua series) that you remain true to the spirit which you capture so well, and although your output is prodigious, you maintain a freshness and write with a great turn of phrase which is true to life in the bush.'

'I am waiting impatiently for your 2016 publication. I enjoyed *Beneath a Rising Sun* and look forward to this year's story.'

'Your stories have brought back precious memories, having been born in Sydney in 1942 . . . I find your selection of characters fascinating not to mention the plots!!! As an ex-serviceman I can really relate to the experiences of your characters.'

PETER WATT

While THE Moon Burns

PAN

Pan Macmillan Australia

First published 2016 in Macmillan by Pan Macmillan Australia Pty Ltd
This Pan edition published in 2017 by Pan Macmillan Australia Pty Ltd
1 Market Street, Sydney, New South Wales, Australia, 2000

Cataloguing-in-Publication entry is available
from the National Library of Australia
http://catalogue.nla.gov.au

Typeset in Bembo by Post Pre-press Group
Printed by IVE

A tribute to Emergency Service Volunteers
who have made the ultimate sacrifice
in the course of their duties.

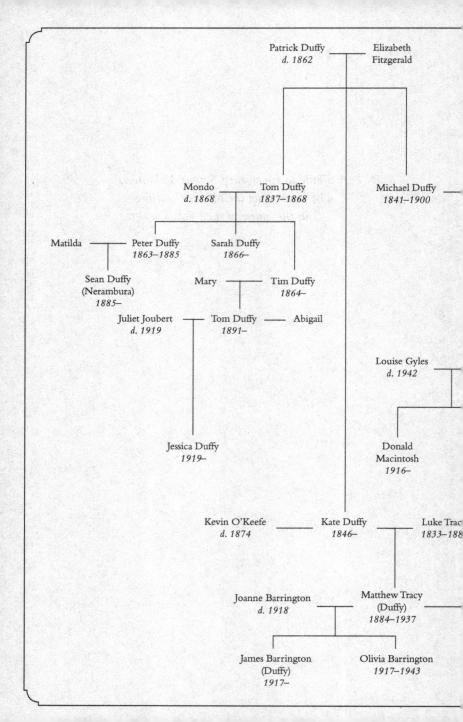

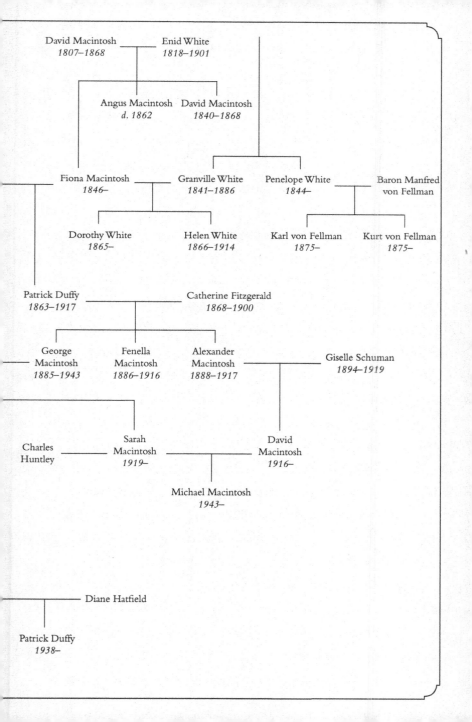

PROLOGUE

May 1945

My name is Wallarie. I was once a warrior amongst my people but now you cannot see me – unless you go out at night and look up at the stars.

A long time ago a whitefella called Donald Macintosh had all my mob killed. I survived – and now I am also gone.

But, sometimes I fly to the earth as the great wedge-tailed eagle, and soar above the lands I once hunted. There, I see my kin who sometimes go to the sacred cave on a hill at a place they call Glen View. The cave has the pictures on the walls made by the Darambal people from a time that goes back to the Dreaming. The old ones were wise. They draw the white warrior on the cave wall. They know the white warrior would come one day, and he did come to us when I was young.

You ask me who is the white warrior. He is more than a man or woman – and more than one person. He and she

1

are the people of my blood who fight as warriors in the whitefella wars. Jessie Duffy, she a warrior. Her father, Tom Duffy, he a warrior.

Tom now walks our land the whitefella call Glen View. He the last who give me baccy before I go to the place in the sky.

But you don't want to hear old Wallarie talk 'bout black-fella stuff. You want to know 'bout whitefella stuff. You want to know 'bout the Duffys and Macintoshes.

Mebbe I fly back to the earth on the wings of an eagle an' visit you in your dreams.

Part One

Rumours of Peace

1945

ONE

Here come the Aussies, to capture Tarakan,
It's just the kickoff, we're heading for Japan,
If you could see the grim-faced men,
And their mates the R.A.N,
And backed up by the Air Force,
We'll capture Tarakan

Lieutenant Donald Macintosh leaned against the forward ramp of the flat-bottomed landing craft. The words of the song, sung to the popular German tune 'Lili Marlene' ran over and over in his mind. Donald's hands were trembling. To his left and right, similar landing craft slapped their way through the tropical seas. He and his platoon had witnessed the massive bombardment against the beach they were about to land on in this backwater of the Pacific war and now the invading force had shifted further inland to seek out and destroy Japanese defensive positions.

Sixteen shilling and sixpence a day was far removed from the income he was used to as a member of one of Australia's richest families. Yet he had always wanted to do his bit in the war, so he had signed up as an officer and now found himself leading thirty men into battle. At least a third of his men had seen action in the Middle East but the rest were as green to combat as he was. Donald could feel his legs trembling now, and hoped none of his men noticed. His biggest fear was not of dying – although he was afraid of that too – but of freezing and letting his platoon down. Ahead was the shell- and bomb-ravaged beach of the tiny island almost on the equator.

He was not particularly interested in why the American General Douglas MacArthur had directed Australian forces to this island off the coast of Borneo. For Donald, the only war that counted was within himself, and the fighting that would take place in the few yards of territory waiting beyond the ramp when it dropped for them to storm ashore.

'Not long now, skipper,' his sergeant said. 'You'll be okay.'

Donald was grateful for the sergeant's words because he was one of the battalion's original members, and had served from the beginning. Donald turned to him and nodded his thanks. The tropical heat was intense and the sun baked the men huddled in the landing craft.

The landing craft beached and the ramp went down. Acrid smoke swirled around Donald as he leaped from the ramp into the oily mud. He struggled forward through the bog to the beach cratered with shell holes. His platoon followed him into the hell that was to be the battle for Tarakan.

Donald's first impression was of smoke and noise: men shouting, ear-deafening explosions and the constant crack of small arms. As they struggled forward he encountered a lone Japanese soldier firing wildly at the advancing Australians. A bullet cracked near Donald's ear and the young officer realised an inch closer would have killed him. Donald froze, and found himself speechless, unable to issue orders. He dropped to the blackened sand and realised that in a small part of his mind this was the thing he was afraid of: he was failing his men. If only the war would go away, and he could return to his comfortable civilian life. He was vaguely aware someone was shouting at him, 'Skipper, skipper, what's your plan?'

It was his sergeant, and he did not have an answer.

★

It was as if New York was in the midst of a massive bout of hysteria. Newspaper headlines blared *GERMANY SURRENDERS!* and those two words had given the population of the great American city permission to explode with joy after the years of pent-up living under the shadow of war.

From his hotel window, Captain James Duffy, a United States Marine Corp fighter pilot, gazed down on the packed streets. Steamers of white paper were being thrown from building windows. It almost looked like a covering of snow. The distant shriek of shipping sirens blended with the singing below. People danced joyously, and men swigged from bottles of whisky, sharing them with strangers.

Colourful bales of silk, rayon and wool were disentangling as they came down from manufacturing shops to drape the crowd. James lifted his own bottle of whisky, saluting the wonderful madness that was gripping the citizens of New York. He was not smiling though. The war in Europe may have ended, but it was not yet over in the Pacific where he was being posted. There the fighting had become increasingly vicious, and the death toll was rising steadily against an enemy who refused to surrender.

James took a gulp of whisky to calm his nerves. Although he did not want to admit it to himself, he was showing signs of battle fatigue – as some called it. It all seemed so surreal to him that despite today's revelry he might not survive the war but instead be killed in the Pacific theatre of fighting.

A rapping on the door brought him out of his thoughts. He was not expecting anyone. and was puzzled.

'Come in,' he commanded.

The door opened and James registered his pleasure and surprise at the figure standing there. It was an older man in his late thirties, wearing an expensive three-piece suit.

'Guy, old buddy,' James said. 'What in hell brings you to my humble – or at least temporary – abode?'

Guy Praine stepped inside, a bottle of champagne at his side. 'I just happen to be in New York, celebrating my release from uniformed service with Uncle Sam,' he said, popping the bottle and glancing around for appropriate glasses. 'I saw your name on the register for returning heroes here to convince us all to buy war bonds. It wasn't hard to track you down, and I can see that you've already got a start on me celebrating our victory in Europe. As a matter of fact, I've just returned from London where Uncle Sam had me working on PR for Ike.'

'Goddamn!' James said, rising from his chair and taking his old friend's hand. 'It is good to see you again.'

'I presume an expensive hotel like this will have clean glasses,' Guy said, as James produced a couple of tumblers. The champagne poured, Guy raised his glass of sparkling wine. 'To the end of one war, and the quick end of another.'

James responded, and both men sat down.

'I tried to call Julianna,' James said after taking a large swallow of the cold wine. 'Her old number has been disconnected.'

'You would expect that after a couple of years of being out of the country,' Guy said. 'You know that she has left LA and returned home to New Orleans? I saw her last year at a cocktail party here in New York, just before I shipped out for England.'

'Is she married?' James asked.

'I don't know, old chap,' Guy replied. 'The last I heard was that she was hooked up with some well-known director.'

'Anyone I know?' James asked.

'That guy whose head you wanted to knock off back on the set of his movie, *Furious Eagles*.'

James remembered the man. It had been the same time he had first met Julianna and been intrigued by the beautiful young woman clutching a clipboard and hovering at the edge of the movie set. He also remembered how she had given him an ultimatum to leave the Marines and be with her: she would leave him if he returned to flying combat missions in the Pacific. He had chosen the latter, for reasons he suspected she could never understand.

'Should have gone ahead and knocked his block off,' James sighed.

'I don't think it would have solved anything,' Guy said. 'I always thought that you two were meant to be together, but you made your choice, and Julianna hers.'

'You're right,' James said. 'All I have to do is survive this goddamned war, and get the chance to show her it is all over for combat flying for me.'

'Are they sending you back?' Guy asked.

'Next week I ship out for the Pacific again,' James

answered. 'I might be getting a posting as a squadron leader – if I'm lucky.'

'Is there an alternative?'

'I could make a telephone call to my grandfather, and ask for a stateside posting until the end of the war,' James said, taking another swig from his glass.

'But you're not going to do that, are you?' Guy sighed. 'James Duffy, you are a stubborn son of a bitch. With a bit of luck you could be with Julianna instead of returning to the shooting war.'

'I have to see this thing through,' James answered, finishing his champagne. 'Hey, let's you and I go out and paint the town red like we used to do back in Hollywood. I think we should celebrate your freedom from the arms of Uncle Sam.'

Guy finished his champagne and followed James from his hotel room. He had a sneaking suspicion that by morning they would either be in a police cell or asleep in the gutters of New York.

*

Sarah Macintosh was irritated by the torn up telephone book pages drifting around her ankles as she pushed her way through the crushing mill of joyous people gathered in Martin Place. People climbed onto the two stone statues of the Great War – the soldier and the sailor, forever back-to-back – watching over the plaza. Singing, laughing and hugging civilians and servicemen mingled to celebrate the end of one war. But for the very attractive woman attempting to walk to her office a short distance away, the celebrations meant very little. The vast Macintosh financial empire, of which she was head, had been established in the Australian colonies long ago by her proud Scottish ancestors. Germany had surrendered, and the secret Macintosh investments in German industry were in tatters, but the secret Nazi connection would remain well concealed in Swedish and Swiss bank accounts, as both neutral nations had a reputation for being very discreet.

She eventually reached her building and was greeted by the old lift operator in the deserted foyer. 'Good evening Miss Macintosh,' he said with a slight nod of his head. 'You wish to go to your floor?'

'Yes,' Sarah said, and he pulled back the metal lattice door to the elevator.

'Has Mr Price arrived?' Sarah asked as they ascended. The lift operator replied that he had, a half hour earlier. Sarah was annoyed. Her lover was supposed to have picked her up, but had instead left her to fight her way through the unwashed throng in Martin Place.

When the elevator reached her floor Sarah stepped out without a word and went directly to her lavishly decorated office.

Inside, William Price stood by a window smoking a cigarette and gazing down on the darkened street. He was tall and suavely handsome, the very picture of a city night-club owner. He had evaded military service with the help of a few well-placed public servants who he knew as patrons of his club. It was quietly rumoured that Bill Price was well connected with Sydney's dark underbelly, and not a man to cross. He was strategically placed to pass on information concerning political machinations and stories of indiscretions of the rich and influential.

'Where were you?' Sarah snapped. 'I was jostled half to death by the crowds in Martin Place. You said that you would meet me in George Street.'

'I am sorry, my dear,' William said, offering Sarah a

cigarette from an expensive silver case. 'The streets were blocked.'

Sarah took a cigarette and William lit it for her with an equally expensive lighter. She inhaled and blew a stream of grey smoke into the stillness of the office. 'Well, you can take me to dinner. I'm sure you have a permanent table at Romano's.'

'We can do that,' William replied smoothly, offering his arm. 'I heard that your husband has been awarded the Distinguished Flying Cross for his service in Darwin. You must be proud.'

Sarah's lip curled. 'I thought that the Japanese might have done me a favour by now and sent his Spitfire into the earth,' she said contemptuously.

'You are a hard woman, Sarah Macintosh,' William said. 'I wonder what secrets you hide. I would hate to cross you.'

'Then don't wonder,' Sarah snorted as they made their way to the door, and had a flash of a memory: she was straddling her father's body, smothering him with a divan pillow until he was dead.

*

Major David Macintosh kneeled in the tall, reed-like kunai grass, examining the map spread out before him as the sun set and a full tropical moon rose, streaked by flames from a burning native hut nearby. Wewak was the next target, and his company of men would be used in the attack on the small town built on a peninsula, located on New Guinea's northern coast.

Behind David stood his second in command, Captain Brian Williams, chewing on the end of a reed and gazing at David's map.

'We just got the news that Jerry has thrown in the towel,' Captain Williams said. 'The war in Europe is over.'

'Nice to hear,' David muttered, and the words were hardly out of his mouth when both men heard the distinctive crump of a mortar being fired. Immediately Captain Williams dropped to the ground and within seconds the enemy mortar bomb exploded a few yards away, shredding the top of the kunai grass around them. It was followed by another five bombs in rapid succession, falling amongst the dispersed company.

'Too bad the Nips haven't got the message about surrender,' David said, attempting to fix the location of the Japanese mortar base plate by ear, and already calculating how his company would find and destroy the deadly tube-like weapon. 'The bloody sun might be rising over Europe and a world at peace,' he muttered, glancing at the flame-wrapped rising full moon, 'while the moon burns here.'

David's battalion was exhausted. They had been pursuing the Japanese along the north coast in mopping-up operations, and losing men to both enemy action and a virulent form of malaria. It seemed to David that he would forever be doomed to live and fight in the tropical green hell all around him, where there were only two seasons: hot and dry, hot and wet. Sometimes the jungle opened up to clearings and the kunai grass took over to shelter the heat and biting insects that made life miserable for the soldiers beating their way through it.

David turned to his radio man sitting a few paces away. 'Corp, get onto BHQ and inform them the company will go after the mortar,' he said. 'Tell BHQ we will move out in one five minutes.'

David turned to his company sergeant major. 'Sar'nt major, get the message to the platoon commanders for an

O group here in five minutes, and find out if we had any casualties.'

The CSM nodded his head and moved away from the position. David knew that the Japanese had a habit of firing on the Australians, then retreating to avoid a counterattack. Speed was essential if they were to catch the enemy and eliminate him. This was a war where no quarter was asked by either side, nor was any given. The war in the Pacific was a fight to the death.

David returned his attention to his map, already working out the advance of his company to the forest line in front of the battalion's advance towards Wewak. The heat of the early evening was oppressive, and sweat constantly dripped from every pore in the body. David reached for his water canteen and took a few sips. While he waited for his platoon commanders to join him he thought how his life had come down to simply surviving by killing as many of the enemy he could. So this was life, he mused, and wondered how much longer he and his men would be caught up before the war truly ended. The good news concerning the surrender of the Nazis hardly meant anything to them in the jungle hell of Northern New Guinea.

*

The news of Germany's surrender reached as far as central Queensland where Tom Duffy sat on the verandah of his homestead, Glen View. He puffed on his pipe as the sun slowly sank over the vast, scrub-covered brigalow plains. The smoke curled away on a gentle breeze and his beloved daughter, Jessica, sat down beside him, nursing a big mug of tea. They both cherished sharing this special time on the ancient plains when the day kissed the night. It was a rarity for them to be together and every moment was precious.

Tom had been surprised and overjoyed to see Jessica step out of a buggy a week earlier, when up until then all his enquiries into her whereabouts and welfare had been met by a stony silence from the military.

But it was not the laughing young woman he had raised as a single father that he saw that day. Not the little girl with dreams of serving either God or her country, but a young woman dramatically changed. Behind her beautiful eyes he could see pain. He knew the agony, he had seen it in the eyes of so many young soldiers who had experienced too much horror, death and mutilation. Tom had only asked the question once, and Jessica had turned to him with a sad smile, informing him that she could not talk of where she had been – or what she had done.

A couple of days after her return to Glen View a telegram had arrived to say Sergeant Jessica Duffy, WAAAF, had been gazetted for the British Empire Medal, and that the Americans had awarded her a Bronze Star for valour. Tom felt a surge of paternal pride, but did not ask why two nations had recognised what she had done. He accepted he had an extraordinary daughter who had, for a short while, been a Catholic nun, renounced her vows, and joined the Women's Australian Auxiliary Air Force to work in the top secret world of codes in General MacArthur's Brisbane HQ.

'I think I'll take young Patrick for a ride tomorrow,' she said. 'He's a great kid.'

'That would be nice,' Tom said. 'I know I'll miss him when his mother returns. She may hardly recognise him now he is going on eight years old.'

'Have you heard from her lately?' Jessica asked.

'We got one Red Cross letter a few months ago to say she was still alive in Changi,' Tom said. 'God knows how she is, from what I know of the Japs' treatment of prisoners.'

'The war has to end sooner or later,' Jessica said. 'I know from friends in the business that our Aussie troops are browned off at being allocated to mopping-up operations behind the Japs' main defensive lines, while MacArthur wins all the glory returning to the Philippines and Nimitz chases the Japs to the north in their grand pincer movement in the Pacific. Our troops are slogging it out against a trapped enemy who could have easily been bypassed. Maybe the Yanks will include us in the final campaign when we have to invade the Japanese mainland.'

'I hope not,' Tom said. 'I know the Nips well enough to also know they will fight to the last man, woman and child to defend their Emperor.'

Jessica gazed across the dusty yard at an old bumbil tree where it was said that Wallarie would sit in the latter days of his life, back in the 1930s. He was virtually blind then, but would still go on a walkabout, only to return for his supply of tea, sugar, flour and his precious pipe tobacco. She still had vague memories of him, and her father had told her how she shared his blood through the family tree.

As she grew older Wallarie seemed to haunt her life, in a nice way, and she had heretically placed him in a pantheon of saints as her protector. Jessica had never been able to shake her belief that he really was a spirit man, and this had caused problems with her religious Catholic beliefs. Wallarie had never really been a Christian – not even with the close friendship he'd had with the Lutheran pastor on the mission station on Glen View many years earlier. They were all gone now. Only some tin and mud-brick ruins were left, a few miles from the homestead.

'You know, Dad, Patrick should be going to school,' Jessica said, returning her attention to life's practicalities. 'He is a bright child who needs a formal education. I know

Abigail has done a wonderful job but he is at an age when only a school can provide an advanced education.'

Tom winced at his daughter's observation. The boy had been sent north to Glen View and had quickly adapted to life on the Brigalow plains. He had learned to ride a horse, and even learned the local dialect spoken by the Aboriginal stockmen. Patrick's best friend was Terituba, an Aboriginal boy his own age. Terituba had told him he got his name from one of his relatives who had been a great Kalkadoon warrior many years ago, and who had come to Glen View after a big battle with the whitefellas. The boys would often disappear into the scrub to hunt goannas and small wallabies with spears they had made.

Terituba had walked with his parents from the Gulf of Carpenteria. Terituba's father, Billy, had served with Tom in the Nackeroos – the North Australian Observation Unit – and had turned up at Glen View one day, simply saying that Wallarie had come to him the night and said that he must go south on walkabout to look after Tom and his family. Tom had immediately put Billy on as a stockman, and Terituba and Patrick had quickly become firm friends.

'I have thought about sending Patrick south to Sydney,' Tom said. 'Sean Duffy has said he is more than happy to look after him for the school terms, and to have him return to Glen View for the school holidays. I know Sean will see him right.'

'Great idea, Dad,' Jessica said. 'I know Uncle Sean is very fond of Patrick, and we have the money to get him the best education. Maybe he could be enrolled at St Ignatius? The Jesuits are wonderful educators. He could even board there.'

Tom tapped his pipe on his boot. 'Everything points in that direction for the lad,' he sighed, not really wanting to give up the boy he had come to love as his own son. 'Poor little bugger has been shifted from pillar to post in his short life.'

Jessica saw the pain in her father's face. She knew what a great father he had been and still was to her. He and his new bride, Abigail, had to all intents and purposes adopted the boy since his mother's imprisonment in the notorious Singapore jail.

Unknown to Jessica and Tom, young Patrick was only a few feet from where they sat. He had been playing hide-and-seek with Terituba, and overheard the conversation about him going south to school. Distressed at the idea of being sent away from the place he most felt at home, he sought out his best friend.

'They are going to send me away,' Patrick said in Terituba's dialect, as the two boys squatted in the dust behind the sprawling homestead.

'That is not good,' Terituba commented in English. 'Whitefella school they give you the cane, and you have to sit in a classroom all day.'

'How do you know?' Patrick asked, also in English.

'The whitefella send away kids to mission schools. I hear things about schools. They are bad places where you have to wash, and do what you are told.'

'Then I'll run away,' Patrick said. 'If they can't find me then I won't have to go to school.'

'I'll go with you,' Terituba said. 'I know the bush better than you.'

'Where would we go?' Patrick asked.

For a moment Terituba pondered the question. 'I don't know,' he finally answered.

'Why don't we go to the hill?' Patrick said. 'There's a creek nearby.'

Terituba looked at his friend in horror. 'Ghosts live there,' he said in a hushed voice. 'Place *baal* – bad. My mother tells us about the lights that glow in the bush at night. They are the old ones who are dead, and come back to grab us kids, and take us away if we're out there at night. Not even the stockman will go there at night.'

'Then if we go there to hide no one will think to look for us on the hill,' Patrick reasoned. 'I'll get a bag and put some food in it until we can catch our own.'

Terituba shook his head and stared at the ground. Patrick sensed that his friend was fighting with his fear. Finally, he looked up at Patrick. 'I will go with you, but if the ghosts get us I will blame you.' Friendship had won over fear.

It was time to take provisions and make their escape as soon as all were asleep in the homestead. The boys arranged a meeting spot at the bumbil tree. After that they would set out on foot in the dark to trek to the sacred hill. It was a simple plan, and Patrick figured nothing could go wrong.

TWO

The two boys trekked through the starlit night, stopping occasionally to sip from the canvas waterbag Patrick had taken from the tank stand, and nibble on the Anzac biscuits Abigail had made for the stockmen's morning tea.

Neither boy had really travelled in the night before. Terituba had often told Patrick that it was a time when the spirits roamed. The prospect of being sent south to school was enough incentive to overcome those fears. Every sound of the nocturnal animals in the dark scrub made them freeze in fright – the howling of dingos, the occasional eerie cry of bush curlews that Terituba said were the voices of the dead. Patrick had often heard them from the safety of his bedroom and would pull up the sheet lest they enter the room and snatch him away.

By sunrise they were exhausted and neither knew exactly where they were. Terituba climbed a spindly tree and called down to say that he could just see the summit of the sacred hill. Patrick was relieved and the boys decided to stop and eat.

They had a good supply of the sweet biscuits made from baked treacle and oats. The water supply was dwindling as Patrick had only been able to carry one of the waterbags. However, Patrick knew from the stockmen that the old creek bed still had pools of brackish water, which would be enough for them. Both were armed with their spears and confident that they would be able to find a goanna or small wallaby to kill, roast and eat.

They napped on the sandy soil as the sun rose to warm them and when they felt strong again they set off in the direction of the only high point on Glen View – the ancient volcanic plug that was a sacred place for Wallarie's people.

★

'Patrick's gone!'

Abigail's cry brought Tom hurrying to the boy's room, where he could see that the bed had not been slept in.

'Maybe he got up early to play,' Tom suggested with a shrug.

'All the biscuits I baked for the men have gone from the kitchen,' she said. 'I strongly suspect that Patrick took them.'

'I had better organise the lads to ride out and make a search of the property,' Tom said, hitching his braces over his shoulders with his one remaining arm – a snake bite and amputation a couple of years earlier had taken the other.

Within a matter of minutes Tom had roused his stockmen.

'My boy, Terituba, he gone too, boss,' Billy said. 'I can track 'em.'

'You lead the boys after them, Billy,' Tom said. He had witnessed Billy's tracking abilities first-hand when they worked together in the Gulf country during Tom's last posting in the army.

Billy gazed around the dusty yard. 'They go that way,' he said, pointing in the direction of the sacred hill. Billy led his horse whilst the other stockmen followed astride their own, with calls back to Tom that they would find the boys. Tom was confident that they would: he had an instinct the boys would be found safely.

*

Patrick and Terituba had reached the old sandy creek bed that meandered amongst stands of scrub and stunted trees. What struck Patrick was how silent the bush was in this place. He felt a growing apprehension.

'Place *baal*,' Terituba said, gripping his spear firmly in his hand. 'My people say a place no one should go.'

'We need to drink,' Patrick said, glancing around fearfully. He had an eerie feeling that they were being watched. 'We can dig here to see if there's water.'

Tom had taught Patrick bush survival skills and had even shown him how to find water in dry water courses. Terituba also knew of the method of searching for water and both boys began to scrape away holes with the ends of sticks.

They dug for some time without success and eventually decided the task was futile.

'Maybe we go further up the creek,' Terituba suggested. Patrick followed him out of the stand of small scrubby bushes where he could have sworn he heard the echo of children at play, laughing and shouting in a language he did not understand.

Eventually they reached a section of the creek that

looked more promising, and began to dig again. This time they unearthed a small trickle. They scooped their hands in the small pool to raise the water to their mouths. When they were sated they climbed the bank of the creek to sit as the sun slowly disappeared over the horizon. They had been travelling now for a night and a day.

'I think maybe we should go back,' Terituba said. 'We're too close to where the spirits roam. They'll get us when it gets dark.'

Patrick tended to agree. Not only because of his fear of the ghosts that haunted this part of Glen View but because he was starting to miss the company of his adopted family, Tom, Abigail and now Jessica.

Patrick knew he would be in trouble with Tom but life in the scrub was growing tedious and today was the day Abigail cooked a haunch of beef with baked potatoes, pumpkin, gravy and peas. He could almost smell the roasting meat, he was so hungry.

He placed his hand on the bank to push himself to his feet and felt something hard under his fingers. Curious, he looked down to see a half-buried old tobacco pipe. What he saw next caused him to shriek in fear; spectres rising as if growing from the ground.

Patrick was on his feet and running. Terituba, also seeing the vision of horror, ran as fast as he could away from this place of ghosts.

It was then that they ran into the small party of mounted stockmen. In their terror they did not notice the search party until they were right on top of them.

'Hey boy, why you runnin'?' Billy asked his wide-eyed, son scooping him up as he ran past.

Terituba hardly recognised that his father and it took several minutes for him to calm down. A short distance away

Patrick stood trembling as one of the stockmen dismounted and handed him a canteen of water.

'What's up?' the stockman asked Patrick, who only stared at the man in silence.

Finally he said, 'I want to go home.'

The stockmen looked at each other and glanced around at the scrub. It had a long-established reputation as a place of the dead, where a massacre had occurred many years earlier. The Aboriginal riders muttered amongst themselves, and the Europeans felt uneasy.

The two boys were pulled up behind the mounted men. It was after midnight by the time they returned to Glen View. Despite his apprehension, Patrick was not punished when the men brought him. Instead, Tom, Abigail and Aunt Jessica were kind to him before leaving him to his comfortable bed.

But Patrick had trouble sleeping as the memory of what he had seen haunted him. It was something he did not want to tell anyone. He knew that Terituba was not about to speak of the terrifying experience they had shared in that terrible place either. He hated the thought of leaving Glen View, but he also now knew that there were things more terrifying in this world than going to the city for his schooling.

*

Just on dusk Major David Macintosh was driven to battalion HQ outside of the port township of Wewak for a briefing. After passing through roadblocks his driver was directed to park the jeep a distance from BHQ. He was guided past cooks preparing a hot stew for the soldiers already in place for the attack on the fortified Japanese positions around Wewak, then through a zigzag tunnel which led underground to the CO's HQ. Here he was welcomed by the smiling Lieutenant Colonel sitting behind a table with nothing more than a field telephone and blazing pressure lamp on it. Behind the CO was his cot, and on it lay a map case, binoculars and a pistol.

Facing the camp bed was a sand model of the area around the town, showing the all-embracing mangrove swamps, a single, skinny track running beside the beach, a plateau of coral cliffs within the fortress, and most importantly, the enemy positions so far detected. David gazed at the model and knew that there would be other well-hidden positions, ensuring deadly consequences for the attacking force.

'Ah, Major Duffy, good to see you were able to make it,' the Colonel said, rising from his table to extend his hand in greeting. 'I was informed that your company were able to neutralise the Nips' mortar this afternoon. Good show.'

'Yes, sir, but I had three WIAs, one serious,' David said. 'I was hoping we might be able to get some reinforcements.'

'Sorry, Major Duffy,' the CO said, shaking his head. 'However, we will have artillery and armour support – as well as those Yankee flame throwers – for the assault. I have briefed your fellow company commanders on the mission, so you are the only one left.'

Using the sand model, the battalion CO briefed David on his mission. David learned that the attack would be from land and sea. A composite force would come ashore in Dove Cove whilst his company would be the vanguard of the land assault.

'I have put you and your men up front because you are my most experienced company commander,' the CO finished. 'We have a reserve if you think you might be getting into trouble.'

David thanked his CO and finished making notes in his field pad. It would be his job now to brief his own company senior leaders before they took the plan to their smaller sections so that each and every soldier knew what his role would be in the attack.

Later that evening when David had rejoined the battalion in its bivouac – a clearing cut from the tall trees of the jungle ringed by gun and rifle pits – and had finished preparing his men for the assault, he had a little time to himself. It was only then that his thoughts turned to Allison, the woman he had fallen in love with in Sydney, and whose constant stream of letters helped him keep his sanity. David took great pains to hide his fear from his men, who considered him fearless. If only they knew, David thought as he looked down at his trembling hands. He often wondered how long he could keep up the charade before he finally cracked. How old was he, he mused, twenty-seven, twenty-eight? Even his exact age was something he had to think about now. Time was measured in minutes and seconds in the jungle. How many good men had he seen die in the years past? He felt a hundred years old.

David knew he had to snap out of these maudlin thoughts. He reached into his pack for the pile of letters from Allison. All he had to do was simply hold them and he knew he had a reason to survive – no matter what. When the sun rose he would be leading his men into a heavily fortified Japanese position. He would once again hear the explosive sound of guns and the screams of men dying on either side, and smell the coppery, acrid stench of blood.

*

Sarah Macintosh sat at her father's desk in his library, awaiting a visitor and pondering the future and the financial empire she had inherited, which spanned the nation and beyond. She had done the impossible, leading this vast enterprise as a young woman, when all the dictates of her time said this was impossible. A woman's role was in the home, and ventures such as the one she had taken on were the sole domain of men. She realised that she was smashing all the taboos about a woman's place in society and relished proving the grey-haired men of the Macintosh companies wrong in their chauvinistic assessment of her abilities. Had not she driven greater profits with her visions in business? Under her leadership the Macintosh name would one day be known to every Australian – and even to the wide world. Such were the aspirations of Sarah Macintosh. The war would end eventually and it seemed inevitable that the Japanese would be defeated. The men would return and her brother Donald would most probably challenge her right to run the great empire. There was also her cousin, David Macintosh, who by law had an equal share in the family company. But thankfully David had never shown any real interest in the world of commerce.

Sarah felt no remorse for murdering her father. In her mind it was something that had to be done. Her father had not recognised how important it was to the Macintosh enterprise for the best person to be at the helm. Donald was not up to being that person, so her desperate measure was justified according to her cold logic. By killing her father she had ensured the great name of Macintosh would dominate into the future.

As Sarah waited she fiddled with the bulging envelope on her desk. It contained a generous quantity of pound notes and she considered it money well spent. Eventually a young servant knocked on the door to say that Inspector Preston had arrived.

The burly policeman entered the room wearing an expensive civilian suit, no doubt purchased on the black market. He did not bother to remove his hat as he slumped into a big leather chair.

'I believe I should be offering my congratulations on your promotion, Inspector Preston,' Sarah said.

'So many of the boys are leaving the job to join up that I was shuffled up the ladder,' Preston said, removing a packet of cigarettes, lighting one. 'I'm sure you realise that my promotion means I'll need a bit more in the packet than you have given me in the past.'

Sarah nodded, pushing the packet envelope to the edge of the desk. 'I anticipated as much,' she said. 'But I expect our arrangement to continue to be mutually rewarding.'

Preston retrieved the envelope, slipping it into his pocket without checking the amount. Sarah Macintosh had always been faithful to their deal, made a couple of years earlier when Preston had concealed evidence proving the coroner's decision to record Sir George Macintosh's death as an accident was not correct. Sarah's regular payments for his services as a corrupt cop had proved more generous than her father's.

Over the past couple of years they had formed an almost amicable relationship. Preston now also did shady favours for Sarah, in exchange for a little more in the regular envelope.

Preston was in no rush to leave. He could read people well enough to see that Sarah had something on her mind. He was patient, and Sarah spoke.

'How hard is it to commit a murder, and get away with it?' she asked, poker-faced.

'Well, you don't want to be related to the person you have in mind,' Preston said, equally poker-faced, blowing a smoke ring into the still air of the room. 'My experience is that the person you think loves you is the one most likely to slit your throat. We always suspect the person closest to the deceased, and we are usually right. Most of the murderers I have arrested over the years have killed someone they love. Do you have your husband in mind?'

'No, no, I was just asking a hypothetical question, Inspector,' Sarah said calmly.

'I have eyes and ears everywhere, Miss Macintosh, and I know you have a considerable list of male admirers. I suspect that your husband is ignorant of that, but no doubt will find out when he returns from the war. I also heard he does not want a divorce.'

'There is always a chance my husband may not survive the war,' Sarah said. 'He has a reputation as a fearless fighter pilot. His luck could run out. As for the divorce – I will find a way if he returns.'

'Just out of curiosity,' Preston said, rising from his leather chair. 'Who have you in mind to do away with?'

Sarah feigned shock at the question, but did not fool the experienced police officer. She looked into his eyes, and could see that he knew.

'Your brother?' Preston continued.

'No,' Sarah answered. 'Possibly someone not related to me. A person who is a threat to what I truly want.'

Preston raised his eyebrows in surprise. Never before in his long career had he met a woman so devoid of all normal human feelings. He had heard that some people were born without a part of them that feels any empathy for others. Looking down on this beautiful young woman, he knew he was in the company of such a person.

'Well, if you decide to tell me I'm sure that, for a good price, accidents can be arranged,' Preston said, shrugging his shoulders. 'Thank you for your contribution to my retirement fund, Miss Macintosh. I will catch up with you.'

Preston let himself out, leaving Sarah to ponder her dilemma. Other than owning the whole Macintosh empire outright, the only other obsession she had was for David Macintosh. He was, after all, the father of her son. The thought of possessing David was overpowering, and she knew he would see they were destined to be together.

But there was one person who stood in her way – the woman David thought he loved. If she was gone then David would realise who he should really be with. Her former best friend, Allison, had to go.

★

The firing stopped as the Japanese soldier, who had barely survived the bombardment, melted back into the jungle.

'He's gone, sir,' Donald's sergeant said with a tone of disgust for the way his platoon commander had frozen in the face of a mere handful of bullets. 'You are safe.'

Donald rose to his feet and noticed the same expressions of disapproval on the faces of his men. He knew he had failed them and felt a shame he had never known before.

'Sergeant, form the men up for the advance,' he said.

The sergeant nodded and the platoon plunged into the dense jungle spread across swampland. They sweated through around a thousand yards of the humid and hot terrain before encountering their first real resistance. A Japanese light machine gun opened up on Donald's forward scout as he crossed open ground at the edge of the swamp. Donald's men did not need an order to go to ground.

Donald raised himself up to peer across the scrubby bush at the edge of the swamp, searching for the location of the enemy machine gun. He knew it was foolhardy to expose so much of himself, but he hoped his men would see him acting with some indifference to the danger.

He lowered himself beside his sergeant.

'Nip pillbox on the knoll ahead, twelve o'clock and a hundred yards out,' he said. 'Corporal Keen's section will provide covering fire while the other two sections flank left and right. Get the section commanders to me for an O group.'

The sergeant crawled away and within minutes Donald was briefing his three platoon section commanders.

'Any questions?' he asked when he had described how they would take out the Japanese machine gun concealed under a log and earth fortification. He could see a little more respect in the faces of his men after the orders group, and they snaked away to brief their own sections on the task ahead.

Donald waited, and at the time he had set for the attack, his section, which had been tasked with providing cover fire, opened up just as the other two sections rose from the long grass to charge the pillbox. It was then that a well-hidden sniper on his flank took out one of his men with a clean shot. Donald saw the soldier stumble and pitch forward. He felt a flood of guilt. It became clear that there was not just one pillbox but several, camouflaged on and around the knoll. Machine-gun fire raked the advancing sections and they were forced to go to ground, returning small-arms fire and tossing grenades. Donald now knew what it meant to be a leader of men. They would live or die on the decision he made next.

THREE

Sarah usually met William Price in her office, but this time she had invited him to dinner at the stately Macintosh mansion overlooking the harbour. She felt comfortable enough with him to invite him into her home. After all, she knew he would be impressed by the wealth the house exuded, from the original oil paintings to the French furniture.

After the servants had cleared away the plates William was invited to smoke cigars and drink port in the library. Sarah selected a vintage wine and the two stood by the great window overlooking the fine white gravel driveway and gardens. Once, magnificent horse-drawn carriages had swept up the driveway, but those days were gone. Now, only William's car was parked in the driveway.

'So, your enquiries amongst your contacts in Canberra have produced some results,' she said.

William took a thick folder of papers from his attaché case and spread them on the teak desk. 'Your man, Mr Duffy, has a rather colourful past,' he said as they both sat down. 'From his military records I was able to ascertain that he enlisted in Townsville in the last war claiming he was of Indian descent, rather than Aboriginal. It seems in the last war Aboriginals were banned from enlisting. He was assisted in his enlistment by a prominent woman in Queensland, a Mrs Kate Tracy. He went on to serve on the Western Front and earned a reputation as a deadly sniper. The Germans nicknamed him the butcher. His company commander features a few times in Mr Duffy's records. He once recommended that Mr Duffy should be considered for the Victoria Cross for individual acts of bravery. However, our government at the time realised that he was a man of colour and downgraded his recommendation to a Distinguished Conduct Medal instead. He also earned a Military Medal with bar.'

'So, Duffy lied about his nationality when he enlisted,' Sarah said. 'I doubt we can use that against him under the current state of patriotism in this country.'

'Ah, but this is where it gets interesting,' William said, flipping a page of the file before him. 'The company commander is a man called Jack Kelly, whose record is a bit shady. Before the last war he was a gold prospector who was caught by the Germans trespassing in New Guinea. As his mother was a German from South Australia he was able to convince the Germans they had made a mistake, and they let him go. I took the liberty of looking into Mr Kelly's life and discovered that there are records of him having dubious contacts in the world of precious stones and metals. I was then able to contact a member of Mr Duffy's battalion, who informed me that Kelly and Duffy were as close as any enlisted man and officer could be. He went on to say that there was a battalion legend that Tom Duffy may have found a fortune in diamonds during an assault on a French village. But my contact was not able to confirm the story.'

Sarah's mind was racing. 'Where do we find this Jack Kelly character?' she asked.

'That will be a little hard,' William sighed. 'He is currently on active service with a Papua Infantry Battalion, somewhere in the Islands. Without corroboration from Kelly we cannot prove Duffy stole a fortune in precious stones. If we could put Jack Kelly before a court and force him to tell the truth we might have a strong case to show Duffy obtained Glen View using stolen money.'

Sarah took a sip of her port and sat down at her father's old desk. 'We can only hope that the war ends soon,' she said. 'That way I can have Mr Kelly brought before a court to answer questions under oath.'

'Why is it so important that you get some obscure cattle station?' William asked.

Sarah stared at William imperiously. 'Because it is,' she answered. 'That property is part of my heritage, and I know Lady Enid would be turning in her grave if she knew it was in the hands of those damned Duffys – especially one with Aboriginal blood. It is not that the property has any intrinsic monetary value compared to the rest of the Macintosh holdings. It's a matter of family honour to regain Glen View.'

William shook his head. 'I reckon you're obsessed with the past,' he said. 'Here you are, the only woman I know who commands so much power in a man's world, and yet all you appear to desire is getting back a heap of useless scrub and dirt.'

'I am who I am because of the blood of those who came before me,' Sarah said. 'I don't expect you to understand.'

William rose from his leather chair to go to Sarah. 'All I know is that you are the most desirable woman I have ever met,' he said. 'I don't know why you don't divorce your husband.'

'You damned well know that is almost impossible without proof in court of infidelity, and I am not about to give the public any sordid details about my private life,' Sarah said. 'All those grainy photographs taken by private investigators skulking outside bedroom windows to prove an adulterous affair. It might be different if I could do that to Charles, but he is up north with his beloved fighter squadron.'

William went down on his knees beside Sarah's chair and took her hands in his. 'You know that I love you,' he pleaded. 'I would do anything in my power to prove that to you.'

Sarah looked into the forlorn face of her lover. 'Love is just a word. The times that we are intimate are real, and that is all I need from you at the moment. Nothing more.'

William rose to his feet. 'I wonder why I stay around,' he said bitterly. 'If I didn't know any better, I would say you were using me.'

Sarah smiled. 'As you use my body for your pleasure,' she said. 'Now you know my rules.'

'Damn you!' he exploded. 'I risked a lot getting my hands on this information.'

'And you will be suitably rewarded,' Sarah said, slowly unpinning her hair, letting it fall around her shoulders. William knew she had this strange power over him, and hated himself for it. Sarah Macintosh was like some evil witch whose sensuality entrapped men.

Suddenly, Sarah ceased her seduction. 'I think you should go,' she said to William, readjusting the clothing she had begun taking off.

Confused, he stared at her. One moment she was ready to make love – or at least indulge in lust – and suddenly she turned cold.

'What is it?' he asked.

'Nothing,' Sarah replied, glancing around the library, and William thought he saw fear in her expression. 'I do not want the servants to know about us sharing in anything untoward that might affect my reputation.'

'That's not it,' William said angrily. 'It's something else.'

'It is nothing,' Sarah said, gathering up the documents on her desk and placing them in the folder. 'I will give you a call for a meeting at a later date,' she said.

He could see that Sarah was frightened but did not ask why. He had already learned she was a complex woman and that it was best to do what she said. He walked out of the library, leaving her with her fears.

When he was gone, Sarah decided that she did not want to be left alone in the library. It had happened as she was beginning to undress. First was a sudden chill that came to the dimly lit room, followed by the strong and acrid smell of pipe tobacco. Her father had never smoked a pipe. With the aroma of pipe smoke had come the uneasy feeling she was not alone in the room with William. Why had William not experienced the subtle changes? Instinctively, Sarah stared at the arrangement of Aboriginal weapons that adorned the library wall. She knew they had been gathered up after a massacre of a clan of Aboriginal people on Glen View during the middle of the last century, and her father would rattle on about a curse on the family. Sarah did not believe in such superstitious nonsense, but the experience just now had been so real. It was threatening, and had seemed to be conjured up by the conversation about Glen View.

Sarah left the library and went directly to the dining room to recover the bottle of port. She hoped that whatever had made its presence known in the library remained there.

★

The law firm of Levi & Duffy was well known to the criminal fraternity of Sydney, thanks to Major Sean Duffy, who was reputed to be one of the best criminal lawyers in the state.

Sean was sitting at his desk, perusing the daily papers for news of the war in the Pacific. He was especially interested in the campaign that had commenced at Aitape in northern New Guinea as he knew David was commanding a company there. Sean had virtually raised David and considered him a son.

Sean's assistant, Allison Lowe, walked in and placed a cup of tea in front of him, attentive as always to his well-being. Allison was a widow and had lost her husband at the battle for Milne Bay. She had resumed her maiden name, and had found a new love: Major David Macintosh.

He flicked through the pages until he found what he was looking for. The first article was headlined *RAPID AIF ADVANCE: BITTER FIGHT ON TARAKAN.* Sean knew that David's cousin and best friend, Donald Macintosh, was leading a platoon in that fight to dislodge the Japanese. Sean was very fond of Donald, whose mother he had loved – and lost to cancer. He had two boys on the frontlines and as a former decorated soldier of the Great War he knew the horror they would be confronting. He hardly had time to search for news of the Wewak situation when Allison returned to his office with a stricken expression and a document in her hand.

Sean looked at her from behind his desk. 'Allison, my dear, what is wrong?'

'I was sorting the files, and this was delivered this morning,' Alison said, thrusting a sheaf of papers at Sean, who took it and quickly scanned the contents. He could see the papers came from the Macintosh solicitors.

'Bloody hell!' Sean exploded, then realised that he had sworn in Allison's presence. 'Please excuse my language.'

'Could they really do that to Mr Duffy?' Allison asked.

For a moment Sean frowned, digesting the two main points raised in the documents. 'They appear to have grounds for declaring the sale of Glen View to Tom invalid,' he said. 'That little vixen Sarah Macintosh has never given up on regaining the property for the Macintosh name. She has had her solicitors question Tom's source of wealth, as they do not feel a person of Aboriginal ancestry is capable of earning the money he has. The other point is about a clause her lawyers found requiring that three persons – not two – must agree to the sale. They say the clause was put in company documents by Sir George before his demise and, conveniently, they've only just discovered it.'

'Can Sarah do that?' Allison asked.

'I'm afraid so,' Sean sighed. 'Or at least take it to court, and drag it out for years. In the end, Tom might win, but it could cost him a fortune in legal fees and, in the meantime, the courts could declare he must vacate the property until the matter is resolved. It would break Tom's heart. He has other properties, but Glen View is his real home.'

'That bitch!' Allison swore.

Sean smiled at her outburst. Alison's descriptive language was not like her normal ladylike ways. But the woman who had once been her best friend was now her worst enemy.

'I hope she rots in hell,' Allison added.

'Hell is in the next world,' Sean said. 'Our fight with her is in this one. I will compose a response to their letter. The last contact I had with Tom was a letter asking me to organise schooling for young Patrick, who will be arriving next week. I may need your help in that matter.'

'It will be wonderful seeing Patrick again,' Allison said, her expression brightened by the news. 'I will be pleased to help in any way I can, Major.'

Sean said she could return to her work and that he would call her when he had time to compose the letter to the Macintosh solicitors. The only thing that concerned him was the reference to Tom's mysterious wealth after he returned from the Great War. Tom had left the shores of Australia poor, and when he settled in north Queensland had suddenly amassed a great fortune. Sean had tactfully never asked how. Tom had wisely invested in property and cattle – even real estate in the southern states.

Was Tom Duffy, war hero and influential land owner, also a criminal?

★

Tom Duffy had learned of the Macintosh challenge to his legal ownership of Glen View. He had also received a letter from his old friend Sean Duffy informing him that Sarah Macintosh had employed investigators to look into the source of his wealth.

Tom sat at the kitchen table, reading the correspondence by the light of a kerosene lantern, while moths fluttered in the dim light.

Abigail sat opposite, sipping a cup of tea. 'You look concerned, my love,' she said.

Tom placed Sean's letter on the wooden table, and looked up at his wife.

'It appears that Sarah Macintosh is out to get me any way she can,' Tom sighed. 'Sean has given me a warning that her hired guns are looking into the source of my wealth.'

'You are a self-made man,' Abigail said. 'I doubt that you would have any cause for concern about anything in your past.'

'That is where you are wrong,' Tom said quietly. 'I had a little help establishing myself.'

Abigail placed her cup on the table. 'Did you do something illegal?'

'It's hard to know how to answer that question,' Tom replied. 'It happened in the last war when I was in France. During one of the battles I stumbled on a fortune in diamonds in a little village. They were meant for the Germans. There was a bit of a fight, and the diamonds ended up in my keep and not the Huns'. So I counted them as spoils of war, and kept them. I was later able to convert them into hard cash through a close friend, Jack Kelly, and then into property holdings. Maybe at the time I should have handed over my find, but I doubt the diamonds would have ever been turned in to the proper authorities. It was war, and moral scruples were in short supply. Jack agreed with my decision and so did others I held dear.'

'My goodness!' Abigail exclaimed. 'I would never have thought that was the reason for your wealth.'

'Well, do you now think I'm a criminal?' Tom asked.

Abigail broke into a smile, shaking her head and grasping Tom's hand across the table. 'I could never think that, my dear,' she said. 'You are a very special man who I love more than anything else on this earth.'

Tom squeezed her hands and knew that he was blessed. He only wished he had two hands to hold both of Abigail's.

Sean's warning worried Tom. How good was Sarah Macintosh at digging deep into a man's past? He suspected that she was very good at destroying people.

★

Captain James Duffy stepped out of the Los Angeles cab and slung his sea bag over his shoulder. He looked up at the plush hotel. It was his last stop on his war bonds drive before returning to active service in the Pacific war. He knew he was only forty-eight hours from a transport flight to a new squadron, and being in LA brought back sad memories of the loss of the woman he had fallen in love with. Julianna was in New Orleans, and the bustling city under a summer sun felt empty without her.

With a sigh, James stepped into the foyer and confirmed his reservation at the desk.

'There is a message for you, Captain Duffy,' the reception clerk said, handing James a sheet of paper.

It was from Guy Praine. It appeared that Guy was also in LA and wanted to meet him for dinner at a restaurant they liked and had often gone to when James was posted to Hollywood a couple of years earlier, to assist with raising morale amongst the many workers in the war industry. Ciro's nightclub on Sunset Boulevard had rapidly become one of the favourite haunts of the big names in entertainment, and was frequented by the likes of Lauren Bacall, Humphrey Bogart and Cary Grant, to mention just a few. James liked the nightclub because it was not as gaudy as some others on the Sunset Strip. Guy had used his influence to reserve a table for them and suggested they meet there at 7pm.

That evening, James arrived wearing his uniform as he had not packed any civilian clothing. His arrival in the club turned the heads of several beautiful young ladies. He cut a fine figure and the wings on his chest added to the glamour. Guy was sitting at a table with a woman James guessed to be in her sixties. James walked over and Guy stood to grasp his hand.

'I have an old friend with us tonight,' Guy said. 'I presume you already know the name Miss Louella Parsons.'

James broke into a broad smile, and Louella cast him an admiring glance. 'Who has not heard of the most famous lady in Hollywood?' he said, taking her proffered hand. 'And I must say, one of the prettiest.'

Louella broke into a laugh at James's unsubtle attempt at flattery. 'Young man, you obviously have Irish blood, with your blarney. I also have Irish blood, as well as German and Jewish. I think Docky would like you.'

James remembered that Docky was Louella's husband, a surgeon currently serving with the Army Medical Corp, who had also served in the Great War as an army medico. He was glad he had some common ground with the husband of the most feared columnist in Hollywood, one whose words could make or break a career in the entertainment industry. People loved gossip about the stars, and Louella gave them what they wanted. She had a keen eye, good hearing and an ability to turn words into weapons.

'I was not aware that you knew anyone of real importance, Guy,' James said with a grin as he sat down at the table.

Almost immediately, a waiter placed three martinis in front of them. 'Compliments of Mr Haver,' the waiter said, quickly withdrawing.

The manager also clearly knew it was important to curry favour with this woman who was larger than life.

The club was crowded and couples danced to the big band orchestra, belting out a song made popular by Jimmy Dorsey and his orchestra, 'Bésame Mucho'.

Louella glanced around the club for any well-known Hollywood personalities. 'I feel my column will be short on scandal.' She sipped her martini, and James saw her eyes light up with delight. 'I spoke too soon.'

James followed her gaze to a couple being ushered to a table not far from the dance floor. His heart felt as if it had stopped beating. Guy also noticed the entrance of the handsome young couple, and blinked in surprise. 'It seems Julianna is not in New Orleans,' he said, looking across at James.

'It is obvious that you two gentlemen know Miss Julianna Dupont and her fiancé, the noted director, Mr Simon Ledger,' Louella said.

'We do,' Guy replied, but did not elaborate.

James continued to stare at Julianna. She looked ravishing in a long, black, body-hugging dress. She was every bit as beautiful as he remembered. She was smiling at the director James had wanted to punch in the face on their first meeting. Every memory he had of the time they had shared welled up, and James realised that he was clenching his fists in his lap.

'I think we should find another club,' Guy said, noticing James's reaction. 'It appears this one is getting a bit crowded.'

'No,' James answered, knocking back his martini 'Everything is Jim Dandy.'

'Are you sure?' Guy asked quietly, leaning forward to his friend across the white linen table cloth.

'It's my last night stateside before I go back to the war,' James said, calling over a waiter for another drink. 'I intend to enjoy it.'

'Do I sense some tension, gentlemen?' Louella asked mischievously, as James downed another martini.

'Not at all,' Guy said smoothly. 'If you want to know, Louella, the lady with Ledger was once a close friend of Captain Duffy.'

'How interesting,' Louella said, leaning forward. 'There is a rumour that Simon Ledger is going to direct a film Miss Dupont has written about an actress, Fenella Macintosh, who was murdered here some years ago. It was a case the police never solved, and she has adapted the screenplay from her book.'

'If you will excuse me,' James said, suddenly rising from the table, 'I should go over and offer my congratulations to Miss Dupont.'

Guy was afraid this would happen but powerless to stop James. He watched as James weaved his way towards Julianna, and groaned. 'Louella, regarding what may occur in the next few minutes, I would ask as a great favour that you do not report it in your column.'

'What do you mean?' Louella asked, intrigued by the request.

'James was more than just a friend of Miss Dupont,' Guy said. 'He was in love with her, but she dumped him while he was flying in the Pacific. James has never got over the breakup.'

'Oh, my!' Louella exclaimed.

Ledger and Julianna both saw James approach at the same time. Ledger's expression was clouded with anger and Julianna's with surprise.

'Hello, Julianna,' James said, standing over the table. 'I just wanted to congratulate you on your success in having your book turned into film. I always figured you had the talent.'

'This is a private moment, Captain,' Ledger growled. 'We do not wish to be pestered by drunken soldiers.'

'I'm not a soldier,' James said. 'I'm a marine, and there is a big difference.'

Julianna was still speechless and was perceptive enough to see the dangerous coldness in the eyes of the man she once loved. 'James, thank you for your kind words,' she said, attempting to defuse the situation. 'Simon and I would prefer to be left alone.'

'I didn't come over to start anything,' James replied. 'I just came over to congratulate you on the story of Fenella Macintosh making it to the screen. I remember how we talked about her at your office one night.'

Ledger pulled away his napkin, rising to his feet to confront James. 'Listen, buddy, I don't care who you think you are, but this is a private affair, and you were not invited, so push off.'

'Simon, Captain Duffy is leaving,' Julianna pleaded, reaching to grip the arm of her fiancé.

'That's right . . . buddy,' James said. He had turned to return to the company of Guy and Louella when Ledger sneered behind his back, 'Not so tough when they are out of the cockpit of their planes.'

Despite the two martinis he had consumed James was able to turn and swing a good right haymaker that caught Ledger in the jaw, causing him to crumble senseless to the floor amongst a scatter of table and chairs. A woman shrieked, and in the ruckus that followed James found himself pinned to the floor of the nightclub by two men. Julianna stood above him with a shocked expression, her hands to her face.

Ledger was helped to his feet by staff, while James remained held to the floor.

'I will see you locked up for this!' Ledger yelled at James.

Julianna was clutching at Ledger's arm, 'No, Simon, you will do no such thing.'

'Better make it quick,' James said from the floor. 'I'm off to the Pacific in the next twenty-four hours.'

Ledger wiped away a trickle of blood from his nose with a handkerchief. 'The man assaulted me! Look! I'm bleeding.'

'You provoked James,' Julianna said.

'Whose side are you on?' Ledger snapped. 'The man is a no better than a common criminal.'

'James is a hero who is returning to the war, Simon,' Julianna said calmly. 'How do you think a judge would feel about someone like you, living a life of luxury, pressing charges against a man like James, risking his life out in the Pacific so you can be safe at home?'

'I suspect when I report this incident in my column, Mr Ledger,' Louella Parsons said from behind Julianna, 'many of my readers, like Ford, Capra and Wyler, might be asking why *you* are not out on the frontlines. I doubt that you will fare well with Hollywood's producers. I agree with Miss Dupont, you should forget the incident.'

Ledger glared at Louella, dabbing his bleeding nose. He knew the power of this woman, and feared her. 'Let the captain go,' he said reluctantly to the two men holding James down on the floor. 'I only ask that he leave now, and not bother my fiancée and myself.'

James rose to his feet, patted his uniform down and turned to Julianna. 'I'm sorry for what happened – but not for what I did. I hope you have a good life.'

Before Julianna could respond, James had walked away.

The next afternoon he was on a cargo plane flying to Hawaii. Opposite James sat a very young soldier reading a Captain America comic book. James knew that the character had been created directly as a response to the war effort. The cartoon character, wearing the red, white and blue, holding a shield, was intended to raise morale.

James leaned forward to the young soldier. 'What happens to Captain America when the war is over?' he asked.

The young soldier blinked in surprise at the question. 'I dunno, sir,' he replied.

James leaned back in his canvas seat. 'Maybe the same thing that will happen to us all when the war is over. We will be without much of a future,' he said quietly, as the twin-engine transport plane flew west towards the war.

FOUR

It had been a long journey on the railway from Queensland to Sydney, but young Patrick had thought it a thoroughly exciting experience. He had befriended Australian and American soldiers returning from the battlefronts of the Pacific. The Americans had given him gifts of chocolate and chewing gum, which he had hoarded away in his small suitcase now bulging at the seams.

The train eventually arrived at Central Station in the early hours of the morning. When Patrick stepped out of his carriage he saw the familiar figures of his uncle Sean Duffy leaning on his walking stick and Miss Allison waiting for him in the fog of steam and coal smoke. Allison rushed forward through the crowd of uniformed soldiers and hugged him tight, while Sean hobbled after her as fast as he could. Any trepidation about coming south quickly dissipated in the warmth of Uncle Sean's welcome on this chilly morning in Sydney.

'It is good to have you with us, Patrick,' Sean said, extending his hand. 'I'm sure that you are weary after such a long trip.'

'Oh, no, Uncle Sean,' Patrick said. 'Some nice Yank soldiers taught me how to play poker last night, and I even won some money.'

Sean and Allison looked at each other with barely concealed grins.

'I suppose snakes and ladders will be a bit dull after poker,' Sean said.

'No, Uncle Sean. I still like playing snakes and ladders.'

The three made their way to the exit gates to enter the cavernous hall that led out to the streets of Sydney. Patrick kept his suitcase close as it held a small fortune in American delicacies that would have to last him for some time. He wished he could stay with Uncle Sean the whole time he was in Sydney, but everyone was insisting he go to boarding school. He supposed it was a good idea but he could not help but think with envy of Terituba roaming freely back home. As far as Patrick was concerned, playing in the bush and learning to make spears and hunt was the only education a boy needed. It was a shame that the adults did not agree.

★

Many miles west of Sydney in the rolling green hills of Goulburn, in a sprawling country house, a two-year-old boy stood naked in front of the great open fireplace where a big log glowed red and warmed the room. His nanny, Miss Val Keevers, rubbed him down with a fluffy towel.

Her mistress had only visited her son once in the two years of the boy's life, and that had only been for half a day when she was en route to Canberra for a meeting. There had been no real bond between mother and son and the only real mother the boy knew was the woman who cared for him. Val had come to love the little boy she was raising as her own, but was reminded when she received her pay from the Macintosh companies that she was merely an employee with the task of caring for Sarah's son.

After Michael was dressed in his pyjamas Val found the battered book about a bear called Winnie the Pooh. She sat him on her lap and began to read the story, which she'd read to him countless times before, and eventually the little boy fell asleep. Val closed the book and ran her hands through the thick mat of Michael's dark hair.

'You poor little mite,' she said quietly, forcing back tears. 'You don't really have a mother – but I will always be with you.'

Outside the sprawling country house the wind whipped up cold sheets of rain that rattled the windows, and Michael Macintosh slept in his beloved nanny's arms by the fire.

*

Patrick was frightened but was determined not to show his fear as he walked beside Uncle Sean up the driveway of the imposing three-storeyed stone structure that was St Ignatius College. They passed a white statue of a strange-looking person wearing a long gown. In the distance Patrick could see green sporting grounds and hear the shouts of students echoing from the rugby fields.

To a boy who had enjoyed the freedom of the bush, where he had lived a life of bare-footed adventure, the school felt restrictive and cold. A bald-headed man wearing a long, black cassock and spectacles welcomed them at a massive entrance door.

'Major Duffy,' he said. 'I see you have our latest addition in tow.'

Patrick wanted to grip Sean's hand but that would not be manly.

'Father,' Sean said, 'may I introduce Master Patrick Duffy.'

The Jesuit priest looked Patrick up and down. 'He looks strong and healthy,' he said. 'Does he play any sports?'

Sean looked to Patrick, who piped up, 'I can throw a spear and kill a goanna.'

'Well, we do have javelin throwing on the athletics team,' the priest said with a hint of a smile. 'Come in and we can settle matters for his boarding with us,' he said, turning to enter the portals of the school's administration.

Sean and Patrick followed him. Patrick felt uncomfortable in the school uniform that had been purchased for him. He had never worn a blazer before, and it felt foreign. They passed other boys of various ages wearing the same uniform in the hallways, who gave Patrick the occasional curious glance as a foreigner in their ranks.

The priest led them to a dormitory, where neat rows of beds and lockers spoke of conformity. Patrick was directed to a bed, and on the adjacent bed he saw a smaller boy sitting forlornly with his hands clasped.

'Why aren't you at sports, Murphy?' the priest asked the smaller boy.

'I don't feel well, Father,' the boy replied without standing.

'Stand up, Murphy,' the priest commanded. Murphy rose to his feet obediently and stood mute. 'You can make yourself useful and help our new boy settle in then.'

'Sadly, Murphy's father was killed last month, somewhere up in New Guinea,' the priest continued quietly to Sean. 'We have to allow him a bit of latitude.'

'Patrick's mother is a prisoner of war in Changi,' Sean said. 'But he has adjusted, and occasionally gets a letter from her. He lost his father before he was born.'

The priest nodded sadly. 'I am sure Patrick will find friends amongst the other boys,' he said. 'He may find things strange at first, but after a time he will settle in. I'm afraid that from your reports about his schooling out in the bush we will have to put him back a class.'

'I understand,' Sean said, watching Patrick looking in his empty locker. 'He is highly intelligent and I'm sure will do well with his lessons.'

'Murphy, you are now in charge of showing young Duffy around the school and teaching him about some of our traditions,' the priest said. 'Say goodbye to the major, Duffy. It is time for him to leave.'

'I'll see you on the weekend,' Sean said. 'I'm not too far away. Chin up and remember that you're a Duffy.'

Patrick fought back tears as he watched the departing back of his Uncle Sean.

'My name is Ken Murphy,' the boy said. 'I come from Hillston.'

'I'm Patrick Duffy and I come from Glen View.'

The boys formally shook hands.

'How old are you?' Patrick asked.

'I'm eight but I had to go back one class. You and I are in the same class. Father John is a real bastard. You'll see. He loves to use the cane.'

Patrick was perplexed by the reference to the cane but did not want to exhibit his ignorance.

'You have to remember when you're writing that you have to put AMDG at the top left on every page or you'll be in trouble,' Ken said.

'What's AMDG?' Patrick asked.

'Aunt Mary's Dead Goat,' Ken replied. 'Not really,' he continued when he saw the confusion on Patrick's face. 'It's something in Latin which means "to the greater glory of God". I hate Latin. You have to decline all the words, and only the old Eyties speak Latin. Come on, I'll take you around the grounds and show you where everything is. We even have an observatory where you can see the stars through a telescope.'

Ken continued to natter about many things which were strange to Patrick, but the smaller boy was friendly, and Patrick thought they could be friends. Maybe when they were he could ask his new friend what the cane was and why Father John was a bastard. It was a word he'd been told he should never use.

They were at one of the green sports grounds when Patrick saw the school rugby team practising. One of the boys on the sideline, who seemed at least three years older than Patrick, was wiping down his face, and spotted Ken showing the new boy the football field.

'Hey, Murphy!' the boy yelled. 'You stopped wetting your bed since your old man got killed?'

Patrick turned to Ken and saw tears welling in his eyes. Without hesitation, Patrick strode over to the older boy.

'You take that back,' Patrick demanded, standing squarely in front of the older boy, who stared at him with an expression of amusement.

'Who are you?' he asked, throwing aside the wet towel, shoving Patrick in the chest. 'Don't you know who I am?'

With all his strength, Patrick delivered a good punch square to the face of the older boy, who stumbled back in shock, his hand up to his bleeding nose. The altercation caught the attention of the boys playing rugby, and they came running to the sideline. The older boy launched himself at Patrick, who was quick to step aside and leap on his back as he had learned wrestling with Terituba at Glen View. As if possessed, Patrick put a stranglehold on his assailant's neck, choking him, until hands reached down to rip Patrick away.

'Hey, new boy, we could do with you on the team when we play Joeys,' a voice laughed, before he was marched off the grounds.

Patrick had hardly been on the school grounds an hour when he found out about Father John and his cane.

News of the fight circulated through the dining room that evening, and Patrick learned he had taken on the infamous bully of the school and beaten him into submission. Ken Murphy stood tall beside Patrick, whose sudden reputation for being fearless was like a suit of armour for them both.

In the weeks ahead Patrick became firm friends with Ken. He discovered a love for the game they called rugby and even a liking for Latin. It was only when he was in bed and the lights were turned out that the young boy stared into the darkness and wondered what was to become of him. No father, and a mother he barely remembered. He tried to cling to the image of his mother's sad face as he stepped aboard a train carriage in Malaya headed south for Singapore. That seemed a lifetime ago.

*

Diane Duffy felt waves of nausea overwhelm her as she kneeled on the concrete floor of the prison ablutions. She dropped the scrubbing brush and leaned forward against the cement wall. Changi had been a criminal prison before the war and now housed military servicemen as well as civilian men, women and children. It was overcrowded and malnutrition had brought with it starvation and disease.

Diane simply dismissed the bout of nausea a result of the appalling food the prisoners referred to as 'slush and ash'. Even the rations had been cut back. But just before VE Day in Europe, the Japanese had strangely doled out extra Red Cross parcels.

'Mother, are you ill?' the voice of her adopted son came to her from the doorway.

Young Sam was Eurasian – the child of a European father and an Asian mother. Diane had agreed to look after him when she was first incarcerated in the POW camp. Although she thought about Patrick every day, she was comforted by the knowledge that he was safe in Australia and being cared for by her late husband's relatives. Sam was about the same age as Patrick. If the war ever ended someone might claim Sam, but secretly, Diane hoped he would remain with her.

Diane rose slowly to her feet and wiped her mouth with the back of her hand. She could see the fear in the young boy's face. He had already seen so many die. He came to her and placed his arms around her skeletal body.

'Sheila's dad is really sick,' Sam said. 'I think he is going to die.'

Sheila Allan was Sam's friend, also a Eurasian. She was a young woman entering her twenties. Her father was an Australian engineer and her mother a Malayan woman. Diane knew that Sheila was bravely keeping a diary of their imprisonment. This was against the strict rules, and discovery by the guards of its existence could result in execution. Sam worked with her in the prison vegetable garden that produced a meagre amount of fresh food.

'Woman, get yourself to the infirmary,' a voice commanded, and Diane saw her friend, the English woman Ann Bambury, appear in the ablutions block. She was both mother and sister to Diane as they faced each uncertain day in the infamous prison.

Diane tried to smile and realised the fever was rapidly returning. She slumped to the floor and was quickly propped up by Ann and young Sam, who half-dragged, half-walked her to the infirmary with its tiny supply of valuable drugs.

As Diane lay on a cot in a world of pain and despair, she wondered if she would ever survive the hellhole. She knew Ann would take over looking after Sam if she died, but if she died she would never again hold her precious son. The war might be won against the Nazis in Europe but that meant very little to those in Japanese captivity. Could it be that the Japanese might kill them all if they thought they were losing? It was a fear expressed by many in the prison. Diane wondered why they all fought so desperately to stay alive when the Japanese might finish them with a bullet or bayonet at any moment.

'Patrick,' she sighed as darkness came for her.

*

Captain James Duffy had not been posted to a carrier as he had hoped. Instead he found himself flying a Corsair fighter bomber from a captured airfield on the Japanese island of Okinawa. Upon his arrival he had been regaled by his fellow USMC pilots with stories of fighting off waves of kamikaze aircraft launched in a desperate attempt to sink the massive fleet of Allied British and American ships off the coast.

The Pacific had seen its own D-day landing on the shores of the enemy homeland island weeks earlier, and the attack had been very costly to the marines and army. The slog along the heavily defended island had seen at least twelve thousand soldiers killed and another fifty thousand wounded.

James was about to lend air support to the crushing of the last bastion of Japanese resistance before the invasion of the Japanese main islands north of them.

The roar of the big fighter bomber engine drowned all sound except for that in his headphones. He waited patiently for his turn to take off and felt the power of the deadly bird of war vibrate through the controls of the machine. He was armed with rockets and wing-mounted fifty calibre machine guns. This cargo would assist the troops on the ground in destroying a dogged enemy prepared to do anything to stop the Allies advancing on the home of their divine emperor.

While he waited, James considered his life. It was obvious that the enemy was in retreat and that the war could end soon enough now that the Japanese allies of Germany and Italy were out of the war. It would mean releasing the soldiers, sailors and airmen in Europe to reinforce their fight in the Pacific.

The command to lift off came through James's headphones, and he raised his hand to signal to his ground crew that he was ready to take off.

Gently he eased the big blue aircraft with the bent wings forward onto the tarmac to join the others. In turn each pilot opened up their aircraft's throttles to gain power. James felt the fighter bounce gently down the strip into the wind, picking up speed and finally lifting off. Ahead was a string of high ground where the Japanese were well dug in, and behind him was his life of memories.

The chatter of his squadron comrades filled his ears as he glanced around the terrain below to identify his target. He watched as one of the Corsairs peeled off, releasing its rockets. Adjusting his flight path James reached down for the trigger to the rockets and fired. The weapons rushed away, leaving a thin smoke trail to indicate their path. He flicked to machine guns and the rockets impacted on the earth below as a stream of heavy fifty cal tracers followed them. Somewhere below James knew there was a good chance men were being killed or mutilated, by the weapons of his fighter bomber, but he did not care. If killing the enemy was what was needed to bring the war to an end, so be it. The war had hardened James, and as far as he was concerned, the enemy below was not even human.

FIVE

Allison was always at her desk when Sean arrived at the law offices, popping his head around the corner to wish her a good morning. When he did so this morning he immediately noticed that she was distracted.

'What is it?' he asked.

'How did you know?' she countered.

'Let's say an instinct,' Sean replied. 'You don't have your usual good morning face. What's going on?'

'It may be nothing,' Allison said. 'I may even be paranoid, but I feel like I'm being followed.'

Sean raised his eyebrows. 'In my business paranoia is good,' he said, stepping into her small office, which was cluttered with manila folders secured with thin pink ribbons. 'I've experienced it myself over the years, and it usually turned out people were actually trying to kill me. Why do you think you're being followed?'

'For the last couple of weeks I've noticed a man following me to the tram, and another one when I get off. They don't seem to be going anywhere, and always wear their hats low over their eyes. Sometimes, it's the same men each day.'

'You are a beautiful young lady: have you considered that they may be interested in that fact and nothing more?' Sean tried to reassure her.

'I understand what you're saying, Major, but it doesn't feel like that,' Alison said, tapping the base of a pencil on her desk. 'I've even seen men standing on the street outside my flat at night. They look a bit like policemen.'

'If it helps, I'll have a word to a mutual friend who'll investigate whether you are just paranoid, or if there is something else afoot,' Sean said. 'If there is something sinister, it may be your old foe Sarah Macintosh attempting to intimidate you.'

'I considered that,' Allison said. 'She has a real obsession with David, and we know what devious lengths she will go to to get her way.'

'There's an old saying that the apple does not fall far from the tree, and in Sarah's case it's very true,' Sean said. 'I thought Sir George was dangerous, but I am coming to think his daughter could be potentially far more dangerous. She has youth and beauty on her side and she uses that to manipulate people. Leave it with me and I'll sort out the situation.'

Allison nodded her appreciation, and Sean left her to comb through the files in her office.

He went to his own office and closed the door. Lifting the telephone receiver he dialled a familiar number and waited.

'Harry Griffiths gym, Harry speaking,' the gruff voice answered.

'Harry, how's your cash flow?'

'Major Duffy . . . Sean, how the devil are you? The answer to your question is that I could do with a job. Things are still slow around the gym.'

'I have a job that is right up your alley,' Sean said. 'I need a surveillance job done on Allison. She thinks that she might be being followed each day to work, as well as being watched in her flat by night. You are on the clock as from this afternoon, and money is no object for your time and expenses.'

'Boss, I would do it for free for you,' Harry said. The former NSW policeman, Great War soldier and sometime private investigator who also owned a gym had known Sean for many years, and Sean considered Harry one of his best friends.

'Well, Harry, old cobber, you get paid for your time and my personal gratitude for taking on the job. I know that you're able to keep an eye on her safety. We're also well overdue to get together for a cold beer.'

Sean replaced the receiver and stared at the wall. Now he had two problems concerning Sarah Macintosh. He did not think that Allison was being paranoid. Sean knew all too well what Sarah Macintosh was capable of, and that included murder. Based on his years of experience handling homicide defences Sean held suspicions about the death of Sarah's father. Sometimes justice came outside of the law, and some deserved to die without recourse to the niceties of the legal system.

★

Sarah did not worry that people knew of her meetings with Detective Inspector Preston. After all, he was famous in Sydney circles as the man most feared by hardened criminals.

There was also talk he was not the most honest copper in town, but the power he wielded was enough to silence any critic through fear or favour.

Preston was as familiar to the servants at Sarah's house as he was to the staff at the Macintosh offices in the city. Today he simply went directly to the lavish boardroom she kept for board meetings and receiving important clients. Sarah entered, closing the door behind her.

'Has my generous allowance to you paid any dividends?' Sarah asked.

Preston shook off the cold of the wet winter's day and looked out a window with a view of the city's harbour. He could see the grey warships of many nations at anchor as little ferries conveying people dodged between them on their way to Circular Quay.

'It depends,' Preston answered, his hands in his trench-coat pockets. 'I can tell you that Miss Lowe leads a pretty boring life. Not even many trips to the flicks.'

'I know she lives a boring life,' Sarah answered, lighting a cigarette and puffing smoke into the warm air of the room. 'What can you do to liven up her life?'

'A bit more than what I heard on the streets. It was a pretty pathetic affair to try to blackmail her with dirty pictures,' Preston said with a grim smile. 'You employed amateurs. You should have come to me.'

'You were in my father's employ at the time,' Sarah replied. 'I had to settle for second-best. What can you do to earn the extra money I pay you?'

'You must really hate that woman,' Preston said, shaking his head.

'It's not of any concern to you what my feelings for her are,' Sarah retorted. 'I just want her to be punished for what she has done to me.'

'Punished?' Preston said. 'You know I have the means to do that for you. I am the law in this city, and I can do what I want. The department is too scared to question my methods as I get results that make those in headquarters look good in the morning papers. Do you really want me to punish this woman?'

'I don't care if you can arrange for her to go missing,' Sarah answered, taking a long puff on her cigarette. 'As a matter of fact, that would be the ideal situation. Perhaps she could have a fatal accident . . .'

'I have other means of getting what you want,' Preston said. 'Missing is a last resort but not one I would dismiss. That situation would require a very big payout.'

'I'll trust you to do whatever you have in mind, Inspector Preston,' Sarah said. 'But you only get the bonus on a satisfactory result for me.'

Preston reached into his coat for a cigarette. Yes, he had a way of satisfying his client's request but he would use the law to do so. It would all be above board and should earn him points with his superiors in the force. Allison Lowe was as good as finished.

★

Tom Duffy watched the two horsemen approaching his front gate. With his keen eyesight he could identify the blue uniformed man as the local police sergeant. The other, he did not know.

When they reined in their horses Tom greeted his visitors.

'G'day Tom,' the police sergeant said. 'I'm afraid I come bearing bad news. The man with me is a court bailiff and he has some papers for you about property obtained with unlawful proceeds.'

Tom looked across at the man standing beside the burly police officer. He looked like an office worker with his pale complexion, and Tom guessed he was a young court clerk. 'I think I know what your mate has for me,' Tom said, stretching out his hand. 'I'll make it easy for him.'

The legal clerk handed Tom the reams of paper with an almost audible sigh of relief. 'I'm sorry, Mr Duffy,' he apologised, 'just doing my job.'

'That's okay, son,' Tom said, barely looking at the papers. 'A man cannot be punished for doing what he is paid to do.'

'You have seven days from midnight tonight to vacate Glen View, Tom,' the sergeant said in an apologetic tone. 'I'm also just doing my job and there is nothing else I can do.'

Tom shook his head in understanding, turned and walked back to the house. The two visitors mounted their horses and rode away.

Tom slumped down at the kitchen table, dropping the papers on the floor.

'What is it, dear?' Abigail asked, entering the room.

'We've just been given notice that we have to leave Glen View within a week,' Tom replied in a weary voice. 'It appears the Macintosh companies are disputing my right to own the property.'

'What will we do?' Abigail asked, sitting down at the table with Tom. 'Where will we go?'

'I'll send you to our station out of Townsville,' Tom said. 'I've not decided yet what I'll do.'

Abigail reached across the table to take her husband's hand in her own. 'You should come with me until this matter is sorted out in the courts,' she said, fearing Tom was considering doing something rash.

Tom looked up at the .303 Lee Enfield bracketed on the wall. He had little faith in the legal system that leaned towards the rich and powerful. As wealthy as he was, he could not match the might of the Macintosh enterprises.

'Maybe it's time I went back to war,' he said quietly.

This was the land of his Aboriginal ancestors. His Irish blood was also buried on Glen View. He had fought the enemies of the British Empire in two world wars. Maybe it was time to fight for something even more important to him: his land.

★

Wewak fell and David's company moved on with the battalion to root out any remaining pockets of Japanese resistance.

David sat with his back against a giant tree in the forest whose entwined canopy blocked the remaining sunlight, resting for a moment as his company spread out around him to bivouac for the night. He had overseen each of the platoon defensive positions, and he was tired. An infantryman was a creature who learned to live on little sleep. David had long learned how to take short naps – sleeping in mud, in the bottom of a trench or, as now, with his back to a tree – his rifle in his lap. Beside him the company signaller sat by the field telephone listening for any signals coming in from battalion HQ or platoon commanders.

'Hello, old boy,' Captain Brian Williams said, crouching down beside his company commander. 'Brought you a coffee from some of those Yankee rations we found back at Aitape.'

David gratefully accepted the battered mug of hot black coffee, taking a sip.

'Do you think we're doing any good out here?' Brian asked, pulling a pipe from his pocket and plugging it with tobacco. 'All we seem to come across are half-starved Nips who are now on the run. The Yanks are getting all the glory and one could feel that they've left us behind to mop the floors of an empty, disused building.'

'With words like that, Brian, you should be writing novels,' David said. 'You know the old saying, ours is not to question why.'

Brian lit his pipe and took a few short puffs to keep it alight. 'We are losing more of our men to disease than to Jap bullets,' he said. 'Once fit men will end up spending years to shake off the effects of every bloody disease known to man – and some, I suspect, they don't really know about. We are short on officers, and that platoon commander we got sent yesterday fought his war at brigade HQ pushing a pencil. He has never really seen any combat. He's a nice chap but I worry what will happen if we really hit something big.'

'No choice in who we get,' David said. 'I asked the boss for an officer with a bit of experience, but he said Mr Markham graduated near the top of his class at Duntroon. It appears that his father is a member of parliament and has some pull in Canberra.'

'Bloody hell!' Brian exclaimed with a short laugh. 'None of us went to Duntroon. We were all civvies when the war broke out, and will return to being civvies when it ends. As for that, the boss was an accountant before the war, and has the best bloody tactical mind of any soldier this war has seen. You know that when this war ends, even you will never be promoted beyond your current rank, because you did not graduate Duntroon. And that is despite your truly impressive record of leadership.'

'We'll give Mr Markham the benefit of the doubt, and I'll trust you to keep an eye on his performance,' David said. 'If he stuffs up, put Sergeant Hayden Clarke in charge of the platoon.'

Brian nodded. 'I'd better go and chase up the CSM about the extra grenades we ordered to be brought up,' he said in his capacity of company second in command. It was not the role most officers desired in an infantry company, but he was also trained to take charge of the company if anything happened to David.

That night was uneventful and the company had time to eat and prepare for the next day. At first light the men moved out, ready to sweep and clear any Japanese soldiers.

As David moved with his small company HQ group, putting two platoons forward and one in reserve, what they saw on the advance confirmed the enemy's pitiful state. The day before, they had come across a small convoy of bullet- and shrapnel-riddled Japanese trucks rusting in the hot, humid air. Scattered about the trucks were the skeletons of enemy soldiers draped in rags. David remembered the strange smell of the rotting earth – and the incense the Japanese liked to burn. It was obvious the men were killed in a strafing by an Allied fighter bomber, and their comrades did not attempt to retrieve the dead for burial. He could see they were mopping up an enemy already on the brink of destruction from starvation and disease.

For the first five miles of the company advance they struggled through swampy undergrowth interspersed by creeks. Then the track began to rise up a long spur into the mountains where intelligence said the main body of the remaining Japanese army were mostly likely to be dug in.

David knew he must send one of his platoons out another two miles to scout and wait for their report. The platoon dragged a signals line behind them, and in the early afternoon the report came back that the platoon had encountered around a section of Japanese. David calculated that even if his platoon outnumbered the enemy section three to one it was better that he get reinforcements up to his clearing unit. Who knew how many other Japanese were in the area? He ordered out the second of his trusted platoon commanders, keeping the newly joined platoon commander, Lieutenant Markham, in his reserve for company HQ protection. Just on dark the report came back over the field telephone: the second platoon had made contact with what they thought was another enemy section armed with light machine guns. The platoon commander requested direction from company HQ and David said to engage them. What followed was a short but sharp firefight.

David ordered his platoon commander to dig in and wait for him to join them in the morning. The platoon did so and David ordered his remaining men to make their way forward to join the rest of the company. At least they would have around a hundred men to take on whatever lay out on their flank. The going was hard in the rugged terrain and marching at night a dangerous venture, but by first light they reached the location of his second platoon.

David ordered three shots to be fired in the air as the prearranged signal, and was challenged over the field telephone. He had to give his full name for clearance, and when this was done welcomed into the second platoon's position, where he met the platoon commander.

'How did last night go?' David asked his young officer as they squatted amidst the pushed-up logs and shell scrapes in the tangle of tall trees and scrubby bushes.

'I had the boys run some jungle vines down the slope to follow in the dark and made contact with the Nips,' he replied, leaning on his rifle. 'From then on a couple of the lads would follow the vines down and fire off some shots in the direction of where we suspected the little bastards to be. Kept this up all night to deprive the Nips of any sleep.'

'Good show,' David grinned. 'I think it's about time our arty support showed how good they are.'

'Yes, sir,' the platoon commander replied. 'I've worked out a grid reference of where we agree the Nips are holed up.' He produced his map and pointed to a marked area.

David turned to his signaller, saying, 'Call up battalion and put in a request for arty support.'

The signaller immediately contacted the battalion HQ in their rear and soon David took over the signaller's transmitter to calmly give the fire orders that would be relayed to the gunners manning the 25-pounders of the artillery support.

'Everyone keep your heads down,' David yelled to those nearest him.

Word quickly spread as the first artillery shell passed overhead to explode deep in the jungle. Satisfied he had accurately called in the first shot David gave the order to fire for effect and soon the explosive rounds fell with their heavy crumping sound, partly muffled by the thick forest. It was still close enough for the men hugging the earth to feel the shock waves beneath their bodies. After a while David called for the artillery to stop and ordered his entire company to advance towards the shelled area. David moved forward with his leading platoon through smashed trees and still smoking craters. He could see three Japanese beating a retreat but they were out of sight before any effective small arms fire could be brought to bear. On the ground were two dead bodies, and blood trails of the wounded leading into the heavy forest further up the hill. One of the enemy had obviously died from gunshot wounds, and the other from shrapnel that had ripped away his chest and head.

'Looks like you bagged one last night,' David said to the platoon commander standing beside him.

'And you got the other one, sir,' the platoon commander grinned.

David ordered a patrol to sweep the area and sat down to organise a report back to battalion. He had not lost any men on this mission. That was all he cared about as the tropical heavens opened and torrential rain came down to wash away the blood of the battlefield.

Two days to kill two enemies, David thought in his weariness. But he also knew there were many more days and Japanese soldiers before them. He had been lucky this time. Next time, they could find themselves in an ambush.

If there was a next time for him.

SIX

Harry Griffiths raised his glass of beer to Sean Duffy and then took a sip. They sat at the bar of their favourite pub amidst a crowd of military uniforms from Australia and the United States. The mood was a lot more festive compared to three years earlier, when the country was thought to be on the point of invasion by an absolutely ruthless enemy. Men pushed and shoved to purchase another round, and beers spilled onto the tiled floor.

'The men tailing Allison are coppers.'

'Coppers,' Sean echoed. 'What the bloody hell is going on?'

'Dunno,' Harry said, 'but she's definitely not imagining things. I recognised a couple of Preston's boys. I got a few good shots on that Hun camera you gave me,' Harry slid a compact German-made camera into Sean's hands beneath the level of the bar. 'Bloody beautiful piece of precision engineering, and sure beats the old box brownie. Where did you get it?'

'David got it off the body of a German officer in North Africa,' Sean said, pocketing the camera. 'He gave it to me as a present when he returned.'

'And you trusted me with it?' Harry said with a smile. 'I could have fetched a pretty penny on the black market.'

'I'd trust you with my life,' Sean answered with his own slow smile.

Harry did not comment on that as he knew the feeling was mutual. 'I don't suppose the Nips make very good cameras, but if you happen to be writing to him ask young David to keep the next camera he takes off a dead Jap for me. You never know, maybe they learned something from their old allies, the Huns.'

'So, if you recognised Preston's boys tracking Allison we can only presume that Preston is behind the operation,' Sean said. 'But I doubt he initiated it. It has to be something Sarah Macintosh would have him do for her.'

'It's no secret on the streets that Preston has been meeting with her regularly. No doubt to get his kickback for his overtime with the Macintosh companies.' Harry said. 'I just wonder what he has on Miss Macintosh.'

'Her father had him on the payroll,' Sean said. 'I suppose she just picked up where her father left off before his unfortunate accident.'

'You know,' Harry said reflectively, 'as an old copper my instincts say the accident should have been looked into more closely. I was talking to an old cobber from our days before the last war, and he was at the Macintosh house the night Sir George's body was found. He said he saw blood smeared on the old bastard's face that didn't seem to fit the situation. He commented to Preston about what he saw, and Preston told him to keep his opinions to himself because he wasn't a trained detective.'

'Do you think that Sarah could have murdered her own father?' Sean asked.

'From my past experience with homicides, the first person you look at is the person closest to the victim,' Harry said, finishing his drink. He signalled to the barmaid for another round of beers. 'It seems Preston accepted Sarah's statement at face value, and the coroner closed the case as an unfortunate accident.'

'What else is Sarah Macintosh capable of?'

'Bloody hell!' Harry exclaimed. 'I think I know, and if I'm right, there isn't much we can do.'

Sean glanced at his old friend. 'I think I know what you're thinking,' he said. 'And if we are both right, Allison is helpless against Preston and his boys. It is going to be a set-up.'

'It would cost a few quid to carry out any counter-operation,' Harry said.

'Money will not be an issue,' Sean replied. 'Whatever it takes.'

'I'll need help if we are to conduct twenty-four-hour surveillance,' Harry said. 'I would need to round up a few of the boys, and convince them that standing in the rain day and night is worth it.'

'I'm sure you'll be able to convince them,' Sean said with a grin. 'After all, half your friends and acquaintances are also clients of mine, and owe me one or two favours.'

Harry raised his glass. 'Here's to a couple of jokers who have been fortunate to have walked the other side of the legal line from time to time.'

★

Patrick Duffy and Ken Murphy found a warm spot in the school grounds during their lunch break. They sat against a wall, away from the rest of their classmates, enjoying the winter sun and a break from the periods of intense learning.

'You were making funny noises last night,' Ken said. 'You sounded like you were frightened of something.'

Patrick remembered the nightmares. There was the ghost of an old Aboriginal man when he and Terituba had found the desiccated body half-buried in the creek bed, and the sudden apparition of many Aboriginal figures. Mixed with the memory of the nightmare was an image of his mother being beheaded by a Japanese soldier.

'I'm not frightened of anything,' Patrick retorted.

'Why were you crying then?' Ken persisted.

'If you're my cobber, you won't tell anyone,' Patrick said.

'Boys, what are you two doing here?' came the voice of Father James. The boys had not seen him approach. 'You should be down on the sports ground with the rest of your class, kicking the footy.'

Both boys rose to their feet. 'Yes, Father,' Patrick said.

'Get your hands out of your trouser pockets, Murphy,' the priest said. Ken immediately removed his hands. His pockets had been warm and it was a cold day.

'You're playing breakaway this Saturday, Duffy,' the priest said in a less stern tone. 'Father Clancy told me you're a natural at rugby.'

Patrick was pleased to hear the compliment and thanked him. Both boys sidled towards the rowdy pack of boys kicking and passing the rugby ball around on the oval. The priest was only a few paces behind them.

'I'll see you down there, Murph,' Patrick said and stopped to let the teacher catch up.

'What is it, Duffy?' the priest asked, seeing that one of his favourite pupils had obviously waited for him.

'Father,' Patrick asked with a puzzled expression, 'are there such things as ghosts?' The priest was also his maths teacher and Patrick liked and trusted him.

The Jesuit looked into the young boy's face and could see the seriousness of his question. 'The only ghost I know of is the Holy Ghost,' he said with just a hint of a smile at the boy's question.

'But are there other kinds of ghosts?' Patrick persisted.

'The Church teaches us that ghosts do not exist.'

'What about devils and demons?' Patrick asked.

The priest hesitated.

'The devil and his demons exist,' the Jesuit finally answered.

'So, there could be ghosts,' Patrick reasoned.

'If there are spirits walking the earth they could only be evil,' the Jesuit countered.

'Wallarie is not evil,' Patrick said.

'Who is Wallarie?' Father James asked.

'My Uncle Tom said that Wallarie is our guardian angel. He is there when we are in trouble. Wallarie used to be a great Aboriginal warrior before he went to the spirit world.'

The priest smiled and shook his head. 'I think your Uncle Tom is just telling you stories.'

'No, Father, I've seen Wallarie's ghost,' Patrick said.

'At your age you have a good imagination, and you only thought that you saw a ghost,' the priest explained patiently. 'As you get older he will go away. Now, go down and join Murphy.'

'Yes, Father,' Patrick replied, unconvinced with the answer given. He knew Wallarie's spirit was real, no matter what other people said.

★

The following Saturday, Patrick took his place on the rugby field. The opposition were tough. Patrick was big for his age, and during a scrum was able to retrieve a loose ball from the mass of grunting and sweating forwards from either side, pushing head to head. He scooped up the ball, saw a space in the opposition and, head down, sprinted for the try line, deflecting two tackles. Even now, he could hear the cheers of his team mates urging him on. With a dive forward to avoid the last defender, he slammed into the ground between the goalposts to score a try, the first for the game.

The try converted with a kick from his team's best goal kicker. Patrick walked back to his position for the kick-off, his team mates' congratulations ringing in his ears. But during a skirmish for the ball that had been kicked towards them Patrick went down in the muddy field as he lurched for the loose ball. Two of the biggest forwards from the other side were on him and everything went black, his world exploding in red sparks when a football boot connected with his head.

He did not know it, but the game was stopped when the umpire noticed one of the players lying face down on the ground. Father Clancy ran forward, dropping to his knees beside him. A stretcher was organised to take the unconscious Patrick to the infirmary. A doctor was immediately called to treat him and Sean Duffy was also informed by telephone of Patrick's condition.

Patrick had not recovered consciousness, and lay deathly pale against the clean white sheets of the bed. Sean sat by his side, in the shadows of the subdued lighting of the room, holding Patrick's hand, not daring to think the boy would not recover from his comatose state. He continued to hold Patrick's hand until he dozed off in the chair by the bed.

Near midnight Father James chose to see how Patrick was progressing. He opened the door to the infirmary room, and immediately froze in shock. In the dim light he thought he could see a dark shadowy figure of a semi-naked Aboriginal man with a long, grey beard, standing beside the bed, holding a wooden spear. For a fleeting second the image burned itself into the priest's mind, and in the time it took to blink the scene was gone. The only two figures in the room were Major Sean Duffy, dozing in a chair, and the boy in the bed.

Father James stood transfixed in the doorway, his eyes darting around the room but saw nothing else. 'Jesus, Mary and Joseph,' he whispered under his breath. 'Save us!'

Awakened by the door opening Sean stirred and greeted the priest. 'Father, are you all right? You look like you've seen a ghost.'

Father James found the strength to move, and stepped inside the room on unsteady feet.

'It's nothing, Major Duffy,' he said. 'I think a conversation I had with young Patrick a couple of days ago triggered my imagination, but it was nothing.'

'You look very shaken, Father,' Sean said. 'You must have a very good imagination.'

'Patrick was telling me a story about an imaginary friend he once had called Wallarie,' the Jesuit replied.

'Ah, but the stories of the spiritual world are strong amongst those of Celtic blood,' Sean said. 'Despite our Catholicism we still have a primeval belief in such figures as the banshee and the old pagan gods. The Aboriginal people of this country share that worldly view with us. What did you think you saw?'

'It was only for a split second, and must have been caused by the shadows of the room, but I thought I saw an old

Aboriginal man with a long spear standing beside the bed, opposite where you are.'

'Wallarie, the old bugger,' Sean chuckled. 'You do have a good imagination, Father James. We know there's no such thing as spirits in our world.'

The priest sensed the Sydney solicitor was being facetious and fought his own self-doubt about what he had seen in the room.

'Uncle Sean,' the raspy voice of Patrick said. 'Where am I?'

Priest and lawyer immediately glanced at Patrick.

Sean immediately gripped the boy's hand. 'You're in the infirmary and an ambulance will be coming to take you to hospital, Pat. You had a bad knock playing footy this afternoon.'

'Did we win?' Patrick asked.

'No, your team lost but when you're well you'll be able to go back on the paddock and win the next one.'

'I saw Wallarie,' Patrick said. 'He came to me and told me to wake up. He was scary because he had a spear.'

Neither Patrick nor Sean noticed the stricken expression on the Jesuit's face. Father James felt he had just lived through one of the most profound moments of his life. Maybe the Church did not know everything about spirituality after all.

*

It was cold and wet standing in the shadows of the streetlights outside Allison's flat. The man Harry had hired lit another cigarette and stamped his feet against the biting drizzle. He was a former amateur boxer who had once trained in Harry's gym but had not fared well as a heavyweight fighter. Too many blows to the head had brought on the condition known as being 'punch-drunk'. This had interfered with his ability to get a regular job, and he knew the generous pay he was receiving from Harry was more than he would get from any other job.

It was nearly 9 pm when the former heavyweight noticed two men appear at the front door to Allison's flat. His years on the street told him that they were coppers. He could tell from the way they dressed and carried themselves. He knew Allison had gone to the movies. The two men opened the door and went inside.

He watched as a light went on in an upstairs room and then quickly turned off. He was now fully alert as the men exited the flat, and hurried down the street to where a car was waiting for them.

What was he supposed to do now? he asked himself. Thinking through situations was not easy.

That's right – he was to go to a telephone booth and ring Harry with the coins he had been given for the job. The former boxer knew where there was a red telephone call box on the next street, and hurried to make the call.

Harry heard the phone jangle and quickly got out of bed to answer.

'Harry, a couple of jokers just went into the place you asked me to watch,' he said. 'I think they were coppers.'

Harry thanked him and immediately telephoned Sean. The phone rang but Harry did not get an answer.

'Bloody hell!' Harry swore.

He guessed a couple of Preston's men had done the deed he had suspected – planting something illegal in her residence. Quickly, Harry dressed and found a late-night taxi to take him to Allison's flat. When he arrived he could see her bedroom light was on. He met his hired man, who briefed Harry on what he had seen. Harry passed him a couple of one-pound notes. The man thanked him and shuffled off into the night.

Harry crossed the empty street and knocked on Allison's door. When it opened she expressed her surprise at seeing him.

'Harry, what brings you here so late?' she asked, clutching a shawl around her nightdress.

'I can't explain everything right now, Miss Lowe, but do you mind if I have a quick look in your bedroom?'

Puzzled, Allison agreed, and followed him up the narrow stairwell.

'What's going on?' she asked when they entered her bedroom.

Harry did not reply. His eyes swept the room, settling on Allison's single bed against the wall. Harry bent down to peer under the bed and reached under it. When he straightened up he was holding a rectangular cardboard box.

'What's that?' Allison asked. 'I've never seen that box before.'

'I know,' Harry replied and opened the box to reveal sheets of ration coupons.

'They're not mine,' Allison said in shock. 'How did they get under my bed?'

Harry stood up with the box under his arm and looked at the shocked young woman. 'I was never here and you do not know about the box. Remember that when the time comes.'

Still confused, Allison nodded. Harry bid her good-night, departing her flat with the box.

Early the next morning four uniformed police arrived at Allison's front door with serious expressions on their faces.

'Miss Allison Lowe?' the sergeant asked.

'Yes,' Allison answered. She stood with a mug of coffee, as she had just finished dressing to go to work.

'We have reason to believe you have unlawful property in your flat and, as such, we'll conduct a search of the premises. Do you have any objections?'

'No,' Allison answered, realising now why Harry had come to her flat so late in the evening.

The four police entered and she noticed they immediately went upstairs to her bedroom. Allison followed, and when she entered her room she could see one of the uniformed officers had been looking under her bed.

The sergeant looked angrily at her. 'Where is it?' he demanded.

'Where is what, sergeant?' Allison replied calmly.

'You know what I'm talking about,' he said, his eyes blazing with fury. 'Do I have to tear this place apart to find what we both know is here?'

'You may do so, but you may also know that I work for Major Duffy at Levi & Duffy, and I can assure you he'll be told of your visit. I promise you there's nothing incriminating here.'

A constable looked uneasily at his sergeant. All the police in the room knew of the formidable Sydney criminal lawyer, and the mention of his name made them think twice about ripping the flat apart.

'You were lucky this time, Missus,' the sergeant said. 'We had a tip-off from a very reliable source that you're dealing in counterfeit ration coupons.'

'Well, sergeant,' Allison said calmly, 'your source must be unreliable, and you were given incorrect information.'

The frustrated police departed Allison's flat. When they were gone, Allison slumped onto a kitchen chair. Her hands were shaking too much for her to hold her mug of coffee, and she burst into tears.

SEVEN

'**R**ound one to us,' Harry said, grinning over the froth on his glass of beer.

Sean Duffy sat beside his old friend at their favourite bar in the city whilst a cold wind blew flurries of misty rain around the people on the street outside the hotel. Inside, the bar was packed with uniformed servicemen and a few civilians wearing overalls and suits.

'We had some luck,' Sean agreed. 'But if the coppers were prepared to plant evidence on an innocent woman then we are up against a formidable foe. I don't think they'll give up just because it didn't work.'

'What happens next?' Harry asked.

'Well, I telephoned the commissioner to protest the conduct of his police, and he apologised profusely, promising it would not happen again. I reminded him that even in time of war we adhere to the rule of law. He said

Inspector Preston would be reprimanded but knowing the way they work I doubt Preston will get anything more than a slap on the wrist. He has too high a public profile for even the commissioner to cross him.'

'Do we presume the attempted attacks on Allison are over by Preston?' Harry asked.

For a moment Sean fell silent. 'Not by any means,' he said. 'If anything, I suspect our obsessive Miss Macintosh will up the ante. I would not put it past her to attempt murder by means of a fatal accident. From now on, you and I have to try to out-think Sarah Macintosh, and be one step ahead at all times.'

'When will her plotting ever end?'

'Sadly, when either one or the other is dead,' Sean replied.

Both men fell silent.

★

Lieutenant Donald Macintosh could not get the ambush out of his mind. At night it came to him in his dreams, a platoon on his flank charging across a stretch of bare ground, only to disappear when a huge explosion from two marine depth charges – concealed by Japanese soldiers in the earth and remotely detonated – caught them. He remembered bodies flung through the air like discarded rag dolls, and as stunned as he was, the ripping crackle of Japanese machine guns opening up on his platoon. But he had reacted well, and with the use of smoke grenades, extracted most of his men from danger.

The war on Tarakan had worsened since that incident, and he had the terrible task of writing letters to the next of kin of the men killed in the devastating ambush.

The company commander congratulated him on his

sound action and said he was worthy of a military recognition – possibly a Military Cross. Donald did not feel worthy. Could he have seen the signs of the ambush? What could he have done better to save the lives of his men? How long ago had that been? Donald reflected as he sat on an ammunition box in the scrub, surrounded by his men dug in and manning their posts. Time had lost meaning. Had it been two or three weeks? It seemed the only time that counted was the present. His past as a highly paid member of the Macintosh companies meant nothing, and as for a promise of a golden future when the war ended . . .

He and the rest of his men spent each day on the island of Tarakan advancing, fighting the enemy in his fortified log bunkers, and going through the ritual of deploying his sections to encircle and destroy the nests of enemy machine guns. Each time, he prayed to any god who would listen to keep his men alive. They were his true family now, each as precious as a brother. It was something he could never have imagined only a couple of years ago in his luxurious office, with its spectacular views of a serene Sydney Harbour.

Now it was the stifling heat, thirst, swamps and scrub, diseases that struck them down, and an enemy who fought to the death, with the intention of taking as many Australian soldiers with him into the afterworld.

The advance came to a halt as he and his battalion reached their objective, a fire support base. They had pushed the Japanese into a corner of the island, and Donald knew they could expect fierce resistance from a well-dug-in enemy. The Australians had named their forward bases Margy and Joyce. Here the battalions had assembled an odd assortment of supporting guns and three Matilda tanks on a flat between knolls, a couple of 25-pounders, a 3.7-inch anti-aircraft gun and a 6-pounder anti-tank gun. The nickname then became HMAS *Margy* or *Battleship Margy*.

'Boss, the boys have been briefed,' came the voice of Donald's sergeant, snapping the young officer's dreams of going home in one piece. He rose from the ammo crate, slung his rifle on his shoulder, and turned to the tired, dirty and fever-racked platoon second-in-command. Sergeant Mat Peene had refused to seek medical treatment for his bouts of malaria. Any sane soldier would do so since that meant being taken out of line and sent to a place with clean sheets and good food to recuperate. But Sergeant Peene was from a breed of soldier who refused to leave his men, and Donald knew he could do no less in similar circumstances. The men of the platoon looked up to their sergeant, and Donald was just becoming accepted by them. Some had stopped calling him 'sir' and started using the term 'boss', which was the Aussie soldier's way of saying 'we accept you as our leader'.

The two men stood watching as the crews of the two 25-pounder artillery guns opened fire on the bunkers in the hills facing them. Donald hoped the shells raining down on the camouflaged posts of the enemy would do the job as he feared sending men forward against them. But his hope would be dashed and his life changed forever.

★

After returning from leave to Brisbane, Jessica had found herself posted to the Atherton Tablelands in Queensland. It was a cipher post and she was bored by the paperwork in the big Nissan hut. Outside she could hear the warble of magpies, and the sun had risen enough to burn away the early morning mist that shrouded the highlands in the tropics.

Around her were other young girls wearing the uniform of the Women's Australian Auxiliary Air Force, chatting as they moved around the office. Despite the fact they were under her command she felt she had little or nothing in common with her compatriots. They were girls who had lived in relative comfort of the cipher station high in the peaceful and scenic countryside. They would chatter about boyfriends and husbands whilst Jessica was still haunted by her mission into enemy territory.

Upon her return from her rescue operation in the islands she had expected another mission with the secretive special forces located down the coast near Cairns, but she couldn't even return to her old posting in MacArthur's HQ in Brisbane, where the pulse of the Pacific war pumped blood into the great campaigns now underway on the slow and bloody journey to Japan. Since she deserted they no longer trusted her.

Instead, she had been posted to this isolated place away from the war. She wore on her uniform the riband of the British Empire Medal. Those around her presumed she had been awarded her decoration for services in Mac's HQ. They did not know it was for valour on her mission to New Britain behind enemy lines. Nor could she tell them, as she was sworn to secrecy.

Many times Jessica would relive the last hours on the beach awaiting extraction, and the sacrifice made by her special forces companion, Warrant Officer Roland Porath. She knew he had sacrificed his life to save her and the American colonel. The painful memory haunted Jessica in her waking and sleeping hours. She would attempt to dismiss the recollections with the sweet memory of Donald Macintosh. In her privileged position she was at least able to quietly discover he was now a junior officer fighting in

Tarakan. She also knew from the coded messages that came across her desk that the campaign in the backwaters of the Pacific was bloody and slow.

'Where do I file this, Sarge?' asked a girl barely out of her teens, snapping Jessica back into the reality of the present.

Jessica glanced at the piece of paper in the young airwoman's hand. 'On the RAAF clipboard for transmission,' Jessica sighed. 'You should know that by now.'

The girl looked sheepish at the mild rebuke. She had been informed by the other girls upon arrival that Sergeant Duffy was a bit aloof, and rarely joined in chatter.

Jessica returned to the ream of papers in front of her, stamping each one with a security clearance and noticed a change in the chatter behind her.

'Attention,' one of the girls commanded. Jessica swung around to see who of commissioned rank had entered the hut.

'Ah, Sergeant Duffy, no need to salute,' the officer said in his usual cultured tone when Jessica stood to attention to salute as the senior NCO in the hut.

'It has been a long time since we last met,' she said. 'May I congratulate you on your majority?'

'Oh, that,' the British officer said. 'Just came as a matter of course.'

'Is the sergeant major with you still, sir?' Jessica asked and saw a sad cloud come over the major's face.

'He went on a mission and I'm afraid it went badly,' he replied. 'Ladies, I'm Major Unsworthy. I had the honour of serving with your remarkable sergeant.'

Jessica noticed that besides the admiring glances for the handsome British officer, his comment also brought on a new look of respect from the girls who had disdained their supervisor. The women recognised the small badge on the handsome major's tropical uniform as that of the Special Air Service, which made him an elite soldier.

'I'm afraid I must take Sergeant Duffy from you,' he continued with a disarming smile. 'I'm sure you'll miss her. Sergeant Duffy, if you'll come with me.'

Jessica had to stop herself from bolting after Major Unsworthy into the bright, clear air of the grounds of the cipher station. Confused but elated, she held her breath as she walked beside him to a waiting jeep where a young, tough-looking soldier sat behind the wheel, sporting the green beret worn by commandoes.

The major stopped walking and turned to Jessica. 'I've already organised for your kit to be packed, and your commanding officer, albeit reluctant to lose you, has signed you off on a transfer to us. I somehow think your talents are being wasted shuffling paper up here.'

He smiled down on Jessica, whose mind was reeling from his unexpected reappearance in her life. 'Well, old girl, take a seat. I know you've learned not to ask questions in our line of work,' Unsworthy said, helping Jessica into the back of the jeep. 'But I also suspect you're just itching to find out what your mission will be. I can promise all will be revealed when we get down to Cairns. Welcome back to our little family of cutthroats, pirates and generally bad people who create mayhem in the lives of the Nips in this Godforsaken part of the world.'

They drove down the narrow and twisting road to the coast. Jessica thought the sights and scents of the rainforest never smelled so good.

*

Tom Duffy had gathered his stockmen and informed them from the verandah that he was to leave the property until a legal matter was sorted. The men shuffled their feet and muttered that it was not fair dinkum that the bloody lawyers could do this to a well-liked and respected boss.

'What happens to us, boss?' the head stockman asked.

'There will be a temporary manager assigned to look after the place until it's returned to me, so you'll still have jobs.' Tom said. 'Are there any other questions?'

The men mumbled amongst themselves, and slowly drifted away to return to their tasks. Only Billy remained at the foot of the steps.

'What is it, Billy?' Tom asked, seeing the worried frown on the stockman's face.

'Gotta tell you sumthin, boss,' Billy said. 'It about my boy, Terituba. He bin see ol' Wallarie.'

Tom stepped down into the dusty yard. 'What about Wallarie?' Tom asked.

'He tell me when they run away they find bones in the creek bed, find them before masta Patrick go south. Terituba say they saw Wallarie standing with a lot of other spirits.'

'You believe your boy?' Tom asked.

'He bin a bit of a little bugga, but he always tell the truth,' Billy said, looking nervous.

'Do you reckon you could find the spot where you found the boys?' Tom questioned. 'I think it's important.'

'Yeah, boss,' Billy said.

'Then we will ride out now and find Wallarie,' Tom said. 'Go and saddle your horse, and saddle one for me.'

Tom returned to the empty house. Abigail had already gone to their property just out of Townsville. He reached for the rifle. Along with the .303, he packed ammunition, filled a hessian bag with tinned food and struggled through the door with the supplies.

When Tom stepped outside Billy was waiting for him astride his mount, holding the reins of Tom's horse. Tom swung himself into the saddle, and they rode away from the station house to the place of death.

★

It was late in the afternoon when they reached the area on the old dry creek bed where Billy said the boys had seen the bones and ghosts. Billy crouched in the sand, searching for bones.

'Nuthin but an old pipe here, boss,' he said, holding up the battered smoking pipe.

Tom reached for it and recognised the pipe as one Wallarie treasured in his last years of life on earth.

'Maybe the dingos dragged away any bones,' Tom reflected, staring at the pipe from astride his horse.

'Dingos don't want old bones,' Billy reflected, looking around with a touch of fear in his face. 'This place, *baal*. Too many ghosts here.'

Tom knew of his Aboriginal stockmen's views on those who were no longer alive and respected their fears. 'I think you should ride back to the station and your family,' he said gently. 'I'm going to stay out here by and by.'

Billy grabbed the reins of his horse grazing peacefully on the dry, winter grass and swung into the saddle. 'Not a good place to be,' he said, glancing at the setting sun. 'Too many ghosts come here at night. We see the lights rolling along the scrub.'

Tom knew what he meant. He, too, had seen the mysterious balls of bright light on the horizon in his early days at Glen View. They were enough to unlock fears and wonder.

'You go now, Billy,' Tom said gently. 'I'll camp out.'

'Okay, boss,' Billy said and turned his mount to ride back. He would reach his family camped near the homestead after dark.

Tom slipped from his horse and pulled out hobbles so that she could graze without going too far from a small copse of prickly bushes beside the dry creek bed. Tom quickly set up camp, made a small fire, and laid out his swag for sleeping.

The sun went down, giving way to a crystal clear, icy cold night. Tom squatted by his fire, eating bully beef from a tin with damper he had cooked in a heavy metal pot. The meal was washed down with black tea. Tom settled back, using his saddle as a pillow to stare at myriad stars slowly swirling overhead on this moonless night.

Around him were the nocturnal sounds of the bush. They were comforting and he thought how times like this cleared a man's view of the world. Here, he could be the only human left on the earth in the vastness of a universe without limit.

He took the old pipe from his trouser pocket and with some difficulty cleaned it. He had taught himself to carry out many tasks with just one arm, and when he was satisfied it was clean, packed it with tobacco from a pouch he carried for his own pipe. Was Wallarie really a spirit man? Tom asked himself. Or was the memory of him still so strong that human imagination made him real?

Tom puffed on the pipe and tasted the strong tobacco in his mouth. If Wallarie were a spirit man, surely he would come to him now.

He waited and waited but nothing, except for the howl of a dingo and the call of an owl.

Tom finished the pipe, pulled blankets over himself and slipped into a deep sleep.

Then Wallarie came to him.

EIGHT

Tom knew he was dreaming. He did not know how, but he was in a world where a familiar voice called to him.

'Tom, time to come with me,' Wallarie said, but Tom could not see him.

With a sudden but gentle movement, Tom felt himself lifted from the earth. He even saw his body asleep below him and then he was flying as if on the wings of a soaring eagle.

Tom looked down and saw where his ancestors were buried. It was not a well-defined cemetery, just a few stone-marked graves.

'Those of our blood sleep here,' Wallarie said in Tom's head. 'You cannot give up this place to the whitefellas. It is land the old people walked, back to the Dreaming.'

'What do I do?' Tom asked.

'You stay, Tom Duffy,' Wallarie said. 'You stay and fight

like our ancestors did. Like I did when I killed Sir Donald Macintosh and his son with my spear.'

'Why don't you show yourself to me?' Tom asked.

'You and I will not see each other again until you join us in the spirit world. The people forget me now. They call it modern times, and all our people are gone – 'cept those with our blood. They will sit by the campfire and tell the stories of old Wallarie when he stood with the people of this land to fight the whitefellas.

'Ah, I remember my time with the Kalkadoons. They were fighting people. I remember riding with the man you were named after, Tom Duffy. We were true brothers. When he took Mondo to be his wife a new people of both bloods was born. It was a long time ago, and now I must remain with the old ones and those I knew. I wish I could sit one more time in the cave sacred of our people and smoke my pipe with you Tom, but they are calling me to join the hunt for the wallaby and kangaroo. You still got my pipe?'

Tom suddenly felt as though he was falling but could not feel the air rush past him as he rejoined his sleeping body.

He jerked awake and blinked at the star-filled sky. Once again he could hear the sounds of the nocturnal animals foraging in the dark. The chill of the winter's night bit into his exposed skin and with his good arm, he pulled up a blanket to his chin. The dream had been so real. But it was only a dream, and all Wallarie could say in it was that he should stand and fight for the land. That might have been good advice for his ancestors but times had changed. He could not be a one-man army.

Awake now, Tom decided to put on the billy and smoke Wallarie's old pipe. He reached for where he had left it but it was not there. Puzzled, Tom took a burning stick from the now smouldering fire. It gave enough light to show the ground around him but he saw no sign of the pipe. For a moment Tom felt the hair rise on the back of his neck. Then he picked up the faint smell of pipe tobacco he recognised as his own.

'Wallarie, you old bugger,' Tom chuckled as he gazed up at the overwhelming display of twinkling stars. 'I bet I don't find my baccy either.'

And Tom was right.

Tom knew now it was time to stand and fight, as he had done in two wars. He was the white warrior of the cave, and the only way Sarah Macintosh would ever possess the land again was over his dead body.

It was time to go to war again.

*

'As far as we know, Mr Duffy has not vacated the property,' said the thin-faced lawyer.

Sarah Macintosh sat before his desk in the Sydney law firm that worked for the Macintosh legal interests.

'He was given notice to leave weeks ago,' Sarah said in an icy tone. 'What can a one-armed old man do to defy the law?'

The solicitor cleared his throat before answering. 'I'm afraid Mr Duffy is a very popular figure in his district, Miss Macintosh,' he replied and removed his spectacles to clean them with a small cloth. 'Our representatives in Townsville have informed us that Mr Duffy is a decorated war hero of two wars, and is a crack shot – even with one arm. He is also expert in living off the land. When one of our representatives approached the police in his area they expressed a reluctance to go out and evict Mr Duffy. They said they would need a small army behind them before they even found the man. I'm afraid, from what the local police told us, it is not likely Mr Duffy will surrender peacefully,' the lawyer said. 'The only way to evict him would be to kill him, and that would not bode well in the papers for us.'

'Damn what the papers might print,' Sarah said. 'I want him off the property one way or another. If he's not prepared to obey a legal decision he could be considered some kind of outlaw.'

The lawyer replaced his spectacles and did not look pleased at his client's decision. 'As yet, we have not established a prima facie case for repossession of Glen View, Miss Macintosh,' he said. 'We require solid proof that Mr Duffy purchased the property with stolen money, and that will not be easy with one of the chief witnesses up in New Guinea on active service. And that's if we can get him to turn on Mr Duffy. At the moment the order is an interim one, and time is running out to renew it in the courts.'

'This Jack Kelly character sounds as shady as Tom Duffy,' Sarah said. 'But I have never known a man who could resist a generous offer. I'm sure he'll turn on his old comrade if the price is right.'

The lawyer was not so sure. It was obvious his client was unaware men of honour existed, and he suspected this Jack Kelly he had investigated was one such man. 'I'll contact our representative in Townsville and see what he can do,' he said. 'But I cannot promise this will be resolved quickly.'

'If that is all,' Sarah said, rising from her chair, 'I expect the good money I pay to retain your legal services will be met with due satisfaction. Good day.'

The lawyer watched gloomily as the young woman swished from the office, deep in thought for how he would organise to remove Mr Duffy. No matter how he looked at it, he could only see bloodshed and bad publicity. Queensland was still a vast region, barely out of its frontier days, and its capital Brisbane was hardly more than a big country town.

All Queensland would ever be was a good place for growing bananas and sugarcane, he mused. And breeding tough frontier characters such as Tom Duffy.

*

Lieutenant Donald Macintosh led his platoon through twisting gullies of tree-covered terrain into the remnants of the Japanese HQ on Tarakan. Artillery shells and air strikes had brought down a tangle of timber. The threat of sudden death from rear parties of retreating enemy soldiers was constantly with them. Men sweated in the tropical humidity as they came across numerous decomposing bodies and scattered papers in the ravines. They were ever wary of booby traps left behind. The operation was taking a toll on their nerves.

Donald had to fight back the instinct to vomit in the putrid, oppressive heat. His men scavenged for any military papers, and brought what they thought might be useful to him.

'It looks like most of them headed north-east from the trail they left behind,' Peene said.

'Then we follow them,' Donald said, stuffing captured documents in a canvas shoulder bag.

The order was given and his men fell into small formations to move forward in a nightmare world of heavy forest. They advanced silently. Hand signals were the only means of communication until a sudden burst of machine-gun fire ripped into their ranks, followed by the crump of small mortars lobbed at the pursuing Australians. The explosions hurled red-hot shrapnel amongst the Australians who had gone to ground. Donald was immediately on the radio to battalion HQ to report his contact and to call his section commanders to keep advancing.

Donald rose to his knees to glance around when the smashing pain in his face flung him backwards. His signaller clambered forward to inspect his officer's condition, and saw a piece of shrapnel from a mortar bomb had landed only a few feet from them and ripped away half of the platoon commander's face. Donald was still alive, but from the expression in his eyes the pain had set in quickly. The signaller could also see other shrapnel wounds to Donald's body.

Donald rose to a sitting position, staring his frightened signaller in the face. He tried to speak but blood gushed from his mouth.

'I'll get a message through to have you evacuated, boss,' the signaller said, removing a battle bandage from Donald's first-aid kit to cover the wound.

Donald shook his head to indicate he did not want to be evacuated as the signaller applied the broad, padded bandage. His men were in contact and it was his duty to remain with them.

'Sarge!' the signaller cried out in desperation. 'The boss has been hit.'

Sergeant Larkin crawled across to Donald, and quickly ascertained the wound was not critical at this stage.

'Give him a shot of morphine,' he told the signaller, by now covered in Donald's blood. 'Look after him.'

Donald was able to remove his field notebook and, despite his condition, scribbled orders to his sergeant.

Sergeant Larkin read them. 'Will do, boss,' he said, and crawled away to meet with any section commanders he could find in the twisted terrain. They advanced cautiously until one of the sections was close enough to view a crew of three enemy soldiers packing up their heavy machine gun, falling back for another ambush. With grenades and small arms fire the Australians killed two of the enemy gunners, whilst the third was able to escape. It at least halted the immediate threat, and the jungle fell silent.

Larkin returned to Donald, who was barely conscious but had been able to write another brief set of orders: they were to advance, and he would continue the pursuit with them.

'Sorry, boss,' Larkin said, shaking his head. 'I'm going to disobey your orders, and have you taken back to the Regimental Aid Post at the battalion. You're in a bad way, and your wounds need to be seen to.'

Donald looked at his sergeant with despair, but understood he was now a burden to his men. He shrugged his shoulders. Within minutes a section was reassigned to make a litter and carry Donald back to battalion HQ. They lay him down and the Regimental Medical Officer, a former surgeon from Perth, examined Donald's face.

'Not pretty, I'm afraid. You're going to need specialised treatment to reconstruct the left side of your face,' he said. 'In the meantime I'm arranging for you to be taken back to a hospital ship, and from there they'll get you back to Australia.'

Donald said nothing. All he could think of was how guilty he felt leaving his men behind on this hell island of Tarakan.

*

The ground support mission had not gone well. A stream of heavy Japanese machine-gun bullets had ripped into the belly and engine of Captain James Duffy's Corsair as he released his bombs on the cave entrance. With a great effort he had nursed his stricken fighter bomber back to the airstrip. Already fire licked at his legs and the thought of being burned to death overtook him in the final approach. He was desperately screaming for help as the crippled aircraft slid along the airstrip, flipping over halfway before finally coming to rest. Hanging upside-down in his harness, the flames began to wrap around him, turning him into a human torch. Hands gripped at him and he felt his body ripped away from the smashed fighter bomber.

After that all he remembered was the terrible pain in his legs, then a series of hospitals that led back to the USA, and eventually home to his grandfather's estate in New Hampshire to recuperate from his wounds.

It was warm outside the bedroom and James could hear the sound of people going about their civilian lives under the shade of the great evergreens. Independence Day was very soon, and that meant the usual round of picnics, fireworks and courting rituals. James knew he would probably miss the social round of celebrations, bedridden while the burns to his legs slowly healed under the watchful eye of the best specialist James Barrington Snr could hire.

'Good morning, Mr Barrington,' the old black servant said, bringing James his breakfast on a silver tray.

James had chosen years earlier to be known by his father's name, honouring the memory of a man he had first hated for the perceived desertion of him and his now dead sister. But he had come to love him when they had finally met in Iraq before the war. His most precious memento of his father was the much worn leather and wool flying jacket now hanging on the back of his bedroom door. The old servant still referred to James by his mother's maiden name.

'Thank you, Samuel,' James said, struggling to sit up in bed. The crisp, clean sheets were a long way from what he had known on Okinawa.

'I also have the morning paper, Mr Barrington. I see your return is featured on the front page. Congratulations on your award of another Navy Cross,' Samuel said. 'We are all very proud of you.'

'I would rather my legs were not burned,' James said. 'The medal was only a going-away present.'

'It says in the paper that you flew your plane low in support of our troops on the ground, drawing fire from the Japs, until your Corsair was riddled with bullets. You are a very brave man, Mr Barrington.'

'I was just looking after the men who deserve all we can do to help them,' James shrugged, not bothering to look at the paper.

'Mr Barrington has said he will be up to see you after breakfast,' Samuel continued, adjusting the curtains so that the summer light could flood the room.

James nodded and the servant left the room. When James had finished his breakfast of orange juice, coffee and scrambled eggs on toast he pushed the tray aside and closed his eyes for a moment. Then he heard a knock at his door.

His grandfather, James Barrington Snr, entered the room, leaning on a walking stick. He settled himself into a chair beside his grandson's bed.

'Good morning, James,' he said. 'You're looking much better than when you first arrived. The doctor has informed me you should be able to start walking again very soon.'

'I'm going to try today,' James said. 'Lying around in bed is driving me nuts.'

'Did you read the article in the paper about you?' Barrington asked, holding up the paper to his grandson. 'It's a glowing account of your war service.'

'No,' James replied, 'probably just a lot of propaganda.'

'You don't realise that people around here see you as a true hero,' Barrington said, putting down the paper. 'I know from my sources in Washington that they'll be discharging you from the marines on medical grounds. You'll be a civilian again, and need to consider your future.'

'If you think I should go into politics you have to remember the idea is yours, not mine,' James said. 'I really don't know what I'm going to do, except get justice for my sister's murder.'

'You have to forget any foolish ideas of seeking revenge for Olivia,' Barrington said, placing his hand on James's bedsheets. 'As you know, our old friend Sheriff Mueller lost the election, and the Wilson family made sure his deputy became sheriff.'

'You mean that goddamned son of a bitch Hausmann, right?' James asked, feeling his rage rise. 'How very convenient that he's a close pal of Edgar Wilson, who murdered Olivia.'

'We don't have enough proof for a case against young Edgar,' Barrington said.

'Who said we need proof?' said James with an expression of cold anger.

'You have too much to lose, James, if you're thinking of taking the law into your own hands,' Barrington countered. 'You're the only family I have left, and very precious to me. All that I have achieved for my time on this earth means nothing if it cannot be passed on to you.'

James turned away from his grandfather and stared out the window at the green manicured lawns and stately leaf-covered trees. He knew all this would be his, but after almost four years of war – the men he had seen killed, the friends he had lost and the harsh way of living in the tropical hellholes – it all seemed so surreal. That night when sleep finally came, he was back in the cockpit of his aircraft, wrapped in flames and fighting for his life.

Now there were only two things worth putting his life on the line for: revenge for his beloved sister's murder, and finding the woman he had never stopped loving, Julianna Dupont.

NINE

Nothing had changed in Jessica's old quarters in Cairns. The only difference was the dust and gecko excrement on the surfaces of drawers.

'Welcome home, Sergeant Duffy,' Major Mike Unsworthy said, standing in the doorway. 'You're the only woman we have on the team and I made sure your quarters were kept intact for your return.'

'I don't suppose you can tell me why I'm here, sir?' Jessica asked, patting down the thin bedspread.

'I cannot tell you at this moment,' Unsworthy replied. 'All I know is that the Yanks asked for you, and I assume they'll also request your transfer to them in the near future. It seems you made a big impression on them when you rescued their colonel. I heard about your bronze medal for bravery. The way you're going, you'll soon have as many medals as your illustrious father.'

'What happens next then?' Jessica queried, plonking her bottom on the end of the bed.

'You get yourself squared away and I expect to hear from our Yankee cousins in the Office for Strategic Services tomorrow. In the meantime you have twelve hours' leave but don't go too far. Report to me at 0800 hours tomorrow. There's a good collection of magazines and papers in the anteroom, and help yourself to biscuits, tea and coffee.'

Jessica thanked her superior officer. After he left she took off her shoes and walked into the anteroom, which was also used as an office. On a small side table rested a recent newspaper. Jessica glanced at the headlines and froze. She scooped up the paper announcing the death of Australia's prime minister, John Curtin, and a memory of meeting him flashed to mind. The quiet but determined man who had led them through the worst of the war was gone. The Labor man, Ben Chifley, was to take his place.

The war seemed so close to ending and the great man would not see the Japanese brought to their knees, Jessica thought with a great sadness. Major Unsworthy must have known of Curtin's death but he had failed to mention it, as if it was of no consequence. Jessica knew many conservatives in the armed forces did not like the Labor PM. When she went to the front door to look at the flagpole she noticed it was not at half-mast but fluttered in the tropical breeze as if nothing had happened.

She returned to the anteroom to look through the paper. On page three she saw a small article about a property owner in central Queensland refusing eviction from his property. Jessica gasped when she saw her father's name, the passing of Australia's PM temporarily forgotten. Jessica felt frustrated she could not simply take leave to help her father.

Leave was not an option when you were posted to the top secret military unit.

★

Sean Duffy was pleased with the reports in the Queensland newspapers, even though they were not considered as important as the war news from the Pacific. He had ensured the local reporters knew of Tom Duffy's stance to retain his land, and also made it known that Tom had served his country in two wars with courage and distinction – only to be targeted by a vast financial empire interested in persecuting a man for private vindictive reasons.

'Major,' Allison said, knocking at the office door, 'the Queensland court has set a date for the hearing about the Glen View ownership.'

'Good,' Sean said, 'I'll ensure I attend on Mr Duffy's behalf.'

'Do you think Tom will win his case?' Allison asked.

'I'll make sure we have the best KC as his mouthpiece,' Sean said. 'From what I've learned, all the Macintosh companies – or should I say, Sarah Macintosh – are basing their case on is that the land was acquired with stolen money. Well, it is a long bow to draw, and I strongly suspect the flimsy case will be thrown out of court. But, for the moment, Tom is in a very awkward position. I just pray he does not do anything foolish to jeopardise his rightful claim to Glen View.'

'What could he do?' Allison asked.

'Shoot someone,' Sean replied calmly.

★

From the top of the sacred hill Tom had a panoramic view of the surrounding scrub. He sat facing the north towards the location of the homestead.

It was near midday and the winter sun warmed the rocks for the lizards to bask. High in the sky a great wedge-tailed eagle soared in search of small creatures. Tom strained his eyes to see the tiny figure of a man on a horse approaching through the prickly, dry scrub. He knew it was Billy from the way he handled his horse. Tom smiled and hoped Billy had included in his supplies a couple of tins of condensed milk. He rose to his feet, picked up his rifle and began to make his way down the ancient track to the bottom of the hill.

After they greeted each other, Billy removed a hessian bag bulging with tins and packets of flour. 'Got what you asked for, boss,' Billy said. 'Maybe have a brew with you now.'

Tom nodded, and Billy set about building a small fire to heat the blackened tea tin. He also removed a tin of bully beef and some freshly baked bread. Soon the two men were seated on a log, eating bully-beef sandwiches washed down with sweetened tea.

Tom took his pipe from his trousers. 'You include baccy in the supplies?' he asked.

'You out of baccy?' Billy asked.

'Bloody Wallarie took my last,' Tom replied and Billy looked at him as if he was joking, only to see an expression of seriousness on his employer's face. He reached into his bag to produce a pouch of pipe tobacco, which Tom used to fill his pipe.

In the dappled shadows of the scrub Tom puffed with contentment and gazed at the horizon. In time the hill behind them would cast its own shadow over the land they now sat on.

'The boys don't like this bloke they sent out to manage the place, boss,' Billy said, poking with a twig at the small fire. 'He says he'll find you an' kick you off.'

'Got to find me first,' Tom said quietly.

'I hear him saying he knows you up on the hill, an' when the coppers come, he'll come out an' get you.'

'He and the coppers can try,' Tom said, watching the grey smoke slowly swirl away on the gentle breeze.

Billy did not ask but glanced at the rifle beside Tom's boot. He knew that his boss was a crack shot, even with one arm. 'When I was little the old people used to tell stories how Wallarie and another whitefella called Tom used to hide up here a long, long time ago. Mebbe you that Tom.'

Tom glanced at the Aboriginal stockman and saw the seriousness in his face. 'Just stories, Billy,' he said. 'I don't think it's true that history repeats itself. That Tom Duffy is long dead.'

'Mebbe,' Billy said sounding unconvinced. 'I heard the coppers from Burketown got him an' now the coppers from all aroun' here come to the hill and get you.'

'We'll see,' Tom said, tapping out the ash from his pipe, and rising to his feet. 'About time you rode back,' he said, slinging his rifle over his shoulder, and reaching for the hessian bag.

With a wave of his hand Billy departed the shadow of the sacred hill, leaving Tom to climb up the track to the cave. As he made his way up the winding track Tom reflected on his situation. He knew they would come for him eventually as the white man's law did not allow any disrespect for its decrees. Tom had been legally informed he must leave, but he had disobeyed. They had not proved him to be a criminal and there was something wrong when the rich and powerful could influence the law. But a loophole had been found, as weak as it was, and he was in contravention of a legal order to vacate until the matter was heard.

When Tom reached the entrance of the cave he looked across the plains at the setting sun. How long before they came for him? And when they did, how much blood would be spilled?

*

Major David Macintosh sat in the torrential rain, trying to keep his map dry under a ground sheet he had placed over his head for shelter. 'You say you saw around ten Japs in the native huts ahead,' he queried one of his more experienced platoon commanders.

'Yes, sir,' said the young officer, crouching in the drenching rain.

'Then we'll flank the huts and fire simultaneously when you report that you're in position,' David said. 'You'll take the right flank, and Mr Jarvis the left. Mr Markham will move into position to cut off any escape to their rear.'

David turned to his company sergeant major standing in the rain beside the platoon commander. 'Sar'nt major, get the message to the other platoons for an O group here in ten minutes.'

The company sergeant major acknowledged his order, and went out to pass on the message for a briefing for an attack on the native village, now occupied by the retreating Japanese soldiers. The country was a tangle of rainforest giants, and low-set ferns easily able to conceal an enemy until the last moment. David wondered if killing one of the retreating enemy actually shortened the war by even a split second. The campaign seemed fruitless as the enemy was now cut off from any support by MacArthur's forces advancing through the Philippines, and Nimitz in the small islands. David slipped his map back into a canvas folder and turned to Captain Brian Williams.

'Brian, you take over running CHQ. I'm going up the track with Mr Jarvis's boys.'

'Do you think that's wise?' Brian cautioned. 'We can't afford to lose you to a Jap sniper.'

'That is why you're 2IC,' David said. 'I doubt there is anything to worry about.'

Brian shrugged his shoulders, and after the platoon commanders had received their briefing for the attack, David informed Mr Jarvis that he would be attached to his platoon. Jarvis looked a little apprehensive at having his company commander travel with his platoon but David reassured him he was not going to take command away from him. He was simply pushing his HQ to the front for any action they may encounter.

The young officer relaxed at David's words and they set out for the native village. David picked up his rifle – he did not carry the traditional pistol of an officer. He knew the Japanese snipers looked for such side-arms that marked an officer, and targeted them first. Even his rank was not displayed on his uniform. All members of the company recognised him by sight as the ultimate commander of their unit.

It was nearly sunset before the platoons moved into position and across an overgrown native garden with run-down huts, long deserted by the indigenous people. David withdrew a set of binoculars and observed the huts. He could clearly see Japanese soldiers setting up a small fire to cook their rice. The order to fire would come from Jarvis. David heard the officer's signaller communicating that they were in position. The reply came back from the other two platoons that they were in place.

David stared through his binoculars and counted five enemy soldiers around a metal pot over a fire. The rain had stopped minutes earlier and others came out of the hut. Either they did not care or they were demoralised, but there did not appear to be any forward sentries.

'Okay, Mr Jarvis, when you're ready,' David said softly.

David lined up a Japanese soldier holding his rifle in one hand and a china bowl in the other.

The eruption of the Australian small arms was sudden and violent, the rapid firing of the Owen submachine guns mixed with the sharp crackling of the Lee Enfields. David fired his rifle and saw the head of the Japanese soldier jerk back as he crumpled to the muddy earth. Bullets tore through the men outside the huts. David and Jarvis were surprised to see a small group of around fifteen enemy burst from a trench behind the huts.

'They are heading Mr Markham's way,' Jarvis said. 'Hope he's ready for them.'

'Mr Markham is in the perfect position to stop them,' David said. 'Meanwhile, we'll sweep the huts for any surviving Nips or military papers.'

They had hardly risen to their feet when they heard the crackle of small arms fire out in the jungle where David knew Markham was located. The radio came to life as a message was relayed to CHQ from Markham's cut-off position. Although the message was veiled David knew exactly what had happened. His stomach was in knots.

Just as the sun fell below the horizon Markham's platoon joined the other two at the former native village. David could see the dark expression on the platoon sergeant's face. He was a man who had seen a lot of combat, from North Africa to New Guinea, and from his barely contained anger David could guess what had occurred when the fleeing Japanese made contact with Markham's platoon.

'Sergeant Harris,' David called to him, 'could I have a word?'

Sergeant Harris slung his rifle over his shoulder and walked over to David, his face still like dark thunder.

'Yes, sir,' he said when David was able to walk him away from anyone overhearing them.

'What happened?' David asked.

'Sir, I don't really want to say,' the platoon sergeant replied.

'Mr Markham lost it, didn't he?' David said. 'I overheard your comms with CHQ.'

The sergeant's shoulders slumped and he looked down at the mud at his feet. 'I had to take command. The boss saw the Japs heading our way, and just jumped up screaming we had to get out of there. I was beside him and when he started screaming for us to abandon our positions, I hit him in the head with my rifle butt to shut him up, so he wouldn't panic the rest of the boys. I then gave the order to engage the Nips with all we had. I think we took out at least half of them before the others got past us.'

'You did well, Sergeant Harris,' David said. 'You did the right thing.'

'Sir, they should never have given us Mr Markham in the first place. I heard he was a logistics officer back at Aitape, and had never been in action before,' the sergeant tried feebly to defend his platoon commander.

'Where is Mr Markham now?' David asked. He had not seen Markham come out of the jungle with his platoon.

'I have a couple of the boys helping him back to us right now,' the sergeant said. 'I'm afraid I hit him pretty hard, and he's still a bit groggy.'

'You take command of your platoon until we find a replacement,' David said.

'Am I in trouble, sir?' Harris asked.

'No, Sergeant Harris,' David answered with a smile. 'Just don't do it too often to any other officers. Promise me that.'

The sergeant could see the humour in his company commander's words, and smiled weakly.

'Promise I won't, boss,' he replied before turning to head back to rejoin his corporals.

David could see Markham, held up between two soldiers. A trickle of blood ran down his face, and his head was swathed in a bandage. David knew he would require medical attention before he saw the officer at CHQ. It was not a situation David wanted. This was serious. No matter the outcome of his talk with the officer, David knew he would never be in a position to lead men in combat ever again.

'Mr Markham, I need to have a word with you,' David said when he walked over to the injured officer. The two soldiers assisting Markham made themselves scarce, and left him with the company commander.

'Sir, I wish to have Sergeant Harris charged with attempted murder,' he said before David could speak.

'I doubt that will happen, Mr Markham,' David responded. 'I'm sure there are many witnesses to you losing it when the men most needed your leadership. In fact, I'm going to report to the battalion CO that you have a case of war neurosis, and have you shipped home.'

The officer stared at David. 'Sir, with due respect, do you know who I am?'

'I'm aware your father is a well-known member of parliament and I'm sure he would rather have his son come back alive than die in this hellhole. Or would you prefer an inquiry into your behaviour today in the face of a numerically weaker enemy force? You will not be the first or last officer sent home suffering battle fatigue.'

The platoon commander considered his options. 'They were on top of us without warning,' he said. 'I felt the only choice I had was to withdraw my platoon.'

'You were in an ambush position, and the Nips stood no chance against the firepower you had,' David countered. 'From what I heard, Sergeant Harris was forced to assume command because you lost it and were screaming in panic.'

'They were on our positions . . .' Markham attempted feebly, but was cut short by David.

'There's no excuse for an officer to panic, and panic you did. You're responsible for the lives of every man in your command and that's why the army pays you a lot more than it does your diggers. You really only have one choice. For the sake of the battalion's reputation and the welfare of your platoon, I suggest you take the battle fatigue option when you head back to the Regimental Aid Post. I'll write a report to substantiate your mental condition, and inform the CO that what happened here today was battle neurosis.'

'Yes, sir,' Markham said. 'But I think you'll live to regret your decision.'

'If that's a threat, Mr Markham, I've had better,' David responded with disgust. 'Just get out of my sight before I change my mind and report your behaviour today to the CO, who I know will want to convene a court martial for cowardice in the face of the enemy.'

Markham knew he was trapped, but still looked defiant.

'Corp,' David called to a nearby NCO, 'assist Mr Markham back to the RAP.'

The corporal slung his rifle, and walked over to the officer he had witnessed attempt to run from the ambush. He glanced at David with a knowing look.

'Yes, sir,' he said. 'I'll make sure Mr Markham makes it back.'

David watched the officer being escorted out of the village ruins, and tried to forget the threat. He knew the man had powerful friends in Canberra and soldiering was as much about politics as it was fighting a war: not all enemies wore the Japanese uniform. David shook his head, as if to dismiss the junior officer's brazen words, then turned to supervise the consolidation of the company. Tomorrow would be the same as today, he reflected. They would continue to pursue a beaten enemy. Men would die, and others would be mutilated on both sides in what seemed a senseless campaign in the backwaters of the Pacific.

TEN

Tom Duffy shook his head. 'You should return to the homestead,' he said.

Billy placed the bag of supplies at his feet. Tom noticed his Aboriginal employee was now armed with an old single-shot rifle from the last century since he last saw him three days ago.

'And where did you get the gun?'

'I found it years ago and cleaned it up,' Billy said with pride. 'Not got much ammo for it though.'

'Bloody hell,' Tom smiled. 'It looks like a Snider.'

'Found it on Glen View in the whitefella quarters with a packet of bullets.'

'You better be careful. It might blow up when you fire it.'

Billy held up the rifle. 'I kill a kangaroo or two with this gun, Mr Duffy.'

'Well, you should still return to the homestead because I'm sure by now I'm being called an outlaw.'

'The new boss, he a bad man,' Billy said. 'He ask all the boys where you are, but they say they don't know. They tell me to take you supplies while the new boss man away, he's going to have the police come out and take you away.'

'Do you know when?' Tom asked.

'I think mebbe in two days,' Billy answered. 'I'll stay with you and fight them.'

'You have a family, Billy. You might get killed if you stay with me.'

'Don't matter, Mr Duffy.' Billy shrugged. 'Better we die like warriors than they take your land.'

'Could have used you beside me in the last war,' Tom said. 'You have the spirit of any of the best I've fought with in the army.'

Tom's compliment made Billy pull back his shoulders with pride. Tom was a good man and boss. Some things were worth risking a life for, and Tom's stand to defend his traditional lands was one of them.

'Mebbe I shoot us a roo for the cooking pot,' Billy said.

'No need,' Tom replied. 'We have enough bully beef and damper to hold off an army from up here on the hill.'

Tom led Billy to the cave entrance and the stockman hesitated. Tom knew of his fears and turned to him.

'Wallarie would have shared his baccy with you if he was still around,' Tom said. 'You are now a part of our mob, just as Wallarie was accepted by the Kalkadoon, and other tribes up north.'

Reassured, Billy followed Tom into the cool gloom of the cave with its centuries of musty smells, lit by a kerosene lantern.

Wide-eyed, Billy glanced around the cave. On the walls he saw the faded drawings and recognised their sacred symbolism.

'This special place for initiated men only,' Billy said in a hushed voice.

'It's a place for warriors,' Tom said, bending down to stoke a small campfire lined by blackened rocks.

That night they sat by the fire, eating bully beef and hot damper. The addition of pickles broke the monotony of the meal. It was washed down with tea, and soon both men settled down on their swags to sleep. Tom knew there would be a showdown. All he hoped for was that no one was hurt or killed. But he also knew he could not walk off the lands of his ancestors without a fight. An unseasonal storm rumbled overhead, producing lightning and thunder, washing the hill with heavy rain. Both men slept through the storm, embraced by the spirits of the cave.

★

The storm rolled across the brigalow scrub, and when the sun rose, left puddles of clear water in the rock crevices of the hill. Miles away at the Glen View homestead a man wearing a suit more in line with a city office stood on the verandah overlooking the yard. Before him were five mounted men wearing the uniform of the Queensland Police Force. They had arrived the night before, just in time to take shelter from the storm. With them was an Aboriginal man wearing the uniform of a black tracker.

'Gentlemen,' the man on the verandah said in a loud voice, 'my name is Edgar Johnson and I'm the lawful manager of this property pursuant to the court order issued.'

Johnson was in his mid–fifties and had a menacing appearance, with his shiny, bald head and square jaw. He spoke with authority, and an English accent.

'You were summoned to remove or arrest the previous owner, a Mr Thomas Duffy, who I believe is probably occupying a hill to the south of our present position.'

'I know the place, Mr Johnson,' a police officer wearing the rank of sergeant said from his mount.

'And who are you?' Johnson asked bluntly.

'I am Sergeant Smith, in charge of this troop, Mr Johnson,' the policeman said. 'I know Tom, and I doubt he'll come peacefully.'

'You are the law, sergeant. If he resists being evicted you'll have to take all measures to protect yourself.'

'If you mean shoot Tom,' Smith said, 'with respect, Mr Johnson, you do not know him as I do. Tom is a crack shot. He was a sniper on the Western Front in the last war, and fought up in New Guinea in this one. He's also one of the finest men I've had the honour of knowing.'

Johnson stepped down from the verandah and walked over to the policeman. 'You are a member of His Majesty's police force, and do not have a say in deciding the orders of the court, Sergeant. Do I have to remind you of the oath you took to carry out your duties without fear or favour?'

'I know what I have to do,' Smith replied, a note of anger in his voice.

'Good,' Johnson said. 'Because I'm coming with you to see that Duffy is apprehended and removed from Glen View. My orders from the court are clear. Plus, we can all imagine how upset Miss Macintosh was when she learned that a place so precious to her was purchased with unlawful means.'

Johnson didn't really know how upset his employer was, but he hoped it helped make his case with the police sergeant to remove Tom Duffy.

The police sergeant waited while a saddled horse was brought to the new manager of Glen View, and they set out for the ancient hill. By late afternoon they reached the hill and made contact with Tom Duffy.

★

'Tom, I know you're up there,' Sergeant Smith called.

'Is that you, Sergeant Smith?' a voice drifted down to the party of uniformed police.

'It's me, Tom, and I'm with the interim station manager, Mr Johnson,' Smith called back. 'We have a court order for you to leave Glen View until the matter is settled in Brisbane. If you do not comply, I'll be forced to arrest you, and I don't really want to do that.'

Dismounting, Johnson pushed himself forward, standing with his legs apart, his hands on hips. 'Duffy, if you attempt to resist you will be shot!' he called in a commanding voice. 'So, come down now peacefully, and leave with the police.'

Johnson did not hear the crack of the rifle but felt the sting of earth erupting between his legs. He leaped sideways in terror and screamed, 'He tried to kill me. Open fire! Open fire!'

'If Tom had wanted to kill you,' the police sergeant said calmly, bringing his skittering horse under control, 'you'd be on the ground with a bullet between your eyes.'

Johnson retreated behind the party of mounted police, most of whom were looking very nervous. They reached for rifles in their saddlebags, and awaited their commander's orders. Smith glanced at his men.

'No need to draw our weapons, lads,' he said calmly. 'I suggest we pull back into the trees over there and discuss our next move.'

The police followed, dismounting amongst a small copse of spindly trees, out of sight of the hill.

'Well, Mr Johnson, I think you have your answer as to whether Mr Duffy is going to comply with this bit of paper I have in my possession. Do you have any suggestions?'

Johnson did not answer immediately, still visibly shaken by his very close call. 'We need to call in reinforcements to assault the hill.'

'With all due respect, Mr Johnson,' Smith said, 'we don't have the manpower, and as a former soldier who served on the Western Front I can tell you now that one man in such a superior tactical position can hold off a small army before he is captured or killed. Is it worth the price for nothing more than an eviction order?'

'As far as I'm concerned, you're the legal representative of the King, and it's your duty to carry out the wishes of the court,' Johnson answered, brushing down his trouser legs to remove the dirt thrown up by the bullet. 'He's defying you, and laughing at us from his hill.'

'I might be able to talk some sense into Tom,' Smith said. 'We've been cobbers for a while. As a matter of fact, we served on the same fronts during the war.'

'It seems to me, Sergeant, that you're too close to the man to be able to carry out your sworn duty,' Johnson said. 'I think it's time someone more capable be employed to do what you appear to be incapable of doing. Rest assured your woeful conduct here today will be reported to the appropriate authorities.'

'Suit yourself, Mr Johnson,' the police sergeant said.

'But I do not intend to endanger the lives of my men over such a piddling civil matter.'

'What about the shot Duffy fired at me?' Johnson asked.

'The rifle might have gone off accidentally,' Smith replied with a shrug. 'After all, Tom only has one arm, and that makes it difficult to handle a Lee Enfield.'

'As you can only find excuses for the man I doubt remaining here will be of any use. We may as well return to Glen View,' Johnson said with resignation.

Even as he spoke he was already formulating a plan to remove Tom – and it would be done outside the law. With her wealth and power, Sarah had been able to influence the courts to appoint the former British policeman to his current role as the caretaker manager of Glen View. But the court officials did not know he was well paid to obey her orders. This was a big country, Johnson smiled to himself, where people disappeared very easily.

★

After being transferred from the hospital ship off the coast of Tarakan and flown south in a specially equipped Dakota transport aircraft Lieutenant Donald Macintosh found his final medical facility to be in his home city of Sydney, near the Parramatta River. It was the 113th Australian General Hospital, newly built in the suburb of Concord to accommodate wounded servicemen. Donald lay in a bed, having nearly forgotten the feel of clean sheets and the taste of good food. But at night he would hear men crying and yelling in their sleep, dreaming of a war that seemed to never end. He wondered if he made the same noises when he slept and re-lived that split second the mortar bomb exploded.

By morning, the chatter and clatter of the ward made him feel lonely. He could not forget his men, north in the rotting jungles, in that place of sudden death and mutilation. His face was swathed in thick bandages and his left hand was still painful after surgery to remove the shrapnel.

'Good morning, Mr Macintosh,' a cheery voice said from the end of his bed. Donald focussed on an army nursing matron who was holding his medical treatment record that had been attached to the end of his bed. 'I see we'll be removing the bandages today to ensure your wound has not become infected. Ah, Doctor Capstan is here now.'

Donald turned his head to see a white-coated man in his middle-age approach, a nurse trailing behind.

'Good morning, Mr Macintosh,' he said. 'We'll remove the bandages, nurse,' he said, and the young woman stepped forward with a metal kidney bowl and scissors. Very gently she cut away at the swathe of cotton until the two halves fell away.

The doctor leaned forward to peer at the tissue of Donald's face. 'Hmm, the wound appears to be healing well. No sign of infection at all. Bloody marvellous drug, penicillin. I think there is no reason to replace the bandages. We'll continue to monitor the healing. With any luck, we'll have you on your feet in a couple of weeks.'

Donald could not help but notice the change in the young nurse's expression when she stripped away the bandages. It was something akin to horror or shock.

'May I see the result, Doctor?' he asked.

'Before you do, Mr Macintosh, you may be a bit upset at what you see, but we have plastic surgeons who do wonders these days. We learned a lot from the last war,' the doctor said. 'Nurse, please fetch a mirror.'

She hurried away to return within moments with a small, hand mirror that she passed to the doctor. Donald was aware the nursing matron had taken hold of his hand as the army doctor held up the mirror.

Donald squeezed the matron's hand when he saw his reflection, and knew there were some things worse than dying.

'At least you still have your vision,' the doctor said, attempting to console Donald, who hardly heard him.

There was a hideous monster staring back at him. He would never be the same again.

ELEVEN

Shrapnel had done serious damage to Donald's hand, and a pretty Red Cross nurse was assigned as his occupational therapist. Donald stood in a large, airy hospital room in his pyjamas, staring out the window at the sun shining in a perfectly blue sky.

'Lieutenant Macintosh, I need to see how much flexibility you have in your left hand,' the nurse said.

Donald held out his hand and attempted to make a fist, but was unsuccessful. The nurse took his hand and examined the healed but badly scarred flesh. She pressed open his fingers and Donald forced himself to restrain from expressing the pain she had inadvertently caused.

'It's all right to feel some pain, Mr Macintosh,' she said sympathetically. 'May I call you Donald? We are both the same rank.'

Donald nodded.

'My name is Rosemarie,' she continued, as she kneaded the palm of his injured hand.

'So, is basket-weaving next?' Donald said.

Rosemarie looked sharply at him. 'Only if you wish,' she said, and Donald regretted his facetious statement when he heard the anger in her voice.

'I'm sorry,' he said.

'There's no need for an apology,' Rosemarie replied. 'You'll have to get used to dealing with your wounds.'

'And this,' Donald said, half turning his disfigured face to her.

Rosemarie shook her head. 'You're alive and still have a face our plastic surgeons can work on. Some of my patients have no faces at all. Some have no legs or arms, so you have got off pretty lightly, considering all things.'

Donald looked more closely at the Red Cross nurse. She had short blonde hair and very blue eyes. He wondered if any woman as pretty as her could ever again look at him with the same expression of acceptance.

'So, where do we go from here?' Donald asked.

'I can work on a program to assist you get your hand working again,' Rosemarie said. 'But I think you should also speak with our resident psychiatrist.'

'What's a trick cyclist going to do for me?' Donald said. 'Tell me my bad attitude was caused because my mother didn't love me? My view of the world right now is coloured by the fact that I'm a physical curiosity who will frighten women and children with this face.'

'Maybe our good doctor will attempt to convince you to come to grips with your injury,' Rosemarie answered calmly. 'You still have many years of life ahead of you.'

A second Red Cross nurse entered the room. She was a captain and looked directly at Donald. 'Mr Macintosh, you have a visitor in the anteroom,' she said.

Donald looked at Rosemarie and shrugged. He was not expecting visitors because his real family was back in the hellhole called Tarakan. The only visitor he had had since his transfer to Concord hospital was Sean Duffy. His visit had lifted Donald's spirits as they could talk together about the horrors of war.

Donald excused himself and went to the anteroom where he saw his sister Sarah, standing with her hand on her hip and smoking a cigarette in a slender holder. She turned when he entered the room. Donald could see the shock on her face.

'My God! Donald,' she exclaimed. 'You look horrible. I hope my friends don't get to see you.'

Donald was not surprised at her response; he had long learned his sister had no empathy for others. 'You could have spared yourself the horror by not visiting me. I doubt you have any real friends, and I don't think you're here out of sisterly concern.'

Sarah walked over to a leather couch and sat down under a portrait of the King. Donald walked over to a window to once again gaze at the gardens outside. Life looked so normal back in Sydney, as if there were no war going on anywhere. His sister was wearing a very chic dress and high heels, her lips a glossy bright red. Clearly the privations of war did not apply to her.

Sarah tapped her cigarette on an ashtray and took a long puff before answering. 'That's not completely true,' she said. 'As soon as I heard from a friend in the government that you were wounded and being evacuated back to Sydney, I made enquiries as to where you would be rehabilitated.'

'That was weeks ago,' Donald snorted.

'I was waiting until you were in better health before I came,' Sarah said, but Donald did not believe her. 'I have a reliable source who informed me you'll be medically discharged in the next few months. He even told me on the quiet that you've been approved for the Military Cross for whatever you did wherever you were.'

'The army's way of compensation, I suppose,' Donald said, surprised by his sister's news. 'The place was an island called Tarakan, and all I did was my job. There were many others who deserved the award more than me.'

'But you're a Macintosh and they know that in Canberra,' Sarah said. 'Which brings me to the subject of what you'll do when you're demobilised.'

'I haven't thought that far,' Donald replied. 'I suppose I should return to my old job in the family companies.'

Sarah stood up and paced across the room in her high heels as she puffed on her cigarette. 'That might not be wise,' she said without looking at her brother. 'With your scarred face, that may prove counterproductive to the wholesome image we wish to project.'

'Image?' Donald snarled. 'Beautiful people doing a beautiful job of making money on the backs of men giving up their lives for the country?'

'Calm down, Donald,' Sarah said, turning to him. 'You have to understand the war will end soon, and people will want to forget the last few years. I'm sorry, but your face is a reminder of those times people want to forget.'

'Bloody hell!' Donald exploded, walking towards Sarah, and thrusting his face towards her. 'Do you think I asked for this? It might have suited everyone if I was killed, and not just wounded.'

Sarah backed away nervously. 'I can understand that you're upset at your unfortunate situation, but I have to think of keeping the Macintosh name at the forefront of business. I'm sure you can understand how important the family legacy is.'

'The bloody family! The family has robbed and murdered its way to the top,' Donald said angrily. 'You only have to look back at the founding of Glen View to see how our illustrious ancestors slaughtered a bunch of harmless people living on their own land to see that. At least the land has now gone back to a man rightfully placed to own it.'

'I can see you're not aware that we've placed an order against Mr Duffy for his illegal purchase of Glen View with stolen money,' Sarah said. 'The courts have declared that until the matter is settled, he is to vacate Glen View. We have installed a temporary manager until the matter is settled.'

'You've what?' Donald couldn't believe it. 'David and I voted that we accept Tom Duffy's offer to purchase before I went away. Has Tom complied with your unscrupulous court order?'

'Er, no,' Sarah replied. 'My last telegram from Queensland informed me that he's armed and holding out on a hill on the station.'

Donald broke into a wide grin. 'Good on Tom,' he said. 'Tom's a warrior, he won't go down without a fight.'

'Your attitude about the matter only reinforces my belief that you do not have what it takes to be a good member of the Macintosh board,' Sarah said. 'You're obviously not aware that there are rumours Mr Duffy may have made his fortune after the last war using stolen diamonds. My investigators are currently trying to find a man close to him, Jack Kelly, and when they do we'll have him put before a court to testify how Tom Duffy made his illegal fortune. I'm sure the truth will come out and Mr Duffy be treated as the criminal he really is.'

'This has nothing to do with how Tom Duffy made his fortune,' Donald said, walking to the leather couch Sarah had vacated. 'It's all about revenge for losing to David and me. It's as if you and father are still together, and cannot admit to defeat against a perceived weak brother and detested cousin.'

'I do not detest David,' Sarah said. 'It's a matter that must be rectified. Glen View has – and always will be – Macintosh land. Our family fought for years to keep the property in our name, and not see it go to some thieving Aboriginal!'

Donald just shook his head. He could see in her eyes that she was grimly determined to regain the property. It was not as if Glen View was unique – the Macintosh companies owned many properties stretched across Queensland and New South Wales. Their agricultural return was not as great as their return from property development and banking.

'I think it's time I return to my basket-weaving,' Donald said, rising from the couch. 'I might return to my old office when I'm demobbed from the army.'

'That wouldn't be a good idea,' Sarah said as he walked towards the door. 'You will not be welcome.'

Donald raised his injured hand above his head in a parting salute.

Donald returned to the dayroom where Rosemarie was working with a soldier in a wheelchair who had lost both legs and an arm.

'I think, after all, I have a use for our resident trick cyclist,' he said with a grim smile as she kneeled in front of the wheelchair.

Rosemarie glanced up at him.

'Not me – my sister,' Donald said. 'She's badly in need of psychiatric help.'

★

129

The constellations wheeled slowly over the sacred hill. Tom sipped his mug of hot tea, gazing up at them. Beside him, Billy sharpened his knife on a whetstone.

'You think you should go to the whitefella court, boss?' he asked, testing the edge of the blade by the flickering campfire.

'I would lose,' Tom said. 'After all, the Macintosh lawyers will point out I'm really a blackfella, and thus not really entitled to any legal rights.'

'But you have fought in two whitefella wars an' the government people give you medals,' Billy persisted.

'They will turn a blind eye to all that,' Tom said, taking another sip of his tea. 'They might even try and use the fact that in the last war I enlisted under false pretences as an Indian.'

'I know blackfellas who went away to war,' Billy said. 'The government looked the other way.'

'Yeah, and where are they now?' Tom countered. 'I knew one cobber who was forced to go back to the mission station after he was demobbed and not allowed to drink with his whitefella cobbers on Anzac Day.'

Billy slid the sharpened knife into a leather sheath on his belt and looked up at the magnificent display of stars. 'Ol' Wallarie up there,' he said confidently, 'he look after us. Wallarie stand by us when the whitefellas come again.'

Tom finished his tea and rolled out his swag. Billy would stand guard for a few hours, and then Tom would relieve him, until the sun once again rose over the brigalow plains.

Tom lay back against the earth, thinking it strange that he should survive two world wars, only to face the possibility of death while fighting a private war no one really knew about.

*

Edgar Johnson badly wanted to lie down and sleep. The railway trip from Queensland had been aboard a troop train, and the men returning from the jungles of the Pacific to their loved ones had been in a festive mood all night. Sleep had been out of the question and upon arriving at Sydney Central Station he would rather have gone to a hotel for a hot bath and a soft bed but he had a mid-morning appointment with his employer, Sarah Macintosh.

Johnson gripped his carpetbag and hailed a taxi that delivered him to the Macintosh offices. He sat in the foyer until he was announced and called upstairs to face the very young, beautiful and formidable woman to whom he had to explain his lack of success in evicting Tom Duffy from Glen View.

He knocked and entered Sarah's office. Her perfume filled the luxurious room, which was decorated in a manner which conveyed understated power.

'Mr Johnson, take a seat. Would you like tea or coffee?' Sarah asked politely from behind her desk.

'No, thank you, Miss Macintosh,' Johnson replied, taking off his hat and placing his carpetbag by his chair.

For a moment Sarah stared at him and Johnson was reminded of his days with a British police unit that had served in Ireland against the Irish Republican Army, fighting a guerrilla war to remove the occupying British army after the Great War. She had a natural talent for making a suspect feel uneasy, and he knew his failure to remove Tom Duffy made him a suspect.

'I paid you good money to carry out a simple task,' Sarah said. 'You came highly recommended. Mr Duffy is only one man.'

'With all due respect, Miss Macintosh, I was not aware he served as a sniper in the Great War,' Johnson said wearily.

'He has the high ground, and any assault on his position would require the services of experienced fighting men.'

'The court conditions require that Duffy not be on Glen View at the time of the first hearing,' Sarah said, leaning forward. 'I don't care how you get him off our land – or even how much it costs. All I care is that I receive a telegram in the next few days saying that the matter has been resolved.'

'I had an idea on the way down to Sydney,' Johnson said. 'I know of three lads from my days in Ireland who are now living in Sydney. They were Black and Tans, and not afraid to do any dirty work necessary to terrorise the Paddies. We used to give them ten shillings a day, but for a couple of quid a day and costs, I know I can employ them to get rid of Duffy. With a Paddie name like Duffy, they would probably kill him for nothing anyway.'

'I did not hear your last statement, Mr Johnson,' Sarah said sternly. 'I would only expect to hear of Mr Duffy's death in the event of you or your men defending themselves against a man refusing to obey a lawful direction to leave my property.'

Sarah had read about the Black and Tans. Apparently they were usually former British soldiers who were recruited to protect the Royal Irish Constabulary from attacks by the IRA. The force was initiated by Winston Churchill in 1920 and gained its name because of a shortage of uniforms – they had to wear mixed army and police uniforms that gave them a two-toned appearance. But fighting in the trenches of the Great War had not prepared them for counter-insurgency warfare, and they soon suffered heavy losses against the more experienced rebel Irishmen. In retaliation they waged a ruthless war against innocent men and women, which only assisted the IRA recruitment. Many atrocities were committed by members of the British paramilitary force, who developed a reputation for being undisciplined and out of control.

'Of course,' Johnson said with a half-smile.

'Just between you and me, Mr Johnson, I'm prepared to pay a very generous bonus to you and your men if Tom Duffy does not survive your lawful attempts to remove him,' Sarah said. 'Do you understand me?'

'Perfectly. I will make contact with the lads,' Johnson said, retrieving his hat and bag. 'I last heard they were working as builders' labourers in the city, and I know where they drink.'

'Good,' Sarah said, retrieving a fountain pen to write a cheque for expenses. She passed it to Johnson, who placed the slip of paper in his jacket pocket. Now, it was just a matter of rounding up his three proven killers. But first he was going to find a good hotel for a bath and sleep.

*

Sergeant Jessica Duffy knew the beach outside Cairns like the back of her hand. She had trained there before her mission to New Britain. Soaking wet and gasping for air, she splashed through the warm water with the Bren gun in her hands. It was a long time since she'd been drilled in hand-to-hand combat, preparing explosives, navigation exercises and using the latest radio transmitters.

'Jessie, working in an office has made you soft,' Major Mike Unsworthy taunted her from high up on the beach.

Jessica came to a stop, leaning forward in her exhaustion and attempting to get her breath. 'Why don't you have a go, sir?' she gasped. 'You might have been too long in the office too.'

Mike Unsworthy stood up and ambled down to where Jessica, wearing the clothing of a male soldier, was still doubled up. 'I've recently returned from an undisclosed place up north,' he said. 'And my office was a clearing in the jungle. Now, strip the Bren.'

Jessica sank to her knees on dry sand and went through the complicated but familiar process of stripping the light machine gun, which was in fact anything but light. 'Piston, barrel, butt, body and bipod,' she muttered to herself as the weapon came apart in pieces.

'Put it back together,' Unsworthy commanded, and Jessica expertly reassembled the gun. She turned to her tormentor. With a grin, he tossed her a loaded, curved magazine. Jessica caught the full magazine and locked it into place on top of the machine gun.

'See that downed coconut tree about fifty yards down the beach?' he asked. 'See if you can hit it with a full mag.'

Jessica lay down behind the weapon, gripping it as she had been trained. She flicked off the safety cap and squeezed the trigger, observing her first burst of three rounds kicking up sand just low of the fallen tree. With a slight adjustment she fired another short burst and was satisfied to see the tree shudder under the impact of the powerful .303 bullets. The Bren gun had a reputation for very accurate fire and, as such, was popular with Australian troops. Satisfied she was on target, Jessica fired three-round bursts until the magazine was empty.

'Well done,' Unsworthy congratulated her, observing the fall of shot. 'I think the last couple of weeks of training has got you back into shape.'

Jessica cleared her weapon and slowly stood up, sweat rolling down her face from under the American military version of the baseball cap, under which she had piled her hair. 'What's next?' she asked.

'A picnic lunch,' Unsworthy said, straightening himself, and taking the Bren from Jessica's hands. 'Officially, lunch will also be your briefing on your new mission up north,' he continued, as she followed him to the edge of the beach under the swaying palms, where a blanket and wicker picnic basket were spread out. Jessica slumped down on the blanket and the British officer produced a lukewarm bottle of champagne.

'Sorry it's not on ice but at least it's the real froggy stuff.' He poured the champagne into two metal mugs. 'To your mission, and returning to the bosom of those who care about you.'

'Do you give the men of the unit the same treatment?' Jessica asked, sipping the champagne.

'As the only woman we have – and do not admit to having – you get special treatment,' Unsworthy said. 'We and the Yanks are sending you to Singapore.'

'Singapore,' Jessica echoed. 'But it's still in the hands of the Japs.'

'We have intelligence from our Yankee brothers in the Office of Strategic Services that as Mac advances, the Nips are killing prisoners. But to his credit he has made a couple of pretty spectacular rescues from POW camps in the Philippines. We need you in Malaya to collect intelligence on what's happening around Singapore, particularly Changi prison. You'll be working with the local communist Chinese resistance in the area.'

'Why was this not a task for our men?' Jessica asked.

'Our friends in the OSS recommended you after your successful rescue of their wayward colonel,' Unsworthy answered. 'They hold you in high esteem, as it seems you also did a classified job for them in another matter they will not speak about. And, I have no doubt, neither will you.'

Jessica knew what he meant. Her mind went back to killing the British traitor to avenge the death of the American officer she had loved. She raised her mug, took a long swig of champagne and let the bubbles go to her head.

Singapore. That was where young Patrick's mother was being held. In the back of her mind, she also knew the mission could be a one-way ticket.

TWELVE

It had never been in doubt that Captain James Duffy, USMC, would apply to return to flying duties. The weeks had passed and the burns to his legs had healed, leaving severe scarring, but they were functional again. James had spent his time convalescing at his grandfather's sprawling estate, undergoing rigorous physical training: running through quaint leafy streets, and working out with weights in the garden.

Many invitations had arrived for his attendance at social and public events but he politely declined. He concentrated on getting well enough to pass a medical board exam to resume flying combat missions in the Pacific. Always at the back of his mind were two other factors: meeting again with Julianna, and revenge for his sister's murder.

As far as he knew, Julianna was with her fiancé in California. Gathering evidence against Olivia's killer was a lot harder since the change of sheriffs in the county. So it had come down to choosing between revenge, love and flying again. Returning to the war was unfinished business. But the other two were not forgotten.

James paced himself and the sweat rolled down his body. He came to a halt in the avenue of great trees, their russet-coloured leaves heralding an early New Hampshire winter. He leaned over to catch his breath, and was aware a car was approaching from behind him. James stepped aside to let it pass, and when it drew parallel to him he saw it was the new county sheriff, Hausmann, alone in the police car. He rolled to a stop beside James, and leaned out of the window.

'I heard that you went for a run down this way,' he said. 'You should be careful that you don't get run over.'

'That a threat, Sherriff?' James countered, glaring at the man he hated above even the Japanese enemy.

'No, no,' Hausmann said with a smirk. 'It's just that the county would be very sorry to lose their son-of-a-gun war hero. So I thought I should patrol along this lane and make sure nothing happens to you. Just the job of a good sheriff looking out for his citizens. After all, that's what your grandfather pays his taxes for.'

'Go to hell, Hausmann,' James snarled, 'because that's where I'm going to send you when I prove you helped cover up my sister's murder for your old pal Wilson.'

'Now, that is a threat,' Hausmann snarled. 'Not a good idea to go threatening a member of the law around here, Duffy.'

'Not a threat,' James said. 'A promise.'

He could see the rage in the sheriff's face and wondered why he had been stupid enough to push the man so far when they were in such an isolated part of town.

'Take care, Duffy,' the sheriff said, engaging the gears and driving away.

James was left with the uneasy feeling that he would have to watch his back. There were many miles of forest in the county and it would not take much to ensure a body was never found. James glanced at the great trees growing along one side of the lane. They had a gloomy look as the light disappeared under a tangle of tree limbs. He turned and started jogging back to his grandfather's mansion before the light went altogether. Maybe it would be safer to return to the fighting in the Pacific, he thought. Julianna and revenge would have to wait.

James arrived home just on dusk and made his way upstairs for a wash and change before dinner. When he went downstairs he was met by the old valet, Samuel.

'Got a telegram for you, Mr Barrington,' Samuel said, handing James the slip of paper.

James glanced at the sender and saw it was from his old friend, Guy Praine. He read the telegram and felt a sick surge in his stomach. Julianna had been married two days earlier in New Orleans.

'Are you feeling unwell, Mr Barrington?' Samuel asked, seeing the stricken expression on the young man's face.

'Tell my grandfather I won't be joining him for dinner tonight,' James said, crushing the telegram into a ball.

'Yes, sir,' the old man replied. He turned and walked downstairs.

James stared at the floor. Now he had only two options left. Returning to combat was his priority. But first, he was going to get himself well and truly drunk.

James spent the evening in one of the less salubrious bars getting drunk as quickly as possible. The night was a blur, and when the sun came up the following day he awoke with the worst hangover he could ever remember, lying on a bed and staring at a ceiling he did not recognise. For a moment

he barely knew who he was – let alone where – and strained
to remember. He vaguely remembered he had been at the
bar drinking, and there had been a very pretty young lady
serving him drinks. He remembered she had informed
him he had had too much to drink and should go home.
James was surprised a young girl under twenty-one was
even working in the bar. Had there been a brawl? James had
flashes of tables being turned over and something hitting
him over the head. After that – nothing.

'Would you like some coffee or orange juice?' a female
voice asked and James turned his head slowly to see an
older woman hovering at the door. For some strange reason
she reminded him of someone he had met, but could not
remember who and where.

'If you would please excuse me ma'am, where am I?'

'You're at my house,' the woman answered. 'I'm Mary
Sweeney and my husband Bernie and daughter Isabel
brought you home from our bar late last night. I'm afraid
that in your condition I doubt you even remember.'

James didn't want to lift his head as he thought it might
fall off. 'I'm . . .'

'I know who you are, Captain Duffy,' Mary said.
'I doubt there's a person in the county who doesn't know
the famous war hero of the Pacific. Getting you safely out
of the bar before the sheriff arrived was the least we could
do to repay you for your service to our country.'

James smiled weakly and rose up slowly, swinging his
legs over the side of the bed. When he looked around he
realised the bedroom must have once belonged to a boy.
There were pictures of a young man in a football uniform,
and later ones of him in the USMC uniform. On a drawer
were trophies for all kind of sports.

Mary noticed James gazing at the trophies.

'My boy was one of the finest athletes in the county,' she said, and James could hear the sadness in her voice. James glanced across at the portrait of the young marine set aside on a shelf and knew the reason for her sadness. The portrait was surrounded by a black ribbon.

'Where?' he asked.

'Tarawa,' Mary replied, tears welling in her eyes. 'My son was a proud marine. He was only eighteen when we lost him.'

'I'm truly sorry for your loss, Mrs Sweeney,' James said.

'I can accept your kind thoughts, Captain Duffy, as you must have lost many you cared for,' Mary said, wiping away her tears. 'You must join us for breakfast,' she said. 'It's about the only meal I have with my husband and daughter. Both work from mid-morning to well after midnight.'

James stood unsteadily and rubbed his face. He felt lousy but realised the actions of this family had kept him out of the hands of a man who might have ensured he had an accident on the way to the county jail. He followed Mary to a small but warm kitchen where a large and tough-looking man sat at the end of a battered wooden table. Next to him was a very pretty young woman he recognised as the girl who had served him at the bar. She had red hair, a spatter of freckles over alabaster white skin and very green eyes. Now he knew why Mary had sparked a memory. Mother and daughter looked very much alike.

Bernie Sweeney rose from the table and extended his hand. Immediately James noticed a fading tattoo on his forearm clearly recognisable as the emblem of the USMC.

'Bernie Sweeney,' he said with a grip that could crush iron. 'You met my daughter last night.'

Isabel nodded at James, who was standing awkwardly at the end of the table spread with condiments and four plates of ham and scrambled eggs.

'Take a seat, Captain,' Bernie said, gesturing to a chair opposite his daughter. 'The best meal you can have for a hangover. Coffee coming up.'

James thanked the powerfully built man, and took a seat. He was not sure if the ham and eggs were a cure for what ailed him.

'You look deservedly ill this morning, Captain Duffy,' Isabel said with the hint of a smirk. 'I tried to warn you, but you wouldn't listen.'

'I apologise if I didn't take your advice, Miss Sweeney,' James said as Mary placed a big mug of hot, black coffee before him.

'Please call me Isabel,' the young lady said.

'Well, I may not be Captain Duffy for much longer, so call me James. It's a pleasure to make your acquaintance – all of you – and I wish to apologise for any bad behaviour I may have exhibited last night in the bar.'

'You were no problem when I laid you out,' Bernie said with a wide grin. 'I had to before the sheriff turned up. Someone called the cops when you swung at one of our star college football players for a derogatory remark he made about the marines. I was able to drag you to a backroom. It's no secret around town that he has it in for you.'

'Thanks, Mr Sweeney, I think,' James said.

'Bernie,' the former marine said.

'Bernie,' James echoed.

James swallowed some of the coffee and picked at his breakfast. It was strange, but in this room amongst these people he experienced a strange sense of peace.

'Are you going back to the Pacific?' Bernie asked over a gulp of his coffee.

'I hope so,' James said. 'I appear before a medical board

next week. All going well, I'll be given a clearance, and back in the islands before this war is over.'

'When do you think it will end?' Bernie asked, chomping into his slab of ham.

'The way it's going, I doubt we'll see an end for at least another year. Maybe late 1946 if we're lucky. The Japs have shown they will die to the last man – and woman – if we invade.'

'I served in the 1917–18 war with the marines and we were saying in 1918 that the war would drag on another year. Hope we get a result before Christmas 1945,' Bernie said. 'The Armistice of 1918 came as a big surprise to us all on the Western Front.'

'I think you should drive James home after breakfast, Bernie,' Mary said, cutting across her husband's war talk. 'I'm sure his grandfather must be worried sick about him.'

'Yeah, sure thing,' Bernie said. 'Better get him back across the right side of the tracks.'

James did not finish his ham and eggs but had another cup of coffee before he thanked Mary and Isabel for their kind hospitality. Bernie's home was set against a row of blue-collar houses, far from the plush mansions of James's life. Many of the windows over porches displayed the strip of stars indicating sons serving in combat. It was from such places that the men and non-commissioned officers were drawn. Officers generally came from the palatial homes and those with social backgrounds on James's side of town.

Bernie had an old Ford truck and James piled in beside him.

'You hear things, working in my bar,' Bernie said. 'I think you'll be safer overseas. That goddamned son of a bitch, Sheriff Hausmann is crooked, but at least I was able to pay him off to allow Isabel to help me in the bar on busy nights. You can't get any good help around here with this war on.'

James stared out the window at the people walking to work. 'Have you ever heard any talk about my sister's death?' James asked, knowing that if anyone had picked up talk it would be someone like Bernie behind his bar.

'I never had the pleasure of knowing Olivia,' Bernie said. 'I know she was your twin and served her country with the Red Cross Down Under in Australia. She must have been a fine young lady. But you must know that a good barman knows when to keep what he hears to himself, like a priest protecting the secrets of the confessional.'

'Does Edgar Wilson ever drink in your bar?' James asked.

'Yeah. When he's slumming to impress his buddies what a tough guy he is,' Bernie said.

'Was he in your bar the night my sister was killed?' James persisted.

For a moment Bernie did not answer, as if struggling with something he would rather not divulge. 'You know, if my son had not been killed serving his country, he had the ability to go to college and make something of his life. He won a sports scholarship to Harvard, but said he would rather use the GI bill to get his education.

'Now we only have our daughter. She is exceptionally bright. I know she did not get her brains from me. Her mother is also extremely smart – except for ever falling for a palooka like me. Isabel turns eighteen next month and wants to go to college to study medicine and become a doctor. She could do it, but you know, it costs a lot of money for her to see that dream come true.

'All I've ever known after my stint with the marines is my bar. We moved from Boston to get our son away from the

Irish gangs in the city, but found that in New Hampshire the Irish were not really welcome. I talked with Mary and we hope I can sell the bar next year to raise the money for Isabel to attend college. Mary and me, we'll live off my military pension. You might understand why I can't say nuthin' about what I hear in the bar. Certain folks around here could make it very hard for us.'

James knew a military pension was little better then living above the poverty line. He understood why the big Boston Catholic Irishman was reluctant to speak in this tight-knit predominantly Anglo Saxon protestant community. They were outsiders. But James was formulating a plan and smiled to himself as they swapped a few marine stories on the way to the Barrington residence.

Bernie pulled up in front of the mansion and James stepped from the Ford. 'Thanks, Bernie,' he said. 'I promise I won't cause any trouble in your bar ever again.'

Bernie grinned. 'Then I promise I won't lay you out again, Captain Duffy.'

The truck drove away, leaving James standing before the columned porch of his grandfather's mansion. What a comparison between where he had come from to where he was.

James strode towards the front door, his mind swirling. He convinced himself they were not really impulsive ideas. But his grandfather would hit the roof if he knew what his beloved grandson was planning.

THIRTEEN

How long had it been since Diane was first imprisoned inside the great stone walls of Changi prison? Three years – or forever? She kneeled in the prison vegetable patch, staring with ravenous eyes at the sparse crop, and wanted to eat them all. But she also knew her Japanese and Korean guards counted the growing vegetables, and to steal any brought swift and painful punishment to the prisoner responsible.

As each day went by the death of another civilian internee meant very little to those who had suffered the cruel captivity. They had long been hardened to death, and many just wondered when and how their own demise would come.

'Something's going on,' Anne Bambury said. The Englishwoman had entered the prison back in 1942 in her early fifties and lost a considerable amount of weight. Like many others, she was gaunt and pale from bouts of malaria.

'The Nips are acting queer. There are rumours they are taking a beating in the Pacific. I heard the news from the men's camp.'

Diane looked at her friend and knew she looked as haggard as Anne did.

'I also heard the Japs are planning to kill us all if our boys invade Singapore. I would not put it past the little yellow bastards. As it is, it looks like they're trying to exterminate us by malnutrition and illness. It has been hard to keep the stiff upper lip,' Anne sighed as she squatted beside Diane. 'I keep dreaming a British soldier is going to walk through the gates holding a big steaming plate of Yorkshire pudding and a bottle of ale.'

Diane smiled weakly. They were all tormented by fantasies of plentiful food.

'I'm sure the Nips know they're beaten and that makes them dangerous. If they know they're going to go out, they will want to take as many of us as they can.'

'You know the bastards caught out the residents of Hut 23 laughing and giggling, and they are now being punished for it?' Diane said. 'Young Sammy has been forbidden to see us because he was caught with a handful of rice he could not account for. What kind of animals punish children who are just trying to stay alive?'

Anne did not answer. Diane could see that the time they had spent behind the Changi walls was starting to break her down. While they might be close to being released, the terrible unspoken fear of their extermination at the hands of the Japanese and Koreans weighed heavily. It was like running a long race, only to trip a couple of yards from the finish line.

'What will you do when the war is over?' Anne asked, to distract them from their morbid thoughts of execution.

'I don't really know,' Diane answered. 'Like you, I was born in England, but my son is in Australia with my husband's relatives. My first priority is to get to Australia and be with Patrick. I still have savings in the bank, but I don't know what we'll do. My airline no longer exists, and all I've ever known is flying. I'll take Sam with me to meet his new brother. I hope to adopt Sam if no one turns up to claim him. What about you?'

'I'm going to return to England, open a fish-and-chip shop, and eat everything I'm supposed to sell,' Anne said, and both women began to giggle.

They quickly looked around to ensure the guards a few yards away did not see them laughing. Their captors were touchy about the Europeans laughing in these uncertain times, thinking the laughter was aimed at them, which was considered loss of face.

Anne helped Diane work the earth around the rows of vegetables. They worked under the tropical sun in a land where it was always the same monotonous hot temperature, broken only by wet and dry seasons.

As Diane grubbed at the earth she also experienced an unspoken fear. Should they survive, would Patrick remember her? It had been such a long time, and he had been so young when she last saw him. Suddenly she felt the familiar waves of the malarial fever wash over her. Diane slumped forward and Anne saw her friend lying face down amongst the rows of vegetables. She called to a couple of women nearby also tending the patch.

'Give me a hand with Diane,' she called. 'We have to get her to the hospital.'

A Korean guard standing at the edge of the agricultural area saw the two women rise to go over to Anne.

'You! Stop!' he shouted, brandishing his bayonet-tipped

rifle. 'You take prisoner,' he said to Anne as the other two were forced to remain in the vegetable patch.

Despite being weakened by malnutrition Anne was still able to heft Diane to her feet using all the strength she could muster, and half-drag, half-walk her to the place they called a hospital with its few beds and meagre medical supplies. Diane had to live, Anne prayed to whichever deity would listen.

★

Donald Macintosh was able to wrangle a leave pass from the hospital. He dressed in a civilian suit and hailed a taxi to take him to the Macintosh companies near Circular Quay.

He was greeted by the doorman downstairs. Donald could see the shock in his expression when he saw the disfigurement to his old boss's face. The doorman quickly recovered and his welcome in return was genuine. He gestured for Donald to take the elevator to the top floor. The elevator operator also looked shocked at seeing Donald's face but said nothing except to ask which floor. Donald did not know the young man.

'Top floor,' Donald said.

'That is the Macintosh companies, sir,' the boy said.

'I know,' Donald said.

'You have an appointment to go there, Mr . . .'

'Lieutenant Donald Macintosh. I think I'm still allowed to visit my family's offices,' Donald said. The elevator boy ducked his head in his embarrassment.

'Sorry, sir,' he apologised and took Donald to the top floor. He stepped out to see the corridor leading to many familiar offices. Donald passed a couple of employees he knew before the war, and who now hardly hid their expressions when they saw his disfigurement. But they greeted him warmly enough.

Donald reached his sister's office reception, where a young man rose from his chair behind a desk. Donald did not recognise him.

'Yes, sir, can I help you?' he asked.

'I'm here to see my sister,' Donald answered.

'Er, you must be Mr Donald Macintosh,' the young man said uncomfortably. 'I'll see if she's available to see you, sir.'

'Never mind,' Donald said walking past the desk, opening the door to Sarah's office where she was alone, poring over a report.

'Hello, Sarah,' Donald said. 'I thought I might drop by to see if my old office will be ready for my return.'

Sarah glanced up in surprise. 'Donald, you should have phoned to say you were coming today,' she said, hardly disguising her annoyance. 'I'm very busy at the moment. I have a board meeting in ten minutes.'

'Good,' Donald said, taking a seat in a big leather chair. 'I think I'll also attend and reacquaint myself with the directors. After all, I still retain a seat on the board, even though you are the managing director.'

Sarah stared at her brother coldly. 'I know you're doing this to upset me.'

'I doubt that anything could upset you, dear sister,' Donald said with a small smile. 'Maybe there are some things that make you angry but you have an ability to disguise your anger and get revenge.'

Sarah rose from her chair and brushed past Donald. He followed her along the corridor to the boardroom. Inside the members were already in the seats, smoking and chatting to each other. All talk stopped when Sarah entered.

They rose politely to acknowledge her entrance and blinked with surprise at seeing Donald follow her.

'Good afternoon, gentlemen,' Donald said, walking directly to an empty chair. A few who recognised Donald greeted him warmly with handshakes across the big, polished table. But half the board members were strangers. No doubt appointed by his sister in his absence. They stared at him curiously.

'For those on the board I've not met, I'm Donald Macintosh. Son of Sir George, brother to our esteemed managing director, and just back from the Pacific, where I had my face rearranged by a Jap mortar bomb on a hellhole called Tarakan.'

Donald's last bitter comment caused a few to duck their heads in embarrassment. All had avoided military service, with the exception of two older men who had served in the last war.

'As my brother has introduced himself to those who did not know him before his entrance today I think I should express my gratitude for his contribution to the war effort,' Sarah said.

Donald knew she did not mean a word of her praise but smiled politely.

The meeting opened and procedure followed, with the reading of the minutes of the last meeting. Donald was bored but determined to give the impression of someone who was preparing to return to management.

'We have the matter of Mr Duffy's removal from Glen View,' one of the newer members offered.

Donald was suddenly interested.

'I've taken steps for Mr Duffy to leave Glen View,' Sarah said. 'I had a meeting with the court-appointed manager of Glen View to recruit some men who can assist him convince Mr Duffy that he should leave until the courts settle the matter for us.'

'How are they going to "convince" Tom Duffy to leave?' Donald asked, aware every board member was watching him keenly.

'Mr Johnson is a former English policeman and has had experience dealing with such matters,' Sarah answered.

Donald could see his question had unsettled his sister.

'Gentlemen of the board,' Donald said, staring down the table at the faces watching him. 'I personally know Tom Duffy, and he's a decorated hero of two wars. He purchased Glen View from us in a fair dinkum way, and I feel he has all rights to remain until the court case is settled. I doubt anyone on this earth would be able to convince him otherwise.'

'Duffy purchased our land with ill-gotten gains,' Sarah flared. 'My late father always expressed his wish that the property never leave our possession, and I still respect that wish, even if you don't, dear brother.'

Donald turned to his sister. 'Maybe you should tell the board how the family first got hold of Glen View.'

'With all due respect,' a younger member of the board piped up, 'from what I know of Glen View it is just one of many Macintosh cattle properties in Queensland. Is it really worth the expensive and time-consuming legal-wrangling the case will cause?'

Sarah turned on the board member who was stupid enough to question her. 'You do not have an appreciation of family tradition, Mr Jenkins. I will educate you after the meeting in my office.'

Jenkins shrank back into his seat. He knew what the invitation really meant, and rued his question.

'I would like it noted in the minutes of this meeting that I do not agree with my sister's decision to pursue the matter against Mr Tom Duffy. If you'd excuse me I have to leave early.'

Donald rose from his chair and walked out of the meeting, leaving his sister flushed and angry. He knew there were things that he must do – and very quickly.

★

'Donald, old son, how the devil are you?' Sean Duffy said, stepping forward to shake Donald Macintosh's hand in his legal office. 'You look a lot better without all those bandages that were wrapped around your head when I last saw you in hospital. You were a bit out of it then.'

'Fair to middling, Uncle Sean,' Donald replied as Sean ushered him to a chair. Sean was not really his uncle but he had been more of a father to him than Sir George had ever been, and the title was an expression of Donald's feelings for the Sydney solicitor.

'Sorry about your injuries,' Sean said, taking a seat behind his desk. 'You have now joined our club of maimed and crippled soldiers. I think this is an opportune time to head out for a cold beer.'

Donald smiled. Sean had not expressed any horror at seeing his disfigured face. The old soldier had probably seen worse in his years on the Western Front.

'I wish I had the time to do that,' Donald said. 'But an urgent matter has arisen. I've just left a meeting at the company HQ chaired by my sister. The matter of removing Tom Duffy came up, and it seems my sister has hired a former Pommy copper to get rid of Tom.'

'I know all about it,' Sean said. 'My informants have told me that, not only has Sarah hired a man called Edgar Johnson, but he was in Sydney to recruit some undesirable characters he once worked with in Ireland against the IRA.

I know the men from my experiences in the courts. They are former Black and Tan members, and from what I know of them, I would consider them very dangerous.'

'Bloody hell!' Donald swore. 'He's going to attempt to kill Tom.'

'That's about it,' Sean said. 'The last I heard, Tom was holed up on the hill near Glen View station with a blackfella. I know Tom is very resilient, but he will be outnumbered – and probably outgunned – if Johnson recruited his old pals.'

'Is there anything you can do to stop Johnson?' Donald asked.

'There is very little I can do, except represent Tom's interests in court,' Sean sighed. 'All Tom has to do is remain on Glen View and stay alive to thwart Miss Macintosh.'

'He needs help,' Donald said.

'How can I be of assistance?' Sean asked, leaning forward.

'I would need to contact Harry Griffiths,' Donald said.

Sean reached for a pen and jotted down an address and a telephone number, passing it to Donald.

'So, he still has his old gym,' Donald said with a smile as he pocketed the paper.

'Whatever you have in mind, Donald, be very careful,' Sean said. 'You and David are very special to me.'

'Thanks, Uncle Sean,' he said, rising from his chair. 'This conversation never happened. Just like I was never here.'

*

'You ever thought about getting back into the ring again?' Harry asked, gripping Donald's hand in a vice-like grip. 'After all, no one is capable of messing up your face worse than the Japs.'

'At least I'm still prettier than you, Harry,' Donald retorted, withdrawing from the bone-crushing handshake.

Here was another man Donald loved like family. It had been his cousin David who had introduced Donald to Harry and his gym to learn how to fight. Harry, too, had served on the Western Front in the Great War.

'The major rang me to say you were coming for a visit,' Harry said, standing by the raised boxing ring. 'What do you need?'

Donald explained his reason for the visit.

Harry listened quietly, then said, 'It will be difficult, but I have a couple of contacts amongst the wharfies. Give me twenty-four hours.'

Donald thanked him and hurried off to a bank to withdraw a substantial amount of cash. His next stop would be the hospital, to apply for the substantial leave he was owed by the army.

FOURTEEN

The battalion had been given its orders to mount a diversionary advance south of Wewak towards Sambakaua in the jungle-covered mountains. At first it was relatively easy-going as Major David Macintosh's company moved forward across a terrain of undulating hills sparsely covered by trees. He had with him a couple of local native guides but he also had heavily reduced platoons of infantry. The main thrust by the brigade was to be made east of their axis of advance so the battalion was protecting the main unit's right flank. So short of men was the company that even the company cook had been pressed into service for the march south. He had insisted the company cook pot travel with them. They were fortunate that native carriers accompanied them, and the cook pot was slung between two poles.

The company was able to spread out in battle formation and were hardly into the march when they encountered their first skirmish with the Japanese. One prisoner was taken – he was so hungry he had attempted to steal food from the Australians.

After a couple of days the country changed and the ever-present mountains and dense jungle forest reappeared to confront the advancing Australians. It was all too familiar to many of the men who had fought along the Kokoda Track.

When the platoon bivouacked for the night, sentries were posted and relieved every two hours.

David squatted at the base of a big rainforest tree, examining the sketch map that was being made of their progress. He used a torch under a ground sheet to conceal the light and was joined by Captain Brian Williams.

'How's it looking?' Brian asked.

'Like it always does,' David replied. 'Jungle, bloody jungle, and most probably Nips holed up waiting for us.'

'At least we have arty support,' Brian said.

'Yeah, but by the time the Nips hit us in an ambush it's a bit too late for our blokes who get caught.'

Brian knew what his company commander meant. Jungle warfare was totally different from what the battalion had experienced in Africa. At least there the artillery forward observer could clearly see terrain that might support enemy troops well ahead of an advance, and lob a few shells to disrupt the enemy's plans to ambush. In New Guinea visual references were measured in feet rather than miles. All artillery could do was react to enemy contact in terrain where a man could hide without much fear of being hit by a direct shot from the 25-pounders.

'I read a paper from home before we left that hinted the war was virtually over,' Brian said. 'A lot of the boys were getting letters from families saying how hard it was living with the rationing. I gather the people back home consider the war over.'

David glanced at his friend. 'Tell that to the Yanks who will have to storm the beaches of the Japanese mainland to make the Japs surrender. I was briefed that they can expect casualties in just one day amounting to all the troops they have lost so far in this war. The bloody war will not be over until next year at the least, unless we get a miracle.'

Their conversation was cut short by the sound of small-arms fire and exploding grenades a short distance away.

'Bloody hell!' David swore, snatching his rifle and flicking off his torch.

A battle was being fought on the perimeter by one of his platoons and he could recognise the shouting voices were speaking Japanese. It was a still, clear night lit by a full moon. When David looked in the direction of the firefight he could see flashes of weapons and exploding grenades. The noise was deafening and every now and then he caught sight of a figure silhouetted by the gun and grenade flashes.

'Brian, get over to the other two platoons and make sure they hold their fire unless absolutely necessary,' David shouted.

It was important his perimeter was not completely revealed to a force that may have surrounded them. Gun bursts gave away their location in the dark. David moved forward in a crouch, following a string line until he found the position of the platoon engaged with the enemy. He recognised the platoon commander shouting orders to his men who appeared to be holding their positions under heavy fire.

'What happened?' David shouted to the young officer.

'I heard rustling in the grass to our front,' he shouted back. 'I stood up to have a quick look, and saw the little bastards crawling towards us. I did not have time to inform you, boss.'

'Well done,' David said, slapping his young officer on the back. After about fifteen minutes the firing tapered off, and the night became quiet again. The jungle creatures, shocked into silence, felt brave enough to now fill the night with their calls and cries. David crawled back to his HQ under the base of the forest giant to await briefings from his other platoons.

When the sun rose the company found the bodies of three Japanese soldiers uncomfortably close to the forward edges of the gun pits. Bloody trails led away from the perimeter. A light machine gun on its bipod had been left behind, indicating that the Australian soldiers had surprised their enemy. The only casualty David's company had to mourn was the big cooking pot, now riddled with bullets and out of action.

The next day, the company's luck ran out. Continuing the advance, a forward scout moved about seventy yards ahead of the advancing company. The rest of the company was assembling into a fighting formation when a single shot rang out. The forward scout took the enemy bullet in the chest, pitching forward. The company immediately shook out into a counter-ambush formation.

David moved forward with the medical doctor. The wounded soldier was treated in the field before being prepared for evacuation down the line to a hospital on the coast.

'Get some shells into the jungle around here,' David said to the captain, an artillery forward. David hoped the barrage of exploding 25 pound rounds might cause the hidden enemy to fall back out of range.

Within minutes the heavy, earth-shaking crump of exploding shells could be heard – and felt underfoot – as guns targeted the nearby area.

David gave the order to continue the advance and near evening his company came under fire from a wooded area near a creek. Another of his soldiers was hit, but survived.

That night David had his platoons dig in, and during the dark hours sporadic fire from the platoon Bren guns kept the enemy at bay. The retreating Japanese were far from a beaten force. The fighting dragged on.

For David, peace was something he had given up on and did not expect to find, even when the guns eventually fell silent on the tropical battlefields of northern New Guinea.

*

Captain James Duffy knew he would be put back on the active roll. It was no secret that an invasion was being planned for the Japanese main islands, and the predicted casualties meant every able-bodied man was needed. There was a shortage of pilots, and his leg burns had healed well enough for him to operate the controls of a fighter plane. There had been no damage to his leg muscles.

James returned from his medical board interview and told his grandfather he was once again to be shipped out to the Pacific war, where he knew he would be facing the deadly menace of suicidal Japanese pilots. The kamikaze pilots' efforts were not in vain – they had taken a very heavy toll on British and American shipping and naval crews off their homeland islands.

James Barrington Snr shook his head sadly. 'You do not have to do this, James. You have done enough already.'

'I have to see out the war, sir,' James replied. 'I have lost too many friends to quit now.'

'You do know that when the time comes to invade Japan, every man, woman and child will meet you on the beaches with anything they can use as a weapon,' Barrington said.

'I expect that it will be no safer in the air above those beaches. When are you due to ship out?'

James knew his grandfather was right. It was well known that the enemy had a policy akin to mass suicide by its civilian population. How would he feel strafing lines of women and children attempting to confront the troops landing on the beaches? He did not want to even consider the possibility.

'I leave tomorrow,' James said. 'I thought I might visit some friends before I leave, so I won't be in for dinner tonight, but will be back to share a nightcap with you.'

James could see tears glistening in his grandfather's eyes.

'I'll read a book and see you when you return home,' his grandfather said. 'Don't be late.'

James shook his head and drove into town to Sweeney's Bar. Inside the dimly lit room he could see Bernie and his daughter behind the bar.

Bernie looked up and broke into a broad smile when he saw James in his uniform. A few patrons sitting at the bar and around the room at small tables also glanced at the handsome young USMC fighter pilot, and the coloured ribands on his chest denoting his bravery. A few raised glasses and mumbled, 'God save America'. James nodded to them.

'What's your poison?' Bernie asked.

'Make it a Scotch on the rocks,' James replied, placing some notes on the wet bar.

'Your money has no value here, Captain Duffy,' Bernie said, pushing the notes back towards James. 'The drinks are on the house tonight.'

'Are we celebrating something special?' James asked innocently.

'You goddamn know we are,' Bernie answered. 'Do you think that we Irish are so stupid that we cannot see through such a badly concealed scheme to send Isabel to college on a scholarship set up by the Barrington Foundation? Don't even try to insult an old gyrene with any blarney about not knowing.'

'Okay,' James said, accepting the tumbler of whisky. 'I may have had something to do with it, but my grandfather has more money than he knows what to do with, and your family has already paid a heavy price with the loss of your only son.'

For a moment Bernie stared at the young pilot. 'I'll be able to sell the bar to pay you back,' he finally said. 'We don't need charity.'

'It's not charity,' James replied. 'If you like, I can have papers drawn up to have a stake in the bar. I kind of like the place.'

Bernie grinned. 'How would it look if it was known that a decorated officer of Uncle Sam was a part owner in a bar on the wrong side of the tracks? I'm not sure your snobby friends in your social circle would approve.'

'They can go to hell – or start drinking in our bar,' James said, taking a swig. 'The main thing is, Isabel gets a chance to follow her dreams of becoming a doctor. She's a good kid.'

James only had two drinks before he left the bar. He stepped out to walk towards his car.

'James!' a voice called to him.

He turned to see Isabel hurrying after him. 'I've not had an opportunity to thank you for the scholarship. I don't know why you have done it, but I will not let you down.'

She was now face to face with James in the dim light of the carpark.

'I know you'll be the best doctor this town has ever seen, although I'm not aware of too many other lady doctors in these parts.'

'Times are changing,' Isabel said. 'This is the second time you have come to my rescue. I guess you don't remember the first time you did, before the war.'

Puzzled, James had no idea what she meant. 'I'm afraid I don't remember.'

'It was almost ten years ago. I was coming home from school when some kids from another school started picking on me. I was very afraid as I was only about eight years old at the time. You came across the boys, who were about your age, bullying me. You looked very angry, and stepped in to tell them to leave me alone. One of the boys was Sheriff Hausmann – but he wasn't a sheriff then – and he challenged you. You hit him so hard that he had a bloody nose and the others ran away, afraid of you. I was crying and you gave me a clean handkerchief to wipe away the tears. I didn't give it back to you at the time. I still have it.'

'That was you!' James laughed softly. 'The snotty-nosed kid with freckles who gave me an excuse to lay out that son of a bitch Hausmann. I'm sorry I had forgotten you. Well, you've certainly grown into a fine young woman.'

'I never forgot how you stood up for me, and I've followed your career as a fighter pilot all through the war. I would say prayers for you at Mass on Sundays so that you'd return safely, and we would meet again.'

James was suddenly aware she was on tiptoe and felt her lips on his own. He fell into the kiss but stopped himself and gently took her arms, pushing her away.

'Isabel, you're still a kid,' he said, and immediately regretted his choice of words.

She stood before him, tears welling in her eyes. Without a word she turned on her heel and ran back to the bar, leaving James cursing himself for being so clumsy. He walked back to the bar to apologise. When he entered he was aware the patrons were less warm in their greeting. He guessed Isabel was much loved.

'What did you do to my daughter to upset her so much?' Bernie growled, stepping out from behind the bar, and advancing on James.

'Mr Sweeney . . . Bernie . . . I swear on my Irish blood that I didn't harm Isabel in any way,' James said, the words tumbling out before he could think of some way to smooth the situation. The big saloon keeper was not a man anyone would want to upset, with his rippling muscles and brawny bulk. 'We just had a misunderstanding in the carpark.'

Bernie glared at James, his arms folded across his chest. He turned to the few patrons in the bar staring at the unfolding scene.

'What are you lookin' at?' he snapped, and they ducked their heads to avoid his cold stare.

Then Bernie's expression changed. 'You'd better come with me,' he said to James in a gentler tone. 'We'll talk in the carpark.'

For a moment James thought this was an invitation to have his head knocked off, but Bernie grinned at his shocked expression.

'I need to tell you something,' he said, gesturing to James to follow him.

Both men stepped into the carpark.

'I think I know what upset my daughter, James,' he said. 'For as long as I can remember Isabel has had a crush on you. I never thought in a million years that you'd ever come into our lives, and that she would naturally grow out of her childish ideas. Did she make some kind of pass at you?'

James nodded his head. 'I realise she's a mere child, and didn't think it was appropriate. I'm ten years older than your daughter, and she should be dating the boys in high school, not someone like me.'

'You're a good man, James,' Bernie said, holding out his hand. 'I heard a rumour that you're going back to the Pacific.'

'I ship out tomorrow,' James said. 'Please make up some kind of apology for me,' he continued. 'The last thing I want to remember is the hurt my clumsy actions may have caused Isabel.'

Bernie clasped James's shoulder.

'I will,' he said. 'Whether you know it or not, you're now a part of our family, with all that you have done for us. When you return I'll help you bring down that goddamned son of a bitch Edgar Wilson. I don't care who his father is or that he thinks he runs this county. I know you're not Catholic, but you carry an Irish name, and you're a brother marine. I think you and I could prove to be a formidable team.'

James disengaged the iron grip and looked at the big Irish American. Who could doubt that between them they would bring Wilson down? All James had to do was survive his next posting to the Pacific, and the upcoming bloody invasion of Japan.

FIFTEEN

'If anyone asks, your names are Larry, Moe and Curly,' Johnson said to the three former Black and Tan members. 'You figure out which name you want.'

'That's the names of those three Yankee comedians you see at the flicks,' said one of them. The three men were in their mid- to late forties and it was obvious from their tough demeanours they had seen a lot of violence. 'I like that,' he continued with a hard smile. 'Theys is always hurtin' each other.'

The four men travelled by train to Queensland. When they arrived in Rockhampton they left the train with their personal baggage. Johnson made them wait until a couple of heavy wooden crates were unloaded from the baggage car. The former Black and Tans stared curiously at the long boxes.

'What have we got here, Mr Johnson?' Moe asked.

'You'll see when we get to Glen View,' Johnson replied,

and looked for the truck waiting for them at the station. Johnson organised to have the boxes loaded onto the truck and the three clambered aboard for the rough and dusty journey to the cattle station.

They arrived two days later.

The truck pulled into the front yard of the homestead, to be met by hostile glares from a couple of stockmen astride their mounts.

'What ya lookin' at?' Curly snarled. 'Bloody colonials.'

Johnson had the two big wooden crates lugged inside, and with a jemmy prised open the lids. Larry, Moe and Curly gathered around and stared with awe at the heavily greased weapons inside.

'Bloody hell!' Larry said, reaching for a Thompson submachine gun with a round ammunition magazine. 'This is some kind of firepower.'

Johnson opened the second crate and from the straw packing produced a quantity of Mills bombs. The hand grenades only needed fusing to become deadly weapons. The rest of the crate contained .45 bullets for the three Tommy guns. Johnson lifted a rifle with a grenade launcher attached and passed it to Moe.

'You're going to need all this to get Duffy off his hill,' Johnson said. 'This country is so big that we can make him disappear.'

'I had trouble with Duffys back in Ireland,' Curly said, stroking the infamous weapon of Chicago crooks. 'Only wish we had these little blighters then. It will be a pleasure killing another Paddy.'

'Don't underestimate Duffy,' Johnson cautioned. 'He knows this country like the back of his hand, and is a crack shot. As far as I know he's armed with a Lee Enfield and will have trouble operating it with just one arm.'

'When do we go after this Duffy?' Curly asked.

'I would say as soon as we can. We clean the Thompsons and test-fire them,' Johnson said. 'We have a good supply of Mills bombs and where Duffy is holed up is far enough away so that any noise we cause will not be heard. We leave in the truck the day after tomorrow. I'm expected to tele-gram Sydney soon after that to say the job is done.'

'With what we got here,' Curly said, 'we could take out a small army.'

Johnson distributed the rest of the weapons and issued grenades and ammunition to each man. He had a pistol with which he hoped to deliver the final shot to Duffy's head.

'Don't let the men here see your weapons,' Johnson said. 'Duffy is well respected by his men, and I don't want him tipped off that we have enough firepower to overwhelm him.'

That night, after the guns had been cleaned and spare magazines loaded, the four men sat around swapping stories of their experiences in Ireland fighting the IRA. Johnson let them get drunk on the cheap whisky he had supplied. He knew they were proven killers, and listened as their stories grew wilder and wilder. In the morning they would drive to an area to test-fire the Tommy guns, away from the hearing of the Glen View stockmen. Then, the next morning, well before the sun rose, they would drive to the hill along the rutted track that led to the string of dry waterholes. From there they would make their assault on the hill before first light. One man against four armed with automatic weapons had no chance at all. Johnson planned to take him from all sides. He'd once heard an American describe a turkey shoot. This would be a turkey shoot.

*

The Criterion Hotel in Rockhampton – only a short distance from the Fitzroy River – was young Cyril Walker's preferred place to go after work. In the past the hotel had been used by MacArthur's staff to plan operations in the Pacific campaign, and he had dropped in from time to time to mix with the patrons, who were mostly military men from the USA.

Cyril was nineteen and had attempted to enlist in the armed forces but failed because of a heart murmur. He was able to obtain a cadetship as a journalist because his father owned the local newspaper. The ambitious young man knew that drinking – albeit underage – in the hotel meant he might pick up information of worth for his editor. There was even the dream he might one day get credentials as a war correspondent, but it seemed time was running out. The Japanese were in full retreat, and after the invasion of their homeland would eventually be overwhelmed by superior American firepower.

Cyril stepped off the footpath from a beautiful, blue sky and balmy day into the smoke-filled interior of the hotel's main bar. He glanced around at the many uniforms of Allied soldiers, sailors and airmen leaning against the bar with glasses of beer in their hands. His gaze settled on a man sitting alone in the corner of the smoky room. What attracted Cyril's interest was his badly scarred face, the scars appearing to be fairly recent. The man was not in uniform but rather the rough dress of a cattle stockman. Cyril guessed the stranger's wounds were similar to others he had seen on wounded servicemen in distant battlefields. Beside the man's leg was a military-issue kitbag, and a single, long canvas bag.

The stranger noticed the young man staring at him and met his gaze with a slight smile and nod.

Cyril turned away and purchased a glass of beer at the bar. The man with the interesting scars might have a human interest story about his service, Cyril thought, and pushed his way through the drinkers to reach the corner of the bar. He stood at the edge of the small table.

'Excuse me, sir,' he said politely. 'I'm a journalist with the local paper here, and I could not help noticing you appear to have been wounded recently. I was wondering if you would grant me an interview.'

Donald looked up at the cadet journalist hovering near his table nervously. 'Have a seat, young man,' he said. 'But I'm not your story. A lot of cobbers were wounded on Tarakan Island. Your story is much closer to home. As a matter of fact, your story is happening now.'

Cyril removed a pencil and notebook from his shirt pocket, ready to write. Donald told him the story of a decorated war hero of two wars standing alone to defend his land from unscrupulous businesspeople south of the border. He named Glen View and Tom Duffy, and could see the young newspaperman's mind working on the angle of the story for his readers. Cyril remembered a story they had run about Tom Duffy's possible eviction from his property, but was unaware the man had chosen to stand and fight.

When he had finished Donald said, 'You know, this story has eerie echoes of events out west of Rockie almost a hundred years ago. If you look back through your records you'll find stories of a bushranger, Tom Duffy of the same name, and an old Aboriginal warrior, Wallarie. Tom is descended from that bushranger.'

Cyril looked up from his notes and Donald could see his expression of genuine interest. It had all the angles he needed: evil businesspeople from down south, a defiant stand against the legal system, and a decorated war hero fighting a new war against his own country.

'How do I get to Glen View?' he asked eagerly. 'It's a fair way west.'

'You find someone who has a plane who can fly us to Glen View, and you'll get your story,' Donald said.

Cyril held out his hand. 'I should introduce myself more formally,' he said. 'Cyril Walker.'

'Lieutenant, Donald Macintosh,' Donald said, accepting the handshake.

'Macintosh!' Cyril exclaimed. 'But wasn't that the name you said was behind Tom Duffy's persecution?'

'Yeah, my sister,' Donald replied. 'Now, the deal between us can only go ahead if you get hold of an aircraft.'

'I know a farmer who lives outside of town who owns a small plane that could fly us to Glen View,' Cyril said. 'But he'd want a lot of money – he has a reputation for being as mean as they come.'

'Money is not a problem,' Donald said. 'Just get us to him.'

'I'll have to clear the matter with my boss first,' Cyril said, going over in his mind a thousand things he would have to do before flying to Glen View. 'If you wait here I promise I'll be back within a couple of hours.'

'No problem, cobber,' Donald said.

Cyril gulped down his beer and hurried from the hotel. Good to his word, he returned within a couple of hours with a small suitcase and portable typewriter. The two men caught a taxi that took them to the outskirts of town and the farmer's property.

Both men left the taxi and Donald slipped the driver a pound note to wait for them. They walked towards the house. The yard was littered with old, rusting agricultural parts and a smallish but solidly built man in his late forties stepped from the doorway of the house.

'G'day, Mr Parsons,' Cyril greeted. 'Do you still have your Puss Moth?'

'Young Cyril,' Parsons said, striding across the yard towards them, 'why do you want to know?'

'I have a gentleman who might be interested in hiring you to take him for a flight west over the hills.'

Parsons stopped before them and looked at Donald's face. 'Last time I saw a bunch of scars like that I was flying with the AFC in Palestine, when my cobber had a bad landing.'

'Infantry, a Jap mortar bomb,' Donald said extending his hand. 'So you flew in the last war.'

'Yeah, got to fly the mail run up this way after the war, but the government grounded me,' Parsons said without elaborating. 'To answer you, young fella, the crate is in the shed.'

Both Donald and Cyril looked over to a large shed not far from the house. Looking beyond Donald could see a flat paddock with a windsock hanging from a tall post.

'I'd like to hire you to fly us to a cattle station west of here, Glen View, as soon as possible,' Donald said.

'Tom Duffy's place. Good bloke,' Parsons said. 'There's a rumour he's in a bit of trouble. Why do you two want to go there?'

'I'm hoping to help Tom out,' Donald said. 'And Cyril is planning on getting a scoop for his paper.'

'Does your old man know?' Parsons asked Cyril.

'Sort of,' he replied, shifting uncomfortably at the question. He turned to Donald. 'My father is also my boss at the paper.'

'It would probably cost you more than you can afford Mr . . .' the former fighter pilot said.

'Sorry,' Donald said, 'I should have introduced myself. Donald Macintosh.'

'Are you related to the Macintoshes who used to own Glen View?' Parsons asked, the tone of his voice no longer friendly.

'I'm afraid so,' Donald said. 'But I'm genuinely concerned for Tom's safety, and need to get to Glen View as quickly as possible.'

For a moment Parsons stared at Donald and then mentioned a price to cover precious fuel he had left in his dwindling stock. Donald did not hesitate, reaching into his pocket and producing a wad of notes. He peeled some off and placed them in Parson's hand.

'That enough?' Donald asked.

'More than enough, Mr Macintosh. For that I will fly you directly to Tom Duffy, wherever he is.'

'The fee also is intended to cover Cyril's passage,' Donald continued.

Parsons nodded. 'You're lucky the Puss Moth can carry the three of us.' He pocketed the pound notes. 'Be back here by 0600 hours and if the weather is right we'll fly out to Glen View.'

Donald and Cyril walked back to the waiting taxi. When they returned to Rockhampton Donald made his way to a boarding house where he had rented a room. The next morning, he was ready to leave with his army-issued kitbag, and the long, mysterious bag.

★

Sarah Macintosh liked to stand by her office window at night and gaze out across the city lights below. It was a quiet time when she could reflect on how far she had come at such a young age. It seemed that all she surveyed belonged to her. It was obvious the war in the Pacific would eventually end after the invasion of the Japanese mainland. The men would return, and she had pushed her various departments to seek out land for urban development around Australia's capital cities. The undeveloped properties would be subdivided into small urban lots for the returning servicemen and their families to settle.

She had also invested in construction companies and their suppliers of building material. Sarah knew it would all pay off when the war ended, and fill the company coffers to overflowing. Money was power, and it was power that really motivated the young woman.

She turned away from the window to ponder the situation in Queensland. Johnson had the credentials to get the job done, and when he reported Duffy was gone from the situation, she could then focus on removing her only competitor in life, Allison Lowe, one way or another. David would be returning from the war, and Sarah's obsession with her cousin knew no bounds.

Her telephone rang unexpectedly. Sarah picked up the receiver and was asked by the exchange operator if she would accept the collect call from Goulburn. Sarah agreed and was connected.

'Mrs Huntley,' the voice of Val Keevers said. The use of Sarah's married name annoyed her. 'I have some bad news. Young Michael is in hospital with severe breathing problems.'

'So, what do you expect me to do?' Sarah asked, annoyed. There was a pause on the other end of the telephone.

'I thought you might come to Goulburn to be with him,' she replied.

'That's what I pay you to do,' Sarah snapped. She could not remember the last time she had held her son. 'Just call me when he gets better,' Sarah said, replacing the handpiece, leaving the nanny flabbergasted at the other end.

Sarah stared for a moment at the telephone on her desk, pondering the situation. Her baby's existence sometimes proved to be an annoyance in her life. Tomorrow she had meetings with her department heads to discuss their progress with the building projects. Her toddler's illness could not distract her from what she must do if she were to corner the market on building homes.

★

Donald Macintosh stood at the edge of the paddock used as an airstrip, watching the sun rise on the horizon and the airsock at the top of the mast fluttered gently in the breeze

The Puss Moth had been refuelled, and Parsons went about conducting his pre-flight checks. The single-engine aircraft, with its main wing placed above the fuselage, was the same model flown by the famous Australian aviator Bert Hinkler when it went down over the European alps years earlier. This thought did not cheer Donald.

Cyril joined him. 'It looks like a good day for flying,' he said cheerily, excited by the adventure that lay ahead on the other side of the low hills.

Parson walked over to the two men. 'Get your gear aboard, Mr Macintosh,' he said. 'We take off in five minutes.'

Donald and Cyril packed their gear in the cramped cockpit. Parsons climbed into the pilot's seat. The engine kicked over with a cough and splutter, and soon roared into life. In minutes they were airborne and rising steeply to clear the high ground of the low range of hills ahead. Donald gazed out at the massive expanse of flat, scrub-covered land that lay beyond. He only hoped he was in time to help Tom. The long canvas case in his luggage might make the difference.

SIXTEEN

Donald had a good idea where Tom would have retreated to on his property. As any soldier would, he selected the high ground, and the highest point on Glen View was the ancient volcanic plug that had become the sacred hill of Tom's Aboriginal ancestors. Donald had visited the hill before the war when his father had exiled him to the family property. It was also then he had met Jessica Duffy.

Donald leaned into Parsons and shouted in his ear that he would like a flyover of the prominent landmark. Parsons nodded and steered a course towards the hill and in a short time was over it.

'God almighty!' Donald swore when he saw the plume of dirty smoke erupt from the summit. He knew what he was seeing and could hardly believe his eyes. It was either a mortar bomb or grenade going off. Parsons also saw the explosion and immediately pulled back on the controls of his aircraft. Donald could feel Cyril's hand gripping his shoulder and just made out his question, 'What in hell was that?'

Donald ignored the question, scanning the earth below to pick up the sight of a lorry hidden amongst a copse of trees at the bottom of the hill. He could see four men clustered around something and guessed it was a rifle with a grenade-launcher attachment. Within seconds he saw another explosion amongst the rocks of the hill but he could not see Tom.

Was he too late? Donald cast about the terrain near the hill and saw the flat, open stretch of ground where it might be possible to land a small aircraft. He gripped Parsons' shoulder and pointed to the potential landing strip about a half mile from the hill. Parsons nodded and turned to fly over the tract to satisfy himself it was a potential landing field, grateful for his years of experience flying in the rugged lands of Palestine during the last war, which had equipped him to undertake unscheduled landings.

Satisfied the strip of land was safe to land, he turned again to make his approach. Donald could feel Cyril's hand gripping his shoulder like a vice as the little plane floated in to touch down on flat stretch of sandy soil and dry grass. There was a line of scrub at one end and Parsons desperately cut back his power to roll to a stop only a few yards from what could have been disastrous. Donald thanked him with a slap on the back and over the noise of the engine gave directions to get airborne again, and take Cyril with him. Already Cyril was attempting to clamber from the aircraft but Donald pushed him back as he dragged out his own kitbag and the long case. Cyril tried to protest but Donald closed the cockpit door and already Parsons was swinging the nose of his aircraft for a take-off. The last thing Cyril saw was Donald pulling out a rifle from the leather bag and slinging his kitbag over his shoulder as he jogged towards the hill.

'I'm to fly you to the homestead,' Parsons shouted. 'Macintosh's orders. He said something about writing your story from there. He doesn't want anything to happen to you.'

On the ground Donald could hear the distant drone of the Puss Moth making its way to Glen View homestead as he jogged towards the hill. He was approaching from the opposite direction to the men lobbing grenades at Tom Duffy. It was warm. Donald hoped Tom had a good supply of water wherever he was holed up.

Very soon he was at the foot of the hill and from there he began climbing, acutely aware the explosions were continuing on the other side of the crest. He dragged the American military-issue .30 calibre Garand, semi-automatic rifle with him as he clambered amongst the rocks. Maybe Tom was safely in the cave where the grenades could not harm him, Donald thought. But that would be foolish as it only had one entrance, and Tom would be trapped if the enemy were able to advance within grenade range. A grenade going off in the cave would be devastating.

Gasping from exertion, Donald finally made the top and was startled when an Aboriginal man wearing the garb of a stockman rose and pointed an ancient Snyder rifle at him.

'Hey, Billy! Don't shoot,' Tom's voice called, just as another grenade exploded only a few yards from where Donald was crouching, causing him to fling himself in the crevice of two great rocks. Shrapnel spattered against the stones, flinging up chips around him.

'What in the bloody hell are you doing here, Donald?' Tom asked, half-rising from behind a small rock wall.

'Came to give you a bit of fire support,' Donald gasped, still getting his breath. 'Have you got the billy on, because I could kill for a cup of tea.'

Tom reached over with a broad smile on his face, spotting the Garand. 'You certainly came prepared,' he said, and Donald immediately passed the heavy rifle to him.

'I figured you could do with this more than me, with the problems you have working the bolt on the three-oh. I'm better equipped to use your rifle.'

Tom accepted the American rifle gratefully as it only required him to pull the trigger and reload when the magazine was empty. He passed his own gun to Donald with a bandolier of ammunition.

Donald settled himself next to Tom whilst Billy moved back to his position between the rocks to observe the ground below.

'I guess you were in that aeroplane I saw buzz the hill,' Tom said, preparing the blackened billy for a brew in his fortified position, relatively safe from small arms fire. 'What in hell are you doing here?'

'I found out about my sister's plan to evict you from Glen View,' Donald replied. 'Sean also briefed me there was a plan to bring in extra muscle, and I figured I should be here to keep an eye on Jessica's old man. What have I missed?'

Tom passed Donald a mug of steaming tea. 'Just before first light Billy spotted a couple of the buggers trying to sneak up the hill. I opened fire and they ran back down the hill out of sight. Next thing Billy and I know, the bastards are lobbing grenades at us. Not sure how many of them are down there.'

'At least four,' Donald said, sipping the hot tea. 'That's about all I know – except they are probably under the command of a former Pommy copper, Edgar Johnson. Sarah will stop at nothing to get Glen View back.'

'I kind of met Johnson,' Tom said. 'I should have put one between his eyes the last time he was here, but there were too many witnesses. How did you get here? Last I heard from Sean, you were in Concord Hospital after being wounded at Tarakan. I can see the Japs made a bit of a mess of your dial.'

'I was able to get a lift on a B24 flying to Rockie,' Donald said. 'In Rockie I met a young newspaperman, and felt your armed stand to save your land was newsworthy for the national coverage it'll get when the young fella has his story of the stand here published. No doubt it will peeve my sister when it becomes national news. By now Cyril should be back at the homestead having tea and scones, asking questions, and writing his story.'

Tom held up the Garand rifle. 'And what's the story with this?' he asked.

Donald shrugged. 'Fell off the back of a truck on the Sydney wharves. Along with around a hundred rounds of .30 cal.'

Tom broke into a chuckle. 'Pity a small mortar didn't also fall off the same truck. We could do with some fire support to even things up.'

'We hold the high ground and that evens up the odds,' Donald said. 'I have a feeling they won't try and take the hill in daylight now that you disturbed their plan to take you by surprise.'

Tom agreed. Billy joined them, and the three men settled down for a meal of bully beef, biscuits and black tea.

*

'The bastard Paddy has the advantage, holed up there in the rocks,' Moe said from the sparse shade of the scrub. 'The grenades must have got him by now.'

'Want to walk out and see if we got him?' Curly said, spitting on the dry earth.

Moe remained silent. Johnson's party had already learned Tom was not alone. They had also seen Billy appear on the crest that day armed with a rifle.

'He's only got some blackfella with 'im,' Larry said. 'Niggers ain't got the stomach to fight.'

Johnson listened to the talk between his men. They were not over-endowed with intelligence, and he knew better than to underestimate his adversary. 'I should remind you all that Duffy has Abo blood, and was a well-known sniper in the Great War. He also served with the infantry in this war up in New Guinea.'

The men fell silent. Their boss had made a statement that contradicted their inborn bigotry against all people who were not Anglo-Saxon. The man who confronted them was part Irish, part Aboriginal – and a colonial to boot. A combination they deemed inferior, and yet, here they were, stuck at the bottom of the hill, impotent despite being armed with superior weapons.

'When I get hold of that black bastard,' Moe said, 'I hope he's still alive because I want to see him die a slow death.'

The others nodded.

'We try again at first light tomorrow morning as we seem to have lost the element of surprise,' Johnson said. 'But this time we'll break up into two teams. Larry and I will give covering fire with the grenade launcher while you two,' he said, pointing at Moe and Curly, 'will make your way around to the right flank of the hill before the sun rises. You have your Tommys, and they should be more than enough to lay down heavy fire.'

The three thugs listened to the plan but still looked uneasy. They agreed it was preferable to an all-out frontal assault against a defended position in broad daylight, and settled down for the day, waiting anxiously for the hours before dawn.

*

Parsons landed his aeroplane on the flat land in front of the Glen View homestead. When the dust settled he turned off the engine and both he and Cyril climbed out in the late-afternoon sunlight. Already a couple of nearby stockman had galloped over to the aircraft.

'G'day, Mitch,' Parsons said to the first horseman who arrived. Mitch was a tall and wiry man with a broken nose, and scars on his face from years of working with cattle in the scrub.

Mitch dismounted and stared at the small aircraft. 'What are you doin' in these parts, Mr Parsons?' he asked. 'Who's the joker with you?'

Parsons introduced Cyril as a newspaperman from Rockhampton.

Mitch stared at him curiously. 'What are you doin' out here?' he asked.

'It seems that Mr Macintosh, who we left on an old volcanic hill, thought there might be a story for our readers,' Cyril said.

'Which Macintosh?' Mitch asked.

'Lieutenant Donald Macintosh,' Cyril replied.

Mitch broke into a wide smile, 'Bloody hell, young Macca is back.' Mitch remembered Donald from his days on Glen View before the war. In fact, they had a stand-up knockdown fight in the round yard, and had become firm friends after the brawl. 'I guess Mr Johnson doesn't know he's back, or he might have something to say.'

'From what we saw when I did a flyover of the hill, it

seems Mr Duffy is in a bit of trouble with a bunch of blokes shooting at him,' Cyril said.

'That would be bloody Johnson,' Mitch growled. 'One of the boys reported he thought he could hear the distant rumble of thunder from that direction.'

'Could you give me something for the paper?' Cyril asked eagerly. There was no doubt the trip had been worth it if a small war was being waged on the cattle station involving explosives of some kind.

'About all I know is that the boys were tasked to go after scrub bulls on the edge of Glen View a couple of days ago. I was ordered to stay here with Bluey, and look after things around the homestead. I can see why now. The bastard was going after the boss with his three stooges.'

'Why do you call them three stooges?' Cyril asked.

'Because they were introduced to us as Larry, Moe and Curly,' Mitch answered. 'You could see they were city types straight off and a bad-looking bunch too. None of the boys took to them, and the rumours started in our quarters that they were hard men sent here to get rid of the boss.'

'Didn't that concern you?' Cyril asked, surprised that men obviously loyal to Tom Duffy had done nothing.

'Nah,' Mitch said. 'There were only four of 'em, and no match for Tom Duffy, even if he only has one arm. Now you say Donald has joined him, so we can expect to see Tom back here pretty soon.'

Cyril was amazed by the stockman's confidence. This was a strange land, far from the comforts of the coastal towns and cities. Cyril remembered the western movies he had seen at the local cinema, and wondered if he was now living in one. All he had to do now was get back to the hill where all the action was.

★

Night was arriving. A silence had fallen over the hill. The three defenders gathered together in a broad rock crevice to eat their dinner. It would be a cold meal as they knew a fire would mark their position. They ate bully beef from a can, and hard tack biscuits washed down with water.

Donald noticed Billy had finished shaping a long hardwood spear, and had also carved a wooden club called a nulla nulla. He had stripped naked – except for his leather belt, into which he had tucked the wooden club.

'What's he up to?' Donald asked Tom.

'He thinks Wallarie has come to him with instructions and I'm not about to convince him otherwise,' Tom replied. 'He's told me he's going out tonight to have a look at the camp below.'

'A bit dangerous,' Donald said. 'The gunfire this afternoon was coming from Thompsons. I know them well from my army service.'

'Don't underestimate Billy,' Tom said. 'He was with me up in the Gulf and is as good as any soldier I've served with.'

Donald shrugged. When he turned to look around, Billy he was gone. It was as if he had become a shadow in the night.

*

Billy moved silently off the hill, aiming towards the campfire he could see burning in the scrub. They were careless, he thought. He could see all four men silhouetted by the light of the large fire. No sentries, and they were standing around confident that they had nothing to fear from those on the hill.

He crept closer, treading carefully, calculating the distance between him and his prey. When he was around twenty yards out he rose from his crouch and balanced his spear in his hand, the woomera sling attached. Bringing back his arm he let the deadly twelve-foot missile go. It whirred through the night, and he saw it strike his intended target.

'God almighty!' Larry screamed as the spear entered his shoulder and drove through the flesh, its point exiting out his upper back.

The sudden and completely unexpected attack caused the others to look about in terror, scrambling frantically to snatch up their firearms. Billy knew what to expect and dropped to the ground as a spray of bullets fired wildly, snapping spindly trees and ripping through the dry leaves above his head. They kept firing until the attached drums of ammunition were emptied, and smoke curled from the hot barrels.

Billy immediately jumped to his feet while the shooters changed magazines and ran expertly between the scrub, away from the enemy camp. Maybe it would cause them to stay awake all night, he mused as he let the night swallow him. Maybe Wallarie was watching and it had made him smile.

★

'Cor blimey,' Larry moaned as his comrades propped him against the side of the truck. 'It hurts like buggery. The black bastard has killed me.'

'You'll live,' Johnson said. 'Lucky for you, his aim was off, and the spear has passed through cleanly.'

Johnson rummaged in the truck toolkit. The best he could find for a medical implement was a sharp axe.

'Lay him down on his side,' he ordered the other two, who seized Larry, forcing him on his side so the spear was now on the ground. With a swift motion Johnson brought down the axe, snapping off the section protruding from the front of Larry's shoulder. Larry screamed in agony as the force of the strike moved the spear in his flesh, grating on nerves. He fainted, and Johnson bent down to grip the section sticking out of the back of the shoulder. He placed his foot on the wounded man's shoulder and with a grunt slid what remained of the spear from his body. Blood flowed and Larry moaned as he regained consciousness.

'It's out,' Johnson said to Larry, lying at his feet. 'All you need now is to have your shoulder bandaged until we get you to a doctor.'

Larry groaned and sweat poured from his ashen face as the other two men lifted him into a sitting position.

'Give him a mug of rum,' Johnson said. 'That should help ease the pain.'

'What are we going to do, Mr Johnson?' Moe asked. 'The buggers are out there just waiting to spear us all to death.'

'There was only one of them,' Johnson replied calmly. 'And I doubt he'll be back tonight. We stick with our plan.'

'I am Wallarie,' a voice called from out of the darkness. 'I will come for all of you whitefellas tonight.'

Immediately the unnerved thugs fired in the direction of the voice until Johnson yelled to cease fire. They were wasting valuable ammunition as Johnson suspected the Aboriginal man was well out of effective range of the submachine guns.

None of the men at the base of the hill slept that night. They took turns at sentry duty as their comrade moaned in pain, unsettling the camp with his suffering.

★

Donald saw the shadowy figure emerge from the night.

'Don't shoot, boss,' Billy said.

'I strongly suspect you caused all that racket down the hill,' Tom said with a grin, passing his friend a mug of cold, sweetened tea.

'Speared one of the buggers,' Billy grinned, accepting the mug. 'But he still alive. Bloody spear a bit off, and got him in the shoulder.'

Tom slapped Billy on the back. 'Well done, warrior,' he said. 'Maybe Wallarie really guided your hand.'

'Nah,' Billy said, drinking his cold tea. 'If Wallarie speared him, he would be dead. Just old Billy throw the spear.'

Soon, the sun would rise. Donald felt for the rifle by his side. It would be modern European weapons that would decide the next few hours, not spears. Johnson still had overwhelming firepower on his side.

SEVENTEEN

Okinawa had changed considerably, thought Captain James Duffy, as he stepped from his transport aircraft onto the tarmac shimmering under a tropical sun. No longer was there the background gunfire of a bloody war being waged inland; now the island now was taking on the look of a well-occupied American shanty town.

'Welcome back, Captain Duffy,' said a senior NCO, jumping from a jeep. 'The boys will be pleased to hear that our favourite officer has come home to his real pals.'

'Thanks, Sergeant Walsh,' James said, hefting his seabag on his shoulder and stepping into stride alongside the armourer who had been responsible for arming James's Corsair with bullets, bombs and rockets when he had conducted ground support missions months earlier.

'You've come back at a bad time,' Walsh said, getting behind the wheel of the jeep as James threw his kitbag in the rear. 'Not much action with our squadron except patrolling against kamikaze, and very few of them lately. But we heard scuttlebutt that we'll be supporting the landings when we go up against the Japs in the invasion. We expect to lose a few of the bent-wing birds over the beaches.'

'Thanks, Walsh,' James said with a twisted smile. 'I just get off the flight from States side, and you tell me I probably won't have much time to live.'

'No, skipper,' the sergeant said. 'It'll be the other poor son of a bitch who'll get killed. You're like a goddamned cat with nine lives. I don't know how you got out of the last crash.'

'I think I used my ninth life,' James said as the vehicle conveyed them to their squadron lines, passing men stripped to the waist playing touch football in the heat, or lazing around in makeshift chairs and soaking up the sun.

James went through the ritual of reporting in, being interviewed by his commanding officer and briefed on his duties. He was then allocated living quarters, sharing a room in a hut only recently constructed.

His roommate was another captain, but part of the ground crew administration. 'Brett Hardy, out of California,' he said, extending his hand. 'You have the misfortune of sharing some sack space with me until the other huts are finished.'

'James Duffy, out of New Hampshire,' James said, shaking the man's hand. 'How long have you been here?'

'Just got in a week ago,' Hardy said. 'I was pushing to get a combat posting in the Pacific, but by the time I got here it was just about all over. So, all a signals officer can do here is shifts in the radio shack. I've heard about you through some of the boys who served with you earlier in the war. Aren't you the flyer who shot down five Jap Zeroes a few years

189

back while flying a Dauntless dive bomber?'

'It was three,' James said with the hint of a smile. 'And one of them crashed himself.'

'Goddamned good to shake the hand of a real hero,' Hardy said, a tone of respect in his voice. 'I was at college when you did that. It was the talk of the campus.'

'Yeah, well, that feels like a hundred years ago now,' James said, sitting down on the edge of his bed.

'That reminds me,' Hardy said. 'A parcel arrived for you yesterday. I put it in your locker.'

James stood up and went to the grey metal closet by his bed and found the parcel just a little bigger than a large envelope. He opened it without looking at the sender's address and found a folded handkerchief along with a short letter.

Dear Captain Duffy,

I must apologise for my forward behaviour the last time I saw you. I have enclosed the handkerchief you gave me those many years ago, as it has always provided me with good luck. Please accept my apology, and I promise such behaviour will never happen again.

Please be careful and return to our town very soon.

Yours sincerely

Isabel Sweeney

James held the handkerchief, aware that Hardy was staring at him curiously.

'Is that all that's in the parcel?' he asked.

'Yeah, I left it at home, and a nice kid returned it to me,' James replied.

'I got to go on duty,' Ryan said. 'No wild parties or broads while I'm gone.'

He left James alone in the room. In the distance James could hear the B29 Superfortress, four-engined bombers roar to life for yet another bombing raid of incendiaries on Japanese mainland cities. Mustang fighters would accompany the high-flying bombers because of the incredible long-range ability of the sleek fighter aircraft.

James knew his war would recommence with the invasion of Japan. He glanced at a calendar hanging in the room. It was 5 August 1945. Tomorrow would just be another day on the flight line.

But Captain James Duffy was very wrong. It was the day that changed everything in the Pacific war.

★

Major David Macintosh sat in the shade of the swaying coconut trees that edged the small beach while his men splashed and frolicked in the cooling waters of the Bismarck Sea. His company had been granted respite leave after their operations, and for a brief but precious moment the war was somewhere else altogether.

David read and reread the letters from Allison. He gazed out to sea and imagined a life away from the hellish world of war. There would be an overhead fan to cool his body as he lay back against clean sheets on a soft bed. A chilled beer in his hand, and the few remains of the biggest steak a man could consume. He would be on a beach with Allison beside him in a skimpy swimsuit, and the world would be at peace. His daydreaming was shattered when he heard Captain Brian Williams say, 'The boss wants us for a briefing in an hour.'

'You know what for?' David asked, dreading the answer.

Brian squatted beside David. 'It looks like we have to go out and join the rest of the division in the bush.'

David slipped the letter he was reading into his shirt pocket. Another operation of sleepless nights, backbreaking climbs up steep jungle-covered slopes, leeches and always the thirst for water. Then there were the ambushes as the Japanese continued to fight fanatically to the last man, and the inevitable killed and wounded amongst his own men. It was never going to end, and the hopes he had of returning to Allison were nothing more than just simple dreams.

Both men walked together towards the HQ area and were met by a signalman flushed with the news the battalion had just received from Brigade HQ. The signalman stopped, and stood to attention before David.

'Boss, we just got news that the Yanks have dropped some kind of bomb on a Nip city called Hiroshima, and blew it off the face of the map.'

'What!' Brian exclaimed. 'When did this happen?'

'Yesterday, sir,' the signalman replied. 'I reckon the Japs will throw in the towel now.'

Neither David nor Brian was so confident. Time after time, they had faced an enemy fully prepared to die rather than surrender, but the signalman's happiness made them keep their thoughts to themselves. The signalman asked permission to spread the news about the new super weapon, and David dismissed him to do so.

'What do you think, Dave?' Brian asked.

'I don't think the Nips will surrender on the strength of losing one city,' he said, gazing at the beach they had just walked away from. 'It would take a war on two fronts before they consider how hopeless their situation is.'

'The Russians have said they would help out,' Brian offered.

'Then, if the Russkies honour their promise, we might

see the Japs consider an unconditional surrender,' David said. 'Until then the war is not over for us.'

★

The news of the first atomic bomb to be dropped on Japan hardly made Sarah blink, divorced as she was from the grand strategy of international politics. Her world was on home ground, and all that mattered was how she could exploit the wartime conditions imposed on Australia. She considered herself a woman of vision, and was already being mentioned as the face of the future, a beautiful young woman chairing one of Australia's biggest financial institutions. She was a part of a successful family dynasty that prospered even more with her touch. A journalist had somehow unearthed the story that Sarah had neglected her sick child and decided to run it in an attempt to shatter her rising star. When she heard, Sarah organised for the journalist to interview her and her charm, along with some hastily arranged donations to children's medical research, had worked. Instead of a smear story, the published article showed her as an angel.

'I read the story,' Detective Inspector Preston said, throwing the paper on Sarah's desk. 'You tell a pretty good yarn for the newspapers.'

'Every word is true,' Sarah protested. 'My duties to the Australian public come before my desperate need to be with my son Michael.'

'You're talking to me now, Miss Macintosh,' Preston said with a hard smile. 'I know what you're capable of, and having real feelings for people is not one of those things.'

They sat opposite each other in the library of the Macintosh mansion, a small table between them, on which lay a plain envelope with the policeman's payment for the month.

'You don't get paid to judge me, Inspector,' Sarah said. 'You earn your place on the payroll by solving problems peculiar to your occupation.'

Preston slipped the envelope into his jacket. 'I expect double the next time I come here,' he said, taking a cigarette from a packet. 'Having someone done away with is very risky business.'

'But you'll do it?' Sarah asked.

'From my experience, I don't think it will be much of a problem,' Preston replied. 'There's a way to do it without attracting much attention. I know someone on the other side of the law who owes me a favour.'

'I don't want to know,' Sarah said, raising her hand. 'Just get it done as quickly as possible.'

'Before the end of the week,' Preston said, rising from his chair. 'Just keep an eye on the morning papers.'

He left the room. Sarah wondered how David would deal with the loss of his beloved Allison. Oh, she would rush to his side to console him when he returned from the war, and David would learn who really loved him.

Loved him, Sarah reflected. *Owned* him was probably a more accurate way to describe how she felt in her obsession for her cousin. As for her husband, Charles Huntley, well, he would sue for divorce by the time she finished with him.

*

The night nurses moved silently in the dimly lit hospital corridors. Val Keevers had been given special permission to remain beside Michael's bed, as the rheumatic fever racked his body. The doctors were able to treat him with the new wonder drug, penicillin. The toddler whimpered in his pain, and Val held his little hand in her own, whispering soothing words to the little boy.

She had trouble controlling her anger as she sat by his bed. Why wasn't the boy's mother here at this critical time? Michael's father was flying Spitfires in northern Australia, but his mother was only a few hours away on the other side of the Great Dividing Range.

'Can I get you a cup of tea, Miss Keevers?' the kindly matron asked.

'Thank you, matron,' Val replied. 'That would be nice.'

The matron disappeared to organise one of her nurses to fetch the drink, and Val continued her lonely vigil.

'No matter what happens in the future I will always be with you, my little angel,' she said softly.

The night passed, and the morning shift found the nanny asleep in the chair, still holding Michael's hand.

★

Daylight blazed across the plains of central Queensland as the temperature rose to replace the bitter cold of the night before.

'He's dead, boss,' Moe said, kneeling beside the body of his former comrade in arms. 'He must have gone before sunrise.'

Johnson leaned over the body, still in a sitting position against the wheel of the lorry. Flies were already gathering on the corpse.

'The spear must have done more damage than I thought,' Johnson mused, observing the large amount of dried blood covering the man's chest. 'You two drag him away, and bury him in the scrub behind us.'

The two remaining thugs obeyed, and after a half-hour returned to where Johnson waited by the lorry.

'We've had a little chat about the situation,' Curly said. 'You either pay us double to go up that hill – or we pack it in, and return to Sydney.'

Johnson glared at the two men still holding shovels. 'You share Larry's pay,' he said. 'He didn't have any kin over here to give it to anyway.'

For a moment both thugs stared up the hill to the shimmering rocks above. 'Okay,' Curly shrugged. 'We're still in.'

Johnson shook his head. 'A couple of blackfellas up there, and you act like you're frightened of them.'

Neither man answered.

Suddenly a fusillade of shots cracked from the rocks lower on the hill, spraying dirt around their feet. All three leaped to the far side of the truck as high-powered bullets ripped through its flimsy structure.

'Bloody hell!' Moe yelped. 'There's more than just the blackfella shootin' at us. Larry's share or not, it ain't worth dyin' for.'

Johnson was stunned; from the rapid fire of one of the rifles, it had to be a semi-automatic.

'Hey, Johnson,' Tom Duffy called across the fifty yards between them, 'how about you toss out your guns and leave Glen View? You know we have you pinned, and the truck is no defence against .303 and .30 calibre bullets.'

Johnson found his mouth was dry. He knew the heavy-calibre bullets could easily pass through the body of the truck and kill them. It was obvious that Duffy and whoever else was with him had used the darkness of the night to come down off the hill and position themselves very close by. Johnson knew that they were in trouble. The threat was real and his mind raced over his options. One was to admit defeat, leave the station and inform Sarah Macintosh he had failed. Another option was to keep trying to kill Tom Duffy. The latter option would not be easy, considering the current disadvantage he and his two hired thugs faced. But the risk was worth it balanced against informing Sarah Macintosh of the failure and the financial cost involved in doing so.

'How do I know that you will not shoot us down if we attempt to leave?' Johnson shouted back. His two henchmen watched him closely.

'Because all I want is for you to leave – that's all,' Tom replied. 'You can take your truck.'

Johnson turned to his men. 'Put down your Tommys,' he said. 'We'll do as the bastard says.'

Neither man protested. They had very fresh memories of their comrade's corpse lying behind the truck. But Johnson had other plans, and quickly briefed his men before they stepped out from behind the truck.

★

Tom, Billy and Donald watched from the cover of the rocks as the three men slowly emerged from behind the lorry, their hands in the air. Tom rose from behind his cover, the Garand levelled at the men.

'Careful, Tom,' Donald hissed, his rifle on Johnson.

'They don't appear to be armed,' Tom said, and stepped out towards the three men standing despondently in a small clearing between the trees at the base of the hill.

Tom stopped about ten paces from Johnson. 'You can go back and tell the courts I'm still occupying my land,' he said.

'You appear to have won, Duffy,' Johnson spat. 'But if you were dead, it would be a moot point.'

Johnson's two men suddenly broke away, one sprinting back to the truck whilst the second ran as quickly as he could away from the scene. For a split second Tom's attention was on them and not on Johnson, who produced a revolver from behind his back. The two shots from Johnson's pistol came in rapid succession, and Tom felt the bullets hit his chest. Tom stumbled from the impact, pulling the trigger of the Garand, but his shot went high. Johnson was turning to regain cover behind the truck when the crack of a rifle spun him around, Donald's shot taking him in the throat. Johnson fell to his knees, clutching his neck, blood pumping between his fingers from the ruptured carotid artery, trying but failing to stem the flow of blood.

The rapid fire of a Thompson submachine gun from behind the truck ripped across the clearing, shattering chunks off rocks.

Donald had already worked the bolt and chambered another round. He could not see his target, and guessed the man firing at him was simply attempting to throw off any repeat fire. Donald took a quick look at the clearing between him and the truck. Tom was lying on his back, clutching his chest. He was still alive.

'I'll get you out of there!' Donald yelled, his words drowned by the rip of rapid fire from the submachine gun. One thing Donald knew about the weapon he was facing was that it was inaccurate at range. It was a weapon designed for trench warfare at close range.

Donald saw Tom raise his arm as if to wave him off, but Donald ignored the gesture. When Donald looked to where Billy had been concealed he noticed with some alarm that he was gone. He hardly had time to think about Billy's absence. Donald wished he still had the Garand, but it lay beside Tom in the red soil.

'Hey, mister,' a voice called to Donald. 'You throw down your rifle, and I will not finish off Duffy.'

Donald could see Tom lying only a few yards from the truck and knew that the man with the submachine gun was not making an empty threat. He also knew everything the man said was a lie. If he revealed himself, he and Tom would be murdered.

'No deal, cobber,' Donald replied. 'My promise to you is, if you do anything to Tom, you'll not get out of here alive.'

There was a short silence. Donald thought he heard a short scuffle and a crunching sound from behind the truck. He raised his head to see Billy emerge, covered in blood.

'Wallarie got the bugger,' Billy said with a smirk.

Donald noticed the hard wooden nulla swinging in Billy's hand, also covered in blood. Billy had used the confusion to leave his position and slipped in behind the lone gunman.

Donald rose from his position and ran over to Tom. Billy was already kneeling beside his friend and boss.

'We got them,' Tom said in a weak voice as blood oozed, soaking his shirtfront.

'Yeah, Tom,' Donald said. 'One of them ran off, but I don't think he was armed. Johnson's dead and Billy took care of the other joker. We're going to use the truck to get you back to Glen View, and get medical treatment.'

'You're wasting your time, Donald,' Tom said, reaching up to grip Donald's shirt. 'I won't be going anywhere.'

Donald knew from experience that the position of the wounds meant Tom had little chance of surviving the next few minutes. 'I want you to make a promise that when I go, you take my body up the hill, and sit me up so I can see all the land around here before you take me to the homestead. You tell Jessie and Abigail that I love them, and they were in my thoughts to the last.'

Donald forced back his grief as he watched the tough old man die.

'Yeah, cobber,' he said, and felt Tom's grip on his shirt relax as life went from the man who had survived two wars.

Tom's eyes were staring up at the sky, where the solitary wedge-tailed eagle floated on the morning thermals over the brigalow plains.

True to his promise, they took Tom's body to the top of the hill and propped him on a ledge overlooking the vast expense of land around the sacred mountain, and sat with him for an hour.

'Look! Boss!' Billy said, staring up at the cloudless, azure sky.

Donald followed Billy's gaze to see a second wedge-tailed eagle joining the other great bird of prey. Both eagles circled the top of the hill.

'Tom, he gone an' join Wallarie,' Billy said with sincerity.

Donald accepted the Aboriginal stockman's statement without comment. It was time to take Tom's body down off the hill, and return him to the Glen View homestead.

EIGHTEEN

When Donald and Billy reached the bottom of the hill they were met by two horsemen, both of whom Donald recognised.

Cyril dismounted, and Mitch followed. Both men stared at the carnage around the truck.

'Bloody hell!' Mitch swore. 'What happened here?'

Donald gently placed Tom's body on the ground. 'We made a stand, and this happened,' he said. 'How are you, Mitch?'

Mitch strode forward and shook Donald's hand. 'I see the Japs have done to your face what I couldn't do before the war,' he said with a grim smile. 'Good to see you back here, Mr Macintosh.'

Mitch then walked over to Tom's body, took off his hat and stood respectfully for a time before the body.

'Who shot Tom?' he asked, replacing his hat.

'That bastard over there,' Donald replied, turning to stare at Johnson's body. 'I believe he was appointed to oversee Glen View, until the court case was decided.'

'Yeah,' Mitch drawled. 'Some Pommy copper who knew nothing about cattle.'

'Well, as a member of the Macintosh board, I'm appointing you as manager until all things are sorted out,' Donald said, placing his hand on the raw-boned stockman's shoulder.

'Thanks, Mr Macintosh. I promise I won't let you down.'

'If I remember rightly you used to call me Macca, when we were running wild in the big smoke of Rockie,' Donald said. 'Nothing has changed.'

'Thanks . . . boss . . . Macca,' Mitch replied. 'I guess we have to get Tom back to the homestead, and contact his missus and his daughter. What do we do about the other one? The one behind the truck looks like he's had his head bashed in.'

'You could say that,' Donald replied.

Mitch glanced at Billy, and saw the blood-stained club tucked in his belt. He was talking to Cyril, who was listening to him great interest.

Cyril detached himself from Billy, and walked over to Donald. 'Billy told me everything about how you three held the hill against Johnson and his men. Will you be telling the same story to the police?'

'It's the truth,' Donald said. 'Johnson and his men came here to kill Tom Duffy. They were armed with Tommy guns and grenades. I think that speaks for itself.'

'Billy said there was another man employed by Mr Johnson who seems to have run away,' Cyril said. 'Will you go in search of him?'

'I'm sure the boys will eventually find him,' Mitch cut in. 'He's probably not far from here, just wandering around enjoying the sunshine.'

The matter of the missing third man was dropped as Cyril scribbled notes and sketches in his notebook. The truck had failed to start, due to bullets that had damaged its engine, so Tom's body was laid over the back of a horse for transport back to the homestead. The horse was led by Mitch while Billy, Cyril and Donald walked beside in a manner akin to a military escort.

A mile or so from the hill a man walked around in circles, desperately trying to find a landmark to guide him back to the Glen View homestead. This was not like England or Ireland with its green fields and streams, but an ocean of dry, spindly trees under a searing sun. It was the closest thing to hell on earth the surviving thug would ever experience before he eventually died of thirst, his body baked in the sun. The two big eagles circling above came to feed on his corpse.

★

Sergeant Jessica Duffy had completed her parachute training, and was in her room conducting an inventory of the items that would go with her for the drop into Malaya. A ceiling fan whirred quietly overhead, and the sun shone with a gentle warmth outside her window.

The knock on the door startled her.

'Sergeant Duffy,' said Major Mike Unsworthy. 'I fear I have some very sad news for you.'

Jessica thought he was going to say the mission was off.

'I think you should sit down.'

Jessica slumped onto the edge of her bed.

'It's about your father, Tom Duffy,' the British officer said. 'We just received a signal that he was killed at Glen View, and that you're to take leave for his funeral. Please accept my condolences. I know what a remarkable man he was.'

For a moment Jessica tried to take in her commanding officer's words. He had said 'killed', not 'died', she thought. How, who? She burst into tears.

'I've already arranged a seat for you on one of our planes flying south,' Unsworthy continued gently. 'You'll be leaving in the next half-hour, so just gather what you need for the trip. It will take you to Rockhampton, where a light aircraft will fly you to your family property. It seems you have some highly placed friends in Mr Chifley's government.'

Jessica was picked up and driven to the airfield where she boarded a B24 bomber flying south. It put down at Rockhampton and when she dropped down from the crew hatch she was met by an older civilian, who introduced himself as a Mr Parsons.

He escorted her over to the edge of the airfield where she saw a small single-engine aircraft she recognised as a Puss Moth.

'I don't know who you know in Canberra,' Parsons said, placing her kitbag in his aeroplane, 'but when I got back to Rockie, I had a visit from a big knob in the army who said I was to fly you back to Glen View where I've just come from.'

'Do you know how my father was killed, Mr Parsons?' Jessica asked.

'I do, but I think you should hear it from Mr Macintosh,' he replied. 'He was with your father when he copped it.'

'Mr Macintosh?' Jessica said in a surprised voice. 'Do you mean Donald Macintosh?'

'That's the man,' Parsons replied. 'Good bloke. He hired me to fly him out to help your old man.'

Jessica boarded the aircraft, and within hours they were circling the homestead. She could see a lot of people had gathered there. Parsons set the Puss Moth down on a cleared area just in front of the house, and switched off the engine. Jessica alighted and saw Donald striding towards her.

'Donald,' she said when he was within a few paces. For a moment she was startled by the terrible injury to his face.

'Jessie,' Donald answered, taking her in his arms, wrapping her in a warm hug. 'I'm sorry we had to meet this way.'

'The last I knew, you had gone to Tarakan,' Jessie replied, stepping back from the embrace. 'I can see you paid a high price for your service.'

Donald grimaced. 'My days as a lady-killer are over,' he replied. 'No woman would want to be with a man as disfigured as this.'

'Not all women,' Jessica said. 'But one who loved you for the man you are would think differently. Mr Parsons said you knew the details of my father's death.'

As they walked towards the homestead Donald described the events leading up to her father's murder, and the role he had played in the defence of the man Jessica had most loved in the world. He did not mention that it was he who had killed her father's murderer.

They sat down on the verandah, and a pot of tea was brought out to them. Jessica could see a uniformed police sergeant and his constable talking near the fence of the house.

After a moment the sergeant came to the verandah and spoke to her. 'Please accept my condolences for your father's death,' he said. 'Tom was one of the finest men I ever had the honour to know.'

Jessica knew the policeman. 'Thank you, Sergeant Smith,' she said. 'I know my father held you in the highest regard also.'

Sergeant Smith turned his attention to Donald. 'Mr Macintosh,' he said, 'from my investigation I'm satisfied that you acted in self-defence, and will be reporting as such to the coroner for Mr Johnson's demise.'

Jessica looked sharply at Donald.

'I hope Billy is also exonerated for his part in defending Tom,' Donald said.

'That goes without saying,' the police sergeant replied. 'I'll be leaving now to make my report, and regret I won't be here for your dad's funeral,' he said, looking to Jessica.

He left to join his constable. Both men rode away.

'You didn't mention that it was you who killed this Johnson man,' Jessica said.

'I didn't think it was important. It cannot bring Tom back,' Donald said.

'Thank you,' Jessica said, placing her hand on his arm. 'At least Dad can rest in peace, knowing he was avenged.'

'I was with your dad to the last, and his final words were to tell you that he loved you,' Donald said gently.

Jessica began to weep. Donald put his arm around her, pulling her to him. She cried for some minutes, the grief finally flowing as she came to grips that the big, strong man who had been the rock of her life was gone forever.

'Hey, Jessie, look at that,' Donald said.

Jessica lifted her head and followed Donald's gaze to the sky where she saw two eagles floating in the air above the homestead.

'Billy reckons that they are the spirits of Wallarie and your dad,' Donald said. 'So your dad is still watching over you.'

Jessica gazed for as long as the big birds were overhead. Deep in her heart she wished what Donald had said was true.

★

Tom was laid to rest in a small cemetery not far from the homestead. The only mourners outside of family and friends were the European and Aboriginal stockmen from the station. Abigail had returned, and stood by Jessica and Donald at the edge of the newly dug grave. A priest could not be found in time, so Donald conducted the service and led prayers for the dead.

When the brief ceremony was over, the mourners walked back to the homestead for the wake. Jessica helped Abigail, who could hardly cover the distance due to her distress. Tea, scones and small sandwiches were served, and the subdued talk amongst the stockmen was about what a bonzer boss Tom had been. Abigail sat in a chair in the corner as the men came up awkwardly one by one to offer their condolences.

Donald stood with Jessica, sipping tea from a fine china cup.

'What will happen to Abigail?' Donald asked.

'She knows she'll always have a home with us here,' Jessica said. 'But her sister in England had said earlier she would like Abigail to return if she ever found herself on her own. Abigail told me she thinks that would be a good idea. Glen View has too many memories of my dad. I'll arrange for her fare home, and make sure she gets Dad's war pension for the rest of her life.'

'I can understand why she's leaving,' he said. 'What about you? What are your plans when the war is over?'

Jessica looked around the room. 'I think I'll return, and take over running the station,' she said. 'I owe that to Dad, and to our ancestors.'

'The Macintosh family also have ancestors in that little graveyard where your dad is now buried,' Donald said. 'This piece of the earth is very special to both families.'

Jessica looked at Donald. 'I know,' she sighed. 'It will not be easy to manage a cattle station. I have little experience in such matters.'

'You have Mitch to guide you,' Donald offered. 'He's a good man and I trust him. He'll see you right.'

'Thank you, Donald, for all that you've done for Dad and me,' Jessica said, reaching up to touch his scars tenderly. 'You have given much for your country.'

Donald was about to flinch away from her hand, but when her fingers touched him he did not feel embarrassed. 'Maybe I could come and visit some time,' he said. 'There are one or two horses I have yet to show Mitch I can break.'

For a moment their eyes met, and memories of their time together before the war flooded back. A time when Donald had professed his love, and Jessica told him she had been called by God. So much had happened to them both since that day when Donald first saw the beautiful young woman laughing at him as he was being thrown by a horse in the Glen View round yard.

'I would like that,' Jessica said.

The stockmen eventually wandered away to their duties, while Donald talked to Parsons about flying back to Rockhampton. From there he would either take the train south the Brisbane and Sydney or, if he was lucky, hitch a ride on a military transport aircraft flying south. It was time to return and put his affairs in order. His leave was running out. He bid goodbye to the men, and Jessica followed him over to the waiting aeroplane where Parsons was carrying out his pre-flight inspection.

'Well, Jessie, old girl,' Donald said, throwing his kitbag in the cockpit, 'I guess this is goodbye for now.'

He held out his hand and was startled when Jessica flung her arms around his neck and kissed him on the mouth.

For a second Donald did not respond, but the warmth of the kiss quickly caused him to react. He returned the kiss, and Jessica broke away with a teasing smile.

'Not all women are repulsed by your war scars,' she said. 'I actually think they make you look even more handsome.'

'Got to get goin', Mr Macintosh,' Parsons called, hoisting himself into the cockpit. 'The wind's about to change.'

Donald turned and climbed aboard, still reeling from Jessica's passionate kiss. As the plane taxied Donald could see Jessica standing alone, watching him. She waved, and he returned the gesture just before the little aeroplane roared down the dusty, stretch of flat ground. Soon they were airborne. Donald could still see the tiny figure of Jessica standing below, gazing up at him. In returning to Glen View it seemed he had found both death and new life.

★

Cyril stood before his father in the Rockhampton newspaper office.

'It's a great story, Dad,' he said. 'I went through our archives and found a lot of stuff about Glen View. What happened there a few days ago was history repeating itself.'

Cyril's father looked up from his desk. 'What's happening right now is more important than a bunch of hillbillies out west having a shoot-out. The Japanese are on the verge of surrendering, and the end of the war will be the headline for our next edition. I'm sorry, but the end of the war is all people will want to know about.'

The Americans had dropped a second atomic bomb on a Japanese city called Nagasaki, and the Russians had launched a massive attack on the Japanese in China. The Russians were rolling up the Japanese armed forces, and the

Americans were poised to invade from captured Japanese territories south of the mainland.

Cyril retrieved the ream of papers from his father's desk and stormed out of the office. He knew that under any other circumstances his backstory about the almost forgotten bushranger Tom Duffy of the 1860s Queensland frontier and his link to the modern Tom Duffy was eerie. The fight for Glen View had all happened well over a half century before, and had resulted in the massacre of the local Aboriginal clan living on their traditional lands. It was as if an ancient curse was upon the property.

Cyril made a decision. His father wouldn't publish his story, so he would send it to a major Brisbane newspaper instead. When the story was printed, he was sure it would cause a sensation and be picked up by all the major newspapers. Then his father couldn't help but be impressed.

*

Allison, like most of the workers in Sydney, had taken 15 August 1945 off to join the rapturous celebrations in the city's streets. The papers had one word splashed across the front page: *PEACE*.

Six years of war were finally over. She waded through piles of shredded paper to join the masses singing and dancing in the clogged streets. David would be coming home, and they would start a life. One without the ever present fear of losing him.

The day flew by as she was swept up in its euphoria. When the sun began to fall over Sydney she decided to return to her flat so that she could just sit and gaze at the photograph of the man she was waiting for. She even thought about their wedding. David had not yet formally proposed, but she knew he was waiting to see if he survived the jungles of New Guinea before considering such a big step.

It was dark in the street, and far enough away from the celebrations to be deserted. Allison was weary and hardly noticed the dark car parked at the end of her street. She crossed the road and was just about to step onto the footpath when she became aware of a car engine revving at high speed behind her. The last thing she saw was the glare of headlights, then the vehicle hit her before she could react.

NINETEEN

Donald stood in front of Sarah in her office. She had trouble concealing her rage. She had not counted on the adverse publicity caused by the violent death of Tom Duffy. It was in newspapers all over the country, next to the Macintosh company name. Under pressure from the board, she had been forced to abandon the case for Glen View.

'Such a shame for you, dear sister,' he said. 'But you have to admit it's probably for the best. My question is, did you tell Johnson to have Tom killed?'

Sarah glared at her brother. 'I only instructed him to remove Mr Duffy from Glen View, not to kill him. What do you take me for?'

'A cold-hearted bitch whose only ambition is to be the richest and most influential woman in this country,' Donald replied. 'I wouldn't put it past you to have ordered Johnson

212

to kill Tom, but since he's dead, I know I can't link you to a conspiracy.'

'You should have been a lawyer,' Sarah snorted, dismissing the accusation. 'My only ambition is to ensure that Mactinosh enterprises remain the biggest and best financial empire in this country, under my sound management.'

'Well, as I will be demobbed very soon, I intend to return to the company and stand against you,' Donald said. 'So have the staff clear out my office.'

Donald picked up his hat and walked out of his sister's office with a satisfied smirk. He could see he had unsettled her – and he intended to ensure she lost her power in the Macintosh enterprises.

★

15 August 1945
ORDER OF THE DAY
BY GENERAL SIR THOMAS BLAMEY CIC
AUSTRALIAN MILITARY FORCES

The JAPANESE have surrendered – our long and arduous struggle has ended in complete victory – the climax has come at the time when all six Australian divisions are fighting strenuously, each on its own far-flung battle-line – NO divisions among the Allies have contributed more to the downfall of our enemies than ours – our general officers and commanders of all grades, our regt officers, our warrant officers and NCOs, have led you unfaltering to victory – under their guidance, the troops have been formed into an excellent and magnificent army to the pride and glory of AUSTRALIA – we have fought through burning days and freezing nights of the desert, we have fought through the ooze and swamp of tropic jungles – we have defeated

the ITALIANS and GERMANS and we would soon
have completely defeated the JAPANESE before us – we
are now planning to go to our homes, having done our part
in ensuring freedom for all peoples . . .

'And the signal goes on a bit longer,' David said to his
gathering of senior NCOs and junior officers standing at
the edge of a beach under swaying palms on the northern
coast of New Guinea. 'Platoon commanders, take a copy of
General Blamey's speech and read it to your men. Copies
will be posted on the company board for anyone to read.
The bloody war is over, and all we have to do is convince
the little Nip bastards out in the jungle it's fair dinkum. The
war's finally over, and we can go home.'

There was an outburst of joyous shouts from some,
subdued silence from others. To them, Australia seemed like
another world and they were uncertain of what awaited them.

David sat down at the edge of the beach, taking in the
contents of the Order of the Day. It seemed so surreal.
He could not think of a time in the past five years when
he had not been entirely focussed on more efficient ways
to stay alive and kill the enemy. Now they were going to
be demobilised to return to a civilian life of quarter-acre
blocks, a wife and three kids in the suburbs.

David knew he could never do that. He had seen too
much death and suffering.

★

At first Anne Bambury thought she was hearing things –
church bells! Then she realised it was true. The war was
really over and the bells were ringing out the news. Already
the Chinese villagers nearby were sending in eggs, butter
and milk for the prisoners. Anne looked up and saw the

Allied aircraft roar low overhead, with no anti-aircraft guns responding to their presence. For some strange reason all she could think of was a Yorkshire pudding, and then she remembered that Diane was still in the hospital. It was imperative that she tell her best friend. On her last visit, Diane had been slipping in and out of consciousness. The news might help her hang on until proper medical help arrived. Young Sam had spent all his spare time sitting by her cot, holding her hand. Anne hoped that had soothed her.

Anne hurried to the hospital, only to see Sam with his head down, tears streaming down his face. He was holding Diane's limp hand. Suddenly Anne felt sick in the stomach.

'No, God, no!' she shouted, looking down on the wan face and wasted body. It was obvious Diane was dead, and Anne fell to her knees to hug the frail body.

'Our boys won,' she cried. 'It's all over.'

A woman walked up behind Anne, one of the heroic doctors who had fought for every patient she had treated. She placed her hand on Anne's shoulder. 'I'm sorry, my dear,' she said gently. 'We could not beat the malaria. She was too weak from malnutrition.'

Anne nodded. She had seen so many people die in Changi without recourse to the drugs and specialised treatment the Japanese had kept from them.

'I believe you were close to Mrs Duffy,' the doctor said. 'Do you know any of her next of kin?'

Anne dried her eyes with the back of her hand and stood up. 'I only know she has a son in Australia, and that her husband was killed before the war in Iraq.'

The doctor glanced at Sam, still clutching the hand of the woman who had been the only mother he had known. 'I see in the records that Sam has no living parents, nor do we know about any other next of kin.'

'I will look after him,' Anne said. 'He's a good boy. I'll see what I can do to take him in.'

'Good luck,' the doctor said, knowing that adopting a mixed-race child would not be easy. She left to tend to the other sick and injured patients in the ward.

When Anne went to hug Sam, he pulled away. What Anne saw in his face frightened her. There was a savage expression in his eyes she had never seen before.

'It's not fair. I hate everyone!' he spat, and stormed away.

Anne never saw him again.

★

Father James singled out young Patrick as he was going to a class.

'Yes, Father,' Patrick answered. The priest indicated he would like to talk to him in private. He led Patrick to his office and closed the door behind him.

The Jesuit priest looked uncomfortable, placing his hand on Patrick's shoulder. 'Patrick, we've just received news from the Red Cross that your mother passed away in Changi,' he said.

'Passed away,' Patrick echoed, the term not quite making sense.

'I'm afraid your mother is dead,' the priest said. This time, Patrick fully understood.

'My mother will not be coming home to me,' he said, gripping his pile of schoolbooks to his chest. The priest nodded.

'I have to go to my class, Father,' Patrick said. 'Can I go?'

'Yes,' the priest replied and watched as the young boy walked away. The Jesuit had not seen any real sign of grief in the boy, and wondered if Patrick really understood what death was.

As Patrick walked along the corridor to his class he had horrific memories of the smashed bodies he had seen on the retreat south to Singapore. He squeezed his eyes shut to make them go away, and wished he could remember his mother's face. She was a blur, someone he had barely known.

He found his desk in the classroom and sat down. He started to shake and tears rolled down his cheeks.

'Look at the sissy,' sneered a boy he did not like. 'Crying like a little girl.'

Patrick slammed his books down on the desk and launched himself at the boy. Only the strength of Father James, who had entered the classroom to conduct lessons, held Patrick back. The priest ordered Patrick from the room.

Before Father James joined Patrick he turned to the young faces watching him. 'Patrick has just learned his mother died in Changi prison at the hands of the Japanese. I want you all to take out your rosary beads, and say ten Hail Marys for her. I will be able to hear you in the hallway, so make sure you say every Hail Mary.'

That evening Father James called Sean Duffy to pick up Patrick and take him home for a while.

★

Jessica Duffy received news that her mission was not going ahead when she returned to Cairns, and that she was due for leave. She travelled to Townsville after receiving a telegram that said the family solicitor would be reading her father's will. After booking into a hotel she made her way to the legal firm, and was ushered into the lawyer's office. He was a rotund man in his fifties, and wore spectacles on the end of his nose.

'Ah, Jessie,' he said. 'Please accept my deepest condolences. Tom was one of the finest men I will ever know.'

Jessica accepted his condolences with a grateful smile, sitting down in a chair opposite the country solicitor. She noticed a thick manila folder on his desk.

'I know you'll be very surprised when you learn the extent of your father's dealings over the last few years. He and I have worked closely while you were on your missionary work in the islands, to restructure much of what Tom owned. For a start, your father sold off almost all his cattle stations in Queensland with the exception of Glen View. Your father reinvested the money into sheep properties in New South Wales and Victoria. He felt wool would be in great demand after the war. He also took out shares in various kinds of companies. I have a list of them here.' The solicitor passed Jessica a couple of sheets of typed paper.

Jessica glanced down the list of companies, and drew a breath. 'Many of these companies are linked to the Macintosh family,' she said. 'Why would my father invest in the companies of our enemy?'

'According to discussions I had with your father, not all the Macintosh family were enemies,' the lawyer said. 'We were also working with your legal representative in Sydney, Major Sean Duffy, and I can see you were not aware that a Mr Donald Macintosh and his mother secretly assisted Major Duffy to identify which Macintosh companies to invest in.

'As a matter of fact, they also paid over their shares to ensure your father became the major stockholder, under the guise of his company, Burkesland Holdings. It appears Sir George was unaware of Tom's incursion into the Macintosh holdings. He only knew a rival was at work, but never suspected your father. I calculated that you probably have a fifth share of the Macintosh financial properties which, I must say, are proving to be very profitable. I have to give credit to their new head, Sarah Macintosh, for pushing their enterprises ahead. She is proving to be one of the most astute players in the world of commerce, and she is so young – and a woman.'

For a second Jessica almost felt an affinity with her hated enemy at the lawyer's obvious chauvinism, but remembered that Sarah Macintosh was behind her father's murder. She placed the sheets of paper on the desk. 'What does all this mean?' she asked.

The lawyer leaned back in his chair, steepling his fingers. 'It means that the way you are positioned, you could cause a lot mischief to the Macintosh millions. The last purchase your father made was in construction firms in Sydney, and according to the papers from down south, the Macintosh companies are going to be heavily involved in the housing business. In a sense, they will have to deal with you.'

Jessica was trying to take in her father's grand strategy. It seemed that he was launching an attack on the Macintosh family from within. Not once had he mentioned his scheme. Jessica shook her head, smiling at her father's tactical skill. 'My dad was a lot smarter than all those fancy whitefellas,' she said.

'For a man of any colour, your father was one of the smartest men I ever knew,' the solicitor said. 'He has also allowed for a very generous allowance to his beloved wife, Abigail, from the dividends of the stocks and shares, ensuring she will never know hard times.'

When the will had been read, Jessica stepped out onto the Townsville street and into a blast of hot air. She walked away with a grim smile, reflecting on how her wonderful father had left her the ammunition to destroy Sarah Macintosh. She would be the gun to fire that ammunition.

TWENTY

Despite the coming warmth in the southern hemisphere, it was cold inside the dank room that smelled of chemicals and death.

Sean Duffy stood at the edge of the metal gurney, where the body of what was once a beautiful young woman lay. He could see the damage the speeding vehicle had done to her body, breaking bones and twisting them into awkward angles.

'It is her,' he whispered, as the morgue assistant held back the covering sheet.

'I'm sorry, sir, but I'll require you to clearly state who this person is,' said the uniformed constable beside Sean.

'Miss Allison Lowe,' Sean replied, leaning on his cane, and hoping his artificial legs would not collapse under him. 'She was my personal assistant.'

The constable scribbled in his pocket notebook.

'All I was told was that Miss Lowe was the victim of a hit-and-run motor-vehicle collision last night,' Sean said as the morgue attendant dropped the sheet over Allison's deathly pale face. 'Can you tell me anything else about the incident?'

'Not really, sir,' the constable replied. 'I was called by a lady who found the deceased in the street. She told me she heard a screech of a car engine, and then a heavy thump. When she ran down from her flat she found the deceased lying in the street, and went upstairs to call an ambulance. I'm afraid with all the celebrations going on last night, I couldn't find any other witnesses. Even if we could arrest someone, it's likely no jury would convict anyway.'

Sean knew what the constable meant. A driver charged with killing someone under such circumstances was rarely found guilty of a serious offence. It was the perfect murder, since it would be written off as an accident. So many people killed in motor-vehicle collisions did not get the attention they should. Juries often went easy on the offenders, perhaps because they thought the person in the dock could easily be them.

'Is there any next of kin I can inform of the lady's death?' the constable asked, his pencil poised to write. 'A husband, fiancé, parents . . .?'

'Not that I know of,' Sean said, turning to walk away. 'I would like a copy of the police report on the matter,' he continued, 'and also notification of when the coroner's court hearing is to be held.'

'I'll make sure you're kept up to date, Major Duffy,' the policeman said. 'I'm sorry for your loss.'

It was a sunny day outside but the smell of the morgue lingered. As Sean made his way to a tram he thought about David. He would have to be informed, but he was still somewhere in northern New Guinea. It would have been better to tell David the tragic news in person, but Sean knew it would have to be a letter from him. How many times had he written letters to the next of kin as an officer in the last war? Too many times.

Sean also thought about young Patrick, who was at home. Should he tell Patrick that the lady he liked so much was dead? No, Patrick was suffering enough from the news of his mother's death.

It was peace, Sean thought bitterly. And good people close to him were still dying. Had Allison been an innocent victim of a hit-and-run? Suspicion ate at the lawyer. He knew Allison had been the victim of a previous campaign to discredit her. Had Sarah taken her campaign to destroy Allison to another level? Sean was convinced the accident was something more, but proving so would be tedious and difficult. Sean was determined to do so, but also knew work on the case could stretch into months, if not years.

*

The heat shimmered over the Okinawa airstrip where the great new giants of the American air force sat idle. James Duffy stood at the edge of the airfield gazing through his aviator sunglasses at the B29 Super Fortress bombers, now redundant since the declaration of peace in the Pacific. It was strange, he thought, that the word Pacific meant peace.

Beside him was his seabag. He was dressed in his precisely pressed summer uniform, ready to board a transport aircraft to fly, first to Hawaii, then onto the west coast of the United States. Points for service had got him an early trip home to await his discharge. No longer would he sit in the cockpit of his Corsair staring through the perspex as his rockets and heavy machine-gun bullets tore into living flesh. No longer would he feel the intense fear and exhilaration of aerial combat.

It was hard to believe that such dramatic events had transpired to bring the Japanese to the peace table. No more the terrible dread of being part of a great invasion of the Japanese home islands, with massive casualties on both sides.

'Goin' home, sir?' a young aircraftsman said, as he loaded a pallet with bags of cement meant for more permanent structures on the Japanese occupied island. Under his breath he muttered, 'Lucky son of a bitch.'

'Yes,' James replied, but wondered, what was home? The past few years, home had been either in the cockpit of his fighter or some foxhole in the Pacific. How could he and his comrades ever really leave behind the memories of heat, jungle rot, sudden death and lost friends? Already his nights were racked with nightmares, and all he could do was hope they would fade with time. An air force senior NCO waved him over to a transport aircraft, and James picked up his bag and wandered over. As much as he was overjoyed the war was over, he also feared what lay ahead in the peace. He was going home to a very uncertain future.

★

Springtime had arrived in the southern hemisphere, an appropriate season to see life return to the land after the winter of war. Jessica Duffy had received her discharge from the air force, and took a train to Sydney to consult with the man she knew had worked closely with her father, and who she considered as close as any family member.

Sean Duffy was delighted to see Jessica walk into his office, and rose to embrace the young woman.

'I was expecting you,' he said when he disengaged himself. 'I regret I was unable to attend your dad's funeral, but time and distance were against me doing so. My learned friend in Townsville rang to brief me that he had read your father's will, and now I feel you have a thousand questions. But first, where are you staying while you're down here?'

'I've moved into our place at Strathfield. It's handy, with the railway station nearby.'

'You were welcome to stay with me, you know,' Sean said. 'I've just sent Patrick back to school. His mother died in Changi hours after the war ended. On top of that, I have to contact David in New Guinea. The woman he loved has been killed in a motor-vehicle accident. On the very night we were all celebrating victory in the Pacific.'

'God help us,' Jessica said, sitting down in a chair in Sean's office. 'It's as if we're cursed, for both deaths to occur so closely in our family circle.'

'It has been said that is so,' Sean replied, taking the weight off his legs by resuming his chair behind the desk cluttered with files. 'Glen View has always been at the centre of tragedy in the Duffy and Macintosh family histories. I remember the old whispers that it all dates back to a long time ago when old Wallarie's people were massacred . . . I should also say, your ancestors were related to Wallarie. With your father buried beside so many others of both families, it appears the curse is not over yet. I know it's not rational to believe in curses, but how do you explain the violent history of the Duffy and Macintosh lineage?'

Jessica tried to smile. 'I feel something in the universe is shifting. It feels as if the guiding hand of Dad's spirit has set up circumstances to finally destroy the family responsible for any curse – if it really exists.'

'Your father certainly spent a lot of time considering ways to undermine them,' Sean said. 'You know you virtually own a fifth of the Macintosh financial empire. It's not enough to destroy Sarah Macintosh, who I strongly suspect ordered Tom's death, and Allison's, but it's enough to worry her when she finally discovers who's behind the associated companies in their portfolio of interests. You now control those companies.'

'Ah, Uncle Sean, there was a time when I could just shoot people,' Jessica said with cold certainty, 'but now my life's ambition is to see Miss Sarah Macintosh on her knees, begging for mercy.'

'You'll never see her beg, but you just might be able to bring her to her knees in the future,' Sean said. 'It's better revenge that she lives a life, where the memory of failure is ever with her. That would be a living hell for the likes of Sarah.'

'Well, I'm here to find out from you the many ways of seeking revenge,' Jessica said.

Sean was only too eager to advise her.

★

Captain James Duffy was now Mr James Duffy. After his discharge he returned to the West Coast where he switched his uniform for a civilian suit. His first stop was a small bar in San Francisco. There were still men in military uniform, but James noticed that civilian enthusiasm for their service was quickly dwindling as peace swept over the United States. Industry was swapping its machines of war for refrigerators and automobiles. The country was experiencing a second economic boom as factories began producing the consumer goods discontinued during the war years.

James sat at the bar with his drink in front of him. From the Wurlitzer jukebox in the corner he could hear Doris Day singing a slow and moody song. It was soothing, and James listened with interest to the song 'Sentimental Journey'.

Although he was in a crowded bar he suddenly felt very much alone. He reflected on the words and recalled Julianna's sweet face. She was now married to a big-shot Hollywood director, and he had seen her latest book in the windows of bookshops he had passed on the way to the bar. How different things might have been had he remained stateside, seeing out the war in Hollywood, raising war bonds.

James finished his drink and ordered another as the song came to an end. A ruckus broke out at the end of the bar, and James turned to see an army sergeant whose chest was adorned with ribands declaring his great combat experience. He appeared to be engaged in a heated argument with a burly civilian poking him in the chest.

'Get the bum outta here!' a voice yelled, and a couple of large civilians wrestled the soldier through the front door.

The saloon keeper who had issued the order moved down opposite James.

'What did he do?' James asked. The saloon keeper, a beefy man in his thirties, blinked at him.

'He started mumbling about being under fire,' the saloon keeper said, wiping the bar top with a cloth. 'He's nuts. He should be locked up.'

'Maybe he has battle fatigue,' James said.

'Don't matter,' the saloon keeper responded. 'Types like him don't deserve to be home in the land of the free. They are a menace. I've seen his type in here before. Some of them just sit and shake like they are possessed by something. It gives my other customers the creeps, so I have to throw them out.'

'Yeah, I know what you mean,' James said. 'They spent all their time and youth fighting for fat sons of bitches like you, and then have the audacity to cause your customers the creeps.'

The saloon keeper went rigid. His eyes flicked to his bouncers, who recognised the signal, and moved in on James. James expected a violent reaction, and spun around on his stool to confront the two goons.

'Any marines in here,' he shouted. Three men rose from their table, one shouting '*Semper fi!*'

The fight was short, sharp and vicious. Blood ran, but mostly from the noses of the two thugs employed by the saloon keeper. Furniture was also broken, and when it was over the four marines in civilian clothes stood looking around the bar that had quickly emptied, before the inevitable arrival of the police. The saloon keeper backed away, and James reached into his pocket to retrieve a wad of money.

'This should pay for any damage to your establishment,' he said, throwing it on the bar. 'Well, marines, time to find another drinking establishment that welcomes returning heroes.'

The three men followed him out onto the street and into another place to drink together. For a moment James was happy as they swapped stories of their time fighting in the Pacific. They were brothers – even in peace.

That evening James found a telephone in the foyer of his hotel and retrieved an old number. He knew he was drunk but dialled the number on the crumpled piece of paper. A sleepy voice answered.

'Who the goddamned is ringing me at this time in the morning?' Guy said sleepily.

'Your goddamned pal who used to be a war hero in Hollywood,' James slurred. 'I've decided to take a sentimental journey before I go back to New Hampshire, and wondered if you have a couch I can sleep on when I visit.'

'Goddamn!' Guy cursed. 'There's always a place to crash for USMC flyboys,' he replied, his voice less hostile. 'Where are you ringing from?'

''Frisco,' James answered. 'I'll see you soon, old buddy.'

James replaced the telephone in its cradle after Guy had given him his address, and noticed the hotel clerk staring at him across the foyer with some concern. James realised that he had blood on his shirt.

'It's okay,' he said. 'I ran into a tram.'

It was obvious that the clerk did not believe him, and shook his head. But the gentleman was known to be of the Barrington family from New Hampshire, and was thus excused any embarrassing questions.

A day later, sober, cleaned up and dressed in newly purchased clothes, James arrived in Los Angeles. He took a taxi to the address Guy had given him, and was dropped in front of an impressive house.

Guy was waiting for him at the front door with a drink in his hand and a wide smile.

'You won't have to sleep on the couch here,' he said to James as he ushered him into the house. The house seemed to be made of glass. It appeared to be all windows, capturing the spectacular view. 'Your timing is impeccable as I'm having a party here tonight to celebrate my latest movie being in the can.'

'I wasn't aware you were in production these days,' James said as Guy showed him to a spacious room with views of the city below. The bedroom had a balcony overlooking the kidney-shaped swimming pool.

'Well, executive production,' Guy replied. 'But all the staff on the project will be here tonight. I have the caterers coming in very soon to set up downstairs. You may even recognise one or two of my more famous guests.'

James threw his old seabag on the bed. 'Do you ever see Julianna around the studios these days?' he asked.

'She's been seen once or twice,' Guy replied. 'Mostly she's down in N'Orleans writing another bestselling book.'

Guy left him and wandered off into the rambling house of many rooms, while James unpacked and lay down on the bed. He fell fast asleep and was woken by the sound of people arriving. When he glanced out the window he could see the sun was going down, and quickly prepared himself to join the party.

When James walked downstairs he could see a host of richly dressed party-goers, amongst them a couple of well-known actors and actresses. At the bottom of the stairs, he was approached by a waiter wearing a white jacket and carrying a tray of champagne coupes.

'Drink, sir?' he asked. James took one of the crystal glasses filled with bubbly. He could see a table decked out with food fit for a king, and decided that he was hungry. Hardly anyone took notice of him as they swapped gossip, and considered who was worth talking to or being seen with.

James selected black caviar from a chilled crystal bowl and spread it on a cracker.

'It should be on a finger of bread,' he heard a female voice say behind him.

James turned and saw a very pretty young woman with long blonde hair flowing over her shoulders. She was smiling at him as she delicately held a flute of champagne in one hand and a cigarette in a slender holder in the other.

'Sorry, I'm more used to eating out of a can,' he said.

'I gather you're one of Guy's friends from his wartime days,' she said.

'I met Guy when I was posted to LA, to raise war bonds

back in '42,' James said, swallowing the last of the imported, salty Russian fish roe.

'I thought only war heroes were given that job,' the young woman said. 'Were you a war hero?'

'Hardly,' James answered, picking up his flute from the food table. 'I was just a marine pilot.'

'I once remember Guy telling me about a fighter pilot he had to chaperone around '42,' she said, looking with some interest at James. 'But you don't look anything like the actors who played fighter pilots in the movies. You are not in the mould of a Hollywood hero like John Wayne.'

James was becoming annoyed with her line of banter. He had long been aware that this was a place where appearances counted more than reality. After all, Hollywood produced the fantasy of what would otherwise be boring real life.

'With all due respect to Mr Wayne,' James said, 'he was booed offstage whenever he visited the frontline. The boys only saw him as a fit, healthy man who had hidden in Hollywood to avoid combat. He was not our hero.'

He was pleased to see his observation had caused the pretty young woman's expression to change. She did not seem so smug. He was about to walk away when he glanced past her to the entrance of the house, where a uniformed valet was greeting guests. For a moment James was transfixed. Wearing an elegant evening dress and laughing at something the man on her arm had said was Julianna.

This was certainly proving to be a sentimental journey.

TWENTY-ONE

Julianna was still laughing when she turned and saw James. Her laughter stilled. James tried to smile but found it impossible. It was awkward for them both of them, and James made the first move, walking across the room through the throng of guests.

'Guy did not tell me you would be coming to his party,' he said by way of greeting.

'I initially declined, but my publisher in LA had me fly up from New Orleans for a sales conference. How are you, James?'

'As you can see, I survived the war,' he replied. 'You're looking beautiful, as usual.'

'You haven't changed,' Julianna said with a smile. 'Still the same charming man I once knew. Is that your latest conquest you rudely left standing alone at the caviar bowl?'

'I don't even know her name,' James said. 'All I know about her is that she's a John Wayne fan.'

'I suppose you'll ensure that you know more about her,' Julianna said with a glint of a challenge in her eye.

'Not as long as she's a John Wayne fan,' James said. 'I'm truly pleased to see you. Is your husband with you?'

'No,' Julianna answered. 'He's on location in Nevada, filming a western, and I came with my publisher. Are you alone here tonight?'

'I decided to catch up with Guy before returning home,' James said. 'He's invited me to stay for a couple of days. How about you?'

'I have a room at the Mayflower,' Julianna said.

'I know it,' James commented. 'Nice place. Only the best for a bestselling author. I read your book about Fenella Macintosh when I was out in the Pacific. It was very good.'

'Thank you,' Julianna said. 'What will you do, now the war is over?'

'I suppose I'll return to civilian life as a boring banker,' James answered. 'Unless another war comes along and I can fly again.'

'You haven't changed at all,' Julianna said. 'There's something in you, always trying to prove yourself.'

'I was kidding,' James said. 'My days of death and glory are over. I only wish you had waited long enough to see that.' James noted that his last statement seemed to hit a nerve. 'I'm sorry, that was uncalled for. I know you must have a great life now, and I do not wish to cause any grief.'

Julianna looked around her. 'I don't wish to talk here,' she said. 'Can we go outside to the pool?'

'Sure thing,' James said. 'It's a bit stuffy in here.'

Outside, under lanterns throwing a soft light over the pool, they found a bench and sat down side by side.

'Can I get you a drink?' he asked.

Julianna declined and stared at the reflections in the pool, as laughter drifted out to them.

'I wish I had waited for you,' she said quietly. 'I've never really been able to get you out of my thoughts. I remember every moment of when we last met, and you punched my husband.'

'I'm sorry about that,' James said. 'I was maybe suffering a bit of battle fatigue.'

Julianna turned to him. 'I thought you did it because you were jealous.'

'Yeah, that too,' James said. 'But you made a wise choice settling for someone who could give you security in those times. I was never certain I was going to survive the war.'

He was aware that even in the dim lantern light she was staring at him in a way he could not fathom. Then suddenly, she threw her arms around him and kissed him fiercely on the lips. He did not resist, and returned her passion. Without any words, he took her hand and led her upstairs to his bedroom.

When they reached his room he did not switch on the lights. The neon city below provided enough of a glow for him to see her slip from her long dress.

'I've dreamed of this moment,' Julianna said in a choked whisper as she and James fell back onto the bed. 'I know it's wrong, but God forgive me for how I've always felt about you.'

The sweet scent of her body against his was all James could think about as they undressed and held each other. Julianna began kissing his body, then hesitated when she saw his scarred legs. James knew what had momentarily distracted her. 'Got that in the burning cockpit of my Corsair,' he said. 'Nothing too serious.'

In the shadows of the City of Angels they made love, and eventually lay side by side without speaking.

'Why now?' James finally asked.

'It was something I had to do, or for the rest of my life I'd always wonder how it felt to be with you in this way,' Julianna said.

'You know I never stopped loving you,' James said. 'I think there must be some truth in what they say about fate meaning for two people to be together.'

Julianna sat up and leaned over James, touching his face with her long fingers. 'I'm a married woman, and what I've done is wrong,' she said. 'I don't care, but I also swore a holy oath to my husband that we would be together forever. I don't expect you to understand, because you're not a Catholic. This was something that had to happen, but I must remain married to my husband. Please understand.'

'All I understand is that we were meant to be together,' James said. 'God is not that blind.'

'Do you believe in God?' Julianna asked.

'Not really,' James admitted. 'He wasn't around when we were out there killing each other.'

Julianna fell back against the pillows, staring at the ceiling. 'There's another reason why we can't be together,' she said.

'What other reason?' James asked.

'I cannot tell you,' she said. 'It's something that does not concern you.'

Frustrated, James turned to Julianna. 'You've admitted that you love me, and you know I feel the same way about you. You could leave your husband, and we could spend the rest of our lives together.'

Julianna turned to face James. 'I'm sorry, but I cannot forsake my marriage vows, so we can never be together.

Please try to understand that, James,' she said. 'I have an important early morning breakfast with my publisher, and I must get some sleep.'

James was also weary, falling into a deep sleep. But the nightmares returned and he whimpered, mumbling incoherent words. Julianna lay gazing at him, occasionally trying to soothe him with gentle words of reassurance, knowing he was no longer with her but flying against the enemy in combat.

When James awoke the next morning he rolled over to see an empty space beside him. Only Julianna's sweet scent lingered on the pillow, and James cursed himself for not waking when she left.

He slipped from the bed, dressing in slacks and a shirt, and walked down to the dining room, which looked as if a bomb had gone off. The remnants of the previous night were littered all over the floor and furniture.

Guy was sitting at a long bench between the kitchen and dining room, sipping black coffee.

'Good morning, James,' he greeted. 'I daresay you had a good night. Your absence and Julianna's were noticed by more than me.'

'Er, ah,' James replied, trying to find an appropriate answer to his friend's greeting. 'Do you have any hot coffee?'

'Help yourself,' Guy said, waving to a pot on the stovetop.

'What happened last night was not something either of us planned,' James said, filling a mug.

'It's not my concern,' Guy said. 'I spoke with Julianna when I called a taxi for her.'

James came to the bench and sat on a stool opposite Guy. 'Did she say anything?' he asked.

'Just the same as to you,' Guy answered. 'But I know why you and she could never meet again.'

James looked sharply at the Hollywood executive.

'That something is a child,' Guy said. 'She and her husband are expecting their first baby. It was broadcast in the social news recently. I thought you knew.'

'Son of a bitch!' James swore. 'Julianna is pregnant.'

'About three months,' Guy said, finishing his coffee, and returning to the pot on the stove.

Stunned, James hardly tasted the strong brew. So that was it. The sentimental journey was at a dead end. There was no way he could win her back when a child was involved.

'Sorry, James,' Guy said, placing his hand on his shoulder. 'It appears it was never meant to be. But I know my philosophy hardly warrants understanding from a man in love.'

'It was never meant to be,' James echoed bitterly. 'Well, time to return home and finish another matter that has to be resolved.'

Later that morning James packed his bag, bid his friend goodbye, and took a taxi to the airport. Within hours he was home and standing in the driveway of his grandfather's mansion. The leaves were already turning red and orange, falling to earth in rich, deep carpets of colour. Fall was something James had almost forgotten. The Pacific was always one colour: green and all the green hues in between.

He was greeted with great warmth by the old valet, and could see his normally stoic grandfather fighting back tears of joy when they met in the great living room with its warm hearth.

'I have a welcome-home present for you, James,' his grandfather said, standing by the fireplace.

'What?' James asked, puzzled by the smile on his grandfather's face.

'It's out in the garage,' said James Barrington Snr, handing James a set of automobile keys. 'We'll go together to inspect it.'

James followed his grandfather out of the house to the double garage and opened the door.

'Son of a gun!' James gasped when his eyes fell on the sleek, red sports car. 'Is that really mine?'

'I felt that a young man back from the war, especially one who is a fighter ace, should have something befitting his status. I had it imported, and now it is yours.'

James turned to the old man and thrust out his hand. 'Thank you, sir,' he said. 'Do you mind if I take it for a spin? I promise I'll keep it to a reasonable speed.'

'Just be back before dinner,' James Barrington Snr said with a glow of pleasure at pleasing his only heir.

'I promise,' James answered, jumping into the driver's seat and inserting the ignition key. He knew exactly where he was going.

★

The young men and women in the carpark of Sweeney's Bar certainly noticed the red sports car drive in. The men looked on with envy, the girls with admiration.

James walked into the bar, expecting to see either Bernie or his wife behind, but saw a stranger who had a vague resemblance to Bernie. James sat down on a stool and ordered a drink. The big barman placed it on the counter.

'Is Bernie around?' James asked. The barman looked hard at him.

'Bernie's me brother. Who are you?'

'James Duffy.'

The hard expression disappeared and the man held out his hand.

'Frank Sweeney,' he introduced himself. 'Bernie said you might be in one day, and he left something for you.'

The barman disappeared and returned a couple of minutes later, passing James a sealed envelope.

'Where's Bernie?' James asked, accepting the envelope.

'All I know is that he sold me the bar, and he and my sister-in-law disappeared from the county after the death of the Wilson kid.'

'Edgar Wilson!' James exclaimed. 'When did that happen? What happened?'

'I guess you've been away a while,' Frank said. 'It was big news around here. The sheriff found the son of a bitch beaten to death and dumped off a road out of town about five weeks ago. My brother was a suspect, but Hausmann got nuthin' on Bernie because he was drinkin' with me at my house. But Bernie thought it wise to make himself scarce.'

'What about Isabel?'

'My niece is at college studying medicine,' Frank answered. 'I hear she's doin' fine.'

James opened the letter of one page:

If you're reading this Captain Duffy, then you made it back alive. Mary and I will be eternally grateful to you for giving my very much loved daughter the chance to get a good education, and one day become a doctor.

You would know by now Edgar Wilson is dead, and that some people will say I killed him. Why would I kill the son of a bitch who boasted openly of murdering your sister? After all, I don't have a motive. However, Mary and I have decided that we would like to go overseas with the money from the sale of the bar to my brother. It must be in the blood of us Irish to immigrate, and start afresh in foreign lands.

At least they speak American where we will resettle. Both Mary and I wish you all the very best in the future, and I know that Isabel would wish the same.

Yours sincerely

Bernie and Mary Sweeney

P.S. It might be an idea to burn this letter once you've read it.

Frank placed a full glass of whisky in front of James. 'Bernie said I was to shout you a decent whisky if you ever came here and read that letter,' he said with a broad smile. James looked up at the big man, who had also poured himself a tumbler.

'To Bernie and Mary,' James said, raising his glass in salute. 'Wherever they may be.'

'To me brother and sister-in-law.' Frank said, and they emptied the glasses in one swift gulp.

'Maybe we should have another toast, Captain Duffy. Me and me brother were both marines in the Great War.' Frank lifted the sleeve of his shirt to reveal the faded tattoo of the marine corps emblem.

'*Semper fi,*' James said, and the refilled glasses were quickly emptied.

James did not make it home for dinner that night.

TWENTY-TWO

All across southeast Asia and the Pacific, Japanese commanders were coming in from the jungles to participate in surrender ceremonies.

Major David Macintosh stood with his company on a parade at the tiny Wewak airstrip. The Australian troops were lined six deep on either side of the strip, and in the centre of the airfield was a table about which were gathered General Robertson, the commander of the Sixth Division, and his staff officers. The morning was clear and hot.

Eventually a jeep arrived at the end of the strip. David watched as the enemy commander General Adachi and a small number of his staff got out and lined up. The Japanese general was marched down with an escort of Australian soldiers to the table where the Australian general was waiting.

The Japanese commander saluted the Australian commander, and then bowed in the tradition of his country.

The Australian commander returned the salute. General Adachi was wearing a sword, which he would hand over, acknowledging their defeat.

To David, the scene felt surreal. For all the years he had been in the mountainous jungles fighting the general's men, he had never dreamed he would one day witness the former enemy admitting defeat. There was a palpable tension running through the ranks of watching soldiers.

The Japanese general was having trouble unbuckling his sword, and a distinctive Aussie voice called out from the ranks behind David, 'Take it orf 'im!'

A chuckle rippled through the ranks, answered by a growl from the Company Sergeant Major to respect the occasion. David suspected the CSM probably had the hint of a smile on his face too.

The sword came off and was handed to General Robertson, who placed it on the table. This was followed by the signing of papers, then the ceremony was complete and David was able to give the order for his company to fall out.

They were transported back to Cape Wom, where all the talk around the camp was of going home.

David made his way to his tent, where he saw a pile of letters on his bunk. A glitch had held up the mail, but now David had the time to read the news from home. He sorted the letters and placed those from Allison at the front. After carefully examining the postmark dates he commenced with the oldest, and read the words of the woman he always kept as the memory of what he was going home to. Her letters were filled with love, and the desire to be in his arms once again, with erotic hints of how they would spend each and every waking hour in her little Sydney flat.

David smiled as he opened one letter after another until they abruptly stopped. The letters ceased about the same time peace was declared. He shrugged, and thought the mail system must have messed up, and that, with any luck, more would soon arrive.

The second-last letter was from Sean Duffy. Sean had been a consistent correspondent throughout David's deployments overseas to North Africa, Syria, the Middle East and the New Guinea campaign. David slit open the envelope and began reading. He was only halfway through the first page when he discovered why there were no more letters from Allison.

David felt his hands begin to tremble, and then his whole body. It was not possible that she could be dead, when it was more probable that he would not survive the war. A bloody car accident had taken her life on the very night Australia was celebrating the end of the war.

For minutes David just stared at the letter in his hand. He did not doubt the news was true, but couldn't accept he would never see Allison again. He also wondered why he couldn't cry. Was it that his soul had been too hardened by all the death he had seen over the years, from Dachau to Spain, North Africa to New Guinea? All he could feel was a loss without limits.

'Hey, David, you want to join the boys down at the beach?' Captain Brian Williams called through the tent entrance. It was only when David looked up at him that Williams could see the immense pain in his expression.

'Is everything okay, old chap?' Brian asked with concern.

'No, not really,' David replied. 'I think I need some time alone. Can you look after things for today?'

'Sure thing,' Brian answered, and stepped back from the entrance. 'If there's anything I can do . . .' he offered.

'Thanks, cobber,' David said. 'I just need a little time. I'll be okay.'

David remained sitting on his bunk, and glanced at his service revolver. Only hours earlier he had watched as the war was officially declared over. Now he felt that so, too, was his life.

The sun was going down when David looked at the last letter on his bed under the mosquito net. The handwriting was vaguely familiar. He opened it.

It was from his cousin, Sarah Macintosh, expressing her sadness at Allison's untimely death. It went on to say that she was always in his life if he needed a shoulder to cry on. David barely registered her condolences.

★

Constable Brendan Wren was ambitious. He aspired to move from uniform duties to plainclothes work, and eventually to gain recognition as a detective. He had been too young to enlist, but had followed in a family tradition to serve as a police officer.

The hit-and-run he had attended on the night of victory celebrations was at the top of his list of cases to solve. As a beat officer he had visited every car repair shop in his area, and finally had a break when he found a black sedan that had damage consistent with hitting a pedestrian.

He questioned the owner of the panel-beating shop, and was informed the vehicle had been brought in a couple of days after the incident. Constable Wren took down the particulars in his notebook. He learned the registered owner was a business, which meant anyone from that organisation could have been the driver. At least he knew where to start asking questions.

His enquiries led him to the head office of Macintosh enterprises. There, he asked at the front counter if he could speak with someone in charge.

The doorman looked him up and down with an expression of superiority, but did call down one of the managers, a young man who normally worked in the accounting section.

Constable Wren asked for the driver's name.

'I'm sorry, constable,' the accounts section manager said. 'I would have to consult with my boss before I release that information.'

'Who's your boss?' the police officer asked.

'Miss Sarah Macintosh,' the manager replied. 'But she is not available unless you make an appointment to see her.'

'You can tell your boss I wish to speak to her as soon as possible. You can tell her I can be contacted here,' he said, scribbling down his details on a piece of paper and handing it to the manager.

'I'll pass on your message,' the manager said. 'If there's nothing else, I'll bid you a good day.'

Constable Wren watched the man walk away. He toyed with the idea of barging into this woman's office, but thought twice when he glanced around at the opulence in the foyer. Whoever ran this financial institution must be an important person, he thought. One of the first things he had learned in policing: the law did not apply equally to the rich and poor.

He left the building and returned to his station for the changeover of shifts.

'Hey, Brendan,' called one of his workmates as he passed the front desk. 'There's a detective inspector who wants to see you in the day room. Are you going to plainclothes?'

'I hope so,' Brendan replied, but he was puzzled by the news.

He went to the day room in the station, which was normally filled with police on changeover of shift. But when he entered the room, there was only one person, a tough-looking man in a well-cut suit.

'You Constable Wren?' he asked belligerently. Brendan could see the Inspector was drunk.

'Yes, sir,' Wren replied. 'I was told that you wanted to see me.'

The detective walked up to the constable, until he was only inches from his face. Wren felt uneasy. 'I heard that you were bothering the boss of the Macintosh companies,' he growled.

'I never got to meet the boss,' Wren said.

'Nor will you, constable, if you know what's good for you.'

'Sir, I was investigating the serious matter of a fatal hit-and-run and . . .'

'Shut your gob and listen to me,' the inspector said. 'The Macintosh family are amongst our most important citizens in this town. I'm telling you now to drop your investigations if you know what's good for you. I also heard in the traps that you want to come to the detective's division some day.'

'I'm hoping to do that,' Wren acknowledged.

'Well, if you keep your nose clean, do what I tell you, you just might have a chance. Let me look at your notebook.'

Wren slipped the small, hardbacked notepad from the top pocket of his tunic and handed it to the detective. He flipped it open until he came to the pages noting the details pertaining to the hit-and-run investigation. The detective took a fountain pen from his pocket, and scribbled under the notes '*no further action*', then signing his name, Inspector Preston.

'Matter closed, constable,' he said, handing the notebook back to the shaken police officer, who had been drilled to obey orders from superiors in the police force. 'I believe you'll be late for the changeover parade if you do not go now,' Preston said, stepping back from the cowed constable. 'Just remember what I told you. Stay away from the Macintosh family.'

'Yes, sir,' Brendan answered, slipping the notebook into his tunic pocket.

The inspector left the room and Brendan hurried to his parade with confused thoughts. It appeared that the senior officer was attempting to interfere in a legitimate investigation. But what could he do? He knew the culture of his job did not encourage mere junior constables to question seasoned, senior members of the service. It was as if the notebook in his pocket was burning a hole into his chest.

★

Sarah Macintosh paced her office, cigarette in hand. The damned police, she thought. At least she had been able to contact Preston to put out any potential fire the lowly constable may have started. But that was not her only worry. She had been informed that some mysterious company had been buying into their public shares, and had done what she thought was impossible. They had taken out a fifty-one per cent share. The only way that could have been achieved was through treachery from within her own family. It had to be Donald.

'Miss Macintosh, you have a visitor,' her personal secretary said, popping his head around the door.

'I do not wish to have visitors,' Sarah snapped.

'It's your husband,' the secretary said. 'Should I tell him you're not available?'

'No, send him in,' Sarah sighed. She had not seen Charles in two years, since his posting to Darwin to fly Spitfires. Charles entered the room wearing his uniform. On his chest were the ribands denoting his conspicuous service to his country, including the Distinguished Flying Cross.

'Hello, Sarah,' he said. 'I can see you're pleased to see me.'

'Welcome home, Charles,' Sarah replied coldly. 'Why are you here?'

'Oh, I thought I might have a job back with the firm,' he said, glancing around at his estranged wife's plush office. 'At least discuss the future with you.'

'You know there's nothing to discuss,' Sarah said, walking back to her desk and stubbing out her cigarette.

Charles walked over to the window, gazing down on the city on the brink of turning from day to night. The activity he saw below was so much like he remembered before he went to war. People had resumed their lives as if the war had never happened.

'I thought we might start with a discussion about my son,' he said, standing in front of the large glass pane. 'I believe you have him at Goulburn.'

'I'm too busy to raise a child and run an enterprise as big as this. Michael is in the capable care of his nanny.'

'Well, I want him back with us in Sydney,' Charles said. 'His nanny can come, and continue looking after him here.'

'What gives you the right to walk in here and start running things, Charles?' Sarah asked. 'You have been off the scene for years.'

'I suppose I can claim the right of a good husband, and father,' Charles retorted. 'I will be demobbed this week, and in need of a job. What better job than being by your side, assisting in running the business?'

'What makes you think I want you back?' Sarah countered. 'If you had any good manners you would accept a divorce.'

'Ah, but that's not as easy as you think,' Charles said, sitting down on the sofa. 'It gets very messy, what with lurid photos produced to the court of infidelity. It would not do your reputation any good should the newspapers get hold of the story. After all, I'm a returning war hero who has risked his life in the skies over the Pacific for my wife and child. No, it's better we keep up the pretence of a marriage for the sake of my son, and the good name of Macintosh. I'm sure your late father would have agreed with me.'

'What do you really want?' Sarah asked, sitting down and leaning forward across her desk.

'The same as you,' Charles said. 'Money and power. I've not fooled myself that you have any feelings for me because you would first have to have a heart. You can live your life the way you feel fit but be discreet about what you do. I can promise you we'll prosper even more as a team. I think it's a good deal.'

Sarah sank back against her chair, and thought about her estranged husband's offer. It had potential, so long as she remained the boss of the financial empire.

'I think we can come to an arrangement,' she finally said. 'The house is big enough for you to have separate quarters. Do as I say, and you'll profit from the arrangement. We are husband and wife in name only.'

'Well, I expect to be able to take time off to play golf, and sit in on board meetings,' Charles said. 'You can make the business decisions, and from time to time, we can pretend to be a loving duo at social occasions.'

Sarah considered what her husband was saying, and saw merit in his words. After all, she was still in a world of old men who saw her as an upstart young woman. A husband and child would show the world that she was a decent and reliable person.

'You can move into the house, and the servants will show you your quarters,' Sarah said. 'If there's nothing else . . .'

'Short and sweet,' Charles said, rising from his seat. 'I expect my son will be with us from next week onwards.'

'I can arrange that,' Sarah said.

Charles nodded and left the room, closing the door behind him. He knew his wife well enough to know his return was not the only thing worrying her.

After Charles left Sarah lifted the telephone to dial a number of an old boyfriend. William Price answered from his nightclub, and she spoke with him briefly about the death of Allison Lowe. He assured her that nothing could be traced back to her. Preston had approached him about the job and it had all gone smoothly, even with the use of a Macintosh vehicle.

Sarah replaced the receiver and stared at the wall. She was not so sure he was right.

TWENTY-THREE

As Jessica was in Sydney, she decided to telephone Donald at his flat in the city and asked after him. Donald explained he had undergone some plastic surgery for his scars, but the operations were unable to fully conceal his injuries. But he was learning to live with the disfigurement. He had also decided to leave Macintosh enterprises, due to his sister's management style. She had been able to manipulate the company to exclude him from all decision-making processes, leaving him with nothing to do but sit at his desk, staring at the walls. Other than that, he felt good about life. His salary from Macintosh enterprises still flowed into his bank account, allowing him to consider another career.

They arranged to meet in the city to watch a movie together. It was a heart-warming film called *A Tree Grows in Brooklyn*. The sun was down when they left the theatre.

Donald could see theatre-goers attempting to hide their furtive glances at the sight of his damaged face. It depressed him. Sensing his melancholy mood, Jessica slipped her arm into his as they walked down the street to a familiar cafe.

'It doesn't worry you that you're being seen in public with a circus freak?' Donald asked as they passed a woman whose young son made no attempt to hide his curiosity, staring openly at Donald.

'You are no circus freak, Donald Macintosh,' she said with a gentle smile. 'You bear the scars of a wounded warrior.'

'It almost sounds romantic, the way you put it,' Donald replied with a twisted smile.

'Like you, I have seen war at close quarters, and those stupid, little people who stare are ignorant. They were huddled in their homes when we were facing invasion. They were very happy to let other mother's sons and husbands go away, with many never returning. Now that it's over, they have forgotten the price men like you paid to keep them safe in their little houses.'

They reached the cafe and stepped inside. There were a few young people sitting at tables, and even one or two men still in uniform. The soldiers hardly gave Donald a second glance, and Donald could see from the ribands on their uniforms they had seen action in the Pacific.

A teenage woman sitting with the soldiers cast Donald a look of disgust. 'They shouldn't let blokes looking like that come to places like this,' she said.

Fury and sadness mixed in Donald's mind. He was about to stand up and leave when he heard one of the soldiers say, 'Shut up, Sheila, can't you see the bloke's probably copped shrapnel!'

'Tarakan,' Donald replied. 'Jap mortar.'

The soldier turned to Donald with an apologetic look. 'Sorry, cobber,' he said. 'Me girlfriend is a bit young to know what it was like for us. I copped some at Milne Bay in the leg. Bloody painful.' With that, the soldier rolled up the leg of his pants, displaying a terrible scar that ran from knee to ankle.

'Well, you can see mine,' Donald said with a smile, whilst the young woman remained sheepishly quiet. For the first time he did not feel any embarrassment when Jessica clasped his hand across the table.

The soldier limped to Donald, stopped and extended his hand. Donald accepted the gesture, and then, without a word, the soldier and his date departed.

'Well, what shall we have with a cup of tea?' Jessica asked without letting go of Donald's hand. He ordered scones with jam and cream.

'What do you plan to do, now that you're out of the army?' Jessica asked, sipping her tea.

'I know this sounds crazy, but I want to go back to the bush and run a cattle station,' Donald said. 'I've always wanted to work on the land, even from my time on Glen View before the war.'

'Funny that you should say that,' Jessica said. 'Mitch is currently in charge, but I think he prefers to be one of the boys mustering cattle. He admits he doesn't have a good head for the paperwork. Would you consider managing the property? I may have to spend some time away on business.'

'You don't think my face will frighten the cattle?' Donald said with his twisted grin.

'You still have a beautiful smile,' Jessica responded, smiling herself.

Then, Jessica said, 'Something has haunted me for a long time. Something I've tried to repress.'

'I hope it's the same thing that's haunting me,' Donald said.

'I know I have always really loved you,' Jessica said. 'Other men may have come into my life, but you always remained, like a rock. I've been told how you and your wonderful mother were working to help Dad establish a foothold in your own companies. You could have told me – but you didn't.'

'If I had, you might have thought I was trying to buy your love,' Donald said, and realised that he was fighting back tears.

He was acutely aware of how strong Jessica's grip was around his hands. It seemed so strange that, at this moment, in this rundown cafe, their true feelings for each other should arise.

'I have always loved you, Jessica Duffy, and always will.'

Now there were tears in Jessica's eyes as they faced each other across the scratched formica tabletop.

'Where do we go from here?' he asked.

'There are wounds people cannot see,' Jessica said. 'I need to let my scars heal first.'

'I understand,' Donald said. 'We'll live each day until you choose to make a decision about us.'

They sat together until the cafe was closed, then walked hand in hand along the street towards the future.

★

Donald was scheduled to attend an extraordinary meeting called by his sister at the Macintosh building. He arrived and went upstairs to his office, only to find it locked and his key no longer working.

He glanced down the corridor to see board members drifting into the conference room. None bid him a good morning. Fuming, Donald followed them into the large room with its great table, and sat down in his chair. His sister entered the room, and Donald noticed the men acknowledged her with polite nods or mumbled greetings.

Sarah took her seat at the head of the table, and without further pleasantries opened the meeting.

'Welcome, gentlemen,' Sarah said. 'I will apologise for the short notice of this meeting. For the last few days my assistants have gathered disturbing information about the ownership of key companies within our portfolio. It appears someone devious from within the company has been deliberately sabotaging us. I'm sad to say that the person behind the sabotage is none other than my own brother Donald. It appears that he and my late mother were selling off their shares to the late Mr Tom Duffy, who was attempting to gather a controlling interest in many critical companies we own. I have consulted with our legal team, and a clause in the constitution has been breached. The breach carries with it a penalty clause that forbids the offender from having a seat on this board. So it is with deep regret that I must order my brother to leave the building immediately, and never return.'

Sarah's statement rippled as a shock down the table. A silence fell over the room and a few eyes looked to Donald, who merely lit a cigarette, blowing smoke into the air. He did not appear to be overly concerned at his sister's declaration.

'Well, gentlemen,' Donald finally said. 'Everything my sister has told you is true. I have been assisting Tom Duffy's companies to take out crucial shares in the family's financial institutions. This empire is founded on the blood of innocent people and my sister, who seems to have an intense interest in the family history, can vouch for that. So I thought I might try and rectify the imbalance by assisting a man whose ancestors were amongst the aggrieved.'

Donald rose to his feet. 'I bid you all a good morning.'

Silence followed Donald's exit from the room.

An hour later he sat in Sean Duffy's office, hat in hand.

'So, the Macintosh dynasty is Sarah's alone, since David has no interest in joining her,' Sean said. 'I guess you're now out in the open as a member of the opposition.'

'Guess so,' Donald said. 'I was going to resign anyway, as Jessie wants me to manage Glen View. I'm due to leave tomorrow night on the train north. At least my sister was not able to strip me of my allowance, which was granted under the terms of my father's last will and testament.'

'You and Jessie were always fated to find each other in the end,' Sean said gently. 'Glen View has more meaning than any financial return it might yield. It is the traditional land of your family, and mine.'

'Jessica has vowed to bring Sarah down,' Donald said. 'She holds her responsible for Tom's death. So do I. My sister may not have pulled the trigger, but she put the gun in his killer's hand. I once read about the people psychiatrists refer to as sociopaths. I fear my sister suffers from that condition.'

'Whatever you call it,' Sean said, 'she's extremely dangerous. I suspect she inherited some of your father's ways. I also have a gut feeling that Sarah is behind Allison's death, although I have no proof at this stage. No one is safe when she sets her sights on them.'

'I know she's obsessed with David,' Donald added. 'Pity help the man who scorns my sister's attention, and from what I hear, David and his battalion will be back from New Guinea soon.'

'I had a letter last week from David,' Sean said. 'He wishes to remain in the army.'

'He could take up a position with the family business,' Donald said.

'Not David,' Sean said. 'He's a soldier through and through. I don't know if I should tell him of my suspicions about Sarah's possible involvement in Allison's death. I fear how he would react.'

'I think it's best he doesn't know,' Donald agreed. 'He has suffered enough.'

*

Major David Macintosh stood on the open deck of the British aircraft carrier, gazing at the twin headlands of Sydney Harbour. The wind whipped at his uniform as the sun rose behind them.

'Ah, but that is the most beautiful sight in the world,' Captain Brian Williams said beside him. 'Home, a cold beer and the biggest plate of steak and eggs any man could imagine. Do you expect anyone to be at the wharf to welcome you home?'

'Maybe my Uncle Sean,' David said. 'No one else. How about you?'

'The wife and kids,' Brian answered. 'Along with a heap of rellos.'

'Lucky man,' David sighed. 'Probably within a week the battalion will disappear off the rolls as redundant. That's going to be hard to take. All those years we belonged to the family we called the battalion, and each and every soldier, our brother.'

'I kind of never thought about that,' Brian said. 'But you're right, when I think about how much we shared. We lost a lot of good cobbers along the way.'

Both men fell silent, lost in thought.

The sun was spreading its spring warmth, its soft shadows falling in the crevices of the sandstone cliffs and sea-washed ledges of rock. The bow of the carrier passed through the harbour headlands. Both men could see distant figures along the shoreline going about their lives with hardly a glance at the aircraft carrier entering the harbour. It had been such a familiar sight over the past few weeks as ships brought men back from former war zones. Some members of the battalion had volunteered for occupation service in Japan, but David wanted to return to Sydney to chase up his continuing service with the army, which he knew would be reorganised to meet the needs of a nation at peace.

The soldiers aboard the aircraft carrier fell into ranks alongside the sailors as the big warship was nudged into the dock by the tiny tugs hovering around her hull. Soon they could see the mass of waiting faces staring up at them from the wharf. They could hear cheering, and the occasional name being called. Then it was time to walk down the gangway to meet the welcoming crowd of friends and family.

David shook hands with Brian before they made their way down. 'Cobber, I just want to thank you for your bloody good support in the company,' David said.

'Mate, we'll have to keep in touch,' Brian responded. 'It was your brilliant leadership that got most of us through alive. You can be proud of that. If there was ever another war, I want to be beside you in the trenches.'

'There will be other wars,' David said. 'We never learn from history.'

The two men parted and went their separate ways. David reached the wharf and immediately spotted Sean hobbling towards him. Beside Sean was Harry Griffiths and a badly disfigured man – for a second, David didn't recognise his cousin.

'Welcome home, son,' Sean said, hugging the big soldier to him.

'Welcome home, young Dave,' Harry said, thrusting out his hand. 'I thought I should be here to see that you keep out of trouble when we go for an overdue beer or two.'

'Donald, I see you ran into some Jap metal,' David said, gripping his cousin's hand. 'I reckon it kind of improves your looks.'

Both men laughed at the joke, as only soldiers could. Together the four men left the wharf and entered the first hotel they could find near the disembarkation point. It was already crowded with disembarked men eager to get their hands on a cold, Aussie ale. David hardly remembered the rest of the day as the beer flowed along with stories of the Great War and what was being now called World War II.

For a moment, when David awoke in a bed in Sean's flat the next morning, he did not know where he was. His head was fuzzy from the alcohol and the unfamiliar feeling of clean sheets and a soft bed. Was he in hospital? Slowly the familiar room focussed around him.

He sat up and placed his feet on the floor, and tried to remember the day before. Outside, he could hear the sounds of a city at peace, of cars, trams, people laughing. He attempted to remember moments from the previous day before.

Donald had said something about coming down from Queensland to marry Jessica Duffy – and David was expected to be best man. Donald was getting married! David recalled the drunken conversation with his cousin, then the memories of Allison swept over him. He had attempted to repress her memory and now felt the tears run down his cheeks. He started sobbing.

The beautiful woman he was meant to return to was gone forever, and so was the battalion he loved so much. Never before had he felt so lost. This was an alien world where he did not belong. He was almost thirty, and nothing in the future seemed certain. From the hills of Spain to the jungles of New Guinea, all he seemed to have known for the last decade was war and conflict.

David buried his head in his hands and continued crying like a child, whispering Allison's name, glad that no one could see him. He would have given anything to see her beautiful face again, and to hear her sweet voice. How unfair life was, that it should take her, and let him live.

In the kitchen Sean paused in his preparation of David's breakfast. He could hear the sound of grief in the tiny flat, and put down the fork he was using to stir scrambled eggs.

Sean remembered how he had gone through the same thing when he returned from the Western Front. It was as if, in peace, a tap was finally turned on, and the bitter tears from years of combat flowed.

'Oh, dear boy,' he said softly. 'The war has finally caught up with you.'

TWENTY-FOUR

The day arrived in late October for Jessica and Donald to be married. David had abstained from his drinking binges to sober up enough for his role as best man, and prepared his wedding speech. Sean had dug out his best dinner suit, and even young Patrick was outfitted in a suit to match Sean and David's.

The wedding was at St Mary's Cathedral in Sydney. David carried out all his best man duties, also ensuring the limousine was ready to whisk the newly married couple to their reception at the prestigious Australia Hotel.

Sean, Patrick and David arrived by taxi at the hotel entrance. Already, guests were streaming in to go to the Emerald Room, with its high ceilings, Italian chandeliers and a marble fountain gurgling water on a raised dais in one end of the dining room. All around the reception area, palm shrubbery created an outdoor ambience.

David, Sean and Patrick walked past the entrance with its polished, red-granite Doric columns and Victorian-era mahogany staircase that led to the many floors above. David could see Jessica, holding a huge bouquet of roses, disappear into the Moorish Room. Her long, white silk wedding grown flowed across the floor, and she glowed with happiness.

'Hello, David,' came a voice behind him. David turned to see Sarah standing with her husband, Charles Huntley.

'Sarah . . . Charles,' David replied, confused at seeing his cousin. 'What are you doing here?'

'Charles and I are on the guest list,' Sarah replied sweetly. 'I convinced my brother to have this one day set aside as a truce. After all, our family has shrunk somewhat.'

David was aware how his cousin's beauty was enhanced by the body-hugging dress she wore to perfection.

'Hello, old boy,' Charles said, extending his hand. David had no issue with Charles, and accepted the friendly gesture. 'I know this is a little awkward, but I think today should be a day of celebration. As a matter of fact, we are booked into the establishment for the night.'

David turned to see Sean standing with Patrick a short distance away. He could see from the expression on Sean's face that he did not approve of Sarah's appearance, although appeared to warm to Charles when he walked over to him, leaving David alone with Sarah.

'You didn't tell me you were back in Australia,' Sarah pouted. 'You have a habit of doing that. I hope you received my condolences on Allison's terrible passing. She was always my best friend, and I miss her so.'

David wanted to say how much his cousin was being a hypocrite but resisted. He did not want a scene at Jessica's wedding. Instead, he said lamely, 'You're looking very nice.'

'I would like to have some private time to talk to you,' Sarah said. David was aware her hand was on his arm.

'I'll be a bit busy making speeches and catching up with a few old friends tonight,' David replied.

'I'm sure we can meet to talk when your duties are over,' Sarah said. 'I have something very important to tell you.'

'We'll see,' David said. 'If you'll excuse me. I should join the bridal party.'

David walked up to Sean and Patrick.

'I didn't agree to that bitch being here today,' Sean growled as the three walked down the corridor of columns to the sound of laughter. The band struck up a tune.

'What's a bitch, Uncle Sean?' Patrick asked.

'Not a nice person,' David hurriedly explained, and both men glanced at each other. They would have to watch their language in the young boy's presence.

The guest list read as a political, military and social who's who. Beer and champagne flowed, and David, at the head table beside Donald and Jessica, gave the traditional speech, interspersed with funny stories of growing up with Donald.

The evening drew to a close and it was time for the bride and groom to leave for their honeymoon aboard a ship to New Zealand. Jessica tossed the wedding bouquet, caught by a young lady David recognised as the daughter of a prominent politician, and the couple went around the room thanking the guests for attending, with the exception of Sarah and Charles. Apparently the truce was over.

David walked with Sean and Patrick to the entrance of the hotel and saw the couple into a taxi. Then David walked back into the hotel, found a bar and ordered a beer. He wasn't alone for very long when Sarah took a seat next to him.

'I thought we might have that talk,' she said, ordering a gin and tonic. 'But I would prefer somewhere less public.'

'Where is Charles?' David asked.

'Charles went home,' Sarah said. 'He worries about young Michael, although the boy is in good hands with his nanny.'

'I thought you might share the same concern about your son,' David said.

'I chose to stay behind to talk with you,' Sarah said. 'I feel we should go to my room, where it's more private. It's very important.'

David turned and looked at Sarah. 'What the hell,' he shrugged and followed her to the grand staircase. Sarah led David into her room, closing the door behind her. They were hardly inside when she threw her arms around his neck, kissing him passionately on the lips.

David pushed her away, holding her at arm's length. 'I thought you wanted to tell me something important,' he said. 'What happened years ago at Manly was a mistake.'

Sarah stood back. 'David, if only you knew how long I've waited to feel your arms around me, and for us to make love again.'

'That's not going to happen,' David said, turning towards the door. 'I lost the only love of my life when Allison was killed.'

'You dare to turn your back on me!' Sarah flared. 'You don't know how I've counted the hours and minutes for your return. You and I were destined to be together.'

David paused. 'Destined to be together?' He frowned. 'We have nothing in common other than our bloodline. If this is a ruse to rekindle old passions, Sarah, it's not going to work. I'm going downstairs to order another drink, and keep drinking until I forget a lot of things that happened in my life.'

David walked to the door and had his hand on the doorknob when Sarah said, 'Michael is your son.'

Stunned, David stood stock still, trying to take in Sarah's words.

'What are you talking about?' he asked.

Sarah stepped towards him until she was a breath away. 'Michael is really your son,' she said. 'Charles is not the father, and I can prove it. Charles believes Michael is his, but Michael was born prematurely, and his conception coincides with our time at Manly.'

'Bloody hell!' David swore softly. 'Is this your cruel way of trying to make me feel guilty and come running back to you?'

'No,' Sarah replied. 'I just wanted you to know that we do share something important. I want you to be with me.'

'Son or not,' David said, 'that's no reason for us to be together. From what I have heard, Charles is a good father to Michael. I may have conceived Michael, but I'm not about to take away the boy's belief in the man who cares for him. Does Charles know?'

'I haven't told him – yet,' Sarah said. 'It's you and me who are destined to be together. I knew that from that very first time I laid eyes on you in that Berlin cafe all those years ago. I've never begged before, but I'm begging you now. Please, consider our future together.'

David stared at Sarah and felt pity.

'I'm sorry, Sarah,' he said, reaching again for the door. 'I hope this will be the last time you and I ever meet. Goodbye.'

He stepped into the corridor and walked away, his head spinning with the news about young Michael Macintosh (Sarah had always insisted that her son be known as a Macintosh). Now he *really* had another reason to drink himself into oblivion.

★

David's leave was over. It was time to report to Victoria Barracks in Sydney for his interview about his continuing service in the army as an officer.

Boots polished and his Sam Browne belt gleaming, he sat outside the office of the brigadier who would decide his future. David was feeling confident as he had served in all the major campaigns and been awarded a Military Cross.

A spit-polished warrant officer marched up to David, and threw a perfect salute that David returned.

'The Brigadier is ready to see you, sir,' the warrant officer barked.

David thanked him, and marched inside to salute the officer with the red tabs on his collar. He then stood to attention, staring directly ahead.

'Take a seat, Major Macintosh,' the brigadier said.

David sat down in the chair opposite the senior army officer. For what seemed like forever, the former brigade commander rifled through a folder on the desk that David knew was his service record.

He glanced up at David with a grim expression. 'I'm not going to pussyfoot around, Major Macintosh, but I have to inform you that we do not have a position for you in the army. I'm afraid you'll be demobbed next week.'

'Sir, I have considerable experience as an officer, and I was made substantive in my current rank,' David said, hardly able to believe what he was hearing.

'I grant you that, Major, but we have more officers than postings. We also have graduating classes from the Royal Military College at Duntroon, and they must be given priority in the new army.'

'I'm prepared to take a reduction in rank, sir,' David almost pleaded.

'I'm sorry, Major, but there is nothing I can do,' the Brigadier said in a sympathetic tone. 'The best I could do is reduce you to a private's rank if you re-enlisted. The war is over, and I believe that your family has its own substantial business interests. I doubt you'll find yourself unemployed on civvie street. If there's nothing else, you're dismissed.'

The senior officer closed David's file. There was nothing else to say. David rose, saluted the Brigadier, and marched out of the office, the word 'dismissed' ringing in his ears. In just a few sentences, David had lost the only real family he had ever had. Everything he had sacrificed for his country had come to nothing.

*

'As of next week, I'm out,' David said bitterly to Sean in his legal office.

'I'm sorry, David,' Sean said. 'I know how much you loved soldiering. God knows why.'

'I feel like I was thrown on the rubbish heap,' David said. 'All those years in the dust of the desert and the stinking jungles came down to a couple of sentences.'

'What do you plan to do now?' Sean asked, feeling David's pain.

'There's not a chance in hell that I would take a position in the Macintosh enterprises run by Sarah,' David said. 'All I really know is soldiering. The allowance I get from my position in the family trust is very generous, and I'm really in a position where I do not have to work anyway. I can afford to travel like I did before the war.'

'There's not much to see in Europe,' Sean said. 'The war took tourism off the map.'

'You know,' David said, 'I've often thought about visiting my mother's homeland. I've never really thought much about being born a Jew. Other than getting circumcised and having my grandmother organise my bar mitzvah. I haven't stepped inside a synagogue since. Maybe I should visit Palestine.'

'Have you read the papers lately?' Sean asked. 'The country is virtually in a state of war. The Poms are caught between Jewish nationalists and Arabs trying to get the Jews out. It's not exactly a place for a peaceful cup of coffee in a cafe.'

'Maybe I would feel right at home under such circumstances,' David grinned. 'I hear the Jewish nationalists need experienced fighting men. I reckon my military experience might qualify.'

'You can't be serious,' Sean said. 'You're an Aussie.'

'I can be both a Jew and an Aussie,' David said. 'But I think it's time I go in search of my ancestral roots. I don't expect you to understand, Uncle Sean, but I hope you'd always be here for me.'

'That goes without saying,' Sean replied, shaking his head. 'It's not against your Jewish beliefs to head down to the pub and join Harry for a cold beer, is it?'

David smiled. 'If it ever was, then I'm doomed to hell.'

Sean heaved himself out of his chair, gripped his walking stick and made the familiar trip to their favourite bar around the corner from Sean's office.

As he walked beside the tall young man, Sean could feel the aches in his joints. How long did he have on this earth, he wondered? After all, he had another young man to raise: Patrick Duffy.

★

'James, I wish I didn't have to have this talk with you,' James Barrington Snr said as he sat in his big leather chair by the fire. Outside, snow was falling. James had appeared after his day in the bank branch office as the manager.

'Is it about the loans I gave to those three veterans?' James asked, pretty sure that was why his grandfather had such a strained expression.

'Yes, it is,' Barrington replied. 'The accountant brought the cases to me yesterday, and expressed his concerns about the viability of lending those men money. They have no collateral and little business sense. I don't think there's much future in selling motorbikes in this part of the world.'

James gazed at the flickering flames in the fireplace. 'They survived the war in Europe as combat soldiers,' James said. 'I think that's the best collateral any man can have.'

Barrington shook his head in despair. 'The war is over, and we now face a time of greater prosperity than we have ever known. But it can only happen if we in the banking business adhere to the principles of shrewd investment and sound judgement. You are letting your heart rule your head. I want you to get a feeling for banking by managing our local branch. I know the staff like you, but you're not thinking like a banker.'

'Maybe I need some time off,' James said. 'I don't expect you to understand, but I need to clear my head. Only months ago I was in the cockpit of a Corsair, and I'm having a little trouble adjusting.'

'At least you're honest,' Barrington sighed. 'There's also the matter of you hanging around that undesirable Sweeney's Bar. People talk in this county. You should be seen attending our church on Sundays and accepting invitations from the country club, not carousing with people of dubious merit.'

'You mean the former soldiers, airmen and sailors returned from the war?' James said. 'I'm comfortable in their company. All the people I know from the country club never served Uncle Sam in the services, but made huge fortunes from the war. They are not my people, sir.'

'What can I do?' Barrington asked in despair. 'What can I do to help you settle back into normal life?'

James turned to his grandfather and saw his anguish. 'There's nothing you can do,' he said. 'I need to find my own path. Maybe I need time to myself, doing something . . . I don't know what. I do have an idea, but it will have to wait until spring. I promise you, until then, I'll try to be a conscientious banker.'

'That's all I ask,' Barrington said. 'Whatever you have planned after winter, I'll support. God knows why!'

James stared at his grandfather. He was growing old, but James could see the love in his eyes. He loved the old man, the only father he had known – until he met his real father in Iraq before the war. The two men were so very different, and both giants in their own way in his life.

PART TWO

Echoes of War

1946–1951

TWENTY-FIVE

The new year of 1946 arrived without the echoes of war in the southern hemisphere.

On Glen View, Donald and Jessica entertained Patrick for his school holidays, and he was reunited with his Aboriginal friend Terituba. It did not take long for the two boys to go bush on adventures. Patrick was proving to be a good horseman, and a crack shot.

Patrick was also one of the first to hear the joyous news that Jessica was pregnant with her first child. Donald fussed, like all first-time fathers, insisting that she travel to their home in Townsville to avoid the fierce summer heat of inland Queensland. She resisted his pleas, saying their child would be born on the soil of her ancestors. With the help of Terituba's mother acting as a midwife, she gave birth to a healthy baby boy. While Donald had married Jessica in the Catholic Church and promised to raise their children as Catholics, he insisted their firstborn boy be called Bryce, an English name with French and Celtic roots which didn't sound too Catholic.

Across the kitchen table at the homestead, under the light of the newly installed electricity at Glen View, Donald and Jessica had their first heated argument. Jessica accepted Donald's nomination of Bryce as their first child's name but added Thomas as his second name in honour of her father. Donald readily agreed, then Jessica moved that Bryce be registered as Bryce Thomas Duffy-Macintosh. She said that having the two family names was a form of reconciliation between the two families. Donald argued his son should bear his family name alone, but realised he wasn't going to win. And so, a new generation began as the moon rose over the semi-arid plains of brigalow scrub, and life went on.

*

David Macintosh knew the streets of Jerusalem. He had visited the holy city before, when on leave from his battalion while fighting the Vichy French forces in Syria. Then, he had befriended a Jewish shopkeeper in the city, Aaron Ben-David. When he stepped off the ship from France he made his way to the shop to find his friend, remembering the sights and smells of the ancient place of three great religions.

'Mr Macintosh,' the little balding man with his spectacles on the tip of his nose greeted him. 'How is it that we see you in our city again?'

David was dressed in a heavy jacket and slacks to ward off the cold of the Middle Eastern winter. He stood in the tiny shop surrounded by carpets hanging from every possible place along the walls.

'I heard my people calling to me,' David replied with a smile. 'Also, I was thinking about buying a carpet.'

'Ah, Mr Macintosh, I think you're pulling my leg,' Aaron said warmly. 'You must take coffee with my family. I'll close the shop.'

David followed his friend into the back of the shop, which was as cramped as his front working area, except it opened onto a pleasant little walled garden where herbs grew in pots. Off that were the kitchen and two bedrooms. Aaron's wife was in the kitchen cooking a chicken stew. She greeted David warmly in Hebrew, which David did not understand.

'You'll eat with us,' Aaron said, pulling out a chair for his guest. 'We're expecting my son Elliot and my daughter Richelle. My son was an officer in the Jewish Brigade, and fought in Italy. My daughter lives on a kibbutz not far from here.'

No sooner had he uttered the words, a young man and woman entered the kitchen. Both were wearing khaki trousers and matching shirts under heavy woollen pull-overs. Aaron spoke in Hebrew to them and the young man held out his hand to David, who guessed he was about the same age as him. His sister was in her early twenties.

'I'm Elliot,' he said with a firm grip. 'My father has told me you're from Australia, and served in Syria during the war as an officer with infantry.'

'Your father told me that you served as an officer with the British in the Italian campaign. I heard it was pretty tough going in the mountains,' David said.

'I'm Richelle,' the young woman said, stepping forward and gripping David's hand. She was dark and pretty. David could see a strength of spirit behind the eyes.

'Pleased to meet you,' David said.

'Why are you here?' Elliot asked bluntly. 'This is a troubled city and not conducive to a visitor seeking a relaxed holiday.'

'My mother was Jewish, and I was half-heartedly raised in her religion,' David explained. 'I just feel a need to find the roots of my mother's faith.'

Elliot stared at David for a moment. 'I'm afraid you'll not find much religion in this house,' he said. 'Our concern is just staying alive in a sea of Arab and English hatred.'

'I read about the concentration camps,' David said. 'I was for a short while an unwilling guest of Dachau back in 1936, before leaving and travelling to Spain to fight Franco's mob.'

'Where are you staying?' Elliot asked.

'I haven't decided yet,' David replied.

'You'll be welcome at my sister's kibbutz,' Elliot said. 'We're transporting a group of refugees there this afternoon, and you can travel with them.'

'That sounds like a bonzer idea,' David said.

'Bonzer?' Elliot queried.

'Aussie slang, for something great or good,' David answered.

David ate with the family and thanked his hosts. He was guided out of the shop and down an ancient, narrow street to an old bus waiting a couple of blocks away. It was filled with dishevelled men, women and children. He could see from their dress and features that they came from different parts of Europe. All David carried was his old army kitbag with a few essential items.

'Who are they?' David asked Richelle.

'They are our people who have travelled by ship from a port in France, seeking a new homeland free of European persecution. Today, we'll take them to my kibbutz and give them that new home.'

Elliot was the last aboard, and sat next to David. Richelle stood in the aisle behind the driver. The other passengers remained silent, and only some whispering could be heard.

'I presume you know how to use this,' Elliot said, withdrawing a German Mauser rifle from under the seat.

David took hold of the bolt-action rifle. 'I spent some time at the other end of the Mauser,' he grinned. 'But basically they operate much like our Lee Enfields.'

'You're now a part of our protection party,' Elliot said, and withdrew a British Sten gun. The small submachine gun was only useful at close range and when David glanced at Richelle he noticed she had a revolver tucked into the belt of her trousers.

'Is it that bad?' David asked, checking that the weapon was ready for use.

'We have to travel on a road through Arab territory to get to the kibbutz,' Elliot said. 'The British are not very helpful at protecting us, and if they do stop the bus we have to hide the weapons.'

'Great,' David said. 'Now the Poms are the enemy also.'

'The Haganah, our national army, do not attack the British but the Irgun and Lehi groups do,' Elliot explained. 'The British conduct operations to find them.'

David had a brief lesson in who's who. 'Are you a member of the Haganah?' he asked.

'Yes,' Elliot replied as the bus ground its way along a road bordered by a bare hill. Cold sleet whipped about the bus as it slowly wound around the hills outside the ancient city.

David peered out the side window at the hills overlooking the road and shuddered. They were sitting ducks should the enemy decide to ambush them. They had seen no other traffic, nor any sign of British patrols. He gripped the rifle's stock tightly as he experienced the fear he knew well as a soldier. Behind him the passengers huddled silently, as if feeling the same trepidation.

'I . . .' David was about to speak when a bullet shattered the window beside the driver's head.

Elliot yelled something in Hebrew to the passengers, a few of whom had begun screaming in terror. They seemed to understand and began lying down where they could. The bus continued and the cold air whipped at David.

'Drop me off here!' he yelled at Elliot. 'I'll see what I can do.'

Elliot tried to grab David but he was quick, and forced his way through the door to fall onto the cold, wet road with the Mauser. The bus continued slowly up the gradient and David was on his feet, running up the slope of the hill bordering the road. Elliot and Richelle watched him from the bus as David scrambled up the steep slope, rifle in hand. Eventually the bus disappeared around a corner, and all David could hear was the wind in his face. He had gained the high ground and found a vantage point from where he could see the bus reappear on the road below him. He also saw what he had expected: two men behind a small stone wall manning a Lewis machine gun. They were dressed in traditional Arab clothing, and oblivious to David's presence a hundred yards away.

David carefully settled himself and took careful aim at the man with the machine gun. He hoped the German rifle fired true, and allowed for the wind as he took aim. He fired, and saw the machine gunner topple to his side. His companion looked about in panic and made a run for it, leaving the weapon behind. David did not bother to try and stop him. He scrambled down the slope to recover the British–made weapon and three spare drums of ammunition.

The bus had been only seconds from being riddled with bullets, had he not stopped the ambush.

David made his way down the slope to the road with his booty. The bus stopped about two hundred yards away. He waved, and saw Elliot running towards him.

'You're a damned fool!' he said breathlessly to David. 'But a bloody brave fool.'

'Thought this might come in handy for your army,' David said, nonchalantly handing the heavy captured weapon to Elliot.

'You'd better get back in the bus,' Elliot said, accepting the valuable gift. 'If the Arabs don't kill you, the winter here will.'

David followed the young Jewish soldier back into the bus. He noticed the passengers staring at him through the windows with expressions of gratitude and awe.

Within a couple of hours they reached the Jewish settlement. David noted it was armed, with young men and women manning sandbagged positions as they drove in.

The passengers disembarked and were guided to a building for food.

Elliot spoke in Hebrew to an older man, accompanied by another very pretty young lady who had titian hair and green eyes. She had a Lee Enfield slung on her shoulder, and David was impressed by her beauty. He smiled at her, but she did not return his friendly gesture. She seemed more interested in what Elliot was saying, and turned to speak with Richelle. Both women were staring at him in a way that made him feel just a little uncomfortable. Then they both smiled at him.

'So, you're a hero,' the titian-haired girl said, disconcerting David. 'Elliot has just explained to my father how you stopped an ambush on the road here.'

'Your English is very good,' David said.

'It should be,' the girl replied. 'My grandfather was from your country. He came here at the turn of the century from the Boer War, and planted all the gum trees around our kibbutz. He served with Allenby's British army during the Great War, and always insisted that the family learn to speak English.'

'Is your grandfather still alive?' David asked. The girl shook her head. 'I should introduce myself,' David continued. 'I'm David Macintosh.'

'I'm Rachel Rosenblum,' the girl answered, holding out her hand, greasy with gun oil. 'My grandfather Saul Rosenblum came from the colony of Queensland. Do you know it?'

David grinned. 'Queensland is now a state in the commonwealth of Australia.'

'Oh, I didn't know that,' Rachel blushed. 'We are very busy learning to work this land and defend ourselves. Geography is not my best subject.'

'I see that you've met my daughter,' the man speaking with Elliot said and held out his hand. 'I am Ben Rosenblum, and I would like to express my gratitude for what you did today. Elliot said that you've accepted an invitation to stay with us while you're here. Do you speak any languages other than English?'

'I speak German,' David replied in that language. 'My family always insisted we learn that language. It came in handy when I was serving in North Africa against Rommel's mob.'

'That's good,' Ben said. 'We have many Jewish German refugees. Some speak Yiddish, which I doubt you do.'

'No,' David said. 'I don't even speak Hebrew.'

'Maybe you'll learn if you stay long enough. But for the moment we can do with a man with as much military experience as you. You can help train the young men and women who speak German and English.'

'I could do that,' David said. 'Anything to help.'

'Good,' Ben said, turning to see Richelle walking back from the bus with the captured Lewis gun. 'Maybe you know something about this weapon.'

David was escorted to the communal food hall, and given a hot meal. Rachel sat with him and asked many questions about Australia. David explained many parts of his country had a lot in common with the arid lands of the Middle East.

Within a couple of days David had his platoon of German- and English-speaking refugees, young men and women, and was feeling very much at home training them to be soldiers. His trainees liked their instructor, whose sense of humour made them laugh – something long absent from their years of avoiding capture by the dreaded German units and their allies tasked with executing them. Rachel would find a way of joining him for meals, as did Richelle. David realised they were vying for his attention. As flattering as it was, he was also aware the two girls had grown up together, and were best friends. The painful memories of losing Allison were not gone, and David was not ready to get involved with another woman.

One morning David was having a cup of coffee outside a room where children were painting pictures under Rachel's tutorship. He wandered inside and picked up a brush, dipped it in paint and outlined a tree in vibrant colours.

'You have a natural talent,' Rachel said, studying his painting. 'Do you paint?'

'Not normally,' David said, surprised by his work. 'When I was at school I loved to draw, but I was also in the first fifteen of the rugby team and the boxing team. Painting was something the creative kids who didn't play footy did.'

'You should practise, David,' Rachel said, handing him another brush. 'I can see that your reputation as a fierce warrior has impressed my little ones here.'

David glanced around at the children, who he guessed to be under ten, watching him with awe. He was humbled by their admiration.

'Their parents have told them how you single-handedly killed a dozen of the enemy on the road here,' Rachel said.

David laughed, 'I've heard the expression Chinese whispers. I guess it's true how stories get exaggerated.'

'Will you remain with us?' Rachel asked.

David remained silent for a moment, looking around the room at the children who came from the four corners of Europe to seek safety in their own land. 'I only intended to visit Palestine for a couple of months, and then return home,' he said.

'You should remain to see spring come to the land,' Rachel said. 'God shakes off the grey of winter, and shrugs off the cold to give us wildflowers and warmth. The orchards become a mass of flowers on the trees, and the promise of life comes to the land.'

'You should have been a writer,' David grinned. 'You know how to put words together.'

'Well, stay and see if I'm right,' Rachel challenged, looking him straight in the eye. 'I think Richelle would like that. She has a crush on you.'

David handed the brush back to Rachel. 'I'd better go and round up my would-be soldiers,' he said. 'It's time to learn how to shoot, run, hide and crawl.'

David left Rachel in her art class, and stepped into the chill of the Holy Land winter.

But he did get to see the spring of 1946 come to Palestine.

★

James Duffy stood in the workshop that smelled of oil, petrol and sweat. Around him were bits and pieces of Harley motorbikes fresh out of wooden crates and still painted in their military green.

'Well, captain, what do you think?' a young man asked, wiping his grease-covered hands on a dirty rag. 'This is where the loan went.'

James ran his hand over one of the modified military motorbikes painted black. It was ready to be put out the front of the shop for sale.

'How many have you sold so far?' he asked.

The young man was in his mid-twenties, and had crewed a Sherman tank under General Patton's fast-moving army in France and Belgium. His two business partners had served as paratroopers with the air force.

'Er, ah, none so far,' the former tanker replied. 'The winter hasn't been a good time for motorbikes. But we expect business to pick up in spring.'

'Well, you've just sold your first bike,' James said. 'This one,' he said, continuing to stroke the metal horse.

The motorbike entrepreneur looked at James to see if he was pulling his leg. 'Hot dog!' he said. 'I'll even throw in a set of saddlebags.'

James produced a wad of dollars from his pocket, peeling off the notes while the young former soldier filled in the paperwork for the transaction. Once the cash was handed over, James sat astride the bike and turned on the ignition. The engine purred over, and James looked satisfied.

'You didn't even take it for a test ride,' the seller said, handing the paperwork to James.

'I didn't have to.' James grinned. 'If I give out a loan from my grandfather's bank, I know whoever I do so to will prove to be successful and trustworthy.'

The former tankman thrust out his hand to James. 'Captain, we will not let you down. We got these cheap through army surplus, and will sell high. We have a feeling there'll be a lot of men who served who will want the freedom only a Harley can give them. A bit like a horse in the old west.'

'I think you're right,' James replied, gripping the young man's hand. 'I have big plans for the first bike you sold.'

James left the shop, riding his newly acquired Harley. He pulled into the spacious driveway of his grandfather's mansion, and parked the big motorbike out the front. The old valet cast the two-wheeled metal horse a look of suspicion.

James went to his bedroom and packed a few things in the saddlebags he'd been given as part of the deal. Then he went to a wardrobe to recover his father's old flying jacket, which he had had professionally restored.

He went downstairs with the saddlebags over his shoulder to meet his grandfather, who was sitting in a chair in the manicured garden. Spring was in full bloom in New Hampshire, albeit still with a chill left over from winter.

'Sir, I'm about to ride out,' James said.

Barrington looked at his grandson. He had on a leather flying jacket with a woollen collar, a T-shirt under the jacket, and his long flying boots. He was also wearing his aviator sunglasses and an old marine officer's cap with its distinct insignia.

'Where will you go?' Barrington asked, looking up at his grandson.

'I don't exactly know,' James replied. 'Guess I'll just hit the road and see if I can find America. I've heard there are many other combat veterans doing the same. Maybe catch up with old friends. I promise to be back before the fall.'

Barrington rose from his chair stiffly, and did something James never expected. He embraced him and said, 'God bless you, son. Just be careful, and come home when you're ready.'

James returned the warm embrace, stepping back to look at the old man. For a moment James felt a surge of guilt for leaving him behind. 'I'll drop you a postcard or two,' he said and turned to walk away, lest his tough and stoic grandfather saw the tears in his eyes.

James Duffy went in search of America, and the words of the Doris Day song rang in his ears over the roar of the motorbike engine.

TWENTY-SIX

By the time spring came to Palestine in 1946, David Macintosh had discovered his hidden talent for painting. Rachel remarked it must have been in his blood.

There were times when his hands would shake and his body tremble when he heard a loud noise akin to a rifle shot. His nights were still filled with the nightmares of war. Painting helped him feel more at peace.

Spring also meant the weather had improved enough for more armed skirmishes with a local Arab population determined to throw out the Jewish newcomers. David stepped up security at the kibbutz and trained his squad to venture out on night patrols into the nearby hills, seeking out armed intruders and setting ambushes.

His aggressive night operations forced the enemy to pull back after a couple of successful interceptions, and David's reputation as a leader grew. When he was not conducting training and operations he would wander through the groves of gum trees. Rachel had told him about her grandfather, Ben Rosenblum, who was from a cattle station in Queensland. He had fought in the Boer War and deserted the army, fleeing to Palestine where he helped settlers recover their once useless land by growing trees. Now there were orchards of fruit and olive trees, making the people both self-sufficient and prosperous. At first they had generally had good relations with their Arab neighbours, but that changed when the Palestine Arabs were forced to heed the calls of their leaders to expel all Jews. Now they were at war, with only the British army providing a fragile stability between the two sides.

Rachel said her grandfather had passed away peacefully just before the last world war. She loved him very much, and missed his colourful stories of the country of his birth. One day she hoped to travel to Queensland to see it for herself.

They sat down amongst the gum trees and watched the sun going down. The air was chilling, but they remained side by side.

David was drawn to the young woman, but fought his feelings. Even now he had an almost over-riding desire to hold and kiss her. He was struggling with his emotions when Elliot turned up.

'David, I hate to break up this touching scene,' he said with a half-smile, sensing that he had intruded on a private moment. 'But you need to be briefed on a mission, scheduled for tomorrow. You'll be going to Jerusalem with my sister.'

David and Rachel rose, brushing down their clothing.

'Maybe one day I'll be able to show you Queensland,' David said. 'It's not all dust and flies as your grandfather experienced. It has beautiful rainforests, mountain streams and coral reefs alive with brilliantly coloured fish.'

'I would very much like that,' Rachel smiled. David resisted the temptation to hold her hand as they walked side by side back to the settlement.

That evening, David huddled with the leaders of the kibbutz, Elliot and Richelle.

'You'll be Richelle's escort to a very important meeting at a location in the Old City,' Ben said by the light of a kerosene lantern.

'Will I be told what the meeting's about?' David asked.

'It's better that you do not know,' the kibbutz leader said. 'It's what your intelligence people call a "need to know" situation. You do not need to know.'

David shrugged. He knew he had the council's respect and could be trusted. Richelle looked pleased at his inclusion.

Details were planned, and the meeting broke up. David stepped outside into the clear, cold night to gaze up at the stars.

He was surprised to hear Rachel's voice in the dark. 'Did you agree to go with Richelle tomorrow?' she asked.

David turned to see her step out of the shadows of the meeting hall.

'Yes, but I wasn't told who Richelle is meeting.'

Rachel was now inches away from him. 'She and Elliot have links with the Irgun,' Rachel said. 'I suspect Richelle will be going to a meeting with them.'

'Irgun,' David echoed. 'I thought they were Haganah members, not Irgun.'

'We tell the British that we do not associate or condone Irgun tactics of terror,' Rachel said. 'But we are facing annihilation if we do not work together. Irgun are fearless, and the British have already killed many of its members. A war is coming, which will decide the fate of all Jews in this country. We cannot afford to lose.'

'Irgun or not, I have agreed to escort her,' David said.

Without warning, Rachel kissed David on the lips, and stepped away just as quickly.

'That's for good luck,' she said with a twinkle in her eye. 'It means stay away from the Irgun, and come back to us.'

Before David could respond, Rachel was gone, leaving him with the sweet taste and memory of her lips.

The following morning David stepped aboard the kibbutz bus and noticed that besides the driver and two young, armed kibbutz men, he and Richelle were the only other passengers. David knew that if they were stopped by a British army roadblock the weapons disappeared into cleverly concealed panels in the bus. He and Richelle were instructed not to carry firearms.

They sat in seats on either side of the bus. David noticed Richelle tuck a map inside her blouse, relying on the British sensibility of not body-searching a female in the field.

The bus made its way onto the road that took them through sometimes hostile hills. All aboard were tense with nervous anticipation of an Arab ambush. But they felt a little more secure when a convoy of British armoured vehicles passed them.

The bus rounded a corner and all aboard felt their heart rates go up. Ahead of them was an army roadblock, manned by British soldiers.

The bus driver said something in Hebrew, and the guns disappeared. Richelle replied and turned to David. 'We have to stop,' she said.

David could see a Bren gun levelled at them from the hood of a vehicle ahead.

'What do we do?' David asked.

'Nothing,' Richelle answered. 'Just have your papers ready.'

David carried papers, his passport, visa and some American dollars.

The bus driver stopped about ten yards from the road-block and opened the side door as two soldiers strolled towards them. One of them was carrying a Sten gun whilst the other a .303 carbine, tipped by a thin bayonet. They boarded the bus. David remained in his seat.

'Papers,' the British corporal demanded. Richelle produced her identification papers.

'Stand up,' the corporal ordered, and Richelle stepped into the aisle. As she did, the map in her blouse slipped from under her shirt, catching the eye of the soldier with the rifle.

'Corp,' he said, bending to retrieve the map. As he did Richelle bolted past the NCO with the Sten gun, knocking him aside, and slipped past the startled private holding the map. She was out of the bus and hit the ground running towards the edge of the road that fell away to a ravine of rocks and small scrubby bushes. David hardly had time to react as the corporal with the Sten gun leaped from the bus after her.

'Stop!' he yelled, but Richelle was already scrambling down the hillside. A long burst from the Sten gun stopped her. David watched in horror as the nine-millimetre bullets stitched her back. She pitched forward as David also pushed his way past the soldier with the rifle.

'You bastard!' David roared, running at the British soldier with the Sten gun standing at the edge of the road and gazing down at the figure of the girl he had just shot. David slammed into him in a rugby tackle, causing the sub machine gun to rattle along the road. He raised his fist to smash the unfortunate soldier in the face when the metal butt of a .303 hit him in the back of the head. David saw a haze of red stars and then nothing.

When he regained consciousness he was still on the roadway, and a few yards away Richelle lay on her back staring with lifeless eyes at the clear skies above. He could see the driver and two young kibbutz men standing beside the bus, their hands on their heads.

David groaned as he forced himself into a sitting position. He felt the back of his head and realised that the rifle butt had split the skin of his skull.

'You're an Australian citizen,' a lazy voice said, and David turned to see a young British lieutenant. He had an accent David knew belonged to the upper classes of England. 'What are you doing with a known terrorist?'

'What terrorist?' David asked, touching the back of his head and feeling the blood oozing between his fingers.

'This woman,' the officer said, pointing to Richelle's body. 'She's a known associate of Irgun.'

'How do you know that?' David countered, his head throbbing and his anger re-emerging.

'We have had intelligence on her for some time,' the officer replied. 'Her death is unfortunate because we would have liked to interrogate her. My man was not aware who she was when he fired. But you're now a person of interest to us. It is not every day we intercept a colonial in the company of a suspected terrorist.'

'I'm here because in 1941 I served in Syria and had reason to visit Palestine,' David said. 'You could call me a tourist, and you better have a good reason to gun down a young woman when you admit you did not know who she was before your man opened fire. I would call that murder.'

David could see the face of the officer redden with rage. 'These damned Jews fire on us on an almost daily basis,' he said. 'And we are here to protect them. They don't deserve protecting. Hitler was probably right when he accused them of trying to rule the world.'

'I can see from your lack of ribands that you did not see any active service during the war,' David said. 'I lost a lot of good cobbers fighting Hitler's forces in Syria, North Africa and Greece. I held the rank of major at the end of the war, and your king gave me a military cross for my service to the bloody British empire – which seems to be shrinking a bit lately. So don't tell me Hitler was right. Also, did I mention that I'm a Jew?'

The British officer looked a little rattled but did not back off. 'Sergeant,' he said, turning to an NCO standing beside him with his rifle levelled at David. 'Take this man into custody and arrange for him to be transported to the Acre jail. I'm sure our people will get something of value out of him.' He turned on his heel and walked away.

'Get up, sir,' the sergeant ordered, but in a less hostile voice than David expected.

David rose on shaky feet.

'I'll make sure you get seen by our RMO before we have you sent to Acre,' the sergeant said in an almost kindly voice. When David focused on him he could see that the sergeant wore a row of war ribands, including the North Africa Star.

'You were in North Africa,' David said.

'I was with Monty for the big bash at El Alamein,' the sergeant replied. 'You Aussies were on our flank when we finally broke through. Your lads were bloody marvellous.'

'I was out of the desert by the time we participated,' David said as he was escorted towards an army truck.

'I saw the war out as a company commander in New Guinea against the Japs. I can see your officer has seen no real action.'

'Pompous little twit,' the sergeant said. 'They send us these Champagne Charlies straight out of Sandhurst instead of battle-hardened officers. This bloody war needs experienced soldiers – not Johnny-come-latelies.'

David grinned as he walked around the back of a tarpaulin-covered truck. He scrambled up the tailgate to take a seat on a wooden bench that looked inwards and was followed by the sergeant.

'The first thing you have to do, sergeant, is get rid of the tarpaulin cover and face the seats outwards in case of ambush,' David said when both men were settled and joined by two other soldiers.

'Mr Ovens says that is not necessary,' the sergeant said, and David guessed that was the name of the young British officer in charge of the roadblock. 'You should be on our side, not with the Jews.'

The truck rolled into motion and bumped its way back down the road towards Jerusalem where David would be prepared for a stay in the prison located at Acre on the coast. The last time he had been in a prison was Dachau in 1936, but that was by the Nazis. Now it was by his own allies, the British. He knew that he had to get a message to Australia concerning his imprisonment. Maybe Sean Duffy had enough clout to arrange for his release. David was leaving behind the body of Richelle and the people he had come to befriend in the kibbutz. And also Rachel, whose kiss still lingered in his memory. Ahead of him was a prison on the coast of Palestine and an unknown future.

When they reached Jerusalem David had a moment alone with the sergeant. Although the British had searched him and taken all his personal papers, they had left the small wad of American dollars.

'As one old soldier to another,' David said quietly at the back of the truck, 'I would like a favour.'

'What would that be?' the sergeant asked suspiciously.

'I'd like you to send a telegram to Sydney, Australia, to my uncle, saying that I'm being held – most probably at the Acre prison. I'm only asking because if I don't write to him he will be worried. That is all.'

The sergeant thought for a moment. 'Just a telegram to tell him you're in our custody?' he said. 'I'll need money.'

David retrieved the Yank money from his pocket and handed it to the British soldier. 'That's all I have. After the telegram you can use what's left over to shout the boys a beer.'

The sergeant could see that David was being generous, and he quickly pocketed the money. He supplied David with a pen and paper to provide details for the telegram, and David was then marched into British army HQ. All David had was the hope that the British soldier believed in the universal brotherhood of men under arms.

With the wonders of modern technology, three days later Sean Duffy received a telegram from Palestine. It was not signed, but did spell out all that David had relayed to the sergeant.

'Oh, dear boy,' Sean sighed. 'You have done it again.'

It was time to call in a few favours from Chifley's government and organise a seat on a flight to Europe on one of the military aircraft ferrying mostly armed forces personnel. He would also arm himself with the appropriate paperwork and references from the Australian government to free David. All other matters would have to take a back seat until he returned from Palestine with his boy home and safe. It was like 1936 Berlin all over again.

★

Six weeks later Sean stood with David outside the Acre prison.

'You've done it again,' David said, taking in the fresh air of freedom. 'Got me out of a prison.'

'My dear boy,' Sean sighed as they walked towards a car waiting for them. 'I'm getting too old to keep running around the world getting you out of scrapes. You have to go home, and get a steady job, and stay away from places where people shoot at each other.'

'I'm sorry, Uncle Sean,' David said as contritely as he could. 'I know this would have taken a toll on you.'

'Damned right,' Sean said. 'But you and Patrick are the only sons I will ever have, and it is a father's duty to look after his kids. By the way, when I was in Canberra chasing up the few friends I have left there I came across something disturbing. Do you know a politician by the name of Henry Markham?'

David frowned. 'I knew a Lieutenant Markham, back at Wewak,' he said.

'That would be Markham's son,' Sean said. 'It seems his father has it in for you and personally intervened when you were demobbed, ensuring that you did not retain your commission. Apparently he has been putting it around you had it in for his son and without any grounds had him sent home. Markham has also raised the matter of you fighting with an international brigade in Spain before the war. He has accused you of being a communist.'

'That's a bloody lie,' David exploded. 'I joined up to fight fascism because of my experience in Dachau.'

'I know that,' Sean said. 'But Markham is very influential in his party and has the ear of powerful people inside the government.'

'God Almighty,' David said as they reached the car. 'I fought a bloody war for my country. What was Markham doing while we were risking our lives?'

'Growing fat on the profits his properties made under contracts from the government,' Sean replied, leaning on his walking stick. 'But we will drive to the best cafe in Acre and enjoy a good meal, which you apparently have not had for the last few weeks, and tomorrow we leave on a ship for Italy.'

David knew that one of the conditions that he be freed was to leave the country on the first available ship. The British administration had declared him a *persona non grata* for his suspected links with terrorism. But David had wanted to return to the kibbutz. Whilst incarcerated he had not received any visitors or correspondence from the community he had worked with. He knew that anyone who contacted him would be placed under a spotlight.

Mostly he wanted to return to find Rachel Rosenblum. Thoughts of her had helped pass his time in the military prison for both Jews and Arabs suspected of subversion. He had been isolated from the other prisoners and frequently interrogated by British intelligence. But he really knew little of the politics of the Jewish underground and that became obvious to his captors. His exile was simply a matter of course upon his release.

Within six weeks David and Sean stood at the rails of a cargo ship staring at the shoreline of Western Australia. Already David knew what he would do with his life. He was independently wealthy – thanks to the Macintosh Trust – and had discovered a talent for art. He would travel to northern New South Wales and buy property on the beach, a large macadamia nut plantation. There he would paint and see if his belief in his ability was warranted. One way or another, he would make contact with Rachel on the other side of the world.

TWENTY-SEVEN

For almost twelve months the letters arrived from Rachel. David had been able to make contact by mail to her kibbutz, and between the lines that expressed her yearning to see him again was the foreboding news that the situation in Palestine had deteriorated. The Jewish population was at war with their Arab neighbours and the Australian newspapers reported on the bloody fighting for land.

Then, suddenly, Rachel's letters stopped.

David sat at the edge of his property on the subtropical coast. His vantage point overlooked the serene ocean below, and a warm breeze stirred amongst a stand of banana trees that came with the acreage and old house he was renovating.

David held Rachel's last letter in his hands, staring bleakly at the rolling sea below. The British were gone from Palestine and David knew that it was now possible for him to return. He would make arrangements to join the fight for the nation of Israel. If ever the tiny Jewish population facing the overwhelming forces of the Arab League needed help, it was now. The odds were against the Jewish fighters as they opposed the professional Arab armies encroaching from every side.

David carefully folded the precious letter and returned to his cottage with its tiny mesh-enclosed sleep-out. It was nothing special and did not even have electricity, but it had a great view of the ocean. He packed his old army kitbag and walked down the hill between the macadamia trees that grew on either side of the track. He hardly glanced at the trees. His aspiration to be a macadamia nut farmer had been a whim. He knew the only life he was suited for was to be a soldier. He was going back to war.

★

Sarah was not happy. She threw her handbag on a side table in the foyer of her mansion and stormed towards the stairs, with her estranged husband stumbling after her.

'Hey, what's up?' Charles slurred.

Sarah froze on the stairway. 'Your damned drinking,' she snapped. 'You're an embarrassment to me when we're in public. I have had enough, Charles.'

Charles gripped the banister to prevent himself from falling and attempted to climb the stairs after Sarah. 'I'm sorry if I have caused you shame in front of your friends,' he said, slumping onto the first step.

Sarah stared coldly at him from the landing. 'You should learn to get over the war and act like a real man.'

'Real man,' Charles echoed, untying his neck tie and struggling to remove his suit coat. 'Like that bastard Billy Price.'

'Shut up, Charles. You made it plain that we are only husband and wife in name for the sake of my public image. All I expect is for you to do your part as the war hero and stay sober.'

'I don't mean to embarrass you,' Charles said, slumping further in his drunken stupor. 'But I have problems forgetting the war. I don't expect you would understand.'

'A real man learns to cope,' Sarah said from the landing. 'You're not a real man.'

'Not like your Billy Price, who I know you're still sleeping with,' Charles said. 'Where was he when I was fighting in the skies over Darwin? Safely in your bed when good friends were dying around me. Is that your idea of a real man?'

'He is twice the man you are,' Sarah snapped. 'You and I have an arrangement and all you need to do is act the doting, sober husband in public. For that you are paid generously by my companies.'

'Mother?'

Sarah turned to see her son next to her on the landing and looking down at his father lying at the bottom of the stairs. 'Is Father hurt?'

Sarah regarded her son. He was five years old and when she looked at him she could see a younger version of David. 'Michael, return to your room. Your father is just drunk.'

Michael didn't move, continuing to gaze down at Charles.

'I said get back to your room, young man.' Sarah repeated, raising her voice angrily.

'I will take him, Miss Macintosh,' Val Keevers said quietly. She had heard the raised voices and gone to protect the boy. 'Michael is a little bit upset at all the noise.' Val ushered him back into his room and remained with him.

Sarah was shaking with rage. The man who should be with her was thousands of miles away in some godforsaken war, helping the damned Jews. David Macintosh was destined to be by her side. Oh but if he could only see that, she thought in her obsession for the man who had rejected her advances. She glanced down at her estranged husband curled below and felt nothing but disgust.

'Do you know that you're not even Michael's real father,' she shouted. 'David is Michael's father, not you.'

Her angry words fell on deaf ears as Charles had fallen asleep. But Val heard her employer's words.

★

The two men stood side by side. Before them was a row of newly dug graves and headstones inscribed with the Star of David. Spring was once again bringing blossoms to the orchards and wild flowers dotted the fields around the kibbutz.

David wanted to cry but remained stony-faced, staring at the headstone inscribed with Rachel's name. He had been too late arriving in the war-torn country to take up arms for the worst of the fighting. But he now stood on Israeli soil, and for some strange reason he recalled the words his German grandmother had often quoted to him when he was a boy growing up on the family copra plantation in New Guinea.

By the rivers of Babylon, there we sat down, and also wept, when we remembered Zion.

'Rachel would always talk about one day going to see you in Australia,' Elliot said quietly. 'I think she was in love with you.'

'Where was she killed?' David asked as he kneeled to gently touch Rachel's headstone.

'She died fighting for the old city in Jerusalem,' Elliot replied. 'Eventually our defenders were forced to surrender to the Arab Legion.'

'How did she die?' David asked, and Elliot shifted uncomfortably.

'Witnesses said she died instantly from a rifle shot. I don't think she experienced any pain.'

How often had David written to families of his men killed in action and said 'he felt no pain' when he knew it was a lie. How could he tell a mother, wife, sister or brother that the person they loved had died screaming in agony. The lie had always been to protect the living as he had now become the voice of the dead. For now he hoped Elliot was telling the truth but he also remembered that Elliot had been an officer with the British army in Italy and had probably written the same kinds of letters to grieving families.

'Are you going to remain with us?' Elliot asked. 'We could do with your experience. This war is far from over as I receive continuing reports of armed intrusions across our borders.'

For a moment David did not answer, contemplating a future in a land so far from Australia. 'I don't think so,' he finally replied, rising to stand. 'I think the nation will be in good hands, and I'm not really very religious. My home is under the Southern Cross.'

'I think we should return to the settlement and share a good bottle of Scotch I have stashed away,' Elliot said, placing his hand on David's shoulder. 'We will raise a glass to the sacrifice we have made for Israel's birth.'

David walked with Elliot towards the cluster of buildings reinforced by sandbags and barbed-wire encirclement. Behind was a row of headstones marking the resting place of many young men and women he had trained. Rachel was in good company. Something else came to David's mind, then. *Lucky in war, unlucky in love.*

★

'Has the mail been delivered?' James Barrington Snr called from the library. Every day for almost two years the old man had waited impatiently for the postcards from all over the USA. He would read eagerly his grandson's latest location and casual job. The postcards had come from logging camps, building sites and fishing trawlers. James had worked his way around the country, meeting men like himself who had returned from the battlefields of Europe and the Pacific, and worked shoulder to shoulder with them in tough and dangerous jobs.

'No, Mr Barrington,' the old valet called from the front entrance. 'But Mr Duffy has returned.'

Barrington almost bolted from his favourite leather chair. Had he heard correctly?

He walked as quickly as he could to the front entrance where he looked out and saw James standing by his motorbike, wearing his father's flying jacket and saddlebags over his shoulder.

'Sorry I didn't call to say I was coming home today, sir,' James said with a broad smile.

Barrington went down the steps and embraced James. 'Welcome home, son,' he said. 'It's been a long time, and no doubt you have experienced many places and things in your travels.'

James disengaged himself from the hug. 'You look well,' he said. 'I missed you.'

Barrington fought back tears of joy and took his grandson by the arm, guiding him into the house. 'I will give you time to settle in before we sit down and discuss your future plans.' he said.

James excused himself and went directly to the room he had left so long ago. It had not changed as he had. Still the same high school sports pennants on the wall and one or two movie posters. He threw his saddlebags on the bed and sat down by the window overlooking the manicured lawns below. James could smell the crisp freshness of spring in the air and hear the distant sound of a tennis racquet connecting with a ball. It was so peaceful compared to his past life and a lot less exciting than being on the road riding to the next town or city. He knew that his grandfather would want to convince him to resume his life in banking, and James had promised he would do so upon his return from his journey in search of America. There would be the expectation that he would meet a nice girl with a good pedigree and settle down to an office job, a house, three kids and a dog.

James sighed as he looked to the future. He was single, facing thirty and assured of a rich and comfortable life. What more could a man ask? It was not as though there would be any more wars for America and a man still on the marine reserve.

James had hardly heard of a place called Korea.

*

It was desperately racing towards a cutting in the foothills like the hunted thing it was. Smoke plumed from its funnel and the engineers in the locomotive piled on as much coal as they could. From a few hundred yards above, the war bird circled, manoeuvring for a perfect shot at the loco-motive trailing a long line of carriages containing men and munitions. The speeding train was not defenceless and small-arms and anti-aircraft fire flew up in an attempt to destroy the American USMC Corsair fighter bomber.

Captain James Duffy ignored the deadly puffs of smoke and long lines of tracer bullets arching into the clear blue sky over the Korean Peninsula. He and the others of his squadron prepared to pounce on the speeding railway train below. James was first in line to attack, and he released his rack of rockets from beneath his wings, watching them trail thin streaks of smoke towards the locomotive. He was already peeling away when they struck their target, and his low-flying aircraft was hit by the concussion of the exploding steam engine of the locomotive. Over the headphones he could hear the whoop of his wingman, 'You got him, Jim!'

But James had also got something else. A heavy calibre, armour-piercing round had ripped through the belly of his bent-winged fighter bomber and slammed into his right leg. He had felt the impact and quickly realised what it was when pain suddenly swamped him. It was so intense that he almost lost consciousness but he realised that he must fight the pain if he was to return to his carrier out in the South China Sea. James transmitted his situation, peeling away from the squadron now strafing the North Korean soldiers who had escaped the jumbled wreckage of the train below, while his wingman escorted him back to the aircraft carrier.

James kept his aircraft on course and swept his instruments to see if anything of vital importance had been knocked out by the AA fire. He thought how ironic it was that only three months earlier he had been sitting in conference rooms of his grandfather's banking empire, wearing the latest fashion in suits, and flirting with the young women he came into contact with. Then the call-up order had been delivered and he was back in the cockpit of a Corsair flying ground-support missions over the hills and rice paddies of some country most of the world had not heard of. The newly formed United Nations Security Council had voted to send in a multinational armed force in a police action to resist the North Korean invasion of South Korea. Uncle Sam had been caught with his pants down: five years of peace had lulled the Western World into an apathy, even living with an uneasy Cold War between the superpowers of the Soviet Union and the United States. The Cold War had grown hot when the Chinese- and Russian-backed North Koreans crossed the 38th parallel in June 1950 during the country's monsoonal season. Men who had thought they had seen their last war were called up to fight, and the situation was desperate for the United Nations.

'Keep your nose up, Jim', a voice said in his earphones, and James fought to focus on his flying. He knew he was losing blood; he could feel the squelch of it in his flying boot.

Then he was over the coast, and the blue sky fell down to join the grey sea. On the horizon he could see the cluster of escorting warships around his carrier.

'Not far now, Jimmy boy,' his wingman said in his earphones, encouraging James to remain conscious. James used the last of his reserves of strength to concentrate on making his approach to the deck of the aircraft carrier. He could see the figures of the crew scurrying to take post and guide him down. James had daylight and the wind in his favour as he made his approach. Everything lined up and with relief he could feel the undercarriage lock into place. Despite his wound, James touched down on the deck, the arrestor cable snatching the hook in the tail, bringing his aircraft to a sudden stop.

James hardly noticed the men clambering up his Corsair

to drag him from the cockpit. All he could remember before he passed out was the smell of his own blood mixed with aviation fuel draining from a jagged rip in the wing of his aircraft, and the smell of salt air blowing across the deck of the aircraft carrier.

★

Jessica Macintosh-Duffy hated being away from her husband and two sons, Bryce aged four, and Kim, now one. Jessica had always loved the Rudyard Kipling book, *Kim*, and had named her second son after the main character. At least Donald was with the boys on Glen View, and she had just learned that she was pregnant again on a visit to her Sydney medical practitioner. She had come to the city to consult with one of the most trusted people in her life, Sean Duffy.

She sat in Sean's office, glancing around the room and smiling at how little it had changed in all the years she had known him. It was obvious from the expression on the aging lawyer's face that he was pleased to see the daughter of one of his best friends.

'Your dad must have had a crystal ball,' Sean said. 'The war in Korea has caused an explosion in wool prices, and the investment Tom made in wool production is paying off in a big way. The way things are going, the Duffy companies will catch up to the Macintosh family enterprises before the decade is out.'

'I guess it's not the return on Dad's investments that counts as much as seeing Sarah Macintosh always looking over her shoulder, knowing that I'm close behind.'

Sean raised his eyebrows. As pretty as Jessica was, there was a deadly coldness in her eyes that could be frightening to those who did not know the gentleness and warmth of her real nature. 'You should consider moving yourself and Donald back to Sydney,' he said. 'Your business holdings are growing, and I feel that you're the best person to be at the helm. I know it would be hard to convince Donald.'

'No, it would be harder to convince me,' Jessica smiled. 'My experiences during the war taught me one very important lesson: there is more to life than making a fortune. Nothing can replace the serenity of sitting with Donald and my two boys on the verandah at the end of a hard day, watching the sun sink over the plains. Money cannot buy that feeling of being one with the universe. Besides, we have you here to look after things.'

'Ah, but that I was younger,' Sean sighed. 'I'm thinking of selling out my share in the firm and retiring north.'

'Donald mentioned that David has re-enlisted in the army,' Jessica said. 'He and Donald have been in contact on a regular basis.'

'David is a lost spirit,' Sean said sadly. 'He met a young Jewish woman when he was in Palestine . . . I should say Israel now. He was forced to leave but kept up a correspondence until the war for their statehood. Her letters stopped coming and he travelled to find her. Sadly, she had been killed. When he came home, his life seemed to fall apart, and he told me that he was returning to the only life he knew. His last letter came to me from Japan where he was serving as a corporal with one of the newly established Royal Australian Regiments. A bloody travesty as he should have been recommissioned.'

'Poor David,' Jessica sighed. 'After all that he has suffered over the years he deserves something better out of life.'

'For a short time while he was up north painting he found peace. But David was born one of those restless men who doesn't realise how much his attitude costs those who love him,' Sean said sadly. 'All I can ever do is be there for him when he needs me. To young Patrick his Uncle David is a hero, but Patrick is only just in his teens and doesn't know anything of war – except in the comics he reads. I have meant to thank you and Donald for having Patrick during the school holidays. He loves Glen View and its way of life.'

'He's not a bother, and Donald treats him like an older son,' Jessica said. 'Patrick loves to work with the ringers mustering the cattle. He has a real knack for it.'

'I just pray that when Patrick finishes school he doesn't follow in David's footsteps.' Sean said. 'The good fathers at his school are pleased to tell me that Patrick is in the top academic three of his class, and that he is probably going to make the first fifteen rugby team and the rowing team. Even so, it's as if Patrick has blocked out his past, and that worries me a little.'

'The Duffys and Macintoshes seem to have had their fair share of tragic stories over the years,' Jessica said. 'I guess the old ones of the sacred cave haven't finished with us yet.'

'That story is almost forgotten,' Sean chuckled. 'By the time your boys have grown up, old Wallarie will be well and truly forgotten. His memory will be swept away on the hot winds of the central Queensland plains.'

'I will tell my children about their ancestral roots, and to be proud of both their European and Aboriginal blood.'

'Spawned by two peoples, spurned by both,' Sean said, and was silent for a moment. 'Back to business,' he sighed. 'I know you have a plane to catch this afternoon.'

Jessica smiled. 'Yes, it's not only Donald and the boys waiting for me. I also suspect that Wallarie and Dad miss me too. We see the two eagles flying around the homestead on a regular basis.'

Sean smiled. The legend of the old Aboriginal warrior would always exist so long as the great wedge-tailed eagle lived.

*

When David Macintosh first heard that Australia would be sending troops to Korea it had hardly rated a mention in the papers. The terrible flooding of northern New South Wales had dominated the news. But David had known that the understrength Australian Army would need volunteers.

He had been holed up in his beach house, watching the rain bucket down. He had put aside his half-finished canvases and packed a few personal belongings. Then, when the waters had receded, he had locked the door behind him and walked down to the railway station with his old kitbag over his shoulder.

That had been months ago, and now he waited with his section of a platoon to advance to a place on the map known as Sukchon, where a unit of American paratroopers were trapped on the high ground by the retreating North Korean army.

Corporal David Macintosh was a curiosity to his section of eight men. They knew he had once been a company commander and had seen action from North Africa to New Guinea, and had won a Military Cross. But what counted to them most was their section commander's ability to lead them and keep them alive.

The Australian battalion moved forward; some travelled on the hulls of American Sherman tanks, whilst the rest convoyed in American trucks along rutted roads, dust marking their progress.

The Australians put on their heavy greatcoats in the early hours of the morning as the bitter chill of the approaching winter bit into their flesh. The autumn leaves had fallen as a russet carpet, and apples lay rotting in deserted orchards.

David sat in the back of the open truck with his rifle between his knees. This was a new war to be fought with old infantry weapons, and the familiar feel of his Lee Enfield .303 rifle brought back flashes of memory of other battlefields. His section was mostly composed of men who had fought in World War II. They were seasoned fighters, with the exception of one young man who had just turned twenty and kept close to David when they were in action.

'It's just about all over, isn't it, corp,' he said to David in the dark. 'Old Doug MacArthur has the Koreans on the run to the Chinese border. Once we trap them there it will be all over.'

'I hope you're right,' David said. 'But in my experience cornered troops fight to the death.'

A rattle of small-arms fire interrupted their conversation, and David gripped his rifle. The firing seemed to be coming from an apple orchard to their right, and the soldiers tumbled from the truck to take up a formation for a counterattack. David could see the valley below, scattered rice paddies, small haystacks and rice stooks.

While David waited for orders, their commanding officer had informed brigade HQ they were going to attack but was warned they could not expect any artillery support because the actual location of the trapped American paratroopers was unclear.

Suddenly the ground exploded in great clouds as enemy mortar bombs fell from the sky. The company commander passed down the order to his platoons to move forward in an attack on the hidden enemy.

'Fix bayonets!' David called to his section. It had always been an order that chilled troops because it meant being within an arm's length of the man and seeing his face before you plunged the bayonet into his belly or chest and killed him.

The company commander led the attack, and the men followed.

They ran through the orchard, unaware that a regiment of North Koreans was in position between them and the American paratroopers. However, to their good fortune, the Koreans were engaged with the Americans and had not posted sentries to their rear, so the Australians fell on the Koreans with the element of surprise. But the Koreans rallied and the Australians were under heavy small-arms fire. David continuously kept an eye on his section to ensure that they were following their battle drills. They advanced up a ridge, calculating that the Americans were somewhere ahead, not knowing that the Koreans outnumbered them almost three to one.

David and his section reached the top of the ridge and could see a beautiful valley below dotted with copses and orchards. There were big vats in the ground for storing apples, and David instinctively knew they were perfect positions for enemy snipers.

He yelled the warning to his men as they moved into a skirmish line and almost immediately drew fire from the Koreans snipers hidden by the vats. David saw the head of one Korean raise above the lip of a vat, brought his rifle to his shoulder and snapped off a shot. He saw the Korean's head jerk back. It was the first Korean he had killed, and for a split second he tried to figure how many nationalities he had killed: Spanish, Italian, German, French, Japanese and Arabs. Now he could add Koreans. Who next? The Chinese?

'Look, corp, farmers,' the young soldier called when a small party of men dressed in the traditional white smock of rural workers appeared. David did not hesitate and called to his Bren gunner. 'Get them!'

The Bren opened up and the machine-gun bullets tore into the party of white-smocked farmers, who replied with a couple of bursts from their own submachine guns, known to the UN troops as 'burp guns'. They were, as David had correctly guessed, North Korean soldiers in disguise.

As they advanced, some of the North Koreans surrendered, whilst others continued to fight. The Australians' battle discipline made short work of those who continued to resist. The Koreans were beginning to learn that the men who wore the slouch hat were battle-hardened soldiers. By midday the Australians had made contact with the badly savaged Americans who were very grateful to be relieved.

The order was given to dig in, and a platoon was sent back to cut off the retreat of Koreans missed in the initial assault.

David supervised the fieldworks for his section and was approached by the platoon sergeant, a veteran of New Guinea who knew of David's excellent reputation as an officer.

'I shouldn't even have to tell you, but well done, Dave,' he said, crouching beside a shell scrape David was digging for himself, stripped to the waist. 'I know the boys back in New Guinea swore by you keeping them alive. You should be a bloody officer and not a junior NCO.'

'Thanks, Harvey,' David replied. 'But now I don't have to worry about keeping a hundred men alive – only eight. We have a bloody good CO, and I know we are in good hands.'

'Were you with the CO back at Wewak when he won his DSO?' Harvey asked.

'No, but I heard from his men how much he deserved his gong.' David said.

Harvey rose from his crouch. 'Keep up the good work,' he said. 'I figure the way things are going with the Koreans on the run we will be back home before we know it.'

David watched him walk away, hardly aware someone had taken a photograph of him standing in his shell scrape. He looked to his left and saw a couple of young soldiers leaning on their rifles.

'C'mon, boys,' he growled. 'Keep digging.'

TWENTY-EIGHT

The pain was intense but the morphine took it all away. Through his euphoric haze Captain James Duffy vaguely remembered a navy doctor leaning over him and saying, 'The leg might have to come off . . .'

James attempted to protest, and the next thing he heard from the doctor gave him heart. 'We'll fly you out to Tokyo, where they might be able to save your leg.'

In a Tokyo hospital skilled surgeons worked for hours to repair the badly injured leg. James found himself lying on his back with doctors and nurses fussing over him. His ward was filled with other servicemen being brought in from the battlefields of Korea. Within weeks, James insisted on walking with crutches. He had been informed that the heavy-calibre bullet had damaged muscle and broken the bone of his lower leg. Chips of bone had to be removed, along with damaged muscle but, with good

315

care and the use of antibiotics, his leg would heal.

After a couple of months James was able to walk with the aid of a cane, and the first thing he did was apply for medical leave to make his way to the bright lights of downtown Tokyo. During the Allied occupation the former enemy had learned to cater to the needs of armed forces members on leave, and the bars and nightclubs had risen from the ashes of a city once bombed to the ground to cater to them. James had marvelled at how industrious the Japanese people were as they rebuilt their country, emerging like a phoenix from the fire.

He asked a couple of American sailors on the brightly lit but bitterly cold street where he could find a bar and went directly to the place they had recommended. It was a Friday night and the small place was packed with officers. In the corner of the smoke-filled room a young and pretty Japanese girl belted out a heavily accented version of 'Rudolph, the Red-Nosed Reindeer'. James was reminded that it was only days away from Christmas, and despite the war on the other side of the Sea of Japan, the bar was warm with merriment. He ordered a Scotch from the barman.

James thanked him and turned to see if he knew anyone in the bar. Through the cigar and cigarette smog of the dimly lit room he spotted a group of navy officers in a corner, surrounding a female navy officer. It was obvious that she was the centre of attention, and James could see why. She was very attractive, with red hair and a smatter of freckles over her alabaster skin.

'Son of a bitch!' James said in shock. There was no mistaking who he was looking at – Isabel! She was laughing at a joke one of the adoring medical officers had made, and all James could do was gape. He was aware that the Japanese singer had broken into the wartime song 'Sentimental Journey' and the words echoed in his head.

Isabel was still laughing when she turned in his direction. She was only about five yards from him and their eyes met. He could see her laughter cease. James knew that she had recognised him. It was a moment James would remember for the rest of his life. Isabel slipped from her stool and made her way to James.

'Well, if it isn't the legendary marine flyer from my old home county, Captain James Duffy,' she said, only inches from him.

'Hello, Isabel,' James replied. 'I'm pleased to see that you've graduated from college.'

It was an awkward and beautiful moment for him.

'Thanks to you, I'm now a surgeon,' Isabel said. 'I was inspired by your wartime record to join up in the navy, and I can see that we're now equals in rank.'

'Ah, but I'm a marine captain and that is superior to a navy captain,' James smiled. 'Where are you stationed?'

'I've just arrived,' Isabel said. 'I'll be at our hospital in our Tokyo before they send me to Korea next week.'

'I'm amazed I've come halfway around the world to meet up with you in a goddamned Tokyo bar,' James said. 'Can I buy you a drink, Captain Sweeney? From one captain to another?'

Isabel glanced at the walking stick resting beside James's leg. 'Have you been wounded?' she asked.

James could hear a note of concern in her voice.

'Not badly,' he shrugged. 'I caught a bit of metal in my leg on a mission in Korea, but the surgeons stitched me up fine. All going well, I should be back in the cockpit of a Corsair after Christmas.'

Isabel frowned. 'I hope not, James,' she said. 'You've done more than all the other men I know put together.

The last that I heard about you, you were a banker back home. Why didn't you visit me at college or at least attended my graduation? I wondered why you didn't take more interest in my progress. I was angry at you, James Duffy.'

James was stunned by her revelations. He had always considered her a young girl, but standing before him was definitely a beautiful woman. 'I thought you'd graduate and find yourself a young man.'

'Maybe I never stopped thinking about my knight in shining armour,' Isabel said.

'Hey, Isabel, come back here,' a voice called from the party of naval officers. 'Peene has a real good story to tell.'

'In a moment,' Isabel replied. 'Where are you staying?' she asked.

'At your hospital, ward B,' James grinned. 'At least until they post me back to Korea.'

'Then I'll see you tomorrow morning, Captain Duffy, when I'm on my rounds,' she said. 'With any luck I might be assigned to supervise your recovery.'

James watched her return to her friends, swallowed the last of his drink, and left the bar to return to the hospital, smiling all the way.

*

Now Corporal David Macintosh had added a Chinese soldier to the list of nationalities he had killed. The retreating North Koreans had been replaced with the might of the Chinese People's Liberation Army. The fighting was desperate in the freezing weather as the massive Chinese army pushed the United Nations troops south. General MacArthur had ignored intelligence that the Chinese were massing on the banks of the Yalu River to resist what they saw as Western imperialism threatening their sovereignty.

The UN troops on the ground were paying the price for the blindness of the arrogant American general. All the gains of the previous months disappeared as the Chinese army counterattacked the UN forces, sending them reeling back down the Korean peninsula.

David pulled back the bolt of his rifle to recharge the chamber, swinging the foresight onto another Chinese soldier struggling up the snow-covered ridge towards the Australian positions. The strategic aims of MacArthur and his senior officers meant very little to the soldiers on the ground whose war was limited to the three hundred yards or so to their front, rear and either side. War was just a tiny part of the big picture to the individual soldier, as it had always been since man had thrown the first rock in the pursuit of killing his fellow man.

David could hear the distant shouts of Chinese officers urging their men on, mixed with the sound of bugles and whistles whose noise was a means of communicating to their troops. The Chinese army were short of modern radio communications and fell back on an age-old system of sound. The crackle of small-arms was deafening, but the heavy fire was hardly stopping the huge mass of Chinese soldiers surging forward across a field covered with snow.

The first wave of enemy fell back but was quickly followed by a second wave, larger in numbers. That also fell back, and the third wave was much bigger in size than the previous assaulting waves. It was a psychological ploy to weaken their enemy's morale – no matter how many were killed in the first fierce attacks, the numbers attacking would only increase.

Between the human waves David checked the situation of his section dug in along the ridge. The bitter cold was nothing like any of his troops had ever experienced before.

So cold that hot food froze hard in seconds. Frostbite was a real enemy as the winter winds blew down from the Arctic Circle.

The rumours that they would be home for Christmas were long gone. David knew this was a bit more than what could be described as a police action. It was a war as bad as any campaign he had fought in World War II. A new American term had come into the language describing the continual retreat from the Chinese army – 'buggin' out'.

When David glanced at the young soldier beside him in his shallow shell scrape he could see that he was shaking, his almost frozen fingers trying to reload a magazine.

'You okay, soldier?' David asked.

'Yes, corp,' the young soldier answered through chattering teeth. 'It's just the bloody cold.'

David knew it was not only the intense cold causing the soldier to shake so badly, because he could feel the same fear, and fought to get his own trembling hands under control. He did not have to issue the order to stand to for the next assault on the ridge they held. The enemy's whistles and bugles did that for him.

*

In the southern hemisphere Christmas Day promised to be a scorcher. Sarah Macintosh sat at the breakfast table, opposite Charles, who was waiting for his breakfast to be served by their maid. At the middle of the big table was seated their son, Michael, poking at his boiled egg with a spoon.

'Eat your breakfast, Michael,' Sarah snapped irritably.

'Yes, Mother,' Michael replied, and pushed the spoon into the soft yolk.

'Look at this,' Charles said, turning the paper to his wife.

'My God!' Sarah exclaimed. 'That's David.' The grainy photograph was of a soldier standing knee-deep in a shell scrape with a small entrenching shovel. His rifle lay beside him and it appeared he was unaware that he was being filmed. The caption read: *Australian soldier digs in on the advance north to the Yalu River with the Commonwealth Brigade.*

Sarah took the paper from her estranged husband and stared at the face of the man she most desired in the world.

'I thought he was still in Australia,' she said.

'Apparently not,' Charles said.

'Who's David?' Michael asked across the table.

'He's your mother's cousin,' Charles said. 'And a really nice chap.'

'What's a cousin?' Michael asked.

'Someone who is related to you,' Sarah said. 'A kind of uncle.'

'Have I met Uncle David?' Michael asked.

Sarah glanced at her husband, who had taken the paper back to read the rest of the news. He showed no reaction to Michael's question, and Sarah felt uneasy when she looked at the innocent face of her son. Would there ever be a time she would tell Michael who his real father was?

Michael was now attending one of the top Anglican GPS schools in Sydney. His academic record was good, but he showed little interest in team sports, although he had proved a talent at tennis and athletics. Michael spent most of his spare time in the school library, poring over books of Greek and Roman mythology.

Most of the boy's time away from his boarding school was spent in the company of his nanny, Val Keevers, who filled the vacuum of maternal love left by Sarah. Val doted on the boy but Sarah had explained to Michael that Val was simply a paid servant. Michael felt confused because Val gave him love and understanding. For Michael that translated to the love of a mother. His own mother was always a cold and distant woman in his life, as opposed to the warm and close nature of the 'paid servant'.

Sarah stared at her son and could see some of David's features. His shoulders were broadening, and his hair was the same colour as his father's, and he had the same eyes. How long would it be before Charles started to notice that the boy looked nothing like him? It was strange, Sarah thought. Michael would be the only real heir to the Macintosh financial empire when the time came for her to step down. Charles Huntley had never been worthy of passing on his bloodline for the future of the family. At least now her legacy was assured in Michael. Still, she felt a shudder of fear when a strange voice seemed to whisper in her ear, *Remember the curse. It has not gone away.*

★

Sean sat by the hospital bed gazing at its occupant. According to the ward sister he was a difficult patient and impatient to be discharged.

Harry Griffiths woke up. 'G'day cobber,' he said, reaching out his hand to Sean's. 'Who told you I was in here?'

'When the legendary Harry Griffiths has a stroke, it makes international news,' Sean joked. 'Your son called me.'

'The little bugger should mind his own business,' Harry said. 'But it's good to see you, old mate.'

'From what the medical people told me here, your stroke was not too severe. You should be out of here soon, and we'll be back working together before you can say Jack Robinson.'

'You got a fag?' Harry asked. 'They have all my stuff locked up somewhere.'

Sean produced a packet of cigarettes, lighting one for Harry, and saw the expression of contentment on his friend's face at the first puff.

'You remember old Inspector Wren?' Harry asked after exhaling a stream of smoke.

'Yeah, he was a bloody good copper,' Sean replied. 'Why?'

'Well, his son is in the job and I ran across him last week. He's working uniform in the city and dropped in to ask me a few questions about some stolen goods trafficking from the wharves. He said that an informant had pointed out my gym as a place to fence the goods. I told him he was free to search the gym. One thing led to another and I told him that I had worked with his dad when I was in the job before the first war. He got a little friendlier and accepted a cup of tea. I told him about the times that his dad and I had went after the gangs before the Great War. I don't know what prompted me but I asked him if he knew anything about a hit-and-run a few years back on VJ day. Lo and behold, he said that he was the investigating officer and remembered it well. He went on to say that he had been discouraged to investigate further by an Inspector Preston. My ears pricked up when he said that. Young Wren said that had come about as a result of identifying the vehicle as belonging to the Macintosh companies.'

'Bloody hell,' Sean muttered. 'That confirms my suspicions that Sarah Macintosh had something to do with Allison's death. I never thought it was just a mere hit-and-run by some drunken idiot.'

'So it was premeditated murder,' Harry said. 'We have to prove that.'

'About as easy to do as removing Mount Everest with a garden shovel,' Sean sighed. 'David has enough problems just staying alive in Korea. At this stage we can't tell him our suspicions.'

'How is our boy?' Harry asked.

'I got a letter last week to say the war is not going well for the UN,' Sean replied. 'But, he has Irish blood, and I hope, their luck.'

For a moment both men fell silent with their memories of the boy they had virtually raised together.

'How is young Patrick faring?' Harry asked. 'He should be spending a bit of time in my gym.'

'The boy is currently up on Glen View station on his school holidays,' Sean said. 'I have to admit I miss him.'

'He's a good kid,' Harry agreed. 'You have to admire his guts, when all he has known is the loss of his mum in Changi and being shuffled around relatives since then.'

The two old warriors of the Great War sat together for a couple of hours, chatting about events and people they knew, until the ward sister came and told Sean that it was time for Harry to have his bath.

Sean left the hospital, stepping into the heat of the summer sun. It was ironic to think that his beloved David was currently living in a world of intense cold, shattered by small-arms fire and artillery. Sean was not a religious man but he said a short prayer that David would survive yet another war and return to Australia without any physical injuries. He already knew he could not say the same thing for the mental injuries David already carried from the years of fighting on so many battlefields.

TWENTY-NINE

James and Isabel took every opportunity to spend time together. For Doctor Isabel Sweeney, United States Navy, it was a time to explore what was being rebuilt of Tokyo. She and James took photos of the imperial palace and rejuvenated public parks. Huddled together against the biting cold on a small bridge that crossed a stream, Isabel completed the kiss she had attempted in 1945. This time James did not resist.

'That was a long time coming, buster,' she said, her face against his chest to ward off the cold.

'I wanted to do that when I saw you in that bar,' James said. 'I was nuts not to admit that there has always been something very special about you.'

'I knew that,' Isabel teased. 'You are just another dumb male who needed to be prompted into admitting how you really felt. I knew that even when you resisted my kiss back at my dad's bar. It was in your eyes.'

'I wasn't sure I was going to survive the war,' James said. 'But by supporting you through medical school I knew I would have done one good thing in my life if I didn't make it back.'

'Well, here I am, Captain Duffy, all grown up and prepared to admit that I have always loved you, from the very first time I saw you as a little girl. That little girl never forgot how a white knight came to her rescue. But she was from the wrong side of the tracks and held out little hope the knight would return for her. When he did, he proved his love in a way that got her a ticket to cross the tracks. I kept tabs on your life while I was at college. I could see that you weren't married, and was even delusional enough to think that you might be waiting to meet me again. I didn't think it would be a war on the other side of the Pacific that would bring us together again. When my time is up with the navy I intend to return to New Hampshire and set up a practice. What will you do after the war? I know your grandfather wants you back. But I also know how you love flying combat mission, and doubt that you'll not try and return to the cockpit of your beloved Corsair.'

James hugged her to him. 'You know, with an attitude like that, I might even propose to you.'

'Why not right now?' Isabel countered, pulling away from him to stare directly into his eyes.

James was stunned. But at the same time he recognised he had suppressed the attraction he had felt towards Isabel from the moment he had first laid eyes on her. 'Would you really marry a messed-up marine flyer?' he asked.

'Is that your proposal?' Isabel asked. 'If it is, then the answer is yes.'

An old Japanese woman scrounging in the almost deserted street looked up to see two foreign devils laughing and hugging each other on the bridge. It was bitterly cold, and she shook her head before returning to her task of foraging for anything useful that may have been discarded by the occupying troops. Why would anyone be happy in this bitter cold, she asked herself.

Before Isabel shipped out to the Korean war zone, she and James made plans to marry when her tour was over. They would marry in Australia so that her parents could be present. Isabel explained that after they had fled the USA her mother and father had set up what the Australians apparently called a sly grog shop – 'A bar,' she explained to James – in a soldier settler region of western New South Wales. Apparently they were happy with newly made Aussie friends, although the business only provided a frugal existence. James liked the idea as he was half Aussie on his dad's side and had distant relatives in Sydney. He even knew who could stand in as his best man.

Isabel left Japan, and within weeks James was able to convince the medical board that he was fit to fly. They agreed, and James found himself on a flight back to a war. The United Nations was not winning against the might of a newly emerging superpower – China.

★

The beginning of 1951 was not a good year for Sarah Macintosh. Already in the corridors of the Macintosh empire mutterings could be heard from board members. It was not a secret that profits were falling.

Sarah was in a bad mood when she met with her principal accountant, who had prepared a spreadsheet listing the profit and loss of every company Sarah owned. He sat behind his desk smoking one cigarette after another, and Sarah sat opposite, waiting for him to speak.

'It seems that from the money we invested in building firms and materials, only the supply of materials for reconstruction appears to be turning a profit,' he finally said, cigarette ash falling onto his white shirt.

'I thought we had both tied up,' Sarah said.

'We did, Miss Macintosh, but there is a large group of building companies undercutting our tenders,' he said. 'From what I can see they are doing so at a loss, but they are still keeping us out of the market. We are losing tradesmen to the other group as well.'

'How can that be? Is it possible that our rivals will run themselves into liquidation?' Sarah asked.

'I'm afraid not,' the accountant said. 'I asked around and it seems this other group – Glen View Holdings – is subsidising its losses with a generous input of cash from the record sales of the wool they have invested in. From what I can gather they are certainly riding on the sheep's back. Do you know anything about this company, Miss Macintosh?'

'That bitch, Jessica Duffy,' Sarah hissed under her breath. Sarah knew she was in a financial war in which whoever blinked first was the loser. She could almost admire her sister-in-law for the ruthless way she had entered into the market. How ironic that she should be a member of the family through her marriage to Donald.

'What, sorry? I missed what you said,' the accountant asked, looking up from the horror of the company's situation laid bare on the balance sheets.

Sarah reached into her expensive handbag and pulled out her silver cigarette holder, withdrawing a cigarette. She dragged in the smoke and then filled the air with white cloud. 'Glen View is the name of my family's traditional property in Queensland,' she said bitterly. 'My brother is married to the woman behind this attack on us.'

'Oh, my Lord!' the accountant exclaimed. 'I didn't know any of this. Surely your brother wouldn't set out to destroy his own family businesses? I know he still draws funds, as does Mr David Macintosh.'

'I regret to say that they cannot be stopped,' Sarah replied, puffing on her cigarette.

'The good news is that we are still turning a profit on the other company investments,' the accountant said, attempting to cheer his employer. 'But I'm afraid to say that wartime taxes have taken a toll on our capital.'

'That bloody Curtin government,' Sarah said, shocking the accountant with her unladylike language. 'My brother was well connected to the politicians in Curtin's administration. I am sure that we can support Mr Menzies in the future.' She leaned over and stubbed out her cigarette in an ashtray on the accountant's desk. 'I don't want the figures known to anyone outside this office,' she said as she rose from her chair. 'I need a little time to present the board with a new strategy to counter Glen View Holdings. If they are at war with us, I know who will win. I thought her father was bad enough, but it must run in the blood.'

Sarah left the office, fury in her step. Her sister-in-law was an adversary she had never expected. Sarah knew her brother and guessed it was not his brains behind the plot to destroy her. It had to be the daughter of the man she had conspired to kill years earlier – Tom Duffy.

The corridor was empty of any staff, and suddenly Sarah felt the warmish air chill. She paused in her walk along the hallway and glanced behind her fearfully. It was as if she was being followed by something unseen and dangerous.

'Superstitious rot,' she said under her breath, and continued towards the elevator. But the chill remained. It had been the mention of the enemy company, Glen View

Holdings, that had sparked her imagination, she told herself. There was no such thing as ghosts.

*

Only days earlier David and his battalion had been enjoying good food, rest and a chance to pick the colourful azaleas growing wild on the hillsides for wreaths to be used in the ANZAC day commemorations of 1951. Spring had come to the countryside, sweeping away the bitter cold of the winter. This was a place where the battle-weary 3rd battalion of the Royal Australian Regiment were meant to have some respite. But now David sat in a slit trench on the side of a low hill named 504 on the maps, facing the Kapyong Valley under a clear blue sky.

Beside him in his trench was the youngster who stared down at the steady stream of refugees fleeing towards the South Korean capital of Seoul.

David scanned the columns of men, women and children with their ox carts and bundles of personal possessions moving ahead of the advancing Chinese army. David could see the men of the 2nd battalion of the Princess Patricia's Canadian Light Infantry digging in on a steep ridge named Hill 667 to their west. David knew from experience that they should have been up in the more defensible position, but it had been deemed that the Australian battalion was far more seasoned and so were given the lower knolls to defend. David knew that his battalion was thinly spread and he had been able to calculate they would be facing an enemy roughly a division in size. David felt sick in the stomach as he knew they would be outnumbered at least five to one. He did not convey these thoughts to his section because, at those odds, the chances of them surviving were next to nil. Would this be his last battle?

All David could do was quietly move amongst his small section of men, chatting cheerfully and checking their weapons. He also made sure their supply of grenades were fused for instant use.

'Have we got any arty in support?' the young soldier asked when David crouched near his trench.

'The Kiwis have some 25-pounders,' David reassured, 'and we have some Yank Sherman tanks, and a Yank mortar platoon to give us fire support.'

'I heard a rumour that the big nobs have put us here to stop the whole bloody Chinese army,' the young soldier said with a worried expression.

'They won't be able to come at us all at once,' David said, gazing down the valley. 'The hills will channel them. All you have to do is stay calm and listen to my orders and we'll be all right.'

The young soldier did not reply but checked his supply of bullets for his .303 rifle.

David was joined in his trench by the section 2IC, Lance Corporal Mackie, with his Owen submachine gun. 'What do you think, Davo?' Mackie asked, resting his weapon on the edge of the earth parapet. 'You think the Chinese will come tonight?'

'I would if I were them,' David answered. 'Use the darkness to assault up the hill and swamp us with their superior numbers. I suspect they have mixed in a few of their troops with the refugees.'

'You're a cheery bastard,' Mackie said, peering down at the valley. 'Did you hear about the poor bloody Gloucesters at the Imjin River? Hardly a survivor got out alive.'

David had heard of the courageous battle put up by the British battalion. Only forty-six men out of six hundred and twenty-two had been able to rejoin the Commonwealth

Brigade. Their brave stand had slowed down the massive numbers of Chinese advancing towards Kapyong but had not stopped the advance of the relentless Chinese army. Now it would be the turn of the outnumbered Canadians and Australians, supported by a handful of New Zealand gunners and American armoured men, to face the vanguard of the Chinese People's Liberation Army.

It was after the sun began to set that David returned his attention to the main road below and noticed that the flood of civilian refugees had turned into a rout when their ranks were joined by panic-stricken South Korean troops fleeing the advancing juggernaut of the Chinese army. It was then that David knew they were about to face the greatest battle the Australians would experience in this police action as the official order came down from the US IX Corps to defend the valley at any cost. If the Canadians and Aussies failed, then there was very little to prevent the Chinese capturing the capital of South Korea and turning the war in their favour.

*

Patrick Duffy sat under the raised tank stand beside Glen View homestead, reading one of the small war comics he collected. Beside him Terituba was looking over his shoulder, attempting to follow the words in the balloon captions. Patrick had patiently taught his friend to read from the comics and, as Terituba was a highly intelligent young man, he had learned quickly. Both were in their early teens and the hard manual work required on the cattle station had turned their puppy fat into muscle.

'You got a 'lation fighting in that place up north of here,' Terituba said, as Patrick closed the comic book.

'My Uncle David is in Korea,' Patrick replied. 'He's a real war hero with medals, and a cobber of Uncle Donald.'

'I'm going to be a warrior like Wallarie one day,' Terituba said quietly. 'My dad says that Wallarie fought here against the whitefellas a long, long time ago.'

Patrick smiled. 'Yeah, but that was in a different war and now blackfellas fight on our side.'

'Mebbe we could go and join the army then,' Terituba said. 'Us brothers fighting together. You an' me are the best riders and shots in Queensland.'

'Maybe we could,' Patrick said. 'But I don't think the army uses horses now. They have tanks like in the comics. But I am going to join the army when I am old enough – like all my family have.'

'Then you and I will be warriors together,' Terituba said. 'We will join up together.'

'A promise,' Patrick said, spitting on his hand and offering it to Terituba, who also spat on his hand, and the pact was sealed between the two young men.

★

'You should accept your brother's invitation to allow Michael to visit his cousins in Queensland for Christmas this year,' Charles said across the dinner table.

'Preposterous,' Sarah snorted. 'Why would I allow my son to be with people I despise?'

'Because the things you hold against your brother and his wife have nothing to do with Michael,' Charles said, looking at his son on the other side of the table. 'I think it would be good for him to meet the rest of his family. Besides, your brother is his uncle, and by inviting Michael to stay he might be extending you an olive branch.'

Sarah picked up a linen napkin and wiped the corner of her mouth. She could not even consider losing to her hated sister-in-law, but what her husband said might have some merit. What was the old saying? Keep your friends close but keep your enemies closer. 'I will consider Donald's request.' She said. 'It might be time Patrick met his cousins.'

'That would be grand, Mother.' Michael said. 'Would Nanny be with me?'

'Yes, she will be with you.' Sarah said. 'That is what she is employed to do.'

'Where do my cousins live?' Michael asked eagerly.

'They live up in Queensland on a cattle station,' Sarah said. 'It has strong connections to our family.'

'A cattle station,' Michael said. 'Would I be allowed to ride horses and shoot guns?'

'I am sure your Uncle Donald could arrange that,' Sarah replied, reflecting that such things were the substance of adventure for a boy of eight years.

'So, you agree with me?' Charles said. 'Michael stays with Donald at Christmas.'

'I suppose so,' Sarah said reluctantly. 'Christmas is a long way away. We will see where my brother's invitation leads.'

'It may be possible for you and Jessica to bury the hatchet and even consider a merger. Such a venture would surely put the Duffy and Macintosh enterprises at the top of the financial ladder.'

Sarah knew her husband was making a good point. But she also knew that while she was alive this would not happen. There was only one seat at the top of the table and that was reserved for her alone. 'We will see,' she said, knowing full well that she would continue her campaign to crush her hated sister-in-law and treacherous brother. Her son was merely a pawn in the game, lulling those who occupied Glen View into a sense of security.

'Has it turned cold in here?' Sarah asked, feeling a sudden chill descend in the room.

Charles looked at his wife. 'No, it must be your imagination.'

But Sarah could feel the chill and cast about, fearing that she would see an apparition. If she did, she suspected it would be of a long dead Aboriginal known as Wallarie.

THIRTY

They came in the dark around midnight. Whistles and bugles blowing. Human waves screaming, yelling and cursing in Chinese. Their raw courage was met with Aussie firepower. Grenades exploded, rifle cracked and machine guns stuttered death into the shadowy figures struggling up the slope.

David worked the bolt of his rifle, sometimes firing blindly, other times picking his target in the flash of an exploding grenade. He did not know if he was feeling fear because he was too busy screaming at the top of his lungs, exhorting his small section to resist. The noise was deafening but occasionally the scream of a man dying could be heard in the constant din of small-arms fire and grenades.

Beside him the Owen gun in the hands of his lance corporal poured bursts of bullets into the human waves.

All David could think about was when would the attacks end. Was it possible that the Chinese would ever run out of troops? He had already learned that they only came on stronger with each wave.

He and his men cared little that the Chinese had driven off the American tank men, nor that the Chinese soldiers had been able to infiltrate behind them, threatening the battalion HQ. Every platoon of every company of the battalion was under attack, and the enemy numbers seemed to be without count.

David was suddenly aware of a shadowy figure to his left. It was a Chinese soldier carrying a bucket of Chicom grenades. He swung his rifle but it clicked on an empty chamber. Out of ammunition, he leaped at the slight figure of the soldier, swinging his rifle like a club, bringing him down with a sickening thud. David leaped back into his trench only to feel a bullet tear into his side. His adrenaline was pumping so hard he hardly recognised his wound and quickly charged his rifle with another clip of bullets.

The lance corporal was tugging at David's arm. 'Almost out of ammo,' he shouted, and David nodded. There was nothing he could do, except slip the bayonet on his rifle. He, too, was low on ammunition, and he feared that his section would have to go down fighting with nothing but bayonets and the sound of defeat ringing in their ears. For just an instant David wanted to lie down and pretend that he was not on the side of this hill in a place he knew hardly anyone in Australia cared about. For David and his section the area they covered with their firepower was the most important piece of ground on the earth, and for the moment there was a slight lull in the enemy assaults.

The pain in his side came in waves. It was too dark to examine his injury and he knew he did not have time to do that when the welfare of his section came first. He did reach down to feel the wetness of his own blood in the chill of the Korean night.

'Get your section back to our other positions,' the platoon sergeant yelled at David, who ignored his wound to pass the order along his front. When he was near the young soldier's gun pit he saw that he lay with his face against the earth, groaning. The Bren gunner beside him looked up at David. 'He's been gut shot,' he said.

'Sling your Bren and drag him back,' David commanded. 'I'll get Bluey to give you a hand.'

Satisfied that he could account for all of his section, David and his men fell back to a new, tighter position and he set about placing his men for what they all knew was coming. So far only he and the young soldier had been wounded, and the Bren gunner watched over the young soldier until it was safe to get medical help.

David and his section were weary as the adrenaline washed away, but before dawn they were given the order to assault their old position now occupied by the enemy. They were to drive the enemy out and reoccupy their position themselves. Time seemed to have lost meaning. Only hours earlier they had been fighting a desperate battle to stay alive and hold a line. Now it was time to move forward and sweep away the enemy with bayonets and bullets.

David led his section as part of the platoon and company attack and was relieved to see that the Chinese had vacated the trenches they had originally occupied. The young soldier had been moved to the rear, joining the other wounded. The platoon sergeant told David that they had incurred fifty casualties in the last few hours. The battle for Kapyong had only just begun and the Australians knew that there would be no rescue for them. A mere handful of Yanks,

Kiwis, Aussies and Canadians stood between the Chinese army and the city of Seoul.

★

This time Jessica gave birth to a baby daughter in a Brisbane hospital. She had done so on the advice of her doctor, and the insistence of Donald, who now held his princess in his arms.

'She will be called Shannon,' Jessica said weakly from her hospital bed. 'That is the place where my Irish ancestors came from – the banks of the Shannon River.'

Donald did not care what his daughter's name was because she was the most beautiful creature he had ever beheld, even with all her wrinkly skin. Her eyes were closed against the glare of the hospital ward lights as he rocked her in his arms. Jessica could see that her daughter had her biggest admirer in her father.

The nurse standing nearby took the baby from Donald and placed her in Jessica's arms.

'I have to leave tomorrow for Sydney,' Donald said. 'Sean contacted me to say that things are hotting up with our enterprises. He said it's getting beyond him to handle alone.'

'I suspected that it would come to this,' Jessica said, nursing her baby in her arms. 'We need to establish offices in Sydney to manage the expansion of the companies. It's not fair to leave it all to Sean.'

'Does that mean one of us will have to live in Sydney?' Donald asked.

Jessica frowned. Her dream of living a simple life on Glen View with Donald and her now-growing family was being threatened by her financial success. 'I hate to say this but it might mean we all move to Sydney,' she said. 'It would at least mean that we don't have to send the boys away to boarding school, and Mitch can take over the management of the property in our absence.'

Donald sighed. He loved working in the open air with the ringers mustering cattle, but he also appreciated his wife's ambition to destroy Sarah. She was also right about the boys' education.

'I'll look around for a place for us to live,' he said.

'We have the house at Strathfield,' Jessica said. 'It's not a mansion but it's a good place to raise children. I know how much you are giving up by us moving back to Sydney. It shows me how much you really love me.'

'That goes without saying, my dearest Jessie,' Donald said, taking hold of her hand. 'After all, we can take holiday breaks on Glen View so that the boys are reminded of where they come from. I know they would like that.'

'Have you had any news from David?' Jessica asked. 'I know you two are close, and maybe David might consider joining our companies when he returns from Korea.'

'I haven't had any letters lately, but knowing David, he will get through the war. He has to be the toughest man alive. But it might be hard to extract him from his place on the beach, and his macadamia nuts, when he does come home. He has a little bit of paradise up there on the north coast.'

'David deserves the love of a good woman and a peaceful life,' Jessica said. 'He's a lost soul.'

Lost soul . . . Donald knew what his wife meant. But at least David was a seasoned soldier and surely this little war to the north of Australia could not kill him – or so Donald prayed.

*

'Battalion HQ has finally made contact with us,' the platoon commander told his NCOs at an early morning briefing. 'It seems that the Chinese have cut HQ off and occupy high ground to our rear. We are too exposed here so there will be a bit of moving around to set up better defensive positions. I have heard some of the Chinese are surrendering which is a good sign that they are as sick of this as we are. We have been tasked with clearing a knoll occupied by a well dug in Chinese force. The only option for us is a frontal assault to clear them off.'

The young officer glanced at his exhausted NCOs and knew he was asking a lot. But they were soldiers and this was their craft – killing or capturing the enemy.

The platoon moved out and waited for their brother platoon to launch the first attack on the knoll. It ran into heavy machine-gun and rifle fire and grenades, forcing them to withdraw after suffering many casualties.

'Our turn,' David's platoon commander said, and the word to fix bayonets was given to the men crouching in the daylight.

David looked to his section and wondered who else would join the young soldier still awaiting evacuation behind them. He could see that they would have to cross open ground and knew that the enemy machine guns would sweep the ground like a giant scythe in a harvest of death.

David remembered running, bullets smacking into the earth around him. He did not consider running away but experienced the terrible fear of being killed. He had been able to hide his wound, packing the injury with a battle bandage that eventually stopped the bleeding. When he had been able to examine his wound he had seen that the Chicom bullet had entered and exited his left side without too much damage. So long as his open wound did not get infected he felt that he would survive.

Then he was on the slopes with his section and, with grenades, bullets and bayonets, engaged the enemy bunkers.

David could see the faces of two enemy soldiers framed by the slit of a gunport. He was on top of them before they realised the threat to them. He stabbed through the slit with his bayonet, forcing the enemy machine gunners away from the weapon they manned. Then he jumped on top of the bunker and tossed a grenade through the slit. He quickly leaped aside to avoid the explosion, and was pleased to see it rip away the timber. Blood splashed his face from one of the men shredded by the shrapnel of the exploding bomb.

From the corner of his eye David could see fleeing Chinese soldiers. Had they taken the hill?

Heavy gunfire erupted from higher ground. Without hesitating, David screamed to his section to follow him in a wild charge against the trenches higher up on the hill. He hardly remembered the killing, as he and his section took one trench after another. Stabbing, yelling, and exploding grenades were flashes in his memory. The constant crash of small-arms fire and the sounds of men dying, calling for their mothers in a language David did not understand. It seemed to go on forever, but eventually the firing died away and after midday the knolls were in Aussie hands. David glanced around. A quick count showed over eighty enemy lay dead on the sides of the scrubby hill.

Even as David and his platoon fought the vicious battle, the Chinese were continuing to attack the other companies. But this time the Kiwi gunners were able to bring their 25-pounder guns into action and pour extremely accurate exploding death down on the massive waves of attacking enemy troops.

All across the Kapyong battlefield that day the Australian infantry held their positions in an heroic defiance of the overwhelming odds against them.

Early in the afternoon David's section was pulled back to the centre of the company's position to form a tight defensive perimeter on the knolls they had captured.

Not far away one of the battalion's companies was fighting its own desperate engagement. An airstrike was called in from a wing of American Corsair fighter bombers hovering nearby. Two peeled off and released their canisters of napalm on the hill, to the horror of the Australian defenders. It was their hill and the result was that the burning mass of petroleum jelly killed two diggers and wounded three more, and the fires it started in the scrub destroyed valuable ammunition and supplies.

Seeing the terrible mistake, the Chinese launched an even more determined attack on the burning scrub concealing the Australian defenders. They came at a run but the Australians fought back with everything they had in their hands and in their hearts, and the Chinese failed to sweep them off the hill.

From his vantage point on a knoll David could see that their previous positions had been once again occupied by the enemy. Already their company commander was planning an assault to clear the occupying Chinese away once more. It would mean another bayonet charge against an entrenched enemy, and David knew it would almost certainly be the death of his weary soldiers. He crouched in his hastily constructed shell scrape, checking the little ammunition he had left. His bayonet was still fixed to his rifle, and David could see that it was covered in blood. He leaned forward against the piled-earth lip and stared across the battlefield. It was a scene of carnage and he wondered if what he saw would be amongst the last memories he had before he, too, joined the ranks of the dead.

'No more,' he groaned. 'I've had enough.' Then David tried to muster the faces of the women he had loved and lost. They became a blur in his thoughts and made David want to cry. His face was smeared with blood, dirt and burnt cordite, and his battered slouch hat torn by shrapnel. Deep in his heart David knew his time had come in the craggy hills of Korea. The next order to attack would be the last in his life.

But they were saved when the order came down from BHQ to withdraw. The CO could see how thinly stretched his infantry companies were, caught between the road and the Kapyong River. They were to fall back to the British Middlesex battalion's area established behind them.

Around mid-afternoon the signal came that they would have to make a fighting withdrawal, and it was not known if the Chinese had positioned a force to cut them off in their retreat.

David and his company began to withdraw under fire. Each company retreated in leapfrog fashion and provided as much mutual covering fire as they could. The Chinese army, supported by their heavy machine guns and mortars, kept coming and they fell back in a running firefight. David experienced intense exhaustion after hours of firing, reloading and screaming directions to his section as the human waves fell on them, only to be repelled at close range.

Suddenly an exploding mortar bomb knocked David off his feet, causing a searing pain in his knee. He lay stunned as a young Chinese soldier ran up to him with a bayonet-tipped rifle. David was powerless to protect himself as his rifle had been smashed by the explosion. The young enemy soldier was only a rifle thrust away. Both men's eyes locked. David had little time to think about dying as the young soldier looked at him with almost pity in his expression. David waited to be killed. But the soldier simply moved on with the rest of his section.

For a moment David could not believe he was still alive. He could see his Bren gunner firing at the young Chinese soldier's section with devastating effect. He watched as the man who had spared his life was cut down by the Bren.

The Bren gunner saw David on the ground and rushed to him. 'Hey, corp, you okay?'

'Caught some shrap in my knee and it hurts like buggery,' David groaned, attempting to stand up, only to fall when his knee gave way.

The Bren gunner gripped David under the armpit and hauled him to his feet. He was positioned to take the pressure off David's shattered knee and he half-walked David rearwards. All the time David tried to shake the image of the young Chinese soldier granting him mercy, only to be killed himself. The face of the Chinese soldier, whom David guessed to be barely out of his teens, would haunt him forever. In such a savage conflict, that an enemy would take pity on another human being did not make sense.

When they were able to disengage sufficiently from the close, bloody fighting, the New Zealanders brought in artillery to drop rounds very close behind the retreating Australians, chewing up the pursuing enemy with red-hot shrapnel. David's section withdrew down towards a ford in the Kapyong River. Then all the survivors of the badly mauled Australian companies were able to pull back into newly established defensive lines.

David collapsed and his lance corporal hurried a couple of the men over to pick him up. It was then that the extent of his wounds was discovered. David would be going home.

The enemy had not finished with its attempt to break through the Kapyong Valley. Now it was the turn of the Canadians on the higher ground on the other side to feel the full fury of an enemy frustrated by the stubborn resistance by a much smaller force then their own. That night they threw themselves against the courageous Canadians in a last-ditch effort to break through. The closeness of the fighting forced the Canadians to direct artillery fire onto their own positions on top of the hill. Sheer courage by the Chinese soldiers was not enough to break the Canadians and they eventually fell away to consolidate their formations. The Commonwealth Brigade had suffered grievously but had saved Seoul by stalling the Chinese advance. The only Aboriginal officer in the Australian army, Captain Reg Saunders, commanding officer of C Company, 3 Royal Australian Regiment, later summed it up: *At last I felt like an Anzac, and I imagine there were 600 others like me . . .*

David's war, however, was over. The shrapnel wound to his knee was severe enough for him to be shipped down the line of field and, eventually, to Australian hospitals for reconstruction. Meanwhile, the war between the United Nations and the Communist North Koreans and the Chinese People's Liberation Army went on without him.

EPILOGUE

Malaya, 1951

The young man in his early-teens gripped the pistol handle of the Sten gun and felt knots in his stomach. He lay prone, concealed by the thick scrub along the dirt road winding its way through the rainforest into the hills of Malaya. This was his first operation as a member of the Malayan People's Army, sworn to oust the imperialist British from the country. Beside him was an older Chinese man who was a battle-hardened member of the communist resistance force that had fought alongside the Allies for years in the war that had seen the Japanese invade Malaya. Other than the chirp of the birds and insects in the surrounding jungle, there was no sound. The ambush had been laid in an attempt to surprise a military truck convoy, kill the British soldiers and recover their firearms and ammunition.

Years earlier the young man had been a boy in Changi prison and had gone by the name of Sam. The loss of the only real mother he had known caused him to flee into the streets of Singapore. In his grief he was soon discovered by a Chinese merchant who recognised that the young boy's knowledge of the English language could be useful dealing with the Europeans returning to the island. The man and his family were kind to Sammy and treated him like a son. Sam became infatuated with their daughter, a young woman four years older than he, who was a nurse and member of the Malayan Communist Party. It was she who recruited him into the ranks of the armed resistance to British occupation.

Now he waited with sweating nervousness a hundred kilometres from the capital of Kuala Lumpur. He was with a large party of comrades off a jungle trail on high ground called Frasers Hill. This was to be a test to see if he was worthy of joining their ranks as an active fighter.

'Listen!' the older Chinese man hissed. 'There are vehicles coming up the hill. Be ready, comrade.'

Sam could hear the sounds of more than one vehicle engine, and he gripped his submachine gun with sweaty hands. The vehicles drew closer and drowned the sounds of the jungle. Then they appeared: a convoy of military trucks – as the ambushers had hoped – and near the middle, Sam could see an expensive Rolls-Royce Silver Wraith appear. It was opposite him when the blast of small-arms fire ripped into the convoy.

'Now, comrade!' the man beside him yelled, forcing Sam to raise himself into a kneeling position and fire a full burst of his weapon into the Rolls-Royce. He saw the side windows shatter and thought he glimpsed an older man in a civilian suit slump forward in the back seat.

The ambush was met with a trained response from the British soldiers in the convoy, and the ambushers knew it was time to fall back. Sam was still kneeling when he felt himself yanked to his feet and unceremoniously dragged into the cover of the surrounding rainforest.

It took days for Sam and his comrades to make it back to their jungle hideout, where his party had a commercial radio.

'Have you heard the news?' a young female fighter said when they joined their comrades. 'You have killed the English High Commissioner to Malaya, Sir Henry Gurney.'

The older Chinese guerrilla fighter glanced at Sam. 'It was Comrade Sam who killed him,' he said, and the communist fighters in the vicinity stared at the teenager with a look of respect.

'You have struck an important blow for our cause,' the young female fighter said. 'You will be a great asset in our struggle to throw the British out.'

Sam did not know what to think. The memory of the man slumping in the back seat of the car did not please him, despite the fact that he was the hated enemy. Still, he warmed to the acceptance his deed had granted him within the ranks of the seasoned guerrilla fighters.

'We will win our war of liberation,' another guerrilla said.

'It will not be easy,' the older Chinese cautioned. 'The British will call on their allies, the Australians and New Zealanders, to assist them. I fought alongside Australian advisors when we fought the Japanese, and the Australians are tough fighters in the jungle. Our war has a long way to go. Maybe even a decade before we win our struggle for freedom.'

Sam listened to his words, but when he looked around the camp hidden in the jungle, the spirit of youth told him that they would win in the end, now that he had proved himself in battle.

★

Young Michael Macintosh did not know whether he should be afraid or excited. He was in a world so very alien from the noise and bustle of Sydney. Even though his nanny stood beside him, he felt alone standing at the steps of the verandah around the sprawling house. There were people on that verandah with welcoming smiles, but he did not know them. The only member of the family he knew was his uncle with the scary face who had picked him up from the railway station in Rockhampton. But he seemed kind and told funny jokes.

The lady holding a baby in her arms spoke. 'Welcome, young Michael. These are your cousins, Bryce, Kim and this is baby Shannon and I am your Aunt Jessie.'

Michael looked at the two little boys gathered around their mother. They looked tough and eyed him with suspicion.

'Hello,' Michael said shyly. 'It's good to meet you.'

'So you've come with Miss Keevers to spend Christmas with us,' Jessica said. 'I think you'll have a lot of fun here. Patrick, come and meet Michael,' she said over Michael's shoulder, and he turned to see a boy in his early teens standing beside a young Aboriginal boy around the same age. Patrick approached and held out his hand.

'Pleased to meet you,' he said. 'I normally live in Sydney but come here just about every holidays. It's a bonzer place. This is my cobber, Terituba,' he continued, indicating the Aboriginal teen behind him.

Michael warmed to the older boy. 'I'm pleased to meet you,' he said, accepting the handshake.

'Aunt Jess said your dad suggested that you come and meet us for Christmas,' Patrick said. 'You get the top bunk in my room.'

Michael could feel the warmth of his virtually unknown

family, and any trepidation about travelling to Glen View began to disappear as he took in the unfamiliar smells, sounds and sights of a Queensland cattle property. For some strange reason he was already feeling at home. They were not terrible people, like his mother had yelled at his father. They were the only relatives he had, his father had pointed out, and he had a right to meet them. It was his father who was right and not his mother.

That holiday at Glen View would prove to be the happiest days yet of Michael's lonely life. He returned to Sydney a different boy. He had learned to ride a horse, shoot a rifle and make a spear. More importantly, Michael had been able to show his cousins, and himself, that he was just as tough as them.

*

The train steamed and puffed its way through lush green hills and plantations of bananas as it travelled north from the town of Casino to the small villages south of the New South Wales–Queensland border.

Corporal David Macintosh stared out the window of his carriage at the green fields and rainforest as the sun rose over the ocean and wondered at how much work he would have to do to restore his macadamia trees. He knew he was wearing his uniform for the last time: his medical discharge for his wounded knee meant that he was no longer classified fit for combat. The doctors at Concord Hospital had done a very good job to save his leg from amputation, but the best they could do was bring his mobility to the stage where he would require a walking stick for the rest of his life.

Whilst he'd been in Concord, Sean had visited on almost a daily basis, with young Patrick by his side, whose hero-worship of his Uncle David shone from his face. Sean had joked with David about the best walking cane to buy and smuggled a bottle or two of beer into the ward for them to share. It was while he was in hospital that David was informed that his actions in Korea had earned him a Military Medal for bravery and leadership.

David recognised there would be no more medals or wars for him. Now and for the rest of his life he knew that he needed to find peace within himself. Maybe it was the incident at Kapyong with the Chinese soldier that haunted him most, although he could not understand why – after all, he had seen many terrible and shocking things in wartime. Now he simply enjoyed the serenity his train trip north granted him, remembering that this time last year he wondered if he would survive the bitter cold of the Korean Peninsula.

The train stopped at a seaside town and David saw the familiar large metal milk containers on the station as people departed the train to return to the dairy farms of the north coast. On the third last stop of his journey a boy around thirteen years old entered David's carriage. He looked around and sat in a seat a few rows ahead, but facing David, and seemed to stare at him with almost a sad expression. David ignored him and turned to gaze at the passing scenery.

'Hey, boy, get outta my seat.'

David looked up to a beefy man standing over the boy in a threatening manner. The carriage was almost empty and there were many seats available. David could see that the boy was frightened.

'Hey, sport, leave the boy alone. You can sit somewhere else,' David said casually.

'Mind yer own bloody business,' the beefy man snarled. 'I sit wherever I choose. And I choose to sit here.'

David rose to his feet, gripping the seat so that the big

man facing him could not see he required a walking stick. 'If you don't shove off, mister,' he warned, 'I will personally rip out your arms, shove them in your ears and ride you off the train like a motorbike.' It was an expression David had heard many times used by drill instructors on the parade ground.

The beefy man saw a soldier with many medals who was big and powerfully built. But more than that, he could see a deadly intent behind the cold grey eyes staring at him.

'Merry Christmas,' he said and, with a wave, departed the carriage for another.

'Thanks, corporal,' the boy said. 'But I could have handled him.'

'Yeah, I know you could,' David smiled, easing himself back onto the seat. The boy left his seat and made his way to David, sitting down on the bench opposite him. He held out his hand. 'I am Craig Glanville. My dad was in the army and served in New Guinea during the war.'

'Is that how you know about my rank?' David said, taking the young boy's hand, impressed by his forthright but polite manners. 'Is your dad waiting for you up the line?'

'My dad is dead,' Craig said. 'He died in an accident last year.'

'Sorry, son,' David responded. 'That has to be tough.'

'My mum is waiting for me,' Craig said. 'I get off in two stops.'

'So do I,' David said.

'Who are you spending Christmas with?' Craig asked.

'I'm on my own,' David replied.

Before the last stop, the uniformed railway guard walked down the aisle between the few passengers left, announcing the next stop. He came alongside David and looked down at him. The guard could see the many campaign ribands on his chest and recognised both the Military Cross and the Military Medal.

'Were you in Korea?' he asked, and David nodded.

'I had a boy over there,' he said. 'He was killed at Kapyong.' The guard mentioned his name, and with a shock David recognised it as the young man who had been in his section. 'Did you know him?' the guard asked. 'I know there were a lot of diggers in Korea.'

'No,' David lied. The guilt of losing the young soldier still haunted him. 'It was a bloody mess.'

'I suppose you'll be glad to get out of uniform when you get home,' the guard said as the train slowed to a jolting stop at David's destination. 'Well, good luck, digger,' the guard said, moving on down the aisle.

David rose stiffly, grabbed up his kitbag and walked to the doorway with the help of his walking stick. The train came to a halt, hissing steam and puffing black smoke.

Craig followed David with his small suitcase and they both stepped onto the nearly deserted platform, taking in the warm air tinted with the strong smell of soot.

'Craig.'

David saw a woman he guessed to be about his own age waving from the end of the platform as she hurried towards Craig. David could see that she was very pretty. She wore a light summer skirt and her long blonde hair was tied back into a ponytail.

'Mum, this is Corporal Macintosh,' Craig said.

'Gail Glanville,' Craig's mother said, "And I know who Corporal Macintosh is. It was in the local papers that you had been awarded a medal for bravery. We're your next-door neighbours up on the headland. My husband and I were given a macadamia farm last year by my father, who owns a lot of land in the district. We hoped that moving here would help my husband deal with his demons from the war. Are you still in the army?'

'Until midnight tonight,' David said. 'Then I turn into a civilian for the rest of my life.'

'Corporal Macintosh does not have anyone to spend Christmas with,' Craig butted in. 'Can he spend it with us?'

'What a grand idea,' Gail quickly responded. 'If you would like to join my son and I for Christmas lunch the offer is open, Corporal Macintosh.'

She was looking directly into his eyes and David felt her warmth. 'I'll accept your kind offer, if you promise to call me David,' he said with a smile.

As the railway station was only a couple of miles from the headland the three walked side by side along a pretty tree-lined lane to the headland. The peace David sought in his troubled soul began to grow in the company of mother and son.

★

The journey on the hard-packed dirt roads west from Sydney seemed to go forever. Isabel sat beside her husband as the car traversed the great flat plains of western New South Wales. On either side of them stretched miles of dry grass, burnt white by the searing summer sun, but the monotony was often broken by the appearance of big kangaroos and emus trotting alongside the narrow road.

'Oh look!' Isabel exclaimed when she spotted a mother emu trailing a brood of young striped chicks. 'They look like ostriches.'

James smiled. Although he had visited Australia during the war, he had to admit that the vast plains were a totally different experience to the crowded city of Sydney.

'Are we getting close?' Isabel asked, sinking back into the front bench seat sticky with their sweat.

'According to the map we're almost there,' James replied. 'Look, I think we *are* there.'

Isabel strained to see a couple of small, solitary fibro houses in the distance and felt her excitement rising. 'Oh God, I hope it's them,' she said, leaning forward to observe the crossroads ahead.

James pulled into a large dirt area in front of one of the two buildings. A painted signed across the front proclaimed *Bernie's Store*. 'This has to be the place,' he said, 'How many Bernies could there be this far into the Aussie outback?'

Isabel eased herself from the sticky seat and stood gazing at the front door of the small store. For the blink of an eye she did not recognise the solidly built man framed by the doorway. 'Poppa,' she shrieked and ran to her father.

Then it was a flurry of tears and hugging as her mother joined the reunion in front of Bernie's Store.

'So you found us,' Bernie said with a broad grin. 'I come to the most goddamned hidden place on earth and you found us anyway.' He shook James's hand in a crushing grip of welcome.

'It wasn't hard when you left your forwarding address with your brother back in Maine,' James grinned, disengaging his hand from that of his father-in-law. 'Good to see you, Bernie.'

Mary gave James a warm hug and kiss on the cheek. 'I wish we could have been with you for the wedding in Tokyo,' she said, tears of joy still streaking her face.

'I think I should get my son-in-law a cold beer,' Bernie said, guiding them into a small room with three battered tables surrounded by chairs. A wooden bench acted as a counter, behind which was a small assortment of tinned foods for sale.

Mary disappeared and within a short time returned with two large bottles of beer.

'I have a big fridge at the back,' Bernie said. 'Most of our profits come from selling beer to the farmers when they all come in at the end of the day to get the dust out of their lungs. This is a soldier-settler area and my customers are all former Aussie diggers. They get very thirsty out ploughing fields and chasing sheep.'

'So, you are back in the business of owning a licensed bar,' James said, gratefully swallowing a mouthful of the chilled ale from a glass, while Isabel and her mother sipped shandies and chatted between themselves.

'Not exactly,' Bernie grinned. 'It's what the Aussies call a sly grog shop, but the local police sergeant gives me a call before coming out so that I can hide the evidence. He's a good Joe who knows that I provide a service to the Aussies way out here. Isabel wrote to us to say you're out of the marines now, and that both of you will be returning to New Hampshire when Isabel's hitch is up with the navy.'

The two men talked until the two bottles were empty and Bernie requested James's assistance to unload some boxes of beer from his truck parked behind the store. James followed and the two men were alone.

'Did you kill him?' James asked bluntly.

'I did,' Bernie said. 'The son of a bitch was talking big around the county how he was going to have Isabel. But not just him, he was going to share her with his pals. So I waited one night when I knew he would be alone on the road. I forced him off the road and finished him with a baseball bat. The sheriff's department had me on their list of suspects, and you know the rest of the story.'

PETER WATT

'You got justice for us both,' James said.

'And the same will happen to you if you don't treat my daughter right,' Bernie grinned. 'Welcome to an Irish family.'

*

So you whitefellas thought the story was over. Well, ol' Wallarie knows it's not. Families jus' keep goin' on. But they do not know the future like ol' Wallarie does. Life is full of tears and happiness. Sometimes the tears are of happiness. You get me some baccy and I will continue to tell you the story of the Duffys and Macintoshes. The new generations hardly know who I am . . . but I know all about them. Who will live and who will die as the new ones go out into the world. Their story is not over yet.

AUTHOR NOTES

The end of the war in Europe was welcomed less enthusiastically in the Pacific. I had the honour of speaking with members of my regiment who had served under its colours in WWII. Their general comment was that it was hard to get excited when they were still out in the jungles of northern New Guinea fighting an enemy who refused to surrender and died to the last man. The incidents Major David Macintosh faced are all drawn from the personal accounts described in 'The First at War; a history of the 2/1 Battalion 1939 – 45', also known as the City of Sydney Battalion.

Near the end of the war Australia's armed forces generally felt that General MacArthur had sent them to Pacific backwaters that could have been bypassed and left out of the push towards the Japanese home islands. That perception was strong amongst the men I met from the 2/1 Bn.

Tarakan was another bloody campaign perceived as a backwater battle. The accounts of Lieutenant Donald Macintosh are actual first-hand accounts of what happened there. I fear that I have not done justice to the men who fought in the Pacific, as they suffered so much to defend Australia. It has been a privilege to have belonged to an Army Reserve battalion in the 1980s whose members from WWI and WWII were able to recount personal experiences not found in history books.

Women served with our elite Z Force and have for many years been overlooked, unlike their sisters who served in Europe with the Special Operations Executive. Sergeant Jessica Duffy and her exploits are purely fictional, but pay tribute to the women who took on highly secretive operations in the Pacific war.

All the rest is pure fiction.

ACKNOWLEDGEMENTS

Many thanks go to my publishers, Pan Macmillan Australia, where a team of people work to produce something readable. I would like to name a few of them. Firstly, Cate Paterson and my publisher, Haylee Nash. On Haylee's team: Georgia Douglas and Alex Lloyd. Also Roxarne Burns, Tracey Cheetham, LeeAnne Walker and Milly Ivanovic. In publicity I have Lara Wallace, who attempts to make me look good to the general public. Not an easy job.

Thanks also to Julia Stiles, Foong Ling Kong and Libby Turner for their work on the manuscript.

Thank you to my literary agents in Australia, Geoffrey Radford, and in the USA, Alan Nevins and Eddie Pietzak. Thanks to the team working on the Frontier TV project; Rod and Brett Hardy, Paul Currie and Suzanne De Passe. A special thanks to Kristie Hildebrand for her continued management of the Facebook site, Fans of Peter Watt Books.

Thanks to all the staff of my local library in Maclean who help me obtain the obscure research material for my stories.

On the domestic front; thanks to the following people who have made life easier, Dr Louis Trickhard and Christine, Jim and Robyn Gilvear, Jan Dean, Kevin Jones OAM and family, Bob Mansfield and his sister, Betty Irons, OAM. Mick and Andrea Prowse, John and June Riggall, realtor Darren Billett, solicitor Daniel Butt and manager of Summerland Credit Union, John Smith. A mention for John Carroll who is not forgotten.

A special mention for a cobber, Dave Sabben MG, and his wife, Di. It has been half a century since the battle of Long Tan, and Dave returned to the battlefield to mark the event in August 2016.

My family; brother-in-law Tyrone McKee, brother Tom Watt and family, sister Lindy Barclay and her husband, Jock. My cousins Luke and Tim Payne and Virginia Wolfe. A special thank you to my beloved Aunt Joan in Tweed Heads.

As always, a special mention to my Rural Fire Service Brigade comrades at Gulmarrad and all those I work with in the Rural Fire Service. I should also mention my friends in the Northern Rivers Retired Police Association and the 1/19 Royal New South Wales Regiment Association.

Last but not the least, my greatest supporter, Naomi, all my love. It was she who suggested the dedication.

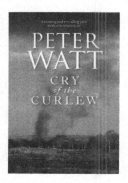

The Duffy/Macintosh Series

Shadow of the Osprey

A riveting tale of love, death and revenge.

Soldier of fortune Michael Duffy returns to colonial
Sydney on a covert mission and with old scores to settle,
still enraged by a bitter feud between his family and the
ruthless Macintoshes.

The Palmer River gold rush lures American prospector
Luke Tracy back to Australia's rugged north country in his
search for elusive riches and the great passion of his life,
Kate O'Keefe.

From the boardrooms and backstreets of Sydney to the
hazardous waters of the Coral Sea, the sequel to *Cry
of the Curlew* confirms the exceptional talent of master
storyteller Peter Watt.

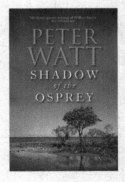

The Duffy/Macintosh Series

Flight of the Eagle

A deadly family curse holds two families in its powerful grip.

Captain Patrick Duffy's passions are inflamed by the mysterious Irishwoman Catherine Fitzgerald, further pitting him against his father, Michael Duffy, and his adoring but scheming grandmother, Lady Enid Macintosh.

On the rugged Queensland frontier, Native Mounted Police trooper Peter Duffy is torn between his loyal bond with Gordon James, the love of his sister, Sarah, and the blood of his mother's people, the Nerambura tribe.

Two men, the women who love them and a dreadful curse that still inextricably links the lives of the Macintoshes and the Duffys culminate in a stunning addition to the series featuring *Cry of the Curlew* and *Shadow of the Osprey*.

The Duffy/Macintosh Series

To Chase the Storm

When Major Patrick Duffy's beautiful wife Catherine leaves him and returns to her native Ireland, Patrick's broken heart propels him out of the Sydney Macintosh home and into yet another bloody war. However, the battlefields of Africa hold more than nightmarish terrors and unspeakable conditions for Patrick – they bring him in contact with one he thought long dead and lost to him.

Back in Australia, the mysterious Michael O'Flynn mentors Patrick's youngest son, Alex, and at his grandmother's request takes him on a journey to their Queensland property, Glen View. But will the terrible curse that has inextricably linked the Duffys and Macintoshes for generations ensure that no true happiness can ever come to them? So much seems to depend on Wallarie, the last warrior of the Nerambura tribe, whose mere name evokes a legend approaching myth.

Through the dawn of a new century in a now federated nation, *To Chase the Storm* charts an explosive tale of love and loss, from South Africa to Palestine, from Townsville to the green hills of Ireland, and to the more sinister politics that lurk behind them. By public demand, master storyteller Peter Watt returns to this much-loved series following on from the bestselling *Cry of the Curlew, Shadow of the Osprey* and *Flight of the Eagle*.

The Duffy/Macintosh Series

To Touch the Clouds

They had all forgotten the curse . . . except one . . . until it touched them. I will tell you of those times when the whitefella touched the clouds and lightning came down on the earth for many years.

In 1914, the storm clouds of war are gathering. Matthew Duffy and his cousin Alexander Macintosh are sent by Colonel Patrick Duffy to conduct reconnaissance on German-controlled New Guinea. At the same time, Alexander's sister, Fenella, is making a name for herself in the burgeoning Australian film industry.

But someone close to them has an agenda of his own – someone who would betray not only his country to satisfy his greed and lust for power. As the world teeters on the brink of conflict, one family is plunged into a nightmare of murder, drugs, treachery and treason.

The Duffy/Macintosh Series

To Ride the Wind

It is 1916, and war rages across Europe and the Middle East. Patrick and Matthew Duffy are both fighting the enemy, Patrick in the fields of France and Matthew in the skies above Egypt.

But there is another, secret foe. George Macintosh is passing information to the Germans, seeking to consolidate his power within the family company. And half a world away from the trenches, one of their own will meet a shocking death.

Meanwhile, a young man is haunted by dreams of a sacred cave, and seeks fiery stars that will help him take back his people's land.

To Ride the Wind continues the story of the Duffys and Macintoshes, following Peter Watt's much-loved characters as they fight to survive one of the most devastating conflicts in history – and each other.

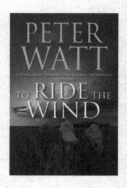

The Duffy/Macintosh Series

Beyond the Horizon

It is 1918, a year when war will end, but an even greater killer arises.

On the bloody fields of the Western Front and the battle-scarred desert plains of the Middle East, Tom and Matthew Duffy are battling the enemy in the final year of the Great War. Even as they are trapped on the front lines, they must also find the courage to fight for the women they love when all hope is lost.

Back in Australia, George Macintosh is outraged by the stipulations of his father's will that provide for his despised nephew, and is determined to eliminate any threats to his power. And in a sacred cave in the far outback, old Wallarie foresees a tide of unspeakable death sweeping through his homeland.

As all nations come to terms with the devastating consequences of the Great War, a new world will be born. But not everyone will live to see it.

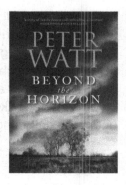

The Duffy/Macintosh Series

War Clouds Gather

Against the backdrop of impending war and the rise of the Nazi Party, the epic saga of the Macintosh and Duffy families continues.

It's 1936. While Europe is starting to feel the shadow of the upcoming turmoil, George Macintosh is determined to keep control of his business empire. He takes extreme measures to prevent his nephew David from taking a seat on the Board. Meanwhile, George's son Donald is packed off to the family station Glen View in Northern Queensland in an effort to curb his excesses.

In Iraq, Captain Matthew Duffy doesn't escape the stain of growing fanaticism. Recruited by British Intelligence, he once more faces a German enemy, although this one has a more pleasing aspect. Matthew is confused by his attraction to Diane and finds himself having to make a hard decision. And just as he is coming to terms with his choice, he meets his estranged son, James Barrington Jnr.

In the middle of all this upheaval, the two families experience loss, love, greatness and tragedy, and find themselves brought closer together and pulled further apart. Romance blooms in the unlikeliest of hearts under the gathering clouds of war.

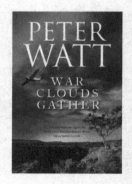

The Duffy/Macintosh Series

And Fire Falls

It is 1942 and the war in the Pacific is on Australia's doorstep, changing the lives of the Duffy and Macintosh families as never before.

In Sydney, siblings Donald and Sarah Macintosh battle for their father's approval, and control of his empire, while their cousin David fights the enemy across the continents.

US Marine Pilot James Duffy defies his grandfather's wishes, and, a number of times, death, protecting Australian skies from the Japanese. Trapped in the jungles of Malaya, Diane Duffy is caught between saving the lives of hundreds of orphaned children, or that of her son.

While Tom Duffy finds himself enlisting in yet another world war, his daughter Jessica narrowly escapes slaughter at a mission station, causing her to revoke her vows and follow in her father's footsteps.

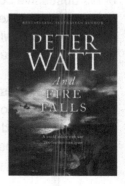

The Duffy/Macintosh Series

Beneath A Rising Sun

As the Allied forces fight to repel invaders in the Pacific, the Duffy and Macintosh clans face their greatest challenges at home.

Sergeant Jessica Duffy relishes her work as a code breaker in MacArthur's headquarters but is also secretly reporting on the Americans to the Prime Minister. When she uncovers treason at the highest levels, neither duty nor dishonour will stop her getting justice.

Captain James Duffy, a decorated fighter pilot with the United States Marine Corps, is expected to wait out the war assisting the bond effort, helping to make movies that gloss over the tragic realities of combat. Despite his scars, he is desperate to return to the cockpit . . . until a chance meeting gives him something new to fight for.

Major David Macintosh has survived prison camps, torture and countless battles, but can he endure the machinations of his obsessive cousin, Sarah? Sarah is prepared to do anything to take over the family companies, and will destroy anyone who gets in her way.

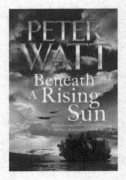

From the frontlines of the Pacific to the back lots of Hollywood, a new generation faces deadly missions, impossible choices and an inescapable family legacy.